Knut Hamsun

The Women at the Pump

translated from the Norwegian by
Oliver and Gunnvor Stallybrass

published by Pan Books

First published in Great Britain 1978 by Souvenir Press (Educational & Academic) Ltd
This Picador edition published 1979 by Pan Books Ltd,
Cavaye Place, London SW10 9PG
English translation © Farrar, Straus & Giroux Inc 1978
ISBN 0 330 25906 7
Set, printed and bound in Great Britain by
Cox & Wyman Ltd, Reading

I

People from the big cities have no conception of the different scale of things in a small town. They think they can come and take their stand in the marketplace and smile their superior smile; they think they can laugh at the houses and the paving – how often they feel that way! But the older inhabitants remember a time when the houses were even smaller, the paving even worse. They have seen the march of progress in the town. Why, hasn't C. A. Johnsen, hasn't Johnsen of the Wharf, built himself a mighty house, a real quality house, with a veranda below and a balcony above, and ornamental carving all the way around the roof? And many another costly building has gone up: the school, the pier for steamships, various commercial buildings, the customs house, the savings bank – there's no reason to smile. The town even has a kind of suburb: on the hillocks out towards the shipyard there live maybe three or four dozen families, in neat little houses painted yellow, red, or white to suit the owner's taste, houses which in their time have eaten up many a nest egg. What's more, even big cities can have their ups and downs, there's no denying it; but who ever heard of Johnsen of the Wharf standing there empty-handed or not knowing which way to turn?

The small town too, then, has its grandeurs, its solid houses with elegant sons and daughters, its immutability and authority. And the small town is fascinated by its great men, it follows their careers with interest; in doing so, after all, the worthy small-town folk have an eye to their own weal and woe; they live and thrive in the shadow of the mighty, as is right and proper. People remember the day Johnsen of the Wharf was made a consul: there were cakes and a drop of something at his store for all comers – and, if the truth be told, there were shameless ones who came twice for their drop of something.

That same morning fisherman Jørgen sat, just as he sits today, hauling in fish for a big dinner. It was a festive day, a glamorous day: for the new consul was still young enough to like a splash, and straightforward and normal enough to have a taste for wine, women, and song – so he gave a party and invited the town. What's more, it was an unqualified success; people remember the newspaper saying so. The women still talk about it around the pump. From time to time a dispute arises over some trifling detail. Lydia may say: 'I ought to know, seeing as how I was helping in the kitchen that day!' The other woman sticks to her guns: 'You can go and ask old man Johnsen himself!' And a third woman puts in: 'Well, I don't need to do that – I've still got the newspaper tucked away!'

But it must be six or eight years since the great day.

Another who could remember that day just as well as the women was Carlsen the blacksmith. Carlsen was a highly respected man, and for that matter a widower with grown-up children – none of your young madcaps. Well, Carlsen it was who stood quietly in his smithy and thanked God for this day of rejoicing along with all the other days he had lived to see. Such was Carlsen: a religious man. Whenever some great or joyful event befell the town, he was at pains to reflect that now it behoved him and his neighbours to thank God. He didn't say much on the subject, and his neighbours would hardly have taken much notice if he had; still, they respected him – stiff-necked and ungrateful they remained, still, say what you like, Carlsen the blacksmith was a shining example to the town.

Oh, and there were any number of other characters: Olaus of the Meadow, fisherman Jørgen, Mattis the carpenter, the doctor, the postmaster – any number of them. Life wears out some of them rapidly, others more slowly; some never change, they grin and bear, grin and bear. The postmaster now – he too is religious in his way, he and Carlsen the blacksmith, that is; otherwise the whole town is worldly, lacking in depth. It's as if there were no parson in the parish: all he does is christen, confirm, marry, and bury his flock – otherwise they have no use for him and never mention him.

Ah, that little anthill! Everyone busy with his own affairs, crossing each other's path, elbowing each other aside, sometimes even trampling on each other. That's the way it is, sometimes they even trample on each other . . .

And now fisherman Jørgen sits, just as he sat six or eight years ago, hauling in fish for a big dinner. Although it is Sunday morning, he sits on and on, anxious to take home enough for a complete meal. From the opposite shore of the bay comes the first hint of a ripple, the morning breeze is getting up. Jørgen drifts away, he has continually to be backing his oars to keep level with his landmarks ashore. Ah, now he is giving up and rowing home. He has sat in his boat since two o'clock.

No one is up yet in the town. Jørgen threads his fish on a line and carries them up through the streets, stumping along in his big boots, a somewhat heavy-footed man in an Iceland sweater and sou'wester, but not large in stature; rather lean in fact, and short below the waist. Still, Jørgen is tough and hard-wearing, never ill in bed, never depressed; his treatment for a cold is to ignore it.

He goes to C. A. Johnsen's great house, hangs his string of fish on the kitchen door, and stumps home.

Aha! – there is smoke rising from the chimney, Lydia is up; she will have kept an eye on his boat and remembered to put the coffee on. Lydia is his wife; she has dark, curly hair and an angry nature – but is capable as they come, a woman who holds the reins.

Jørgen stumps in. 'Walk quietly!' whispers Lydia with suppressed anger, looking with every sign of alarm at the children, at the boy and the two girls as they stir in their sleep. Jørgen pulls off his boots and sweater, drinks his coffee, has his meal, and goes off to the bedroom for a sleep. 'Don't let the door creak!' hisses Lydia through clenched teeth.

But now, of course, the older of the two little girls wakes and sits up. This is the normal pattern. Then the little girl at her side wakes, too. Their mother, furious, flings open the bedroom door and yells at her husband: 'Look, now you've gone and woken them all for me!' And goes on yelling until she wakes the boy, too.

Lydia's anger is easily roused, and quickly spent; as the children strike up their chatter, she is tidying the room and starting to hum. She opens the bedroom door with extreme caution and says: 'Hullo, not asleep yet? What I was going to say – you had a good catch? Did you hear what sort of party they were going to give?'

'No, they weren't up.'

'Well, now you must stop talking and go to sleep,' says Lydia, closing the door again. And she raises the roof getting the children to be quiet.

She resumes her tidying and humming, she ponders, she broods over the party. In former years, they knew how to give a party at Johnsen of the Wharf's: the preparations lasted for days, and extra help was needed in the kitchen; Lydia herself was sent for. About today's party she's had no word, so maybe it's nothing special — probably just the son, young Scheldrup Johnsen, inviting some of his friends.

Later in the morning, when people are out and about, the rumour goes round that C. A. Johnsen's steamship is to sail today. Lydia stops brooding; it seems that there is to be a roaring party for the captain and the town dignitaries, but that they intend to manage without her in the kitchen. Fine, good luck to them! She dresses her children nicely, removes the odd stain, brushes their shoes with lard and soot, and herself puts on some suitable clothes.

Afternoon comes, and with it a great pilgrimage down to the quay. Spring is already far advanced, so people are dressed in thin, light clothes — a lovely spectacle. The *Fia* is loaded and ready to sail.

This ship is no longer new: she was built in the days when a moderate-size cargo vessel cost a couple of hundred thousand* and no more; now she has been bought in Göteborg by Johnsen of the Wharf, who has done her up and rechristened her the *Fia* after his little daughter. What it must have cost to buy such a ship and do her up and make her look like new! The rechristening alone is said to have eaten up a tidy sum. But what's a tidy sum to Johnsen of the Wharf? And now the *Fia* lies there, the town's sole steamship, its wonder of wonders.

Naturally, with her ship about to sail, little Fia herself is on board, sitting in the cabin with her parents and the captain. Naturally, also, her brother, young Scheldrup, comes aboard. Already tall and nearly grown-up, he wears a light suit with the black velvet coat collar that fashion demands — a splendid, dashing fellow, the Johnsen son and heir, with his father's brown eyes and a line of down on his cheeks. Hats are raised, he raises his own in return: his head is bare most of the way to the cabin.

The ship lies with steam up, belching smoke. Up on deck, all is calm; first mate and crew stand by the rail, spitting into the sea and exchanging small talk with their acquaintances ashore. Young Oliver Andersen, deckhand, knows his place and keeps farthest forward; he has served for a number of years on sailing vessels – an

* The unit in question is the *krone* (plural *kroner*). A rough equivalent in dollars may be obtained, here and elsewhere, by dividing by four. Trans.

ordinary, blue-eyed, working-class lad, but a sturdy fellow and a daredevil, with a widowed mother. He is below middle height, but compactly built – he used to resemble pictures of Napoleon, but now he had grown a beard and struck out on his own. This very year he has seen his way towards giving the cottage back home a new roof of red tiles and building an extension at one end. Doubtless he is thinking of the future.

'Sure,' he says to his mother, the widow, who is standing on the quay with her hands under her shawl, 'sure, I'll write from the Mediterranean.'

Bravo – spoken like a grown man! In point of fact, no doubt, he is addressing others on shore: the girls, Petra, whom he's about to leave behind. There she stands, engagement ring and all.

'And don't forget to water the garden,' he adds; but now of course he is only joking, it doesn't mean a thing, God knows, everyone knows, that Oliver has no garden; his mother has merely sown a few carrots and turnips close to the house. She smiles wanly, she knows her son; he's never at a loss for a joke. Is that boy ever at a loss for anything? She knows nothing but good of her son: he has a good head and uses it well.

The second mate takes a turn forward; doubtless he too has a girl on the quay. 'Coil that, you!' he calls with exaggerated authority, pointing at a rope end.

Oliver coils away. Mind you, he would have liked to slip ashore for a moment, for half a moment, and present his girl with a bag of raisins he's got in his pocket. He would dearly have liked to go ashore. Well, at least he will make his presence felt where he is.

'Carlsen!' he shouts to the blacksmith. 'Lucky I saw you. I owe you for those clamps for my gutters.'

Carlsen, embarrassed at finding every eye on him, answers: 'That's all right, take it easy – time enough when you come home again.'

But Oliver already has his purse out and hands the money over the ship's rail. 'That's right, isn't it?' he asks.

Such a display of punctiliousness in full public view puts Oliver right on top of the world. Who is present to witness his conduct? Petra, the lot. Oh, and Lydia is there with her children, keeping an eye on everything, sharp as a razor. Her husband, fisherman Jørgen, is there too, somewhere on the fringe; but as soon as the

9

town dignitaries start to arrive, by a route which takes them right past his corner, he drifts gently away along the quay and finds a safer place.

And now come the big shots, the shipowners, the doctor, the highest-ranking merchants; some are still festive from their dinner with the consul and arrive with flowers in their buttonholes and top hats on their heads. Here comes lawyer Fredriksen; the moment is not yet ripe, but lawyer Fredriksen needs to be on his toes, poised to say a few solemn words. He is used to holding forth; it is he who organizes public meetings in the town and holds forth at them.

The Johnsens appear from the cabin: C. A. Johnsen himself, with his lovely brown eyes and his paunch of prosperity, and Mrs Johnsen holding little Fia by the hand. As they step ashore, everyone makes way; not a child blocks their path. People who own steamships are entitled to plenty of elbow room on their own quay – that is only right and proper.

The captain climbs briskly up on the bridge and signals to the engine room. 'Let go there!' The hawsers are taken in. He raises his cap, family and friends on the quay wave back, the ship vibrates and glides out. At the last moment Oliver throws his bag of raisins ashore; no doubt he sees that it more or less hits the target.

And now the moment is ripe: lawyer Fredriksen steps forward and, raising his silk hat aloft, invokes success and good fortune on the ship, her owner, and her crew. Cries of 'Hurrah!' from the quay.

And so the *Fia* sailed for the Mediterranean.

The bag of raisins hit the target all right, but it was an unwelcome bag of raisins, an outrageous bag of raisins; for the bag burst as it landed, and the raisins spilled out over the planks of the quay. A fine state of affairs! Petra gave an indignant smile and stood with tears in her eyes, while Oliver's mother started gathering the raisins in her shawl; it was all she could do to keep the children away with dire warnings against trampling on God's gifts. The town dignitaries and even the Johnsen family came past the miniature battlefield – most notably, young Scheldrup Johnsen came past, smiling and murmuring to Petra: 'Pick up your raisins!' Petra went scarlet, hung her head, and wished the earth might swallow her ...

The women at the pump remembered that occasion for many a long day. They might differ on this or that detail, but by general agreement Mrs Johnsen had been in elegant black silk, with a silk-fringed shawl around her shoulders. And her hat was one of those with a thin, wide brim that fluttered up and down a little as she walked, and a single large feather.

Whereas no one had made much effort to remember what happened next, because now daily life took over. Oliver came home again in the autumn, but not on the *Fia*. Quite so, he was reduced to pulp, he was almost reduced to a corpse; he was crippled. That's the way it was. If you fall out of the rigging and smash your ribs in, you may survive, but it's certainly an event that sticks in your memory. As for Oliver, though, *he* got a barrel of whale oil on top of him, and broke his pelvis and a thigh; he was mutilated; he survived. Then he lay in a hospital in a little Italian coastal town, where no doubt he was inadequately cared for. The leg had to be amputated. It was seven months before he came home.

Petra, his girl, kept her chin up and showed her mettle under this monstrous ordeal. She was as ordinary as they make 'em, a run-of-the-mill sort of girl, but she had her good points too, there's no denying it.

Mattis, who had been apprenticed to a carpenter and was now working as a journeyman, big-nosed Mattis came to Petra and said: 'That was a terrible calamity!'

'What calamity's that?'

'I mean, Oliver coming home like this. Haven't you heard?'

Petra answered, with loyal indignation: 'Of course I've heard – I've had letter after letter, haven't I?'

'He was injured,' said Mattis.

'Yes,' said Petra.

'And now he's the type who can't even fend for himself, let alone for others – so what's going to happen now?'

Petra answered curtly: 'You don't need to concern yourself with that!'

She showed no conspicuous sorrow, no self-pity; perhaps she felt no great pity even for her sweetheart. 'Welcome home!' she said to him.

Oliver remained silent, but his mother answered: 'Well, now you can see the state he's come home in.'

'Oh, you've got yourself a peg leg,' said Petra.

Oliver gazed at a wall and answered: 'Well, of course.'

His mother added: 'And a crutch.'

'That's only to start with, while I'm weak.'

'Does it hurt?' asked Petra.

'Not on your life.'

'Well, that's a blessing at any rate.' Petra got up to go. 'Well, I thought I'd just drop in.'

So of course he never managed to give her a couple of presents he had ready, a white angel and a small inlaid wooden tray. Why was she so dry and curt? Surely she knew he was in the habit of bringing her something when he came home from distant lands – and he hadn't forgotten her this time, either. The wooden leg had made a very disagreeable impression on her, of course; that was only to be expected. But curt and cold – was Petra cold? Anything but. As Mattis now began saying to anyone who would listen: 'That Petra now – I've no desire to be saddled with her. When a girl's the type who stands there panting and quivering at the nostrils – no, thank you!'

Oliver had to start thinking of something to do. As long as there was food in the house he ate his meals, gathering strength, regaining his powerful chest and shoulders and his formidable health; but when his mother could no longer draw on his wages, supplies of flour, fish, and meat all began to dwindle. Maybe he was not too old to learn a trade; he could turn watchmaker or tailor, or he might go to college and become a teacher. But what kind of woman's work was this for hands like his? And what was his mother to live on during his apprenticeship? Besides, the sea was his element, and nowhere else.

He was young and unused to his sudden helplessness. Mostly he sat still, using his hands to propel himself from chair to chair if he wanted to move about the room. He was preoccupied with thinking up a new way of life – a strange occupation for a born sailor; sometimes its singularity pulled him up short. Him decrepit, him a cripple! As a stopgap he'd better get himself a boat and catch some fish for the larder. He had received a nasty injury, his body had an incontrovertible and authentic flaw, but having shed his gangrened leg and survived the consequences, he was left sitting with a substantial remnant, a net balance of strength.

The fishing was no very splendid affair: frost set in, and the bay became so completely icebound that even the mail boat was unable to keep the channel open but had each time to butt her way in through the ice. Oliver could have copied the other fishermen, hacked a hole in the ice, and fished through that, on foot – one might almost say, on shore. That was what Jørgen did, and even old Martin, who lived on the heath. But Oliver was too new a hand; and besides, he was not prepared to go to such extremes. People must get the impression that he fished, not from necessity, but for pleasure, to help pass the time.

Grim days set in; Christmas was truly dismal. But with the new year there came a change in the weather: there were storms at sea, the ice in the bay broke up. Day after day Oliver rowed out and fished, staying out longer and longer, sometimes till late in the evening; what is more, he returned home with fish. Not that he fished from necessity!

His mother said casually: 'Come to think of it, they asked me at old man Johnsen's if you could supply them with a little fish.'

'Me?' said Oliver. 'They did, did they? Well, I don't go fishing for other people.'

'No, that's what I thought,' his mother agreed. She let the matter drop, oh, absolutely, as if the mighty Johnsen of the Wharf could do his own fishing. Finally she said: 'Ah well – but they did promise to pay a good price.'

Silence. Oliver mulled it over. 'Old man Johnsen can pay me first for my leg,' he said.

Throughout this period Petra had scarcely been seen: she had dropped in a couple of times, had received her presents, had chatted on indifferent topics, and had gone away again. She still wore her ring, and showed no sign of wanting to end the engagement – no sign whatsoever; but deep down inside him Oliver may have had this and that fear. Rightly considered, he was no longer much of a prize: a half-man, a kind of freak who owned nothing – even his clothes were wearing thin. You see, like the rest of them, he had been too carefree in his sailing days and had put very little aside. The only thing which he had done with an eye to the future, and which before his fall he had been rather proud of, was now perhaps of small account: the extension to his house, the two new rooms on the other side of the passage. God alone knew if he would ever find a use for this showpiece now.

The winter just wouldn't end; it got on his nerves and sapped his courage.

One Sunday afternoon Petra called and behaved with unwonted friendliness. 'I saw your mother going into town,' she said to Oliver, 'so I thought I'd pop in and see you.'

Oliver smelled a rat; his girl was so unlike herself. She said tenderly, 'Poor Oliver!' and hinted that God had visited them both with affliction.

'Yes,' Oliver assented.

'I suppose it's our destiny,' she murmured with a sigh.

Pause. 'Well, what do you think?' he asked.

'What do *you* think?'

He gave in at once, partly from ancient pride, partly because he realized that at bottom she was right. It was impossible to shut his eyes to how things stood.

They talked it over together, and although she used only gentle words, her meaning was clear. 'I don't wonder at you,' he said, gazing at the ground.

When the moment came for her to leave, she knew the worst was still to come. She got as far as the door, but then she turned, went right up to him, stroked both his cheeks, and lifted his head. 'Now, you're not to put us both out by saying no. I've thought it over. It's not just yourself, you have your mother as well. Things aren't so easy for you.'

He looked at her uncomprehendingly: they had gone over this already, he wanted a respite from it. 'I know that,' he said.

'And without the use of your limbs or anything—'

'I know that too!' he broke in irritably.

'No, you mustn't take it like that, Oliver!' she coaxed. But when she saw him about to snap at her again, she too frowned and came abruptly to the point: 'It makes no difference what you say, things aren't so easy for you right now; still, they're bound to get better. Look, I'm putting it here, you can turn it to account; it makes no difference what you say, I'm putting it here on the table. It's heavy and expensive. I'm sure there are lots of people who'll buy it.'

'What is it? Oh, the ring. Put it there,' he said, nodding.

She might have spared herself all her beating about the bush; at this moment he seemed to have no objection to getting the ring back – at least it was worth something. When Petra had gone, he put it on the first joint of his little finger to see the effect.

But now he was seized by sentiment: sell the ring, turn it into cash? Never. He would sooner sink it in the ocean waves. He could keep this memorial all his life, he could take it out on Sundays and look at it. Not that his life had all that long to go . . .

2

After this Oliver no longer went out fishing every day. Not every day. No doubt his showdown with Petra had had an inhibiting effect; he put off doing any work, he made no decisions. His mother would ask: 'Are you going out today? No, I suppose not?' And Oliver would counter by asking: 'Are you out of fish, then?' 'It's not that,' his mother would answer, and fall silent.

Yes, but she could have done with a little flour, and one or two other things: soap, coffee, lamp oil, firewood, butter, matches, syrup – absolute necessities.

Mattis, the journeyman carpenter, was busy building himself a house. Doubtless he was thinking about the future. Oliver limped over to see him one day, chatted with him, and twirled the ring on his little finger. There was no quarrel between them.

Oliver said: 'I had two doors made for my new extension; in your master's workshop it was.'

'I remember,' said Mattis. 'It was last winter.'

'You could buy those doors from me and put them in here.'

'Do you want to sell them?'

'Yes – since they're no use to me any longer. I've had second thoughts.'

'I remember those doors well; it was I who made them,' said Mattis. 'So you've had second thoughts, have you? Not going to change your circumstances, uh?'

'Not for the time being.'

'How much do you want for the doors?'

They quickly came to terms. The doors were secondhand, of

course, and not even painted, but Oliver had paid for the lock and hinges; so he got his price.

Only now he had nothing left to sell – he could hardly sell the staircase. For a time he and his mother lived nicely on the money from the doors; but now spring was in the air again. Oliver was young, his clothes were threadbare, he could give a better account of himself in new ones, and now that misfortune had made him a landlubber for life, he hankered after a boater. His mother, who looked more and more despondently at the future, suggested that they might have taken in lodgers in the extension, if—

Well, Oliver had nothing against that.

'Yes, but now there are no doors.'

He thought for a moment, then answered carelessly: 'Doors? I can always get a pair of doors made.'

His mother shook her head. 'There's no stove, either.'

'Stove? What would they want with a stove in the summer?'

'They'll be cooking for themselves, surely, so they'll need a stove, won't they?'

Clearly, something had snapped in Oliver; his mind no longer functioned the way it used to.

He dragged himself over to Mattis again, chatted with him for a long time, and finally said: 'Well, what with all this building and painting and putting in doors and windows, I suppose you're intending to change your circumstances?'

'I don't rightly know how to answer that,' said Mattis. 'But the fact is, I haven't exactly closed my mind to it.'

'I understand!' Oliver nodded and looked on while the carpenter worked. There was still no quarrel between them. Oliver continued: 'Well, whoever she is and whoever she may be, she'll have a good billet with you. What was I going to say – have you bought the ring?'

'The ring? No.'

'I see. Well, when the day comes, I've got one.'

'Let's have a look,' said Mattis. 'But hasn't it got your name on it?'

'Yes, but you can get that filed off.'

Mattis looked at the ring, weighed it in his hand, valued it, and ended by buying it. 'Provided it fits, of course,' he said.

Oliver answered meaningfully: 'That's the least of my worries. If I understand correctly.'

Mattis glanced quickly at him and asked. 'Well, what do you say?'

'What do I say? It's not my affair any longer. I suppose I'll get my chance, too – I'm not dead yet.'

'No, I know that all right,' assented Mattis.

'Well, what's you opinion?' said Oliver, flattered. 'Won't I get my chance?'

'You must be joking, Oliver – your chances are as good as mine.'

Mattis was visibly relieved. They exchanged flatteries, talking without reserve but without trust, either.

'What happened, exactly, when you got your injury?' Mattis asked. 'Did you fall?'

'Me?' exclaimed Oliver, bridling. 'I've been around a bit too long for falling.'

'That's what I thought.'

'No, it was a wave.'

'I'll bet it was a wave all right – could have finished you off, uh?'

'It was just about the most God-almighty wave you ever saw,' Oliver boasted. 'Swept the cargo off the deck – I got a barrel of whale oil in my lap – it came hurtling through the air at me like a cannon ball.'

'Through the air – wow!'

'Then I heard a blood-curdling scream from the others.'

'Didn't you scream yourself?'

'Why should I scream? What use would that have been?'

Mattis shook his head, smiled, and said: 'Ah, you're the boy!'

Yes, Mattis was so visibly relieved, it was a pleasure to have dealings with Oliver. Could anyone be more cooperative than this man? Half his lower region gone, everything gone, but the rest a Napoleon! Put him in a carriage with the apron up, and he'd be flawless ...

For a time Oliver and his mother again lived well; he even did a little fishing, so they had fish for themselves and the cat, while the ring brought in flour and lamp oil. Only now he had nothing left to sell – he could hardly sell the chimney off the roof.

His mother's mood grew more sombre: this could not go on!

She started hinting that something must be done; later she ventured on a little discontent. The cupboard was bare. 'Perhaps you could make nets, surely you could make nets?' she asked. But Oliver could do nothing, had learned nothing, had never bothered to learn anything – had gone to sea when he should have been learning something.

'I badly need a porridge stirrer,' his mother said. 'You could make me a porridge stirrer if you were a handy man.'

Oliver could only interpret this as fretting and nagging on his mother's part. He retorted: 'You'll be wanting me to make mittens next!'

He pondered, he weighed innumerable pros and cons; something must indeed be done. He continued weighing pros and cons.

Nothing more could be extracted from the house than had already been extracted; it had long been mortgaged to lawyer Fredriksen. True, the new extension was unmortgaged, and on returning home Oliver had at once applied to Fredriksen for a loan on this, too, but had been refused. The extension? Fredriksen regarded it merely as a valid form of upkeep of the property. And the new tiled roof? asked Oliver. Upkeep! said Fredriksen. And when Oliver suggested that he could go elsewhere and raise a loan on the extension, the lawyer threatened to terminate the mortgage and put the house up for auction without more ado. They argued this way and that, till the lawyer asked in surprise: 'Are you really reduced to this?' '*Me*?' said Oliver, acting the big shot. Ah, that was what the lawyer had thought! And since it was only the extension and the new tiled roof that gave Fredriksen reasonable security for his money, Oliver ought to sign a declaration that all the new bits of the house were included in the mortgage – would he mind doing that as an honest man? Oliver, newly arrived home, accustomed to open-handed dealings in seaports, and born good-natured, signed the agreement. He and the lawyer parted the best of friends.

At the time, that is.

He often regretted this stupidity, which there was no undoing. Or was there? Could he simply sell the house, repay lawyer Fredriksen, and be rid of him? Would the money go so far? The only certainty was that he himself would be homeless.

Oliver weighed innumerable pros and cons; Oliver pondered.

At times he toyed with the idea of turning religious, and perhaps getting a wheelchair and making the rounds of the congregations.

His mother would come home from town and tell him this or that; she heard more than he did, picking up snippets in the street or at the pump – gossip, incidents, truth and lies – tucking it all away and carrying it home. Sometimes it just remained in her head and came to nothing, but sometimes a scrap of casual information would prove useful. As when she told Oliver about Adolf, son of Carlsen the blacksmith, a lad they knew, who had just signed on to go to sea.

'Where's he signed on?' asked Oliver.

'On that barque of Heiberg's. They said he was out fixing himself up with a chest.'

After a while Oliver nodded and said: 'He can buy my chest.'

'That too!' sighed his mother.

'What good is it to me? I've sailed it out and sailed it home again time after time, and now it's just standing here. No, you get young Adolf to buy the chest – I'm sick of the sight of it!'

Besides, he was sure Adolf would be glad to have the chest: it had made many a voyage and was used to the sea, a well-tried sea chest, and one that brought good luck. Why, before every voyage Oliver had positively yearned for his chest. It wasn't alive of course; still, it was a companion and a servant – yes, a loving friend. Well, good luck to it, let it go now! On his last journey home from Italy, it had been a sore trial to him, for he was a cripple now and unable to handle it. On the railway it had been overweight, and had cost him money. It was almost as if it had taken the bread from his mouth and preyed on him, the monster – out with it!

Ah, but Oliver was not entirely indifferent when his mother arrived with Adolf. His sea chest stood there, an ugly, heavy object when all was said and done; but useful. It had been kicked and knocked about; there it stood, with numerous scars on its green paint; the lid had even been used for shredding tobacco – but, God, what a piece of work that chest was, all the same!

'She's just as you see her,' Oliver told Adolf. 'She's never kowtowed to captains or brokers or consuls; she's stood her ground and never budged unless she was forced.'

Adolf bought the chest and settled down to hear Oliver's words of wisdom. The former sailor was able to tell the boy about the life he was about to embark on: ah yes, a free and healthy life, but not in every respect a life to boast of. Ungodliness and depravity and lavish shore leave in foreign parts and lands. Not that he himself, he boasted, hadn't always been lucky enough to find nice sweethearts in the ports; still, things hadn't always gone off without a fight or a battle. But then it was just a matter of getting one hand on the fellow's neck and the other on his behind, and making a hole in the window with him – one, two, three, and out into the gutter! Oh no, one hadn't always sat in a chair and been a cripple.

Oliver began to philosophize. His old salt's talk was empty and commonplace, neither better nor worse than that of other old salts: truth mixed with bravado, boasting, sanctimoniousness, and white lies. He enlarged on the temptations, slipped in some English words, warned Adolf against drink. 'You see now, Adolf, the state I've come home in. It's almost beyond belief. "But do you mean it was due to drink and debauchery? You're sober enough now!" God bless my soul, it was on the stormy ocean, and what had I done? So never succumb to drink like so many of them, and let our Lord do his will with you – you have no say in the matter. And if they see you've got money on you, see you taking English sovereigns out of your pocket, they're after you like gulls after roach – that's when you need a waistcoat pocket sewn in before you sail.'

'Did you have one?' interrupts his mother.

'Didn't I just!' Oliver opens some buttons; he has no sewn-in waistcoat pocket. 'It must be in my other clothes, my shore-leave clothes,' he says.

'Shore-leave clothes?' asks his mother.

Oliver ignores her and continues: 'Be that as it may, young Adolf here is to take heed of righteousness and not of unrighteousness. Well now, just remember what I've said, Adolf, and keep your mind on God when you're on the night-watch and are standing at the helm. And then you'll learn to speak English and to express yourself in the language wherever you go, all over the world. They'll understand you whether you go into a bar and order a glass of beer, or whether you go to church or to the consulate. But take my chest now and treat it fairly and squarely all your life – it's never known anything else.'

'What shore-leave clothes were those?' his mother asks. 'Have you any clothes beyond what you're sitting in?'

'Who says I've no other clothes?' Oliver retorts. 'They were made in Italy. How you do talk!'

But his mother is bolder in the presence of a third party and merely gives a little snort. Oh, the cupboard has become so bare.

And now Oliver had nothing left to sell; the sea chest was the last item, and there was nothing for new clothes or a boater. But the days went by, and one day he seemed to wake up a little and actually dropped a hint about selling the boat.

'The boat!' shrieked his mother.

He checked himself and changed course: no, it wasn't a boat for selling, he'd get nothing for it, it was an old tub that was only held together by the tar it was lined with. He himself had bought it for a song.

'I suppose I'll have to try and row out myself,' his mother threatened. 'Since you've given up.'

Whereupon, with the utmost indifference and contempt for his mother's words, Oliver took his crutch and hobbled out into the street.

Fine weather; he sniffed the smell of the sea. A whir of pigeons settled in the street; children were playing with a skipping rope. He himself had once played with a skipping rope.

He took to going into the shops. 'You *are* a stranger!' people said everywhere, and in their kindness provided the cripple with something to sit on. Again and again he had to tell how he came by his injury. He became a practised narrator, embellishing his tale more and more, with some particularly interesting accretions about his spell in the hospital, about which none of his mates from the *Fia* could come home and put the record straight. One of the nurses had not been averse to marrying him . . .

'Well, why didn't you take her up on it?'

'What, go and become a Catholic?'

But gradually they stopped lionizing him in the shops; the novelty had worn off, he had to find himself a crate to sit on, or else stand leaning with his elbow on the counter. And no one inquired about the nurse any more.

Time passed, his visits to the stores petered out and he started doing a little fishing again. Johnsen of the Wharf in person had asked if he would sell him whatever he could spare from his catch. 'Well,' said Oliver, to avoid an outright no. That Johnsen of the Wharf knew his way around all right: the sort of shipowner who could get a mutilated man home, and even employ him on a boat again. But, no, thank you, Oliver ate his fish himself!

He met fisherman Jørgen out on the water; they laid their boats alongside and had a chat. Well, what were they to chat about? The weather, the fishing, their earnings. Jørgen was a demon for work.

'Why do you stay here in the bay?' said Oliver. 'If I had your splendid boat I'd go farther out. How much can you earn in a day?'

It varied so much. Sometimes a lot – there were good and bad days – sometimes very little.

'Let me tell you something, Jørgen: here you stick in the bay, just like us amateur fishermen. Now I don't count myself – I'm disabled and no use for anything – but if you put out to sea you could catch halibut and big fish.'

Jørgen agreed: yes, then he'd catch some whale.

They both laughed; for of course this putting out to sea was only a joke, mere friendly chatter on Oliver's part. Jørgen hadn't the boat or tackle for it, and in any case was only one man.

'Suppose we clubbed together and got ourselves a seagoing boat,' said Oliver, still in jest.

Like everyone else, Jørgen was patient with the cripple. He sat discussing various ideas with him: a seagoing boat, why not, and heavy tackle, deep-sea lines – they could sweep the market in fish. It was Oliver who had the ideas; they flashed into his head and were not worth much; he had been in foreign lands and seen and heard fantastic things; he had brains in his head. 'Here I sit talking,' he said, 'but I dare say I'll end up having a try for the light-house service.'

'Well,' said Jørgen, 'you could easily do worse.'

'I don't know. But a disabled man has to do something.'

'Look after the lamp, keep the logbook, guide seafarers on dark nights. If you had someone to put in a word for you . . .'

'Sure, I can get old man Johnsen to put in a word for me. Well, shall we row home?'

'No, I must stay a little longer; I've promised the judge enough for a dinner, and I've got very little so far.'

'What does the judge give you for a catch like that?'

Jørgen mentioned an average price.

Oliver shook his head at the paltry sum; then he rowed away and began fishing again on his own account. He sat for another half hour, then rowed home with what he had caught.

He rowed like a champion. Perhaps he wanted to show off and astonish Jørgen with his strength; and in this he succeeded. In reality Oliver might have been made, or remade, for life in a fishing boat: he sat holding the oars like a heavy weight that moves backwards and forwards – and he had all the limbs he needed. Perhaps it was this truth that dawned on him a few days later; for now he grew industrious, setting out each morning and fishing all day, rowing farther and farther out, and finding new fishing grounds, returning home with two or three strings of fish, and selling quite a few in the town. The money he put aside.

'You row like a steamer,' said Jørgen. And Martin said the same: Martin, who lived on the heath and was the oldest fisherman in the town.

'Do you think so? Ah, well – it's a fact that I've sailed most of the world's seas and seen a thing or two.'

To which Jørgen replied with his usual maxim: nature was full of mysteries that we could learn from.

'It's a good thing I can use the oars,' said Oliver. 'I've planned an expedition for myself one of these days.'

He didn't say where he was going; his project was not entirely legal – gathering eggs on the islands. While he was at it, he might salvage some driftwood to take home. It was thus a two-way speculation, with the legal search for driftwood as camouflage for the illegal egg gathering.

3

Fisherman Jørgen, on the other hand, was no speculator; he was a fisherman who had got along by matching his wants to his modest earnings. He owned his house and a bit besides, his three children were nice and plump, Jørgen was doing fine in every way.

Lydia for her part was impetuous, her anger easily roused; but she was capable: sharp as a razor, with a tongue like a grater, and something of the saw, the plane, and the scrubbing brush about her, but indispensable to her husband and children. People made stealthy fun of her; her enormous vanity and her genteel pretensions bordered on the ridiculous – her children were prettier than other people's, she herself prettier than the neighbouring housewives. It was an infection she had picked up as a girl and carried around with her since: she had served exclusively in the best houses, first at Heiberg's, then for several years at Johnsen of the Wharf's – did she not then belong to the upper classes? Had not C. A. Johnsen himself cast an eye on her in her younger days? How well she remembered that! He got nowhere with her of course, but it wasn't for want of trying.

Then she got to know Jørgen, kept him dangling for four years, but finally married him. He was not exactly a portrait painter's dream, but his face was innocuous, with small, unremarkable features, and his beard – full, dark, and soft – had a certain distinction. His failings included being heavy on his feet: he was no dancer. God knew, everyone knew, whenever he came or went; and his sedentary life in a boat was hardly calculated to make him more nimble-footed. But Jørgen was a steady, loyal man, and Lydia had never regretted taking him on.

Jørgen was a worker; indeed, he positively fretted when the weather kept him from his boat. Spring and early summer were a sad time of year, with all those endless holidays to endure; Easter and Whitsun were a sore trial. It would have been all right if his fish hadn't commanded a sale; but small as it was, the town was always short of fish, and the price rose every year. Oliver might sniff at the profit as much as he liked, but small-scale fishing was a good livelihood, an excellent livelihood. Moreover, Jørgen had read in a newspaper that fishing had the same blessed character as farming: that it was a gathering of the harvest. He too was in the service of the earth.

But now he was weatherbound. The major festivals were over at last – Ascension Day, Constitution Day,* Prayer Day† – but God had raised a storm at sea. God wanted a three-week break in the gathering of the ocean's harvest, for whatever good it might do. Jørgen wandered around holding his small boy by the hand; they managed to get a good soaking from the rain, they climbed up to high ground, gazed at the sea, and counted the steamships in the distance; then they came down again and looked at the boat, to see if she lay securely and whether she needed bailing out. Jørgen fretted badly during this idle spell.

He bumped into Oliver. Having nothing else to do, they were free to find themselves a quiet corner for a chat. Oliver was far from fretting: he was in good bodily health, the bad weather allowed him to remain in idleness, his industry had deserted him. It was like the hand of Providence: no sooner had he resolved to earn the money for some new clothes, and even begun to acquire a genuine taste for work, than there came this long spell of being weatherbound and his good resolutions faded away. His only regret was that he couldn't go on that expedition of his; day after day he was obliged to go home and wrangle with his mother.

He had become quite a champion at philosophizing. He was young, and at times he would testify insistently and vehemently to his own existence. Look here now, was everything so beautiful and diamond-studded as we learned in the Scriptures? Take that fellow Olaus, who got a charge of dynamite in the face one year and went blue. The next year, after he had found work in the shipyard, a winch had come and taken off his hand. Now he drank like a fish and fought with his wife. 'Take anyone you like, Jørgen, misfortune can change and corrupt us all, however much we're God's creatures.'

'Well,' said Jørgen.

'Well, isn't it true? You can be the kindest of souls, but if you get a cannon ball in the crotch it does you no good. It does you no good whatsoever. Perhaps you think it does you good?'

* The Norwegian constitution was signed on 17 May, 1814. Trans.
† The fourth Friday after Easter. Trans.

'It's – well, it's a chastisement, sort of,' said Jørgen mildly.

'And you're a dolt. Chastisement? You can tell yourself that when you meet with a God-almighty wave like I did.' Oliver was suddenly white with rage, but when Jørgen showed signs of wanting to go, he regretted his outburst and felt in his pocket for his pipe. 'Would you like to have this? I've been meaning to give it to you.'

'Have you given up smoking?'

'Long ago. Since the hospital. I bought it abroad once upon a time. So if you'd like to have it—'

'No. You keep it.'

They set out for home.

'Oh, you needn't bother to make yourself look pious with that drooping mouth, Jørgen – you needn't bother, I tell you,' said Oliver in another burst of anger. 'I don't care what you say, you have your problems to wrestle with, and I have mine. Right now, for example, your not being able to go out to sea – is that because you're so full of riches and wealth that you can't take any more? I can tell you, He's strict in His reckoning, our Lord is, it's almost as if He's stealing from you.'

Jørgen frowned and opened his mouth as if to answer, which for a moment gave him, too, the appearance of an angry man. But he stopped at the preliminaries and said nothing.

Oliver subsided and veered round again. 'But everything rests in His hand, I know that, of course. And if we try to walk according to His precepts, then we have no say in the matter. Won't you have the pipe?'

Jørgen squirmed and answered: 'You oughtn't to give it away.' But when he saw the cripple's pleading face, he changed his tune and said: 'Why should I have that valuable pipe of yours?'

'You *shall* have it!' Oliver declared. 'I *want* you to have it, I've thought of you all along. You'll have plenty of chances to do me a favour in return, and I know you'll take them.'

And indeed the house of Oliver had recently provided its neighbours with several chances of doing it a favour. Oliver himself had kept in the background, but his mother would go out of an evening, when the shops were shut, and borrow a cupful of coffee beans or a bowl of rye flour 'till tomorrow'. There was nothing the old girl couldn't borrow: one evening she was obliged to borrow a codling from fisherman Martin.

She was in perpetual conflict with her son. 'But what on earth have you done with the fish money you earned before the bad weather set in?' she asked.

'Wouldn't you like to know!' he retorted.

But his mother persisted; she never let up until she had brought him to the boil, and one day he came and slammed the money on the table; all he had salvaged from it was a blue tie. All right, it was not a great sum – coppers laboriously scraped together fish by fish; but much or little, it was money for clothes and a boater – and now these would go by the board. Naturally he would not have handed it over if God Himself had not messed things up with His bad weather and thwarted his good intentions – goodbye to the lot! Bold as brass, he said to his mother: 'And now let me have some peace for a while!'

His mother was not exactly overwhelmed: so that was all! 'Oh, you'll have peace from me, all right!' she said. 'But if I'm to pay our debts, this won't go far, you know.'

Whereupon he came out with something that had long been smouldering inside him: 'It's not myself I'm worried about, don't imagine that. If you can manage, so can I.'

'What do you mean?'

'What do I mean? I mean just this: that I'm a disabled man without the full use of his limbs. Have you no eyes in your head?'

'Am I to go on the parish?' she asked indignantly.

'On the parish? Not exactly. But couldn't you get a wee bit of assistance?'

'Well!' she exclaimed, and set her jaw firmly.

'Well, would that be so unspeakable? Disabled as I am?'

'Disabled?' she raged. 'Now listen to me: you don't *want* to do anything, you don't *want* to perform God's will. Why didn't you take the opportunity of going out fishing yesterday, when the sea was calm? Today it's rough again.'

'It was quite rough yesterday, too.'

'Oh. Then can you tell me why Jørgen was out?'

'Was Jørgen out? It's all very well for Jørgen, he has a good new boat,' sighed Oliver.

Silence. But by now his mother was in a fury and making no

attempt to hide it. 'You sell the doors off the house,' she said. 'It's a wonder you don't sell the walls. I wish I was in my grave.'

'So do I.'

'You!' she snorted. 'All *you* ever do is lie around the house. And I know very well that if I started drawing assistance I'd have to feed you, too.'

Oliver exploded with laughter at his mother's preposterous talk. 'No, really, do shut your trap! Ha-ha-ha, no, really, so help me God, you can talk to yourself from now on.'

After a while there was once again no fish with the potatoes, and no wood for the stove. There had been the occasional day of good fishing weather, but each time Oliver had missed his chance, and each time the white horses had been out again next morning; in fact, the weather got worse rather than better. What did it all mean? Heaven was merciless; never before had it thundered so rudely over the town.

Oliver threw himself from chair to chair in the living room, and sprawled at the table for long periods, asleep or dozing, with his head on his arms; from time to time he would lash out at the cat with his wooden leg. One day he went up on the roof over the living room. Old sea dog that he was, he wanted to go aloft once more. He tinkered with the lightning conductor, put a few tiles straight, and came down again.

By now he was in dire straits; regular meals were a thing of the past. One day his mother took herself off and stayed out all day. When she didn't come back the next day either, Oliver called on an expert and said: 'You must do me a favour and come and look at my lightning conductor – I'm afraid I may have damaged it when I was straightening the tiles on the roof.' 'Do you think it's urgent?' the man asked. 'Perhaps you'd be so kind as to come with me here and now,' Oliver answered. 'The fact is, this weather makes me scared of lightning.'

The man went with him; like everyone else, he felt obliged to help the cripple.

The man went up on the roof; Oliver remained below. The man called down to him: 'Well, if there'd been a disaster you'd have had yourself to thank for it!'

'How's that?'

'Good heavens, the conductor's gone – goes as far as the roof and then stops. It's taking the lightning straight down to the stove in the living room.'

'The way I look at it,' said Oliver, 'it's a good job my old mum's been away on a visit all this time. I would have been the only victim.'

The man put in a new conductor; when he had finished, Oliver asked how much it cost. 'Nothing.' 'Oh, but I want to pay.' 'It can wait. Any time you have a codling left over, you can let me have it.' 'You shall have a whole string!' said Oliver.

He spoke loud and clear, for the benefit of someone who was passing by – of Petra, who was just passing by. He wanted it known that he was offering to pay, and to pay well. Yes indeed, Petra was passing by – presumably on her way to Mattis's new house, to her own new house. Oliver remained standing there. He should at least have had a new boater to raise to her. He had nothing.

Still no sign of his mother – where had she taken herself? Had she really gone on the parish? Oliver resumed his drifting around the stores; he had stayed away for quite a while; once again he was given a crate to slump down on, an occasional ship's biscuit to gnaw. Look, he ate these granite-like rusks for fun, purely as a joke; no need for anyone to feel surprise – the old seadog still had a taste for ship's rations, and splendid teeth.

When he had done the rounds of the stores, he extended his circuit, went up on the heath, and had coffee and bread with old Martin. They chatted about the weather, and Oliver told Martin's womenfolk about his spell in the hospital and about the nurse. A right fool he had been not to take her. But the fact was, a man preferred to live and die in the faith he'd been brought up in. And besides, at the time he'd had a girl back home that he'd believed in. 'Is it all over between you and Petra?' asked the womenfolk. 'I forbid you to mention her,' he replied.

He hobbled over to a new house that was nearing completion, and sat down for a chat there, too. Yes, it cost money to build, that was for sure. Not so much the house itself, but the windows and doors took your breath away, they were so bloody expensive. If they wanted to buy a pair of doors, he had a specially fine pair.

From the heath Oliver made his way to Mattis's place. The carpenter was busy as usual, but put down his plane in order to provide a seat for the cripple. They talked about the long spell of bad weather on land and sea; a poor wretch could hardly keep body and soul together. Still, it was the same for everyone; old Jørgen and old Martin were stuck at home, too.

'If only I had my pipe, I'd have made you a present of it,' said Oliver.

'You shouldn't do that.'

'Before you could say Jack Robinson! But old Jørgen's got it.'

'What, old Jørgen's got it?'

'Brand-new pipe. I bought it abroad some place or other. What was I going to say – when are you changing your circumstances?'

'Well, you know,' said Mattis, almost bashfully, 'it'll be any day now.'

'I see,' said Oliver, and fell silent and pensive. Oh, yes, Oliver could show patience and profound wisdom; he could resign himself to the inevitable. The carpenter felt sorry for him; after all, he really was a Napoleon. There he sat, gazing at the floor, experiencing no doubt a melancholy moment; his eyes were almost closed. But suddenly a ripple broke the calm surface: he still gazed at the floor, but he pointed with his crutch and said: 'I could do with those doors back!'

Mattis gaped and said: 'What?'

'I could do with those doors back!'

'Doors? I see.'

Oliver slowly raised his eyes and said: 'You can *give* me them back.'

They stared at one another.

'I'll try and find time to make you a pair of doors,' said Mattis.

'No,' retorted Oliver, 'it's those doors or nothing.'

Was this a threat? Oliver rose and stood erect – yes, he used the crutch only as a walking stick; his whole bearing was now one of haughtiness. A performance like this was just the thing to confuse the carpenter's ideas about the cripple; Mattis looked almost totally blank; his great nose seemed to grow even longer; he was visibly shaken.

'Well, you can have the doors,' he said.

'You're doing me a favour,' said Oliver. He went home, leaving Mattis in a thoughtful frame of mind.

More sitting at the table, sleeping or dozing, giving the cat an occasional kick, keeping an eye on the desolate street. The days passed slowly. The doors had come; there they stood in the passage, not yet back on their hinges, but all ready to hang. Mattis in person had carried them there on his head, first one door and then the other. The carpenter was, not surprisingly, inclined to be taciturn. Oliver said: 'There's not much wrong with your muscles, Mattis!'

Shortly afterwards his mother came home again. She walked in without a word or a gesture of greeting, but without overt hostility, either. 'Have you got the doors back?' she asked; doubtless she already found her home rather more inviting.

'Where have you been?' asked her son.

'Oh, I've been wandering around a wee bit.'

'Well, you see,' said Oliver, 'even if you're away I can still get a thing or two for the house. I've got the doors now.'

'As far as I'm concerned, you can please yourself whether you have doors in the house or not,' said his mother, compressing her lips.

'Oh, so you don't care what it's like here – right, you can whistle for your next set of doors!'

Oliver rose, picked up his crutch, and hobbled rapidly out of the house. What an opportunity – he would really go berserk! He took the road up over the heath, back to the new house. While he was out his mother had a meal; before coming home the old woman had hidden a variety of foodstuffs under her shawl – waffles, blood sausages, smoked herring, eggs, pork fat, bread. She packed it all up again carefully and stowed it away at the bottom of her bed.

When Oliver returned, he had a man in tow. The man came and carried away one door on his head. No words passed between mother and son. The man came back for the other door and carried it away in turn to the new house. Perhaps Oliver began to think he had gone too far, and to pacify his mother he said: 'When you want to buy a door, it costs the earth, but when you want to sell it again, you don't even get the price of a decent meal for it.'

'You're not telling me you've sold the doors again, are you?'

'What good are they to me?' Oliver shouted. 'And in any case, you didn't care about them.'

'Well, God preserve me from you!' his mother exploded.

For a moment he may have thought of flaring up and laying all the blame on her; he stumped around the room with needless haste, banging his wooden leg on the floor. Ah well, since he was born with wits he had better use them. 'That's for the doors!' he said, laying the money on the table. 'You can take the lot.'

Again his mother didn't seem exactly overwhelmed; she looked askance at the money and gave a little toss of the head.

Oliver asked indignantly: 'What – perhaps you think I've boozed away the rest? I've merely kept back a wee bit for my expedition.'

'What expedition?'

'Because if I'm going on an expedition, I shall need a wee bit for provisions, I take it.'

'Yes, it's just the weather for an expedition,' said his mother incredulously.

'It's calming down now; the wind's changed. But in any case,' he muttered, still the man who was born with wits and had better use them, 'in any case, I'm not going to pick a quarrel with you.'

'Indeed,' said his mother in an injured tone.

'No. Because whatever I do is wrong.'

Devil take Oliver if he wasn't the injured party in the matter of the doors!

4

At last there came a fine day followed by another; the weather seemed to be set fair. Oliver called on fisherman Jørgen and said: 'Look, you must be so kind as to swap boats with me tomorrow.'

'Whatever for?'

'I need to go quite a distance, and I don't care to rely on my own boat. Ah, you're using the pipe, do I see? How is it?'

'The pipe's all right.'

'Good, just carry on using it – I want you to have it.'

Lydia offered him coffee, but he had a few coppers in his pocket and was able to refuse. 'I had some just before I left home. Well, how about it, Jørgen, will you do me that favour?'

Jørgen had no choice. He answered: 'I suppose I'd better. But make sure you look after the boat properly.'

And so Oliver set out on his expedition.

The older inhabitants remember to this day what happened next; it was no small matter. Far from foundering or doing himself a further injury, Oliver came home with a ship, a derelict, and demanded his salvage money. He was not alone in this meritorious deed: when he found the ship drifting beyond the islands, abandoned by her crew, he had had to row to the nearest land and fetch help. But Oliver was the discoverer, Oliver the able seaman who could take charge of the salvage operations. It was he who set to work with the pumps, took in the remnants of sails and the dangling ropes, and later directed the towing from the helm. No one could tell that he was a cripple now.

If only he had brought a cargo of coffee ashore! No such luck: the derelict was loaded, one might say ballasted, with bricks – a Danish vessel, making probably for the nearest city with these bricks when she was blown out to sea by a violent gale. The old tub was not worth much; still, there she lay, a find, a gift; battered admittedly, with no boats, no trimmings, a stinking wooden trough, but not a total write-off. She must have been at sea throughout the bad weather; the crew seemed to have abandoned her for lack of provisions – there was virtually no food aboard.

Someone had spotted the strange spectacle, and now the whole town gazed out curiously over its mirror-smooth bay. What was it? A kind of procession: tugboat and ship, with a boat in tow behind. People wormed their way down to the quay, Jørgen came and recognized his boat; the ship was a stranger, but Oliver stood on board.

Oliver stood on board, thickset, erect, not overdoing the strong words, but giving the occasional order to the two fisherman he had roped in to help with the salvage operations. Then he asked the people on shore to send for the consul. Jørgen called out a subdued question about what ship this was, but got no answer, Oliver having many other things to see to. Olaus, who was always loafing about the quay when he wasn't drinking or fighting with his wife, said in his loud, rough voice: 'He's stolen the ship!'

Oliver was incensed by the arrival, not of the consul himself, but merely of his son, young Scheldrup. 'Where's your father?' he shouted.

'Dad? What ship's that?'

'Go and fetch your father. Take my word for it, he'll have to write a report and seal everything on board.'

'I said, what ship's that?'

Oliver shouted to some small boys on the quay to fetch the consul; only then did he turn to young Scheldrup and explain: 'You see, this is a Danish ship, a foreigner, as far as I can make out.'

The consul arrived, C. A. Johnsen himself, and the crowd made way. He came somewhat reluctantly – he had no intention of being a man that anyone could send for. But, of course, with his superior intellect he soon sized everything up. A couple of questions sufficed. 'I've brought an unusual guest!' announced Oliver. The consul glanced at the ship with his brown eyes and was unimpressed – it was not a steamship, not his own *Fia*. He sent young Scheldrup for writing materials, then went on board and concerned himself with statements and reports.

This took an hour, while the crowd waited. Half the town had come down to the quay. Petra had come, lawyer Fredriksen had come. He asked, 'Who's the hero, who rescued the ship?' Young Scheldrup allowed himself a little joke: 'Oliver – in case you want to make a speech!' Young Scheldrup joked with Petra also; that boy was getting a bit too grown-up. 'That's what I call a true sailor's deed,' said lawyer Fredriksen.

To be sure, a true sailor's deed; it got Oliver into the newspaper, and many were those who discussed it. Oliver himself made relatively light of the affair. He had to explain all the details to these landlubbers, but he didn't boast, or make a fool of himself by aping the town dignitaries. Naturally he took great satisfaction in his exploit; he at once went and ordered new clothes – he had earned the right. Velvet and silk were not his style, but no one could grudge him a blue sailor suit. 'How it happened?' he would say to the landlubbers. 'Just like when you're strolling down the road and you find a gold ring and pick it up!' And they would all laugh at his pleasantry – a true sailor's deed couldn't be as easy as that! He was like a king who descends to his people's level and makes himself accessible to all; he was not the one to ignore those who only sat at home while he was rescuing the ship.

But after a few days he felt the need to make rather more of it and said to Jørgen: 'As you know, I was looking for driftwood. Then it seemed as if someone was telling me to row farther and farther out. It was just as if I was inspired!'

Jørgen nodded reflectively at this; nature was full of mysteries.

'I don't want to exaggerate; I'd never dreamed of a whole wreck coming in from the great ocean. But as I sat and rowed, it came over me: farther out, far, far out! Besides, the fact is, as you know, I've been knocking about the world ever since I was fourteen. I've seen the other side of the globe, so now, I don't mind telling you, it's almost as if I don't belong to this little town any more. Still, now I shall have to live and die here, God help me – there's nothing else for it.'

It was remarkable how Oliver's morale improved. His stroke of luck with the derelict altered his entire outlook: the bitterness left him, he became milder and more patient. Not that he pulled himself together to the extent of turning industrious, but he began taking the air in his new clothes; the trouser might flap vacantly about his wooden leg, but he no longer cursed his misfortune. 'You can buy what you like, as far as I'm concerned,' he would say to his mother, the soul of tractability. One day he came across an old woman who was going around selling raffle tickets for a tablecloth. 'Let me look at that fine tablecloth,' said Oliver; and he bought some tickets out of charity. It was almost as if a kind of piety had come over him.

This continued for a week or so; then it continued no longer. Consul Johnsen of the Wharf had given him an advance on the salvage money; but it was beyond the consul's power to sell the ship and its cargo without more ado, and pay out the entire proceeds. Had Oliver imagined he could go on receiving advances? At all events, he had expected them to last a little longer; things were fine now, these were blessed days; Oliver could strut down to the derelict and pump her out daily and practically own her.

But now the crew turned up – turned up from much farther south, a skipper and three men, the ship's lords and masters. No question of condemning the vessel; they set to work at once repairing her. Having come all the way to Norway, they were not keen on sailing their bricks back again; they sold them to the consul and loaded up with planks instead. Then they settled up for everything and sailed.

The golden age was over; Oliver was again thrown back on his own resources. Really, now, how had it all happened? The salvage money could not be withheld, of course; but Oliver had to share it with the other two, the two fishermen, so none of them made his fortune. 'Don't I even get the lion's share?' asked Oliver. Yes, he got the lion's share, and a bonus for the pumping. But he had received the whole sum in advance – how had it all happened?

He had had a fine old time with his little piece of good fortune, but now it was over. He was a much-wronged man. What did Jørgen think, what did old Martin think? He dropped in on Mattis to hear his views.

Mattis was strange today – a riddle. He neither answered Oliver's greeting nor offered the cripple a seat. He seemed angry; and indeed, when a man grinds his teeth and keeps hopping about, his frame of mind can hardly be in question.

Oliver was full of his own woes: he had been made a fool of, he had been taken for the most God-almighty ride! 'Listen to this, for example: it was I who found the ship and brought her in, and what do I get out of it? I'm sorry now I ever took a cent, and what's more, I mean to sling it back at them again, so help me God!'

'Oh, stop your blathering!' the carpenter suddenly yelled.

Oliver looked at him: he was working like a maniac, his hands were trembling. Was he drunk? If he wanted enmity he could have it; Oliver straightened his broad chest and shoulders.

'I want those doors of mine back,' said Mattis.

'Oh,' said Oliver . . . 'What was that you said? Doors?'

'I want them back!' snarled the carpenter. 'I paid you for them – they were mine. Do you understand? The doors!'

Oliver was almost speechless at such an unreasonable demand, but he managed to answer: 'You gave me the doors. As well you might, after all we'd had in common.'

Mattis flung down his work and stood erect. 'Had in common? I don't wish to have one morsel in common with you. No. Not so much as a crumb. What have I got out of it? No, it's like I said: when they're the type whose nostrils go in and out – no, thank you! In any case, I can do without you hanging around here, and I want my doors back!'

How unreasonable can you get? Oliver had come here in a spirit of peace, just wanting a little sympathy, and instead had been chased out. It must have something to do with Petra. He said: 'If you've been let in for some sort of hanky-panky and scandal by the womenfolk, it's happened since the time when I was going to have her. It's nothing to do with me.'

The carpenter began working again and gave a scornful, devil-may-care toss of the head. 'You can have her yourself, now,' he said. 'In the state you've got her in,' he added.

Oliver understood not one word, but since he had been as good as ordered out of the workshop, he got up and banged his way to the door.

'It's beyond belief!' said the carpenter, laughing savagely to himself. 'They thought they'd lure me into it!'

'What are you talking about?' Oliver asked.

'Why, you've been as cunning as foxes, the whole pack of you,' the carpenter continued, laughing still more to himself. 'But old Mattis looked where he was going – enough was enough. Old Mattis wasn't willing.'

Oliver paused a moment with his hand on the door handle, in case there was more coming; to his amazement he saw that now the carpenter was weeping, his whole body shaking. As he opened the door he heard an unrecognizable voice behind him: 'You can have her now! And I'm coming to get my doors back!'

Oliver had long been used to the idea that a cripple was let off lightly – and here he was, being spoken to as if he had no wooden leg. The carpenter's behaviour hurt his feelings; exercising great restraint, he nevertheless snorted and said: 'You can get *me* back instead if you want! Do you think I'm afraid of you?'

The carpenter became a man again; he snatched his jacket from the hook and said: 'I'm coming with you now and getting them!'

Seeing that he was in earnest, Oliver relented again, opened the door wide, and made a quick exit. 'I haven't even got the doors,' he admitted. 'I've sold them up on the heath.'

After this there was silence behind him; no doubt the carpenter still stood there speechless. Let him stand, let him stand in his doorway and never again find words!

But perhaps Oliver felt insecure, for he loitered a while in the streets before he thought of making tracks for home. The carpenter might still decide to seek him out – what a way to treat a cripple!

There was Petra, crossing the street; she looked at him and nodded. Yes, whatever it was, it must have something to do with Petra. Perhaps she had decided against the carpenter, decided against Mattis and his nose. And damnit if he didn't stand weeping in full public view, instead of taking it like a man! It occurred to Oliver that he really should rise to another expedition, the last having been interrupted so strangely. Though doubtless Jørgen would again have qualms about lending his boat; people could be so odd. Supposing he made a real expedition, out beyond the islands! By now it was much too late for eggs, but he might find some driftwood. Besides, there was no knowing what he might stumble on; fortune might be lying in wait for him.

Again that afternoon he saw Petra in the street; and again she nodded. Curiously enough, during the following days he chanced to see her more and more often – Petra, who had been invisible for weeks and months. It wasn't that he made any effort to cross her path; it just happened that way. He cut more of a figure now that he had rescued a ship and been in the paper, he wore new clothes, and raised a yellow boater in greeting; but he was far from running after the girls or putting himself on display; on the contrary, he was bent on his deep-sea expedition.

Once again he began having little disagreements with his mother, and one day things came to a head, when she asked, 'I suppose you want me on public assistance again?'

'Who am I to decide for you?' he shouted back.

'Your father should have lived to hear you!' she exclaimed, on the verge of tears.

'Indeed.'

'Yes. Because he wasn't the man to lie around idle. He toiled morning, noon, and night – *and* he was open to reason.'

Oliver gave an inward sniff of scorn. His father open to reason? Yes, *now*. How like a woman: wait till you were dead and buried, and then pull a long face over losing you. Oliver recalled his childhood, and all the battles his parents had fought – they were no small matter.

'You sit there whistling,' said his mother, 'with your snob hat over one ear, and you don't give two hoots about anything. But I'd like to know how you think this is going to end.'

'I'm not worried about myself,' he replied. 'Not on your life! Right now, I'm putting out to sea again. I've also been thinking about a post in the lighthouse service.'

Provisions were scanty this time; still, he managed to borrow Jørgen's boat, took some fishing gear and a pot with him, and rowed out to sea. Doubtless he meant to live off the fish he caught. During the three days that he was gone, his mother too was away; she had found herself some place and taken herself off there. Oliver returned to an empty house.

This time he had met with no very special luck; it seemed he hadn't even caught many fish. So he put a pot of potatoes on the stove.

Mind you, his trip had not been entirely pointless: he had a good big load of driftwood in the boat, not to mention a great fistful of eiderdown carefully concealed in his armpit – and besides, they were indolent, carefree days he had spent out beyond the islands. When he had eaten the potatoes, he felt tolerably content, went down to the boat again, and sold most of his driftwood to people who weren't going to haggle with a cripple. Now he had a little money in his pocket again.

Day followed day.

One evening Petra called. At first he thought he must be mistaken – she was wearing a new grey coat, and surely Petra could hardly be coming to see him, her old sweetheart, after breaking off with him. 'You *are* a stranger!' he said in some embarrassment.

'I just thought I'd pop in for a moment. Where's your mother?'

'Your guess is as good as mine.'

'Oh. Who's cooking for you?'

'Who do you suppose?' he answered evasively. What business is it of yours? he may have been thinking. Sitting there in her smart coat – fine, but he wasn't going to get in a flutter over her. 'What's up between you and that fellow Mattis?' he asked, by way of taking her down a peg or two.

'That fellow Mattis? How do you mean?'

'He was crying over you,' said Oliver with a scornful laugh.

'Over me? You're joking. No one cries over me.'

He had really found his mark; her face gave her away. He treated her and her new coat to an even more discouraging laugh.

She said quietly, 'Why are you like this?' and stood up.

'Well, it's no concern of mine,' he said, to show how remote she and her affairs were from him.

'I read about you in the paper,' she began again.

Now surely he should have been grateful to her for reading about him in the paper; but no. What had come over Oliver? So unlike himself, virtually another person, a changeling. She was all at sea; she tried various lines; finally she asked if she could borrow the paper – she would like to read it again.

Evidently he carried it on him; he took it out of his pocket, neatly packed in brown paper, and said: 'You can take it with you, only I'd like it back again.'

Two evenings later she came again to Oliver's house; it was Sunday evening, so she was smarter than ever. Perhaps because he was expecting her, he made some artless preparations: first he wiped the floor and brushed the top of the stove; then he stacked the dirty cups and dishes in the new extension. And fortune came to his aid: in the pocket of his old waistcoat he had actually found some small Italian coins, which he now took out and scattered over the table to smarten the place up. Then he settled down to dozing at the table. When Petra came he gave a listless stretch and a yawn.

'I'm returning the paper,' she said. She knew the passage by heart, but she read it aloud for him to hear. There, that was what the paper said: great stuff, he could go a long way on that.

'I've knocked about the world a fair amount, you see,' he said, preening himself.

'Yes, there's no denying that ... Who's been washing your floor?'

What business was it of hers? Had she come here to queen it over him? He answered slyly: 'The girls.'

'What girls?'

'Who told you to ask?' he countered. That would put her in her place.

'I could have done it,' said Petra. Incidentally, she wasn't quite the picture of health; indeed, she looked a little wan – no bloom on her cheeks. 'If you'd wanted, I could have made you some coffee,' she said humbly. 'I brought some coffee on the off-chance.'

This was by no means displeasing, but ... 'Oh, you needn't bother,' he answered.

'Goodness gracious, surely I could do that much!' she said, and set about it forthwith.

He noticed that she supported herself on a chair; once or twice she turned away and spat. 'Why do you keep that coat on, can't you take it off?' he asked.

'It's only a light spring coat. That's a peculiar sort of money you've got lying there. What kind of money is it?'

'It's from foreign parts.'

'All the places you've been to!'

'It's from Italy. That's what they have there, soldi. Would you like them?'

'No, you mustn't part with them.'

He gathered up the coins and dropped them into her coat pocket.

Next they talked about his mother – she'd be back soon, probably; then about his last trip out beyond the islands – pretty daring that, to row so far out in an open boat.

He fetched some cups from the new extension, and she washed them and poured coffee for him; she herself had just had some, she made out, and couldn't manage any more just now. She sat down on a chair; the perspiration broke out on her face.

Oliver, on the other hand, began to feel really good; he even chaffed her about the carpenter, without malice, having nothing against either of them. 'Well, so there *was* something between you and that fellow Mattis, uh?'

'What nonsense you do talk! That fellow Mattis?'

'Well, weren't you going to take him?'

'That fellow *Mattis*?' Petra clapped her hands together; she rid herself of Mattis, she washed her hands of Mattis, she even made fun of his big nose.

'How strange!' said Oliver, by no means averse to hearing this assurance. 'That's what I understood,' he said.

Petra looked down her coat and murmured: 'There's only one man I'd ever have taken.'

Oliver became pensive; suddenly he asked: 'Are you still in service at old man Johnsen's? What's young Scheldrup like?'

'Young Scheldrup, how do you mean?'

'I was only asking. He behaved like a kid that time I brought the wreck in and needed a report about it all.'

'Oh.' Petra poured him some more coffee and sat down again. Then she began: 'Listen, Oliver dear, what do you say to . . .?'

'Well, what is it?'

Silence.

'Oh, I don't know,' she said, shaking her head, and sat there fingering the Italian coins. 'But don't you think we could be like we were before?'

The question made no profound impression on Oliver; perhaps he had expected it – doubtless he thought his own thoughts. 'What gave you that idea?' he asked.

'It's what I've always thought.'

'I'm no use to anyone now.'

'Don't say that. Surely you could get a job of some kind from the consul.'

'The consul!' he snorted. 'No, I've been toying with the idea of a post in the lighthouse service.'

'Yes, or that. Something will turn up, I'm sure.'

Silence.

'It's out of the question,' he said. 'A disabled man and an empty house. Well, I suppose I could get hold of a couple of doors to put in, but . . .'

She could see it wasn't impossible, and she didn't press the point; but she hinted gently that she herself could afford a couple of doors. And she showed him that she still wore his ring; everything was just as before. Oliver certainly stared and gaped somewhat when she began talking about the ring; he may even have been a trifle embarrassed. The only line to take was a flippant one.

'Ha-ha – well, I suppose there's another name on it now?'

'No, I've had it filed off. Want to see?'

That girl Petra, in all sorts of ways she was infernally bright, not to say brilliant. But this was almost too much. 'Aren't you going to give him back the ring?' he asked.

'The ring? That's what you think!'

Oliver laughed heartily; he needed to save his own face as well as hers.

'Returning the ring?' she said. 'Feel how heavy it is! It must be pure gold, isn't it?'

Oliver bridled. 'How you do talk! Do you suppose I'd buy you a brass ring when I was in foreign parts? That ring's genuine carat gold.'

'So I understand. It shall never leave my hand.'

But it couldn't be allowed to pass off quite as smoothly as this. Presumably she meant that, right, she was engaged to him again. But hadn't they better think about it, think it over a little? Not that the carpenter would die of it – he had been the one to back out, and besides, it would pay him back nicely for behaving so badly towards a cripple. All the same, there was plenty of food for thought.

'Look at me sitting here!' she exclaimed, jumping up for the coffee pot again. 'I hadn't noticed your cup was empty.'

Oliver let her pour; it was good, strong coffee. All in all, Petra brought with her a blessed sense of well-being – even the way she leaned on his shoulder as she poured. 'There's more coffee where that came from!' she said, and proceeded to sit on his knee. 'Can you still support my weight?'

'Can't I just!' he said manfully. 'I can support every bit as much weight as ever I could.'

'There, you see! So why shouldn't we make a go of it?' She snuggled up to him, coat and all, kissed him, and whimpered importunately: 'Well, what do you say, Oliver, will you have me?'

Really now, this was almost too much; but never mind, all things carefully considered, maybe it wasn't such a bad idea. How she wanted it, how she wanted it!

'Hm!' he said. 'Sitting here and thinking it over, it seems to me' – here he paused and allowed a moment to pass in deadly silence – 'that perhaps it could be managed.'

'Yes,' she panted.

'Since you want it.'

'Yes,' she panted.

5

And now once again the days went by, and things were by no means worse than before; indeed they were better: Petra brought this and that item for the house when she moved in, and Oliver fished with increased application. A certain craving for adventure never left him: on a fine day he might row far out to sea in his own ramshackle boat, lie there for twenty-four hours, and then come home. He was an eccentric in this respect.

No, things were by no means worse than before, and as long as he was not confronted by actual want, Oliver was content. As now, for example, when his mother returned from her outing and, far from coming empty-handed, carried a sack on her back containing foodstuffs and articles of clothing. Not so long ago such a sack would have been the cue for a fine old row; now that they were three in the house, they shared and shared alike, if only for the sake of appearances. As a fiancé Oliver was beyond reproach.

One day an old woman called; Oliver recognized her and was all set to take some more tickets off her – but no need, he had won, and the woman had brought the tablecloth. 'Would you believe it?' laughed Oliver. 'Our Lord has not forgotten me!' They had a tablecloth, Petra did indeed provide doors for the two rooms, they had this and that item. In earlier years whenever Oliver came home from a voyage he had brought a variety of presents for his girl, and now these knick-knacks came in handy; there they all stood, on her chest of drawers, from the china dog and the mirror to the white angel and the inlaid wooden tray.

After the wedding he allowed himself a couple of lazy days, while he lived well off the remains of the feast; then, from old habit, his mother began reminding him to row out again. Right, so he rowed out. As he would have done, he pointed out, without being reminded – he knew what had to be done! Truly, life was better than it was made out to be, and Oliver had no complaints; he was a married man and all, everything was settled, nothing nebulous or unresolved. It was lucky he hadn't rented the extension that time, because now he needed it himself.

The only thing was that Mattis turned up one day and sent a message by a small boy that he wanted to speak to Oliver. But

Oliver had nothing left to discuss with this man, not on your life! 'What does he want with me? Tell the fellow he needn't bother coming to my house!'

They could see the carpenter strutting up and down, chest out, in front of the window; ah, this was evidently not his first encounter with Napoleon. 'He's crazy enough to go for a cripple,' said Oliver. 'Those of you who have any accounts to settle with him had better talk to him,' he informed the living room. Petra gave her hair a pat or two, made herself a bit nice, a bit irresistible, and went out into the street.

From the living room they see the carpenter's face fall. What has come over the fire-eater? Out there they exchange question and answer, nothing happens. If they're talking about the doors, good luck to them, but more likely they're talking about the ring. Oliver sits in the remotest corner of the room, with only his nose projecting, and observes the scene. The carpenter begins to show his paces, he rallies and looks Petra in the face, he wriggles as he talks, he weaves a circle around her. And Petra – even though she happens to have spots on her face and not to be at her prettiest – manages to soothe the agitated man with muffled, mournful words. Why, as she stands there she even musters a sweet, seductive smile. As for Mattis, he ends up gazing at the pavement, and when Petra offers him her hand, he takes it without looking up, and after standing like that for a while, he goes. Exit Mattis. Oliver, sitting in the living room, almost feels sorry for him.

And now no more annoyances occurred.

No more?

Well, time passed of course, all sorts of things happened, autumn gales put an end to fishing; Petra's time was taken up by the child, by the boy she had had; the old mother allowed her household cares to slip from her hands, she no longer went out into the world and returned with a sack.

Not that Oliver was ever in need; he and the cat flourished. Oh, that old tomcat! He was fit for nothing but to lie around the living room and eat, till he grew potbellied with fish and the women began to suspect him of being a tabby. As for Oliver, he too sat there and made the best of things, rocking the infant and keeping an eye on the street. His hands had grown smaller and whiter, his looks had improved. It irked him that he couldn't see his way to a fur cap for the winter; on a winter's day was he to go rowing in a straw hat? 'Can't you get yourself a sou'wester?' asked his mother. '*You* can get yourself a sou'wester,' he retorted. 'I'm getting an otter-skin cap.' Vain, that was Oliver. The once-smart blue tie had lost its colour – a sad state of affairs, but surely it could be covered up. If the tie couldn't be dyed, maybe Petra could turn it? But the reverse proved equally faded. Then Oliver became a little, well, fretful and said: 'I seem to remember your thinking I could get work from old man Johnsen – what became of that?'

Poor Petra said she would have a word with the consul.

'Why do you always call him the consul?' he asked irritably.

'We always called him the consul when I was there.'

'Yes, but there are others who've been made consuls – old Heiberg's a consul, old Grits-and-Groats Olsen's a consul. So you can spare your breath.'

It was true: there were so many consuls nowadays, so many of these vice-consuls and consular agents, so many of them fighting over the same bone, the town was crawling with them. Nor did they always make the grade without strife and envy: much surreptitious sabotage took place, tradesman X would not allow tradesman Y to blossom behind his back. Johnsen of the Wharf lived to see equals by the score, and as for what Mrs Johnsen lived to see . . . God was her witness!

Petra may have chosen a particularly unfortunate moment to call on C. A. Johnsen; at all events, he had no work for her husband. Or would she have fared better if she had been looking the least bit pretty or dainty? Poor Petra, she was gaunt and grey, and the consul said straight out: No, really, Petra – she must excuse him. She had better try some of these newfangled consuls – what exactly was their line? Couldn't her husband go and weigh groats for that fellow Olsen? Still, she was right to come to him in the first place, to C. A. Johnsen; he would try to find work for Oliver later on, only not just now. No, she mustn't look so downcast, there were others besides her feeling the pinch at present; these were difficult times, even the steamship *Fia* had not done anything very special. And why wasn't Oliver fishing?

The consul looked at Petra and her problem with his good brown eyes, and he saw her out not without compassion, though without helping her.

What next? Merely that Oliver pulled himself together again and fished like a man – morning, noon, and night. He'd show 'em! And never did he bring a fish to Johnsen of the Wharf; instead, he gave him the go-by, for all to see. Later, when he caught more fish than he could carry, he installed himself with some empty crates on the quay and created a fish market, created a sensation. There he stood: the big shot. For a few days people shrank from the long trek down to the quay, but since they were always short of fish, they had to surrender and be grateful. Oliver's eyes had lost all their lustre, and to look at he was on the fat and feeble-minded side – but not always: when it came to a trick or a piece of sharp practice, he was crafty enough then. There he stood with his fish, not bawling out his wares but quietly jacking up the price till it reached unheard-of levels. 'Do you want it? All right then, forget it!' Oliver knew he could always sell the fish on the coastal steamers; he also knew that decent people were incapable of being too stingy with a cripple.

All that autumn Oliver and his family lived better than ever. The womenfolk appreciated their breadwinner and gave him the best of everything; the breadwinner got syrup on his evening gruel, the breadwinner got waffles for his Sunday breakfast. It was only right and proper. He improved his position, he paid a few of his old tradesmen's bills, he could afford to paint the two doors to the new rooms, he began to rise in the professional esteem of his fellow fishermen, Jørgen and Martin. All these years they had been content to drag their fish from house to house, until Oliver taught them to stand still behind a counter on the quay – they too – and jack up the price. They thanked him for his brain wave. 'The fact is, I've knocked about the world a bit' was Oliver's answer.

The growing respect of his family and of others influenced him for the good. When he came home from his day's work and passed the living-room window, he could hear a bustle of activity indoors and Petra saying to the child: 'Here comes Daddy!' It was remarkable how these well-chosen words melted Oliver; he even maintained that the infant lying in the cradle understood them. And perhaps this was not so impossible: the words were repeated every day at a fixed time and were regularly followed by the creaking of the door, a cold draft of air, and the entry of a man who nodded from above the cradle. When the boy was a few months older and sat playing by himself, there could be no doubt that he followed events in the living room with all his faculties – just look at the prodigy, the rogue: the moment his mother unbuttoned her blouse he began to smack his lips, and when she said, 'Here comes Daddy!' his brown eyes sought the door.

Oliver made no small fuss over the boy. When the child started stretching out his arms and wanting to come to him, the cripple was quite overcome. The tiny creature – did you ever see the like? – this cipher, this rascally brat, hee-hee, a devil of a fellow, so help me God! It was simply too dreadful when the child started crying as Daddy left, simply too dreadful – Daddy couldn't stand it, he could have cried himself, so he yelled at Petra: 'Give him the breast, I tell you!' Then he and his wooden leg hopped rapidly out of the house.

Ah, many's the time he fell out with the womenfolk over what the child understood and didn't understand; he struck blow after blow on its behalf, showed it pictures and letters of the alphabet, and gave it every conceivable object to play with. They were children both of them, idiotic and quaint. 'Have you taken leave of your senses?' the womenfolk would scream – 'Giving the child the coffee pot to hold!' 'Well, what can he have to bang on?' Oliver would ask. He would bring the boy the ornaments from the chest of drawers, and when the child threw a little mirror on the floor, Oliver took the blame, making out that he himself had dropped it.

Happy days, blessed days! And Petra got her looks back and was keen to go out for a bit on Sundays. By all means, let her go, Oliver had no objections; Granny could go too – he couldn't understand healthy people with the use of their limbs sitting indoors. He himself stayed in the living room, dozing at the table while the infant slept. Did he dream? Did memories of the past come sailing through his sluggish brain? He had reason to brood over his fearful fate, but perhaps it had already blunted him.

Petra came home at dusk – about time, too, because by now the youngster was squealing like a piglet. You see, Oliver wanted to teach him to read, but halfway through the lesson the boy began to yell, whereupon Daddy swung him majestically up and down and spoke kindly to him: 'There, there, there, it's all right, you mustn't lose heart, you'll learn as sure as my name's Oliver Andersen!' But the boy, of course, was yelling for milk and for nothing else.

Now if only Petra had been meek and remorseful over coming home so late – but don't you believe it. No doubt it was a sudden comedown for her to shut the door on the street and on life, and be met with infant wails. So young and already so tied, so quelled. 'There, be quiet, you, I'm here now!' she said to the child. Yes, but she took her time taking off her Sunday finery, looking at herself in the mirror as she did so; all in all, it was a sickening performance, and Oliver showed the patience of a saint in not taking the crutch to her.

After gazing at her for a while, he shouted furiously: 'Why the devil don't you take the youngster?'

'Why don't I take him? Look, I *am* taking him.'

'Yes – after he's yelled himself blue.'

'Let him yell. It's not a matter of life and death.'

No, you couldn't get away from it: Oliver should have used the crutch. Not a matter of life and death? God, what a cow! No, it was a matter of food. See: as soon as the child got what it needed, peace reigned. 'You should use your wits,' said Oliver sanctimoniously.

But Petra tossed her head, Petra grumbled. What had got into her? Didn't she realize what she had let herself in for? She was no longer a girl, she was married and done for – all hope abandon, ye who enter here! Poor Petra – she had got in a scrape, been forced to make a bad bargain, and oh, what a cross she had taken up! She couldn't endure it, couldn't put a decent face on it. Would other girls have borne such a cross? Would they, hell! At the consul's she had held a position of trust: twice they had raised her wages, Scheldrup had been in love with her, and doubtless still was. And now to be stuck like this!

'At times it's just as if you don't remember the child,' said Oliver judicially.

'I remember him night and day. Am I to carry him on my back when I go out?'

Petra snorted. Oliver looked at her more and more attentively; then he got a whiff of her breath and understood better – she had called in somewhere and had a drop of something. Hee-hee, priceless! That was what had given her courage and loosened her tongue.

'Where have you been?' he asked.

'Oh, nowhere very much.'

'Well, you've certainly paid a call and had a drop of something.'

'Can you tell? Yes, I've been at the consul's. They were having a party, and I gave a wee bit of help. It was the Mrs who offered me a glass.'

Petra was no drinker, and her explanation was adequate if it was true. If it was true. She didn't shrink from a white lie, a falsehood – far from it; and since she was not particularly inventive, she carried it off with the aid of sweetness and impudence instead. Believe her or disbelieve her about being at the consul's, what difference did it make? There she sat now, giving her child the breast, a bit dim, but young and attractive, wild maybe, irresponsible maybe – so what? No, she was not exactly a genius, she was commonplace and insignificant, a wench in a pair of shoes; still, she had her good points, she was warm-blooded and damnably alluring. She had come home now, this was where she lived, she belonged to Oliver, she provided nourishment, she had milk in her, he could see her teats.

But now Petra had had a drop of something, and maybe she had had it on an empty stomach and couldn't take more than one glass without growing bold, without growing unmannerly and reckless. Look at her now, tossing little Frank, tossing the child, something she knew Oliver would object to. A fight ensued, and Petra showed her teeth, indifferent even to the fact that old Granny had come in from the street and was listening. 'What?' Granny was evidently wondering; 'are they quarreling in earnest?' She heard the young wife say to her husband: 'What have you got to boast about?'

'Me?'

'Yes, you. Aren't you ashamed of yourself?'

'I'm what you see with your own two eyes.'

At which she laughed and said: 'Well, if only you were *that* even!'

Granny understood not one word of all this; but she was surprised at her son's not doing something violent. There he sat. Petra's words so strange – what was she getting at? Oliver said nothing.

'What's going on?' asked Granny.

Neither of them answered.

Suddenly Oliver asked an ominous question: 'Why did you come here wanting to marry me? That's what I don't understand.'

To which Petra replied: 'You understand all right.'

'What did I understand?'

Silence.

Granny walked about the room; she too took off her Sunday finery and hung it up. But she was all ears. What more could Petra know about her husband than was there for the world to see? Was there some secret blemish? Had he been in prison? Or was he going there? Now she remembered that for some time Petra had been in the habit of taunting her husband, half in jest, half contemptuously; she would laugh and drop unseemly little hints: that he was about as much use as their tomcat, that he ate fish.

Now all was quiet in the room: the child slept and the others fell silent. 'What's the news in town?' asked Oliver, to show how easy-going he was.

As Petra remained silent his mother answered: 'Speaking for myself, nothing. Oh yes, there's to be a new senior school.'

'What, there's to be a new senior school?'

'So they say. And it's to be a huge stone building.'

But since it was his wife that Oliver wanted to draw into the conversation, he asked her point blank: 'Who was at that party?'

'What party?'

Ah, she had forgotten. So it must have been a cock-and-bull story. He resolved to sort it out in the morning.

'You mean at the consul's? All the gentry were there.'

'And their wives, too?'

'No. Oh, I don't know.'

'Ah, so you weren't waiting at table?'

'Why do you ask questions all the time?' she exclaimed with a laugh. 'Perhaps you don't believe me?' Ah, but she was evidently not quite at her ease, her laughter rang hollow. They were doing a balancing act, each of them poised on a tightrope. Suddenly she made up her mind, rumpled his hair, and said jokingly: 'No, you should have married that nurse of yours in Italy, Oliver! She'd have made a man of you.'

And Oliver, half in earnest, joined in the joke: yes, he really did regret that nurse.

6

The winter wore on, day by day.

But of course Oliver lacked the staying power, his industry was an artifice, he grew tired of the everlasting fishing. He laid the blame on the child.

Step by step he acquired the habit, when he got home from his fish stall, of ostentatiously examing the child in its cradle, listening to it, satisfying himself that it was breathing. And he would ask insulting questions: 'I don't suppose they've given you any food, Frank? I don't suppose they've thought of that, uh?' At first the womenfolk just laughed and took it as a joke, but Oliver solemnly declared that he was anxious. Later he was unabashed in using the child as a pretext whenever he wanted to give the sea a miss: its cries were too heartrending when he left it.

His place on the quay he made over to fisherman Jørgen, offered it to Jørgen unasked. 'It's the best place, and I want you to have it. You and I, you know, Jørgen!'

Was he giving up fishing?

No, but he wouldn't sell; he would fish for himself and for no one else. Jørgen could have the place for the whole winter at least; come the spring, Oliver might want it back. He explained to Jørgen more fully: he hadn't the heart to stay away from little Frank, they'd have to see how things worked out, the child wanted him every minute of the day. It was wonderful in a little fellow like that – and could Jørgen tell him why Daddy was preferred to Mummy and the rest?

Something implanted in the child, perhaps?

Just what he'd been thinking himself: the father was the real author of its being, and the child clung fast to that; the mother was merely the soil it was planted in. Wasn't it clear as daylight? Grass grows, a ship floats on the water, the sky is full of stars – it all made sense. But now here was another question, and surely nobody on the face of the earth could explain to him how Frank – how a child – why, he was only *so* high, and already he had all his wits about him!

Empty chatter, dogwatch ruminations – on a par with the nattering of women over their crochet work. But Jørgen, a man of fewer words, had to fall back on his usual explanation: nature was full of mysteries.

The town took a different view of Oliver; the town, predictably, thought he should be put on bread and water for his idleness. Whoever heard of a man being kept ashore by a child?

But nature is full of mysteries, and Oliver's was no exception. And on this occasion he justified his lapse from industry in his own eccentric way: of course he was lazy – but might he not have a reason for being so?

One morning he noticed that Petra was in a cold sweat over the coffee pot. 'Are you poorly?' he asked. 'Yes,' she answered. He let it pass, helped himself to food, went out fishing, and came back late in the afternoon. Petra was in a bad mood, and seemed to have a pain in her mouth; Oliver observed how carefully she chewed; she couldn't stand the sight of coffee and kept spitting surreptitiously. 'Are you still poorly?' he asked. 'Yes, I tell you!' she snapped.

At this point he gave her a sly look, and scrutinized her slowly from head to foot, not furtively, but with the blatant intention of her noticing him. That done, he lowered his glance and heaved a sigh.

Oh, Petra had eyes in her head, she had got the message. 'Do you want more coffee?' she asked; and she poured him another cup.

He made no answer; indeed, he seemed so lost in thought that he neither saw nor heard. Had his sigh gone home? At all events, she remained silent as she busied herself about the room. 'Drink your coffee now, before it gets cold,' she said.

Oliver returned from far away – from the land of oranges, no doubt, or perhaps from the nether regions – and stood up. By now the scene was heading for a grave and moving dénouement, when a chance occurrence spoiled the whole effect. 'Well, Frank, I'm going now,' he said to the sleeping child. So far, so good. But then he started feeling his hips for something, and failed to find it. 'And I'll come back to you this evening, Frank,' he added. He rummaged on a shelf, opened a drawer – and failed to find it. Eventually he found it in the cradle: his sheath knife, that sword-like monster that he used on the fish he caught, down at the quay. The evening before, he had given it to the child as a toy and then forgotten about it. No, it was no good. Petra clapped her hands and burst out laughing. Oliver's sign was completely wasted, and he slunk to work like a beaten man.

But why this scene at all? What a paltry game! Was a married woman debarred from feeling unwell or detesting coffee? Suddenly Oliver found everything too much for him, too dismal and desperate to bear – so little sense had God granted him. He threw in the sponge. Not that he now took to blaming his own laziness for anything, or complaining of others; no, he blamed the child. And this gave him a reason for taking time off.

Thus the winter went by.

And thus more than one winter went by – in idleness and domestic strife, in bad food, in rags, in darkness.

In the spring Oliver would wake up and fish regularly until the autumn, and their life at home would improve again; he would pay the tradesmen by instalments for the winter's flour and margarine, and scrape through somehow. It was one way of coping. The reputation he had once built up was squandered, and he was consistently slighted and despised, as perhaps he deserved – God knows.

When Frank got a little brother, a brown-eyed squirrel in the cradle, Daddy took it like a man and staved off despair; he was good to both children, although Frank, the first-born, was and remained his boy, while Abel, the second, he largely ignored. Even the mother preferred Frank as being perhaps the prettier; and as his clothes became too small for him, his brother had to take over what was left of them, so that year after year Abel went around in ragged trousers. Not that this upset him; quite the reverse, since he generally found something in the pockets of these cast-offs when he inherited them – a pocket knife, a pipe, a pencil stub, buttons, fish hooks, nails – all of which he would instantly swap for others items, prudently letting them change hands. This was one of Abel's ways of acquiring worldly goods, though he had others, too. He was perpetually running around with Jørgen's son, Edevart, who being rather older had plenty to teach him, and the pair of them earned money from errands, odd jobs, and occasional lucky 'finds'. Once, indeed, they found coffee in Grits-and-Groats Olsen's warehouse – how could they help doing so? There it stood, on the bare floor, obviously forgotten by somebody, a whole sack, newly opened; the boys reckoned it must be worth quite a bit. Pockets were altogether inadequate on this occasion, but pockets had never come in so handy, either. On the way home Edevart had a few qualms about taking his share of the goods home, but Abel walked straight into the living room with his. His mother took the coffee, promising him something in exchange – though she also forbade him to find more coffee. Next day, when Abel turned up again at the warehouse, this time with a suitable container, his partner had a scandalous tale to tell; first he had been made to sneak the coffee back into the sack, and on returning home he had received a thrashing. Edevart was now of two minds whether to retain his parents any longer.

This coffee, which might have been a source of lasting prosperity, proved instead an annoyance to Abel also: his mother defaulted on her promise to give him something in exchange. He tried both fair means and foul, but no. So he went to Oliver, to his daddy, and cried.

'When someone's been promised something in exchange, then you should give it to him,' said Oliver the righteous.

'Oh,' retorted Petra, 'so I'm to buy the coffee he's stolen, am I? That's a fine way you're bringing him up!'

But Daddy had been flattered by his son's appeal, he had had a good day's fishing, and so he gave Abel a shining new krone. 'I won't have them doing you an injustice!' said Daddy for all to hear. And thanks to this generous treatment, Abel saw his way to acquiring a secondhand fishing line next day. The vendor was Olaus, the selfsame Olaus who got a charge of dynamite in the face and went blotchy-blue and lost all his beauty from that day forth. Later he had lost a hand, too. He drank like a fish and sold all his belongings; now he sold his fishing tackle to Abel.

'Have you got any money?' asked Olaus.

'A krone.'

'*One* krone? I wouldn't sell if for five.'

They looked at the line; Olaus smoked and spat.

'It isn't rotten, is it?' asked Abel, feeling it.

'Rotten? It's a brand-new line. You could hang yourself with it. But whatever it is; *one* krone – no.'

'It's all I've got.'

'Then be off with you. What the hell are you standing there with *one* krone for?'

Abel went.

Olaus shouted after him: 'You – what's your name – is that all you've got?'

'Yes.'

'Here, come and get it. But it's worth five.'

Now Abel was on top of the world. For fishing was what the two friends, Abel and Edevart, really had on the brain. They had both been out to sea with Edevart's father, they knew the fishing grounds; but they had no gear – their fathers hadn't dared to lend the boys their lines and let them loose on their own. Now they were on top of the world; and that evening they rowed out in Oliver's boat.

How excited they were! Two tiny figures, wary as thieves, they crept along the shore so as to get around the headland and out of sight; small as they were, they swelled like turkey cocks as they made their plans. It was undecided how much they would make the first time, but whatever they made was to go towards a line for Edevart, so that each would have his own. Of course they were thoroughly at home in a boat, they had known how to row and scull and back their oars almost since they could walk – no one need keep an eye on Edevart and the squirrel. For Abel indeed this was a red-letter day: he was wearing boots, great jackboots, and he was as proud of them as if they had not originally belonged to his father and subsequently been worn out by Frank.

Then they fished.

Or rather, then Abel lowered his line to the bottom and took it in a fathom; Edevart kept the boat steady. They knew what they were up to all right. From time to time Abel would lower the sinker to the bottom again and take it in a fathom, in order to keep the right depth. Once again he let it go to the bottom; but this time, when he wanted to take it in, it stuck fast. Yes, it stuck fast. Hey – row north, back your oars! Try rowing east, west! The line was caught fast in the bottom. 'Here, take the oars and let me have a go!' said Edevart, who was bigger than Abel. They rowed and they hauled, and at last the line went slack. 'I've got it!' called Edevart. But when he took it in, the line was bare; it had snapped in the middle. The hook and the sinker still lay at the bottom of the sea.

They looked at each other blankly, they couldn't take it in: the line had broken. 'Hell!' said Edevart, who was bigger than Abel. Abel himself didn't exactly swear, but when Edevart did, it expressed his own deepest feeling. Neither could blame the disaster on the other – but could Olaus have sold them a rotten line? There was no option but to row home again.

'You'll get your krone back,' said Edevart consolingly.

'I won't, you know,' muttered the crestfallen Abel.

'Won't you? I'll come with you!'

'Will you really?' How Abel relied on his faithful friend, his proven friend! His spirits revived. Edevart sat there, pursing his lips severely, and nodding his determination to come too and sort things out. In the morning they would waylay Olaus as he arrived at the quay; he was always loafing around there.

Yes, but Olaus refused to cancel the deal – get packing, you young whelps! Abel started to cry, but this didn't help. 'That line was never intended for plunging into the bottom,' said Olaus – 'it was intended for fishing with. Be off with you, I say!'

But little Edevart was bigger than Abel, and an old hand at monkey tricks. The friends put their heads together and agreed to smuggle some gunpowder into Olaus's pipe and give him yet another scorching. Oh, the youngsters in that town – they were hardly out of the cradle before they were possessed by seven devils. Well, Edevart bought the tobacco, and tobacco was something he wanted now in any case, so there was no waste; and he found a nice lump of blasting powder where the men were working on the road. Thus armed, he sat with his friend on the quay and bided his time.

It was a choice packet of tobacco, too: bought at a price, with silver paper and all; it lay invitingly open and ready to use. The blasting powder was underneath.

Olaus turned up. 'What's that trash you've got down there?' he asked.

'Do you mean my tobacco?'

'Is that tobacco? Let me fill my pipe.'

'No, you'll only take it from me,' answered Edevart, making as if for flight.

'Are brats like you allowed tobacco?'

'And besides, how can you fill your pipe when you've got only one hand?'

Olaus realized he might lose out altogether and said: 'All right, take it and fill it yourself. What kind of tomfoolery is this?'

As Edevart plunged the bowl of the pipe in the tobacco and rammed it full, Olaus continued to prattle: 'Are brats like you allowed tobacco? Where did you get it?'

'I bought it.'

'You stole it, more like. If you were a youngster of mine . . .! Go on, fill it properly and don't be stingy!'

Edevart handed back the pipe, and Olaus prepared to light it.

Now the boys retreated ten paces and started examining a horse that stood there, tied to a post. There was something peculiar about this animal; it looked exactly like a horse, it was brown, and all in all there was no fault to be found with it, yet the boys exchanged question and answer about the horse and aired their views on the subject. All at once there came a crackle and a flash from Olaus, and the boys saw him leap in the air – whereupon it seemed they had to hurry off to some other strange spectacle in some other part of the town. But behind them they heard a series of furious yells, threatening that somebody would 'get' them – just wait! Abel, unluckily, was in his jackboots, and was nearly caught at the outset.

This was not the last of the two friends' pranks, or the end of their fishing: it was not long before they acquired proper lines and used the boat with Oliver's full knowledge. Sundays were good days for the boys: there were no religious differences between them, and so they readily agreed to fish then, when the boat was free from morning to night. Sometimes they would come home with a small string of fish each – believe it or not. Disposing of the fish was no problem, dear me, no: the doctor's household was ready to pay the price they asked and a little more, merely for being given precedence over the Johnsens, with whom (there's no denying it) they were on rather bad terms. Sometimes the boys would receive into the bargain a huge hunk of bread and butter, the finest possible offering after an eight-hour fast. They were also liable to be asked in the doctor's kitchen if they had permission to fish on Sundays when people were at church; but they seemed not to have acquainted themselves with the town's congregational life.

Happy days, prosperous days! Reckless, unbridled urchins up to every kind of escapade, twenty-four hours a day, waking or sleeping, their heads chockful of adventures! Was there something of the dreamer, or a certain dignity, about Abel? Not a scrap. A tiny squirrel, as quick as lightning, a daredevil with every limb in a state of commotion. He would be seen simultaneously up by the church and down on the shore; he never walked if there was the faintest possibility of running. It was hurry hurry, his great boots thundering along the street. Such was Abel. Nor was Edevart exactly decrepit with age either, but he was older and took the responsibility; in addition, he always had enough to eat at home, so his body was more rounded. Not that his plumpness did him any disservice – he could show a remarkable agility when the pharmacist came storming out into his garden yelling, 'What the devil are you doing up that apple tree?' When Edevart started at school in earnest, he lost a bit of weight, but not enough to matter – if anything, it was Abel's substance that was diminished still further by this event; Abel who now became a decidedly lean and lonely character. From force of habit, he continued to haunt Jørgen's home, where some years back there had appeared on the scene a third little girl, with whom he sometimes played; but this little girl was a far cry from Edevart and the world of men. She was called Lydia after her mother, or rather Little Lydia, and for a girl she was quite good fun, except for her tiresome habit of screaming about nothing.

Yes, Abel had become lonely; his brother, Frank, was also at school, and in any case, Frank had always been too learned and superior for Abel; they had never had much in common. Their outlooks on life were so ill-attuned: what fishing was for the one, books and newspapers and other such frills were for the other. Frank started early at school and was a genius. He was to become a telegraph operator or a senior bank clerk; it was his mother's ambition that he should one day go to the senior school with the better-born children and learn everything. We all have our ambitions; why should Lydia, fisherman Jørgen's wife, be an exception? Yes, but what was worse and caused the town to smile, was her foolishness: she entered her little girls for a dancing class. In this, of course, she was acting far above her proper station.

And indeed, the upshot was that Henriksen of the Shipyard, the customs officer's family, and Mrs Johnsen of the Wharf all found it necessary to withdraw their children from the dancing class – not, of course, on account of the fisherman's children, certainly not, but because, well, Fia Johnsen, for example, was getting anaemic and had grown distressingly thin and spindly. It became a political issue. The poor dancing teacher, who was new to the town, wrung her hands and racked her brains, for she had much to lose. Finally she hit on the answer: the first course of lessons was fully subscribed – fancy not thinking of that before! – but she would start a second; yes, the demand had been so unexpectedly heavy that she might even run two additional courses. So all was well again.

And now the town witnessed a remarkable boom in dancing; the women stopped laughing at Lydia, the children streamed in. If Lydia's children had joined, then why not the cooper's children and Holte the barber's children, too? Never had the dancing lady clapped her hands so much; she had mastered the politics of the dance and was full of *joie de vivre*. Edevart too was enrolled; likewise Frank, whose father, Oliver, was fishing at present and earning money. 'That's right ,Frank,' said Oliver, 'you learn all there is to learn!' As for Edevart, however, he turned up just once, after which he went to Abel and asked him to dance in his place. Well, Abel was willing enough to do his friend this favour, but since he wasn't properly dressed, or even washed, he was flatly refused admission. Thus they both kept their freedom.

7

The town thundered with dancing. Had a great boom period started, thanks to a sensational catch of herring along the coast or to an unprecedented scarcity of timber and tonnage for some new British war? Neither. Outside the town, peace reigned.

It was this dancing lady who had come and corrupted the entire congregation. She met with Christian opposition, prayer meetings were held against her, but it was too late: the sickness had spread too far. Not only had it taken hold of the parents on their children's behalf, it threatened to do so on their own. What an epidemic! At first it engulfed mainly the menial class; but then the infection started to spread upwards, to the town's respectable folk: there was waltzing in the dining room at Consul Grits-and-Groats Olsen's and Henriksen of the Shipyard's; the town dignitaries warbled as they walked the streets.

Outside the dancing school you could always see listeners, indecorously rocking to the music within and dreaming they were there; but Police Constable Carlsen did nothing, arrested nobody. Petra was found at the top of the dark staircase up to the ballroom, sitting there wistful and shameless and dreaming to the scrape of violins and the stamp of feet inside. Ah, but Petra's dreams were utterly in vain: she was married and done for. And to crown everything, she had grown so heavy again that it was all she could do to stand. For many years she had avoided putting on weight, her figure had been as pleasing as any girl's; now that too was past and gone. She ought to have been at home, invisible to the world; instead, here she was, found on the staircase, and it was Scheldrup Johnsen who came and found her.

'Is it you sitting here, Petra?' he asked sympathetically.

'Yes. Oh, do go away. Scheldrup!'

But Scheldrup became still more sympathetic – whereupon Petra rose to her feet and gave him a resounding box on the ear, Scheldrup Johnsen or no Scheldrup Johnsen. That was what she did. And in no time someone farther down the stairs who had heard the smack came and saw the sequel: Scheldrup slipping quickly into the ballroom, and Petra, in tears, lumbering down the staircase and out into the street.

It was all the dancing lady's fault – why couldn't she have stayed in the next town? What's more, the disturbance she had created was very far from having begun to subside; and on the night of the final dance more than one piece of spite found vent among the families in the town. Jealousies came to a head over silks and tulles; parents were consumed with envy of each other's children.

The doctor and his wife accompanied the C. A. Johnsens home.

Fia had had her evening of fun and was due to take her weary limbs to bed, whereas the adults could well sit up a little longer. Anyway, several of them came, including lawyer Fredriksen, whom Mrs Johnsen rather liked because of his attentions to her. The Henriksens of the Shipyard were invited also, although they were not really part of the inner circle. 'Yes, fetch your wife, Henriksen, and come and join us. And you, Postmaster!' But the doctor and his wife were invited with the full ceremony that was *de rigueur* in their case; they were the cream, as the consul and his wife well knew.

Oh, the hidden enmity among these friends, these bosom friends! It seldom came to an honest explosion, but it was there, latent and smouldering. There was much lively chatter as they went home, walking four abreast and sweeping the street before them; from time to time they stopped and blocked the traffic, forcing all others to squeeze past them. It was a really glorious summer evening.

'I must congratulate you on Fia,' said the doctor's wife. It was easy for the doctor's wife to be impartial, to avoid siding with any parents in particular, since she herself had no children at the dancing school; indeed, she and the doctor were childless. 'Fia looked so nice this evening. But don't you think, Mrs Johnsen, that a bright, neat dress would have suited her better?'

'She was set on silk,' Mrs Johnsen replied; 'and besides, there were plenty of cheap dresses around. Did you see how the Heibergs had dolled up their Alice?'

Someone else said: 'Wasn't there one with a great watch chain?'

'That was one of Consul Olsen's daughters.'

'Well, yes, poor child, those grocery people are not quite *comme il faut*,' Mrs Johnsen acknowledged indulgently. No, she could never forgive Grits-and-Groats Olsen and his wife for having a consulate of their own and being in the money. Curious: one might have thought it a great advantage to Mrs Johnsen to be able to meet more and more ladies of her own rank in the town; but no, she found it intolerable. And how did she get that yellow complexion? Her face was so yellow, perhaps her stomach was troubling her.

'To change the subject,' said lawyer Fredriksen, the platform orator, stopping all conversation – his voice was as loud, in the stillness of the evening, as that of a sailor in a wine bar – 'To change the subject: are you expecting your steamship home soon, Consul?'

Johnsen of the Wharf was not slow in answering. 'Yes, the *Fia*'s on her way home. She's been away a long time.'

'I wouldn't mind having the money she's earned,' said Henriksen of the Shipyard wistfully. He understood that the sum in question was not exactly peanuts.

Consul Johnsen puffed out his feathers, but said: 'If I didn't comment on that, my silence might be misunderstood. In point of fact, the *Fia* hasn't earned all that much. I've often been glad I had the resources to keep her afloat. But the last few years, of course—'

'Oh!' exclaimed Henriksen, wagging his head.

Suddenly the doctor pronounced: 'Of course the business ethic has got an undeservedly bad reputation.'

'How do you mean?'

The doctor went on, as though not hearing the question: 'Because if a man like Consul Johnsen can get along with it, it must have its uses.'

'Business ethic? How do you mean?'

A long, ponderous silence – the doctor did not choose to say anything that might be ridiculed. Nor did the doctor choose to converse with Henriksen of the Shipyard. So he proclaimed to the assembled company: 'It's a libel to say that business is akin to exploitation.'

'Well, I never—!' exclaimed Henrikson in astonishment. And he raised his eyebrows as if he had just heard some brilliant epigram.

Ah, but now Consul C. A. Johnsen showed the man he was: not a man to model yourself on in every detail, perhaps, but a man of enterprise and stature. The town wits called him the First Consul, to distinguish him from later and less important consuls.

Consul Johnsen answered: 'Business is labour that is worthy of its hire.'

'I quite agree. And so it's not right to call it speculation.'

'It is, in a sense. We all speculate. Before a doctor takes up medicine, he speculates on being able to earn his living from it and then gets down to it. You shake your head?'

'I most certainly do.'

'Ha-ha!' laughed the doctor's wife.

'Medicine is a science,' explained the doctor. 'But whether the *Fia* earns a little or a lot—'

'Shan't we move on?'

'Well, it's only reasonable; it's things like the *Fia*'s business dealings that people call speculation. Wrongly in my opinion.'

'Then we're all agreed,' put in the the postmaster, that man of peace.

'He'll live to regret his spiteful tongue,' the consul refrained from answering. Slipping away to Mrs Henriksen of the Shipyard, he struck up a conversation with her. She was young and attractive, of lowly origin like her husband, the mother of two little girls at the dancing school, but still under thirty. Consul Johnsen was at his most amusing and chivalrous with her: at times, indeed, he pitched his voice legitimately low to prevent the others from hearing. You see, the consul's daily life could hardly have been all peaches and nectarines; he had to seize his opportunities. Was he not still a vital force? Greying, but still a man? It irritated him that his hulking great son, Scheldrup, was walking alongside, listening. 'Go on ahead and tell them to get things ready,' he told Scheldrup.

As for Mrs Henriksen, so deeply honoured by the company she had kept that evening, so intoxicated by all the splendour she would see when she crossed the First Consul's threshold – 'Will you promise me something?' she asked.

Inspired by the devil to skittishness, he answered: 'I daren't make you any promise.'

'But – why not?'

'A promise? To you? I might keep it, you know!'

The lady laughed, understanding nothing except that he was cute, that the First Consul was cute. Then she came out with her request: that the consul would drop in on them some time, drop in on the Henriksens of the Shipyard, he and Mrs Johnsen.

'Are you coming?' called Mrs Johnsen, turning around and waiting.

There was nothing else to do: they had to catch up with the others. But the consul promised himself that he would resume his conversation with Mrs Henriksen later, when her husband was well and truly occupied with mixing whisky-and-sodas. He would be the perfect host, say: 'Yes, help yourself, Henriksen, make yourself at home,' and then chat up his wife.

The postmaster was talking about offspring. He was a lean, indigent man, thought to be something of a failure. He was also thought to be religious, and was given to saying with a pensive air, 'Ah, what is one to believe?' As a young student he had dreamed much about art, castles and cathedrals, architecture; but he had never managed to settle on a career and had ended up in the post office. Now he spent his leisure hours designing houses for God and man; it was he who had designed the senior school, the handsome stone building with columns that was visible from far out in the fjord; he took nothing for his work, only the compliments of the town council. His wife was in no sense a failure, but no beauty, either – just a good soul and a blessing to her home. She was older than her husband, though not enough to signify. She was silent in company, and this evening as usual she walked along saying nothing unless prompted.

'Offspring . . .' said the postmaster. His theory was that the parents should in general be regarded as less important than the children. Absolutely. Everything should hinge on the offspring. 'This evening the parents have sat on hard benches along bare walls, getting their enjoyment, their fun, from their little ones. The mothers weren't all dressed up – it was the children who were to look smart! I thought: Once upon a time these mothers looked just as smart, when they were young daughters themselves. That was thirty years ago, when ladies wore tremendously full skirts. "Dear me!" I thought as I looked back over the years.'

'An elegy!' said lawyer Fredriksen – a bachelor, by the way.

'Precisely!' echoed the childless doctor. And since it was the harmless postmaster, who was after all a gentleman, he deigned to add a few words. 'Offspring—' he said, 'what do you want with them? Is this a world to bring offspring into? How long and for what object do we live, if not for ourselves? Let us use our time well, Postmaster. Death awaits us, we shall soon be ground into pulp. We lie between the upper and the nether millstone. Some are mild and peaceable by nature, and let themselves be kneaded without a murmur; others squirm, like you, Postmaster; they jerk their necks back and try to protect their faces – ah, but the next moment they too are ground to pulp. It must feel strange – and we're all going to feel it sooner or later; if it starts at the feet, we shall feel our legs and stomachs gradually giving us the slip.' By now the doctor had his audience with him, so he continued to embroider his jest, the witty rogue, and to send shivers down their spines. 'Finally, I suppose, there'll just be a bit of toe left that will give one last impersonal twitch. It's all too good to be true, it's just perfect.'

Silence.

'It's so dismal to think like that,' said the postmaster. 'But even on that assumption it's good to leave—'

'Offspring! To be ground to pulp in their turn! Dismal? I don't know. Speaking for myself, I manage to keep up my spirits; sometimes I catch myself arranging my hair over the bald patches – making good the ravages as best I can. And I whistle.'

'Well, well,' said the postmaster, evidently at a loss for words.

But Consul Johnsen took up the cudgels – he certainly had no intention of giving way to this supercilious fellow. 'Without offspring the human race would die out.'

'Fair enough. It's none of my business.'

'But surely your whole aim and object is to preserve human life, isn't it?'

'Mr Consul, Mr First Consul Johnsen, are you offering logic to people caught between the millstones?' sneered the doctor, a little put out. 'Where is the logic of life, the logic of the cosmic principle?'

The consul retorted: 'I'm merely pointing out, Doctor, that personally you favour the extermination of the human race, whereas your trade, your livelihood, consists in preventing this extermination.'

The doctor would have much preferred not to score points off a half-educated man, but the First Consul had grown too big for his boots, and it was necessary to answer him. 'Surely this transcends business somewhat, doesn't it? It's a question of one's outlook on life. When a doctor bends over a sickbed, I suppose he's motivated mainly by compassion for suffering humanity.'

'Ah, yes!'

'You may well sigh. At least he doesn't speculate.'

The consul said recklessly: 'He stands there and earns his five kroner. The doctor is like the rest of us: he speculates in fives, whereas I speculate in thousands – that's the only difference.' And with this the consul laughed and looked around at the others in a way that embarrassed them still further.

The doctor was constrained to laugh, too. 'You've certainly set us all at odds, Postmaster,' he said.

'Me?'

'With your offspring.'

So the postmaster was obliged to join in again: 'Yes, but my dear doctor, we simply must have offspring. You can say what you like about the millstones, but they can't be our goal.'

'Our goal lies within ourselves. When I die, I die – lock, stock, and barrel. Do you believe in God, Postmaster?'

'What are we to believe? Don't you?'

The doctor shook his head. 'Never met Him. Do you think He comes from these parts?'

'Ha-ha!' laughed the doctor's wife.

The postmaster asked: 'What sort of a goal is that – a goal that lies within ourselves?'

'One makes the most one can out of existence. Enjoyment, for example.'

'A poor goal, a short-term goal. In that case it's perfectly true, everything ends with oneself. But one can think of a longer-term goal: immortality through offspring. Seriously now, what's your opinion? I take it you've been pulling our legs up to now.'

'Absolutely not.'

'Take my own case. I'm the postmaster in this town. One job may be as good as another, for that matter. But what can a childless man hope for when he dies, if he himself had never done anything much? Not that it would be any satisfaction to me to better myself now; on the contrary, I'm glad now that I never did anything very much, because it means I've saved my abilities for my children. If I live to see signs that my children will outshine me in everything, then naturally I shall feel profoundly grateful to the Almighty. Among the saddest things I know are the sons and daughters of great men, the children of famous parents. They're a sadder sight than children with no parents at all. But, thank God, it's easy to believe that even if I'd gone twice as far, my children will go still further. And that is what I will hope for when I die. I mean, that I myself will have risen with my children. That my sons didn't have Goethe for their father.'

The postmaster's theory found favour with nobody. It was a theory and a consolation for failures and nonentities, not for those at the top of the tree. 'You're a pious man,' said the doctor amicably. As for Consul Johnsen, he was something more than the father of his sons – he was one hell of a fellow in his own right, yes, and might rise higher still: he stood erect, lights at green, some new target held between his sights. Still, Consul Johnsen wanted to show that he too could address the postmaster amicably, and not even patronizingly. He nodded and said: 'In my poor opinion, there's a lot in what you say, Postmaster.'

'Opinion!' scoffed the doctor.

Lawyer Fredriksen, who up to now had been saddled with Henriksen of the Shipyard, broke in with: 'Why, yes, opinion. But we bachelors and childless men have our opinions, too.'

At that moment they must all have feared that the fun was over, that no one would get another word in. The consul lengthened his stride, threw open his door, and welcomed them in. 'We'll try to agree about a glass of wine at least!' he said with a smile.

As the party entered, young Scheldrup slipped out through the kitchen door. Presumably he had no taste for these futile arguments that the postmaster would insist on starting. You could hardly blame him: at that age life is not a riddle. The summer night belongs to youth.

8

The elderly remember bygone days and dates, they have a wonderful way of hoarding in their heads all manner of trifles as if they were valuable, as if they might one day stand them in good stead. They hoard newspaper cuttings.

And now people stand listening to an unfamiliar steam whistle out in the bay. It isn't one of the mail boats, nor is it the little cargo boat that pulls in once a week at every door; so people go up on their roofs to get a good view. 'It's the *Fia*,' they say. 'Just look at all her flags!'

And at once they recall the great pilgrimage down to the quay one Sunday long ago; they do a mental calculation and work out from their children's ages which year it was. A great popular pilgrimage there was, they recall, and the occasion was the *Fia*'s departure for the Mediterranean. Now she is back after many a long voyage; it's a festive occasion on board, and hearts must be swelling with pride. And wasn't Seaman Oliver Andersen once a member of the crew?

Now Oliver hobbles down to the quay, throwing himself strenuously forward on his wooden leg; he is innocent enough to believe that his shipmates will be scanning the quay for him, awaiting him above all others. But no, they are not awaiting him; he is forgotten. They look down over the rail at this cripple, they recognize him, but they show no joy, and it is he who has to hail his old friends and make the first approach. Oliver stands there now, hair thinning and greying a little though he is still a young man; but what strikes the eye is the weight he has put on, how his cheeks hang down. Has he basked in the sunshine so happily on God's earth? Was his accident an accidental blessing?

The lads on deck exchange a few sympathetic words with him – after all, he is a cripple – but they don't waste too much time on him, they can't afford it, they are too busy looking up and down the street; ah, here comes their girl, their mother, their wife and children, having hastily spruced themselves up a little before setting out.

Olaus is there, of course, pipe in mouth, drunken and swashbuckling as usual. If the *Fia*'s crew have thought to cut a bit of dash in the town with their homecoming from inexpressibly distant lands, they are brought down to earth by Olaus's total lack of respect.

'Where have you come from?' he asks.

'From a country they call China.'

The name does nothing to Olaus. 'From China, uh? Well, the earth's shrunk,' he says. 'In the old days a sailor could say he'd come from far away. Last week there were two fellows wandering around the town begging for money and food. I asked where they came from. From Persia, they said. From Persia that we used to read about in the Bible and nobody knows where it is! Have you got a fill of tobacco?'

He is given a fill, which he acknowledges, not with thanks, but with 'I've known worse!' As he hoists up the gangplank with his one and a half arms, he yells an order: 'Make her fast there!'

Such is Olaus. Fate has dogged him, too, the man with one hand and a permanent blue face; but has it made him placid or fat? – the hell it has! He is not gross and listless like an animal, but neither is he delicate and wizen of mein like an aristocrat; no, he is drunken and radiant. Is he draining away his reserves? Well, what are reserves for if not to be drained away?

Oliver clambers on board – a mistake, this, for they make no fuss over him; they merely take his hand and say the routine minimum. They are wrapped up in their own affairs. Is Oliver expected to marvel at men being able to return from China? The old seadog has been there himself, of course, for him there is nothing new under the sun. No, it was a mistake going on board; he has even forgotten his English and cannot converse with them in the approved style. The forecastle is unchanged, a malodorous well of darkness even though it has been swabbed for the occasion. He sits at the familiar table, chattering on and on about himself; at first they listen to him, but what they really want is to ask about their own kith and kin and about the town dignitaries, and one by one they go up on deck and scan the horizon for their relatives.

Oliver says: 'For example, take the way I got disabled.'

'Weren't you put right out of action in the crotch?'

'What, me put out of action in the crotch? I'm a married man with a swarm of children. A barrel of whale oil can't put a man out of action in the crotch.'

'Barrel of whale oil?' asks Kasper.

Oliver recollects himself and shows confusion.

'Didn't you fall from aloft and get the derrick bang between your legs?'

'No.'

Oliver has talked about this barrel of whale oil for so many years that perhaps he believes in it himself; but now it appears that there was no barrel of whale oil. What has he hoped to achieve with this lie? Has he been trying to conceal something? He collects his wits and resumes his chatter; the captain is nowhere in sight, the lads are aloof and reserved – ah, they must have had word in letters from home about all his recent doings; he has behaved badly, there has been gossip in plenty about him and his household. Poor Oliver, not even when he rummages in his pocket and produces the newspaper report of his true sailor's deed does he make any real impression. No, because now the relatives are starting to arrive.

There is a sullen glow in Oliver's eyes. Maybe he is on the fat and feebleminded side, but at times he shows flashes of animal cunning. He draws nearer to Kasper, his old friend and contemporary, and says: 'Isn't your wife coming, Kasper?'

'I guess she is.'

'Yes, she must be back home by now.'

'Why, where's she been?'

'I don't know. It was only a year she was away. Abroad, they said.'

'What's that you're saying?' asks Kasper uneasily.

'What? Oh, you needn't bother to take any notice of what a poor chap like me says. But then it doesn't matter to you or anyone else whether it was a barrel of whale oil or a derrick that did me in.'

'No, of course it doesn't,' Kasper agrees. 'What was she doing abroad?'

'They said she was a stewardess on a boat.'

'No! Why, I've had letters from her every year, from this very town.'

'Well, well,' says Oliver.

On the way home he meets Kasper's wife, all dressed up and innocent, on her way down to greet her husband. As they pass, Oliver mentions that Kasper is standing there, waiting; but whether because she is too dressed up to answer or too innocent, the woman merely hurries past.

Oliver goes home, to his hearth and his family. His visit aboard the *Fia* has been a decided mistake. Good luck to them, he won't go there again! As for Kasper and his wife, he expects no repercussions from that quarter; the whole town is in the know. And besides, a cripple is protected by his pitiable state, even if he has set a married couple at odds.

He sits down at the head of the table and starts abusing the crew of the *Fia*: riffraff they are. In the days when he had the use of his limbs he'd have flogged every man jack of them.

Petra doesn't answer, doesn't look at him, she is so weary of his talk and of his person. Oh, that lump of fat in the chair – it breathes, it wears clothes that someone has sewn, it has buttons on its clothes; on its upper end it has a hat, tilted at an angle. She knows it all inside out, the sprawling wooden leg that projects into the narrow room and blocks the way, his conversation, all the lies, the bombast, the voice that grows more and more like a woman's, the lustreless, watery-blue gaze, the mouth that is perpetually moist. Year by year he seems to be going to pieces; only his appetite remains intact. And there isn't always enough to eat.

Strange! The life of the town continued its course; indeed, it was decidedly on the upgrade. By the time the dancing lady had fulfilled her mission and gone her way, a regular Saturday-night dance was established in the courtroom, and the improvement in people's clothes and life styles was unmistakable. But with Oliver and Petra nothing whatever was on the up and up, everything was on the down and down, until it reached rock bottom. If the crazy man didn't suggest selling the knick-knacks from off the chest of drawers – the white angel and the piggy bank from foreign parts! And one winter's day Oliver went out into the town and sold the house he lived in. This was a reckless thing to do.

More than once he had wanted to sell the house; the owner, lawyer Fredriksen, must surely have a heart where a cripple was concerned. But lawyer Fredriksen evidently thought he had helped him enough already by making him famous with his report of the true sailor's deed; why didn't he perform some more exploits? What – sell the house, sell another man's house—

In short, Oliver found himself reported to the police.

You see, these Oliver Andersens should really have been evicted long ago, but the town had protected the cripple. Now by breaking the law he had finally put himself beyond the pale.

Oliver pounded his way to the lawyer and asked for mercy. He would cancel the deal, which indeed had hardly got under way. This didn't help: the lawyer meant to seize the chance of getting vacant possession. No, it didn't help – until Petra was constrained to go to the lawyer and ask him nicely. It didn't even help Petra at the first encounter.

Here was a fine state of affairs – their home on the edge of the abyss. What if Petra now sneaked out and sat on the staircase up to the ballroom, dreaming away a blissful evening hour? Her husband, Oliver, far from dying of shame and want, was keeping up his end and grumbling about that Scrooge of a lawyer, who had no heart even where a cripple was concerned. Not that Oliver was any worse ruined than before, even if he had been cheated of the money for the house; and he was never short of solutions when he sat talking at home, surrounded by his family. The lighthouse service – no, he'd dropped that idea; but what was there to stop him from getting a wheelchair and making the rounds of the congregations? Or supposing he went to one of the cities and took up organ grinding?

'Oh,' said Petra to this, 'just you try!'

'Well – and what would you and the family live on, then?'

Yes, what would they live on, then? Unless he earned enough to send money home. But on this score Petra had her doubts. So did Granny; indeed, she said straight out that Oliver would be certain to eat up all his earnings in food.

So nothing came of the breadwinner's travels, and the family's standard of living remained as before. Still, they lived from day to day; like many another, they lived and survived.

Why should things go so badly? The breadwinner had a physical defect – so what? Hannibal was blind in one eye, Alexander was lame. Oliver was not entirely lacking in good qualities – what was all the fuss about? Basically he was a peaceful soul; he didn't go around with bloodshot eyes and gleaming rows of teeth waiting for babies to grow nice and fat and ready for the slaughter – indeed, he was kind to children. Disabled, certainly – witness that empty trouser leg that flapped so disconsolately when he walked. But he wasn't like, say, the hunchbacks, who look as if they are carrying themselves on their backs when they walk. Lacking in good qualities? He didn't drink, not on your life, he didn't even use tobacco any more; as far as that went, he had grown just like a woman.

And of course things were made worse, rather than better, by the arrival of the third child, a little girl who yelled at night and woke the weary breadwinner. Oliver now took to indulging his wanderlust again, disappearing from home, rowing out to sea, and staying away for days and nights on end. God knows what he was looking for or what he found! His favourite time for making these expeditions was after a storm at sea; he may have been childish enough to hope for another derelict. For that matter he did once find a suitcase floating in the sea; it contained only underclothes and a few women's gewgaws, but Oliver carried it home in triumph, and never dreamed of doing any more work that day. On another occasion he found an empty paraffin can with the stopper in; and from time to time he brought home a wad of eiderdown that he had plundered from nests out on the skerries. He knew that this down was valuable, but dared not try getting rid of it in the town, and could only hide it.

The maddening thing was the way Petra completely failed to appreciate his finds, indeed turned her nose up at them. He would creep up from the quay unobserved, walk in with a swelling chest, and lay his loot on the table. 'Here's something to make you open your eyes, uh?' And Petra would mutter: 'Three days' earnings, that's supposed to be. What are we to do with eiderdown? Or an empty paraffin can?'

Oliver came down to earth again with a jolt and answered in injured tones: 'I see you're in one of your tantrums again.'

Petra flared up. 'Oh, I'm in a tantrum, am I? Look at her in the cradle, do you think she's lying on eiderdown?'

Oliver glanced at the child: it was lying in rags, but there was nothing wrong with it – only teething made it cry. But suddenly Oliver got up and looked more closely; it was the first time he had really looked at the child.

'What the devil – has she got blue eyes?'

Petra gave a little jump and answered: 'You can see that, can't you?'

'How does that come about?'

'How does that come about? How should I know! You and your questions!'

Oliver stood there staring, utterly bewildered and utterly stupid – was a child of blue-eyed parents not to have blue eyes? But the others, the boys, didn't they have brown eyes? There was some new mystery here. Mind you, Oliver had doubtless thought his own thoughts all these years, had harboured them in sluggish indifference; now he was faced with a riddle. Where had Petra

been? At home. At home. A woman who boxed Scheldrup Johnsen's ears didn't go out.

She didn't go out – or did she?

A fierce, unnatural jealousy blazed up in the cripple; for the first
time he experienced that strange stab of pain, a stab so violent that
it distorted his features and terrified Petra; she covered up the
child. Oliver staggered to the window and looked out. If brown
eyes were now the proper thing, the family eyes – how could the
same be true of blue eyes? He was well aware of all the gossip
about himself and his household, which had hardly been so subtle
or innocuous as to prevent him from understanding it; the latest
item to reach his ears was that boxing Scheldrup Johnsen's ears
had apparently not always been Petra's style. So what? Scheldrup
Johnsen had brown eyes, the baby in the cradle blue.

A serpent gnawed at Oliver's heart. Hitherto he had lived contented; now it was no longer granted to him to keep uneasiness at
bay. Uneasiness? Call it rather distress, call it torment. He took to
lurking at street corners; he was liable to jump out at Petra, grab
her by the breast, and ask where she was going. Night and day he
was on the watch; his peace was gone, his hair withered away. The
only place to which she had free acess, now as before, was Johnsen
of the Wharf's, his house and his store; there she could go at any
time, with no objection raised. But he followed her and saw that
the terms were observed.

His madness went on and on; he neglected the sea in order to
lurk in hiding, he begged fish from the other fisherman that he
might not return empty-handed. And foolish Petra lacked the wit
to alleviate his sickness; instead, she made it worse. When it had
lasted for a while and she realized that no danger to life or limb
was involved, she began goading him to ungovernable, white-hot
rage. Suspecting, perhaps, that the blue eyes came from Mattis
the carpenter, he was lost for words to express his contempt
for that man, that rhinoceros, that lady's lapdog. Petra took his
part.

'Well, hasn't he got a terrible nose?'

'No. That nose suits him.'

'Be quiet. He's a carpenter – he should build a stable for his
nose.'

Curiously enough, those blue eyes seemed to cause jealousy, so to speak, in others besides Oliver – though of course Consul Johnsen was laughing and joking when he spoke to Petra about it. 'I hear you've got a little girl, Petra.'

'Yes.'

'With sky-blue eyes this time.'

Petra looked down and said nothing.

'It's not everyone that can have sky-blue eyes,' said the wag. 'No,' he announced suddenly, 'I haven't got a place for your husband, you understand. Try that fellow Olsen.'

Once again Petra had to go home with her mission unfulfilled, home to her family and her misfortunes. The way things were, no one was so sorely tried. From time to time she would cry and feel sincerely sorry for herself, but she was too young and robust to lose courage completely; quite often she would stand in her doorway laughing and chattering with the passers-by – her wounds went no deeper than that.

Time passed, the seasons came and went. The boys were both at school: Frank was as bright as they come, winning a scholarship and the highest grades, but that squirrel Abel was no fool, either, merely an unmitigated rascal whose interests lay elsewhere. Life went on, habit helped, God fortified the family with a certain stubborn refusal to go under. Thus, for example, little Abel mostly fed and clothed himself around the town. Yet at times he found it a somewhat shameful business, being a little squirrel: one day when he had gone out into the country he badly needed a bite of food, and when he failed to get it, or to scrounge a jacket he had found hanging on a clothesline, he asked bluntly if he could buy a cup of coffee. It was then that the farm people behaved disgracefully towards the squirrel, asking him if he was allowed to drink coffee. Allowed indeed! He would never go to that farm again until he was grown up.

His brother, Frank, never got up to adventures; he was too clever for that. He too got many a garment and many a meal in the town; and once a year he was given a complete set of clothes at Consul Johnsen's store, and came home refurbished from top to toe. That was Johnsen of the Wharf all over, a great man for living himself and for letting others live.

Life went on. Sometimes, again, Granny would go on a little outing, and perhaps return with some good things: potatoes, pork, a bag of flour, a cheese. No, Granny was not to be sneezed at. As long as she kept off public assistance and avoided becoming a scandal with the other women at the pump, she could roam a score of parishes, and the country fare she brought home was a valuable contribution. Truth to tell, it was often due to Granny that the family wanted neither for food nor for fuel, so industrious had she become.

The worst sufferer was Oliver himself. His sickness would not leave him. For a brief period he took up fishing again; this because he had acquired a new boat. You see, he had gone someway out and found this boat adrift. Could you beat it? It must have been moored somewhere – probably a great distance away, perhaps in some foreign land – and come adrift. Of course he should have reported the boat, no question of that; be that as it may, he kept it, and incurred no trouble thereby. No one called him to account; the cripple needed the boat, he might go to the bottom any day in his own wretched tub. At first, to be sure, he had thought of selling the boat and getting money for it, but over this the town put its foot down – this was going too far. 'No,' said the townspeople, 'if you found her, you must keep her.' So Oliver spent all his free time fishing and using his new boat.

All his free time.

Not that he was often free; his sickness tied him to the land, tied him to the house, where indeed Petra was again showing faint signs of an aversion for coffee. By now he was almost overcome by his guard duties. Had he not stood in corners and alleys and passageways month after month, spying and listening? He was wretchedly clad and badly fed, but jealousy kept him at the post hour after hour, standing with his heart in his mouth, consumed by his suffering, while the wind played with his trouser leg as with a flag that has wound itself around the mast, Indeed, he was *never* free: he felt no safer by night than by day; he worked overtime, worked like a slave. If it would even cast him on a sickbed and kill him, but no. Guarding a woman, forsooth! Instead of letting her cut and run, and then bolting the door! What was one to do with this combination of impudence, unfailingly innocent eyes, and tireless mendacity? He might expect her from one direction and she might come from another; so where had she been? She might turn up singing to herself, there was nothing to prevent her; but what she was thinking of on these occasions, what memories was she licking her lips over?

Instead of sinking into the ground, Petra would merely say, 'What are you hanging about here for?'

'Where have you come from at this hour of night?'

'From the consul's, of course. What's that you're holding, a knife?'

'You've got eyes in your head, haven't you?'

'Your fish knife. What are you doing with that?'

'I've been using it on the quay.'

'You haven't – you're just trying to frighten me.'

'Be quiet!'

'But you're wasting your time.'

No, Petra felt safe: he was a coward, he was repulsive, he was beneath contempt. Without more ado she walked past him into the house, leaving him to follow. In the entrance she stopped for a moment with the intention of shaming him: she would show him that she, the night prowler, was the orderly, vigilant one, the one who – look! – bolted the front door after them both.

'What, are you bolting the door?' said Oliver. 'I'm certain young Abel's still out.'

'He can stay out, then!'

'He'll do nothing of the kind!' yelled Oliver in a fury, sweeping her aside with a lunge of his heavy body.

Her heart gave a thump and she said: 'Why don't you kill me and have done with it?'

Another fine old row develops; they go inside and raise the roof. Granny, who sleeps in the old part of the house with Frank and the baby, raises herself on one elbow and listens, then lies down again; it's the old story, she knows it all. Oliver's jealousy has run its course for the moment; furthermore, he is well satisfied with his performance: sweeping her up against the wall, light as a child! He feels he is a man, ho-ho; his chest expands.

The nightly tussle between his parents stands Abel in good stead: he thunders in as quietly as possible from the street, and is in bed before an angry word has reached him from any quarter.

9

Nothing could have been so unmanageable or so painful as this suspense. Oliver had played truant for days on end, pacing the streets, a man who had utterly lost the blessed gift of peace. Now skirts and aprons had been hung in his windows, so that he was prevented from peering in and was reduced to pacing up and down in front of the house like an idiot.

At last he got hold of Granny, who said: 'It's another girl.'

This was of no interest; he could not have cared less. But he kept on talking in order to hear more. 'Oh, another girl. Has she got all her limbs and so on?'

'Yes, as far as I could see.'

'So she hasn't just one leg?'

'No.'

'Well, that's something to be thankful for. It's no fun having a wooden leg. What was I going to say – has she opened them? Her eyes?'

'Why?'

'I was only asking. Why isn't she crying? She's not stillborn, is she? Let me see her.'

'She's fallen asleep.'

Once again Oliver had to wait, play truant from his fishing, pace the streets, wait. Late in the afternoon he was able to see her awake; he carried her over to the window and satisfied himself as to what kind of eyes she had. Petra lay looking at him complacently: there was no problem – the child had brown eyes.

It was remarkable how this trifling fact calmed the tormented father; he boasted about the child and even made a friendly joke for Petra's benefit: 'You're tops when you choose to be!' Although night was setting in, he went out fishing. All these months his heart had been filled with rage against Petra; it seemed that she had again behaved badly, appallingly. Now he saw things differently: she hadn't been so crazy after all, she'd been tremendous in fact, so help him God! If there was fish in the sea, she should have it and welcome! Here come the brown eyes again, the genuine family eyes; nature has triumphed, all's right with the world.

Poor feebleminded man, God knows what arguments he used!

One day, meeting Scheldrup Johnsen, he says to him: 'Now that the winter's coming on, you must be so kind as to think of me.'

'I'm to think of you, am I?'

'Yes. Seeing that I'm a cripple.'

'What's that got to do with me?'

'And that I have a large family.'

'How stupidly people talk!' says Scheldrup uncertainly.

Oliver smiles deferentially and gazes at the ground. 'Well, be that as it may,' he says, 'you must now be so kind as to give me a job.'

'Me? What sort of a job?'

'At the warehouse.'

'That's something you'll have to ask Dad about.'

Oliver slowly raises his eyes, looks hard at Scheldrup and answers: 'No, that's something for you to do.'

Is this a threat? Young Scheldrup takes a step back and meets the cripple's eye. But his glance is vacant; or rather, it begins as a very abrupt, extremely angry glance, but then turns into a vacant one. Evidently he has had second thoughts; he has remembered his conduct, the box on the ear, the gossip, and he has no desire to have it all dragged up again. So he says: 'We-ell, I'm perfectly willing to ask Dad if that's what you want.'

'Precisely,' answers Oliver.

A few days later he again meets Scheldrup, who asks: 'Do you think you could take over the warehouse?'

Take over the warehouse? This is mere pretentiousness and bluster on Scheldrup's part; there has never been any such regular post at Johnsen's warehouse before, one of the shop assistants simply trots down there in the course of his work – so surely a full-time Oliver should be up to a bagatelle like that?

'Dad wants to see you,' says Scheldrup.

Oliver goes home as nothing less than a warehouse supremo. 'Am I correct in thinking that old man Johnsen refused to give me a job?' he asked Petra.

'Yes. And I don't intend to ask him again.'

Silence – a silence that Oliver draws out to immense and momentous proportions. 'Right, I'll have a word with him myself,' he says and goes out.

The women look at each other. Well, it won't make any difference if Oliver does go; and perhaps he isn't really going at all. As for Petra, she tosses her head in scorn.

Oh his return he is silent for a long time, silent and looming. The women are not going to question him, but they smile faintly, and Petra goes so far as to say: 'I wonder who's been seeing the consul.'

At last Oliver breaks the silence. 'I must have my Iceland sweater darned this evening. It'll be cold for me in the warehouse.'

Petra almost shouts: 'You mean you *are* going to the warehouse?'

And even Granny's mouth drops open.

But Oliver looks up in total astonishment, total incomprehension; really, women are a mystery to him. 'But of course?' he answers questioningly.

They clap their hands.

'Of course I'm going to the warehouse. Any day now. I start tomorrow, in fact.'

They talk it over and over: the difference it will make, the regular wage, prosperity; one could go on all night! And there sits the man who has brought it about, the master, swollen with pride, quite the dandy, hat tilted, preening himself. Then he says: 'I told you I was going to have a word with him, didn't I?'

'And all the times I've asked the consul!' Petra pouts.

Oliver answers: 'It's not the same as when a man comes and asks.'

It made a difference all right. But Oliver, who knew what he had let himself in for, sat there thinking, perhaps, that it didn't exactly mean a savings-bank book or a Garden of Eden; old man Johnsen of the Wharf was no spendthrift. On the other hand, he was First Consul, which made him seem to Oliver's family like a fairy godmother.

The work at the warehouse was hardly strenuous; for days on end Oliver might have nothing to do but go there and be around. His busiest days were when a cargo boat put in at the little quay and unloaded flour, syrup, coffee, paraffin, and linseed oil in exchange for fish and whale oil; on such occasions Oliver had to get the goods under cover in warehouse and basement, and by evening might succeed in feeling tired. Otherwise his job was to sweep and keep the place shipshape. Open sacks of coffee must not stand forgotten in the middle of the floor, a potential find for small boys. And when customers turned up with a note from the shop, Oliver would read the note and hand out a sack of flour, twenty fathoms of rope, or a specified weight of fish, as the case might be. The warehouseman was also responsible for filling the drawers in the shop with groceries from the warehouse every morning. Finally, he had to note those goods which were running low, to enable the office to reorder in good time.

All in all, it was no mean position that Consul Johnsen had created for Oliver; and once again his conduct earned applause. True, it was on Johnsen's ship that Oliver had been crippled, but this entailed no obligations, only ordinary kindness and compassion. And with such qualities the First Consul was well endowed; he was a great man and a philanthropist.

So where was the catch? Nowhere. A nasty smell of ancient fish and rotting liver might pervade the warehouse; in summer especially the stench in there attained the highest quality – well, what of that? By and large, Oliver was the same undemanding soul as before, content to earn margarine on his bread, Sundays spent in idleness, a little finery, a resplendent tie, polish on his shoes, a new hat cocked at an angle. But the effects of Consul Johnsen's munificence were more far-reaching than this: from various small indications Oliver became aware that the town no longer looked down on him; even lawyer Fredriksen, unwilling to lag behind the others, held his peace about the house.

Ah, the benefits of prosperity! But the best of it was that Oliver ruled over his warehouse, his little kingdom; indeed, he was virtually an executive, a person of rank one might say. This was greatly to his taste, and it was like a friendly nudge in the ribs when the townsfolk came as his customers and wished him good morning before presenting their slips of paper. 'Good morning!' he would respond, for neither was he the kind of man to look down on another. And it can't be denied that it paid to be a bit polite to the cripple nowadays: he had plenty of opportunities to vary the odds appreciably, to be stingy or generous with his weights and measures.

Fisherman Jørgen brought him slips of paper; Kasper – the former member of the *Fia*'s crew who no longer dared to leave his wife for fear of tempting her to fresh voyages of her own – this same Kasper brought him slips of paper; so did Martin who lived on the heath, and Mattis the carpenter, and Police Constable Carlsen, and a host of others; and Oliver it was who received them at the warehouse door and heard what their business was. Verily, it was a case of Pharaoh setting Joseph over all the land of Egypt.

'Well, you've gone up in the world,' fisherman Jørgen would say out of the kindness of his heart.

'I can't complain,' Oliver would answer. 'Providence has placed me here and not forgotten me.' And now he made over to Jørgen for all time his place in what he called the fish market. 'Just take it all, the cases, the position, and good luck with it! You've given me many a catch of fish when I've been too poorly to put out to sea,' he added sentimentally. 'As for myself, I and my family have our daily bread, praise God, and what more, for example, can anyone want? Then there's your children and my children, Jørgen, they're well behaved, and young Frank's going to senior school and becoming more and more of a scholar; it's a real marvel, he can read German the moment he sets eyes on it.'

Jørgens nods: that's right, his own boys and girls speak of Frank with great respect.

'It's fantastic, it's like something out of a storybook. He can get any job he likes, he can go straight into a bank or an office, there's no denying it. If you'll just wait a bit, Jørgen, we'll walk home together.'

Oliver takes out a handkerchief and wipes the sweatband of his hat, removes the flour and dirt from his face, polishes his shoe, brushes his clothes, and lets Jørgen wait. He is, of course, anxious for Jørgen to take good note that he's a changed man, that his new position is not that of any Tom, Dick, or Harry. Jørgen waits patiently. Finally, Oliver locks the warehouse door for the night; the hinges emit a piercing creak, but for Oliver this is a friendly sound, a warehouse door's nightly swan song. He puts the great key in his pocket and is ready.

They walk home, Jørgen faithfully carrying a heavy can of linseed oil and listening to Oliver's steady flow of talk, which has an underlay of humility but is full of boasting. 'So you're going to paint your house, uh?'

'Yes.'

'Lucky you to be able to do it yourself! I'll have to employ painters on mine, I don't have the time.'

'No.'

'But there's no denying it: my luck's turned. I'll be able to paint and spruce the place up by and by. It'll cost money, but that can't be helped.'

Jørgen, who has something weighing on him, says: 'We must try to keep our boys at home more.'

'Our boys? Why?'

'They were out rowing again last night. I worry about them at times.'

'About young Edevart and young Abel? There's no need for you to do that, Jørgen!' Oliver answers with a lordly air. 'Those fellows are capable of looking after themselves.'

'They come in at all hours. I wish you'd refuse them the boat.'

'Let the lads be,' says Oliver. 'When I sailed to foreign parts and visited every town you can think of, all I ever saw was small boys in boats. You should go to the Pacific; there they dive off boats and swim like eels.'

'But then they don't learn their lessons.'

The two fathers discuss this sagaciously from their respective viewpoints, Oliver being the man of more experience, a circumnavigator to whom Jørgen needs pay attention. But suddenly Jørgen says, 'Still, it's no use denying that they steal fish.'

'I see,' says Oliver. Then it dawns on him that thieving is incompatible with his new position, and he pulls up short. 'They *steal* fish?'

'Not from me. But old Martin's been on about them.'

'Right, I'll speak to the boys,' Oliver declares, with a nod to show that he means business.

These two, fisherman Jørgen and Oliver, have had many a chat over the years, and they know each other so well that they always part without a good night or anything; but on this particular evening Oliver says: 'Won't you come in and pay us a visit?'

As an intellect Jørgen is slow and not of the brightest: what's his neighbour, the warehouseman, up to?

'I don't know whether Petra has a cup of coffee and a bun or two – we could try.'

'Thanks a lot, but it's too late for tonight' is Jørgen's response to this extravagance.

'Fair enough. Well, remember me to them at home.'

Jørgen has never heard anything like it – remember him to them at home!

Arrived there, he couldn't resist sharing this event with his wife; and Lydia, the razor, the grater, was not slow to see it all. 'They're going crazy,' she said. 'Not that the coffee costs them all that much, I dare say, when they can find it in the warehouse; but buns! And that Petra's just been to the headmaster in person to ask if young Frank shouldn't become a parson.'

Plain, blunt Lydia – she could not escape a twinge of envy. To be sure, Petra had something to be high and mighty about – of course, it was all those brown-eyed children of hers, ha-ha! No, she needn't bother. That grey coat she got before her marriage was, as you might expect, no longer fit to be seen; but then again, a married woman had no business with a light fawn coat like the one she'd just had as a windfall from Mrs Johnsen. It was quite unsuitable, she looked a fool in it!

Poor Petra, they all had their knife into her – an unhappy creature when all was said and done, a tethered animal driven mad by being tied up. Worst of all, for herself and for others, she was so hard to satisfy, so discontented by nature. After all, she had a home and a livelihood, a husband and children – she hadn't done too badly in life, had she? Well? Had she deserved any better? What reason had she for not being happy with a man like Oliver, who had risen to be manager of Consul Johnsen's warehouse

Enter Oliver. He hangs the heavy key on its nail over the windowsill. He has personally provided the coppers for the sugar buns from the baker and ordered them to be bought, and now sure enough they are duly brought forth; but not many, not a whole heap for Oliver as the breadwinner – furthermore, Petra shows no manners whatsoever, but puts them down on the bare table. To teach her what's what, Oliver lifts his cup, puts the buns on the saucer, and then looks up. But Petra simply says in her cussed way, 'I didn't know it was to be a party!' The way Oliver is nowadays, he doesn't squabble if he can avoid it; he gives a bun to each of the two little girls, and has one left for himself. Yes, he's as sweet-toothed as any woman; he enjoys his bun in peace, and drinks coffee with it, after which he tucks into his evening meal of loaf end and margarine.

'What was Jørgen carrying in that great can?' asks Petra.

'Oil for painting.'

'Oh, is he going to paint?'

'I guess that's the idea.'

'Well, some people can paint and do their place up nice.'

No comment from Oliver.

After a while she starts again: 'That fellow Mattis is so posh now, he's got a red mailbox on the front of his house.'

'How do you know?' Oliver instantly asks.

'How do I know? I walked past and saw it.'

'What were you up to in that part of the town?'

Petra snorts. 'I suppose I have to ask your permission to go outside my own front door!'

'Why didn't you take that fellow Mattis?' asks Oliver. 'Then you'd have had a red mailbox.'

No comment from Petra.

The fact was that Oliver had grown benign and grateful to Providence for the eminence he had attained; he no longer philosophized in godless fashion over his misfortunes (while thinking it a sin and a scandal if others did so); he was an unashamedly happy man, was Oliver. Mattis, however, was the poisonous fly in his ointment; oh, if only that man were removed from this earth, say into the midst of outer darkness, so help me God! Really, Oliver was behaving like a downright buffoon, an imbecile: he connected the carpenter with his blue-eyed little girl. Just wait, he intended to keep an eye on the child, to see if she grew a horse's nose.

In point of fact, Mattis the carpenter was very hard to fault; he had no reputation as a Lothario. This solid citizen, who now owned his own house and workshop, and employed a journeyman and an apprentice, had refrained from 'changing his circumstances': he had no wife. Out-and-out bachelor. It was as if he said to himself: No, thanks, I've had my nose put out of joint once, I don't want my beautiful big nose disfigured any further – enough's enough! Now he had as his housekeeper Maren Salt, who was well over forty and unlikely to tempt anyone. There he stood in his workshop, year after year, sawing and planing; the corner of his mouth drooped, his aspect grew ever sadder and simpler, but he did his job.

However, the very fact of his not marrying must have made Mattis an object of suspicion to Oliver. What was the man hatching? Was he creeping in on Petra? Every time his name was mentioned, Oliver had a recurrence of his sickness.

'Can you tell me,' he asked, 'what's so marvellous about having a mailbox on your front wall?'

'Well, it's a kind of an ornament – it cheers you up, like. You won't find one on everybody's house.'

'I've knocked about the world and I've seen *gilt* mailboxes.'

'Gilt!'

'From top to toe. With imperial crowns, too.'

Ah, but Petra had heard a thousand times what Oliver had seen while knocking about the world.

10

It was just as well that Oliver didn't deprive them of the boat. A fine thing that would have been, interfering with people's livlihoods!

As for the four small fish that had occasioned libellous gossip, they had found them, quite correct, in old Martin's fish crate, as they now went and acknowledged to Martin in person with nods of the head. But they had borrowed them to make up a score of frying fish they had promised for the doctor's kitchen. 'And please, here they are back again, we've brought them of out own accord, and we'll gladly lend you four another time, Martin.'

Poor Martin, who was indeed a little sorry for his loose words about honest folk, mumbled that he hadn't really been in any hurry over the loan.

'Oh yes,' they said, 'here are the fish, and thanks for your help.'

But it was Oliver who had spoken to the boys, as he had promised; or rather, he had given them a shining new krone to make good their loss. Oh, Oliver was not such a bad sort, he was kind to children in his way, and children in turn were fond of him – Abel would sometimes buy candy for his father.

What did he buy it with? Why, Abel earned a little money by fishing.

The boys went through a phase of being much preoccupied with their business affairs. They never discussed their lessons or their teachers, only their balance sheet. The accounts were all in their heads: a small sum might have been lent to a friend who was in straits, another small sum lost at marbles, but the rest was intact. Neither of them was badly off, they owned silver and even notes, but they also had heavy expenses. Edevart now had to keep himself supplied with tobacco wrapped in silver paper (otherwise, he maintained, he got seasick), while poor Abel was no better off, with disbursements on syrup cookies, pistol and caps, plus red chalk for writing on walls. These were no trifles. But the boys stuck diligently to their boat.

At a later stage, when school closed in on them with a vengeance, they lost their passion for work, owing to the scandalous amount of time and energy they were obliged to spare for their lessons. They made up for it by seeking adventures in town, and succeeded in meeting with quite a few. Their greatest joy came from angry owners of gardens. Good-tempered owners of gardens, such as the postmaster and Grits-and-Groats Olsen, they found less rewarding, but the pharmacist was first-rate. Last year he had shot salt at them when they pursued a mouse into his garden; this year they had their revenge, terrorizing his poultry without mercy, hauling down his flag halyards, and keeping his garden reasonably well stripped of fruit.

For these pranks they had now recruited a third hand, and although she was only a girl, a crazy creature called Little Lydia, she was keen and quick-witted, with a special hawklike talent for keeping a lookout and giving the danger signal.

Now it so happened that Edevart was the biggest and best at making plans, while Abel was light and well-starved and thus indispensable for climbing or for squeezing through narrow gaps. They had a lot of bother getting down some splendid black cherries from a tall tree in the pharmacist's garden; it could only be done by Abel getting up on the outhouse roof and operating from there. It was late in the evening, but the moon was up, all were at their posts, Little Lydia raking the area with her eyes, Edevart piling up empty crates for Abel to climb on, and Abel himself going up aloft. It took time to scale the steep tiled roof, but the squirrel advanced with the aid of his fingernails; at last he was astride the ridge, after which he had a longish traverse in order to reach ... and when he was almost there the hawk gave a low cough. She had seen a chink of light from a door being opened in the pharmacy. Just so. But now the squirrel, having reached his target, ventured to linger for a moment; the hawk coughed louder – and suddenly the pharmacist was down by the outhouse. 'Ah!' he yelled, 'come down there, you devil! Now you'll see!'

But it was the pharmacist who did the seeing.

Roof tiles began cascading down on him, as the squirrel left the roof by the other side, pursued by an avalanche, pursued by the terrestrial globe itself rolling after him; he missed the crates, spearing himself instead on a wooden paling, whence he finally jumped down into the street, a saved if bleeding man. To crown everything came a volley of salt through the paling, triumphantly piercing Abel's thin trousers. But worst of all was the pharmacist's laughter.

And how did it go when the boys tried to reclaim the money they had lent?

To help one or two friends in an hour of need they had opened a reasonable cash credit for them; but the days and the weeks slid by, and the debtors showed no sign of wanting to repay. Finally, a precise day and hour were appointed as a deadline, and a fair-sized crowd assembled, the offenders among them – a supercilious pair of boys who merely smirked at their creditors in order to goad them. But by now Edevart and Abel had determined to get the matter cleared up, if necessary by force.

Edevart first.

He went right up to Reinert, who as the sexton's son wore the latest thing in knee breeches and had his father's watch chain dangling across his waistcoat – went right up to him, perfectly correctly and as if nothing was up, indeed as if he wanted to shake hands with him. But this was only Edevart's fiendish cunning; for suddenly he shot out an arm and a fist and fell headlong on his adversary. The crowd watched the scene in breathless suspense, watched them rolling around, getting to their feet again, dancing all over the place, flashing fire at each other. Then came the unhappy moment when Reinert discovered his watch chain was missing; whereupon everyone started hunting for it and Little Lydia, the hawk, found it in the gravel. 'Give it here!' shrieked Reinert. But Little Lydia had too much sense, and ran with it to her brother Edevart, who stuck it in his pocket. 'Oh!' gasped the crowd. If Reinert had had more time at this juncture, he might have recaptured the chain, but he needed to go straight to the brazier with it if he was to escape going home with a broken chain. 'I'll pay!' he shouted to Edevart. 'I only wanted to tease you a bit!' This denouement was greeted with loud applause from the assembled company.

That left the squirrel and a funny little runt known as the Thumbtack. But when Reinert, his mentor and hero, had to leave the battlefield, there was no one to steel the heart of the Thumbtack, and feeling himself betrayed and abandoned, he muttered, 'I'll pay, too!'

Thus, they were always having one adventure or another, not all of them so straightforward and honourable, but each one instructive and in its way improving.

Now came a time when Abel started to grow and to develop an enormous appetite; at the same time he lost all taste for work, having prematurely reached the slouching age. And this was not good for Abel. When he had spent all his ready cash, he could no longer obtain his own supply of fodder from the baker's; so he signed on with the municipal engineer as an evening errand boy and woodcutter. In this capacity he acquired a taste for stolen rides about the street, hanging on to a wagon by the last half inch of his ass, ready to jump off the moment he was discovered. Hitherto no great lover of horses or of driving, he now heard the rumble of a vehicle a long way off and would wait for it, showing no small art in boarding it at the right moment.

At the municipal engineer's, his modest wage was supplemented every evening by some blessedly thick slices of bread and butter, which helped greatly to fortify his animal spirits. He kept this position for winter month after winter month, during which time he met Edevart at school but had no adventures with him. On the other hand, he did have an adventure with Little Lydia: at the age of twelve he offered his hand in marriage.

He had, of course, known Little Lydia all along as a nice girl, and had attached himself to her; of late, moreover, she had grown painfully pretty, and the sexton's son Reinert had unmistakably been showing off to her in his knee breeches. So Abel decided to take swift action.

One Sunday, over at fisherman Jørgen's, with the hens wandering around the little yard, Abel and Little Lydia were chatting away together. To mark the sabbath she was wearing a smart yellow dress, while Abel was the same today as yesterday and every other day, and gave the matter no thought. She had just been explaining that she couldn't understand how Grits-and-Groats Olsen's Ragna could still care for dolls. 'If I look at my doll now, it's not so much as to cast my eyes on her.'

It was doubtless at this point that Abel concluded she was so grown-up that it was high time to act, and laid his heart at her feet. Although he spoke plainly enough and said all that needed to be said, Little Lydia didn't understand him and questioned him in turn. This was his worst moment. Not that he doubted her answer; she would say yes straight out – they had been through so much together. But on hearing his entreaty once more, she frowned and said no. An unvarnished no.

He gave her a searching look, to see if she was sober.

Little Lydia appeared to be thinking it over; truth to tell, she was somewhat embarrassed by her suitor. They had been friends, had known each other well, but to get engaged to him – no. True, he was still a bachelor, as far as that went there was no impediment, but actually to get engaged to him – no.

Oh, women, women! Unfortunately, it was a fact that for the moment he had nothing to support a family on but a place as errand boy to the municipal engineer; still, he might rise – what was there to prevent him from rising? Nor should she overlook the fact that his intentions were honourable – whereas God alone knew what she might get up to with Reinert and his knee breeches. But women, women! No, she answered, with a shake of her head.

'Well, well!' he said in reply.

He stood there so crestfallen that he couldn't even contrive a departure; he just wanted to sink into the ground. What should he have done? Taken off his cap and bowed: Your servant, madam? Well, he had to say something, some word of farewell, especially as

– surely – she was not entirely depraved. 'Well, well, goodbye!' And when he tried to thank her for everything, he couldn't manage it, he felt his face going distorted, and, oh, how he pitied Little Lydia for all the sorrow and misery she was bound to meet with Reinert.

His spirits were sorely affected; even the municipal engineer's hunks of bread and butter no longer helped; he became all skin and bone, numb with cold, disinclined for anything, hiding in dark corners, eaten away with melancholy and gloom. These were the worst winter months he had ever known. School and lessons – sure, he just about scraped through. Fishing – not a hope. Nobody to confide in, alone in the wilderness; sorrow and rags. No overtures from Little Lydia, either. Had she forgotten him so soon? It looked like it; she seemed to be avoiding him. Nothing could have been easier for her than to indicate that she too was heartbroken; but no, not once did she come rushing up to him and throw herself on her knees in remorse.

He asked his father if he could be confirmed at once and then go to the military school. Father discussed it with him and by no means pooh-poohed the idea; but it was a bit too soon, he said, not all that much too soon, only a bit; they had better wait a few months, and a few months would pass in a flash, just you see, Abel! And soon it would be spring, when he could go with his father on a long Easter or Whitsun outing.

But Abel no longer cared about long outings, he would sooner sit in a hole ashore and brood. What use had he now for the sea or boats or eggs from the nesting rounds or driftwood or adventures? From all such things he was utterly remote, his little vessel caught in a dead calm.

He struggled through the winter. The night (and no more) he spent at home; the day brought school, with now and then a deadly piece of homework; in the evening he had his job with the municipal engineer. The little warrior, it was lucky he stayed in one piece! His brother Frank, of course, went straight ahead with never a detour – what a difference between two brothers! He continued to be the bright boy who justified his free place, the genius whose brilliance everyone saw, acknowledging that here was something out of the ordinary. What a difference between two brothers – it was hard to believe that they came from the same stock. For all that, Frank's parents were the same as Abel's, though truly they seemed unrelated to him. Even at home he was extra-ordinary, so serious, so finicky and industrious. With Abel he was insufferably grown-up. 'You ought to know that at your age,' he would say, like any pedagogue. He had got into the habit of impressing certain civilities on Abel with needless nicety: 'When the teacher comes into the class, you are not to remain standing but to sit down again.' 'Jackass!' said Abel.

When Frank had taken his intermediate examination, the question arose, what he was to do next. Do next – he? The same as before, what else? Was one to extinguish the shining light of genius? Not with the consent of the person directly concerned! But while his destiny was being decided, Frank was advised by the headmaster and the doctor to take an invigorating trip to the mountains, along with other youngsters who had been reading too hard. Before setting out he weighed his rucksack on a steelyard, took a few things out, and put a few things in to get the weight right; he also weighed his shoes in his hand; they were over the permitted maximum, still ...

Now if Abel had been equally industrious and had read himself into the ground, he would not have missed out on this trip to the mountains; it would have done him a lot of good, filled him with fresh vigour. But Abel wasn't that sort, damned if he was, and besides, he was sunk for the moment in grief and inertia.

One day Edevart proposed that they should go out rowing again; there were quantities of whiting offshore. Abel proved so glum and apathetic about everything that it took his friend an hour to talk him into it. Even so, he didn't secure Abel's company then and there. Truth to tell, Abel was quite hopeless at breaking off a connection or saying goodbye to a place, and if he was to start fishing again, he would have to give notice at the municipal engin-eer's. His pay there had been wretched, the municipal engineer himself found it hard to manage on his meagre salary, but bread and butter had been liberally served in his house, and everyone had been kind to the squirrel – how could he walk straight in there and say goodbye? He knew it couldn't be done without his stomach turning over inside him, so he put it off from day to day.

Whereupon Edevart grew angry and said he'd better find another friend.

'Oh. But where will you find a boat?' asked Abel.

This brought Edevart to heel again, for it was Abel's boat, Oliver's boat.

And for the first time in many a day Abel could enjoy a small triumph, could stand in the street and spit like a grown man, and not be a mere cipher. Moreover, it would be good for Edevart's soul – Edevart, who was Little Lydia's brother.

However, he did after all abide by his old friend, and after considering it more thoroughly, he set to work in earnest and said goodbye at the municipal engineer's. All might have been tolerably well had not the engineer's wife taken his hand maternally and said: 'Poor Abel, what a skinny little hand you've got!' He emerged into the street blinded by tears. Somebody shouted to him. 'Ho-ho, have they been thrashing you in there?' It was the Thumbtack.

So here he was, sitting once more on his thwart, and starting to return to his normal self. You see, he had become a regular landlubber and horse fancier, so that now he put a bridle on the boat and drove her, and if he encountered a bit of rough sea, he would once more hang on by his eyebrows and balance on a razor's edge. Ah yes, the two friends were in their element; they had their lives in front of them once more and were again earning money. There was a new small tradesman, Davidsen, an excellent man to deal with, who sold them quality lines and took fish in payment. No fisherman now was better equipped than they. At the end of a week or so Abel could see a wagon and remain untempted.

But for a long time yet he was tormented by the memory of Little Lydia; he went out of his way to avoid her and never mentioned her name. No, but he got Edevart to do so, to speak her name if nothing more.

Abel would ask: 'Isn't that Alice walking over there?'

'Where?'

'There. In the yellow dress.'

'No. That's Little Lydia.'

In the old days he had been entrusted with carrying heavy things for her if he met her when she was out on an errand; all this was now over – he didn't even offer any more. Let her go! And now that the dancing lady was back in town and Little Lydia went to dancing classes, which Abel did not – now more than ever their ways had parted. Destiny had taken a hand.

After two weeks neither boy could think of anything but the sea again. Abel's military school might be all right; they discussed it as a possible recourse, but later they heard that a military school meant lessons and teachers again. No, the moment they were confirmed they would sign on and go to sea. It was the only course for a man.

'Where are we taking fish to tonight?' asked Edevart.

'Tonight I'm taking the whole string home.'

'Aren't you going to sell it?'

'No. Dad's asked me for enough to make a meal tonight, because Frank's come home.'

Edevart was lost in thought for a moment. 'Oh, so he's come home, has he? You know, if that Frank of yours becomes a parson, he'll be able to get us damned.'

'Get us damned? Can he do that?'

'Yes, he'll learn how to work spells.'

For both of them, Frank had become something mysterious and rather dangerous. It might be advisable to give him a wide berth.

I I

What was that new sign they were putting up over Consul Johnsen's door? Another shield or coat of arms – had he been made an out-and-out aristocrat? He had been made Belgian Consul.

It had been apparent that he had something in mind, some target held between his sights. So this was it: to be twice the man the other consuls were, to be a double consul. Just think what it meant: another coat of arms on the wall, for Mrs Johnsen another ring with a stone in it.

The headmaster read the new sign, dusted his threadbare coat, and entered the double consulate. He showed some guile in choosing this precise moment for an interview with the consul.

He offered his congratulations in gracious and respectful words: so the Herr Consul had been chosen to represent yet another government.

Well, yes, indeed – though for that matter it only meant more work, not to mention considerable expense. But one couldn't very well refuse. 'To change the subject, may I thank our headmaster on behalf of little Fia? I'm glad the exams are over. No doubt she might have done a little better, but it's no use worrying now, and it's not as if she were going to become a teacher.'

'Since you mention it, Fia could well become a teacher; there are several subjects she could teach, yes indeed. Herr Consul, I have come to you as being our leading light in everything; I have come on a mission.'

'Really?'

'On a solemn mission. It concerns a pupil of mine whose brilliant progress must not be halted or allowed to go to waste. I refer to Frank, Oliver's son.'

'What about him?'

'You have given him clothes year after year and shown great interest in the whole family—'

'Nothing of the kind!' interrupted the consul.

The headmaster looked at him in surprise. 'First you had his mother—'

'In my employment. Certainly, Petra has been in service with us.'

'Yes. And more recently you have given work to the father. I consider therefore that your benefactions to this family have been many and great. But now it's Frank who needs help, needs it badly and urgently. Do continue helping him, Herr Consul!'

At first the consul was far from enraptured by this application; on the contrary, his brow contracted. He was the town's leading citizen, by now he had risen as high as he could rise, and perhaps he had no desire for any further greatness. So he said: 'When you reckon up my benefactions – as you are good enough to call them – do you think there is any reason why you should come to me now?'

'We were very keen to begin with the first name in the town; we can try the others afterwards. But we fully realize that in doing so we are ... well, that we are ... trading on the obliging nature of a man who finds it hard to say no.'

'What is the boy to be?'

'A boy as diligent and hard-working as that can be anything he chooses. However, he has a special flair for languages.'

The consul pondered, gazed into space and pondered. Then he spoke these remarkable words: 'If I gave the family any further help, it might be misunderstood.'

'Misunderstood?'

'Give rise to gossip. Have you not heard whisperings already?'

'What whisperings?'

The consul shifted his ground. Since the headmaster had evidently heard nothing about a certain box on the ear, he said: 'Oh yes, there've been whisperings all right, people have gall enough for that. I perform my little benefactions from sheer vainglory, they say.'

The headmaster had never heard such nonsense, never. 'Ah, but a man like the consul rises above that sort of thing, soars above it. All the better elements in the town are on your side.'

They discussed it further, the consul still uneasy about gossip, about public opinion, but finally he gave way a little and said: 'Well, I suppose I'd better bestow a helping hand.'

It was now, perhaps, the headmaster's turn to feel a shade uneasy; if so, he expressed his feelings cautiously: 'Oh, *thank* you: I knew I would not come here in vain. Ah, this is an opportunity for people with the wherewithal to practise magnanimity. Otherwise these exceptional gifts will be lost to cultural life and to our country.'

'Look, it was a helping hand you wanted, wasn't it?' asked the consul.

'Yes. Precisely. The kind of munificence that the consul calls a helping hand. That's to say, an annual allowance during the boy's student years.'

This was evidently more than the consul had had in mind. He said 'Hm!' and wagged his head in token of reluctance.

A gloved hand knocked at the door and Madam Consul Johnsen entered. 'Excuse me, I won't be a moment!'

What infernal bad luck for the consul that his wife should come in just then! And of course the headmaster in his innocence was bound to lose no time in initiating her into his great plan for the boy Frank. 'Well,' said the lady; 'well, well,' she added.

But her presence proved the very fillip needed to further the plan. Mrs Johnsen too must have been in a somewhat festive humour, having that very day become twice the woman the other ladies were; she glanced at her husband and said: 'Well, I suppose you'll have to step in here.'

A tremor of relief passed through the consul: whatever the cause, he now had his wife's wholehearted support for a benefaction to the Oliver family. 'It's a great blessing to have an understanding wife,' he said. 'I very much wanted to hear your views, Johanna.'

'Mrs Johnsen being the lady she is,' interjected the headmaster.

Was this too much for her, was this more than she could stand for? She lost her head to the extent of asking: 'Has the boy renewed his baptismal covenant?'

'He's going to be confirmed now. And then the idea was that he should start at college straightaway.'

The consul asked: 'Who else had you thought of roping in over this?'

'Consuls Olsen and Heiberg—'

'I think not,' said the lady.

'No, no, perhaps not. Then we'd thought of lawyer Fredriksen. He owns Oliver's house, the house could be his contribution to the cause.'

But by now Consul Johnsen had been lifted so high on the crest of a wave by his wife's attitude that he shrugged his shoulders and said: 'What, a lawyer like that! He's dabbling in politics these days, wants to get into Parliament – let him get on with that, it's about all he's fit for.'

To this the headmaster agreed with a respectful smile. But then he mentioned Henriksen: they should try to rope in Henriksen.

'Which Henriksen?' asks the lady.

'Henriksen of the Shipyard.'

'Oh, him. Mrs Henriksen sometimes sticks a "von" in front of the name.'

'Well, we oughtn't really to laugh at her,' says the consul, trying to curb his wife.

But Mrs Johnsen is clearly not standing for much today, and certainly not for being curbed: her jaw sets.

The consul continues: 'No, but the real point is, we've no idea how much Henriksen can afford to give away.'

His wife pays heed to this. 'Indeed we haven't. But we don't really mix with them.'

The headmaster is on tenterhooks until he has everything straightened out again. The three of them discuss the Henriksens of the Shipyard and agree that they're ordinary decent people, in their own way, that is; though not quite out of the top drawer of course, a little underbred, and the man likes his glass.

'Well,' Mrs Johnsen finally breaks off, 'I only came in to ask you for a scrap of money.'

The consul goes to the safe. '*One* scrap?' he asks.

'Yes. If it's big enough.'

When his wife has gone, the consul sits down again and confers with the headmaster. 'An annual allowance, yes. That's really what I meant by a helping hand. Have you discussed this with the doctor?'

'Yes. He too would like to chip in as much as he can. But I dare say that's not much.'

'I should think not! Listen, I may as well come straight to the point: I'll defray these expenses. You can go home and sleep on that, Headmaster.'

'Oh!'

'That's what I'll do,' the consul confirms as he rises. 'I shall bestow this helping hand, this annual allowance, alone.'

The headmaster, rising with him, murmurs, overwhelmed: 'In this I recognize the Herr Consul!'

And behold, young Frank was saved from sinking back into his environment, into the darkness from which he had risen. Everything worked out right; the headmaster was enabled to wax triumphant, to stop each better element in the street and tell him the news, and to go in person to Oliver's house and announce it. It was a happy day for him; it was as if he himself had been granted one more exam-room victory by endurance. He knew no greater joy than to be able to do good in this way, asserting the supremacy of scholarship and the printed word. It was his livelihood and his passion. Some passion a man must have, and there are men who will brave fire and water for the reward of conjugating verbs.

The headmaster happens to meet a flock of his charges

returning from their trip to the mountains, a flock exhausted by its drudgery, footsore, sun-baked, full of indignation against bad-tempered bulls and farmers. The headmaster is recognized a long way off; his flock hails him, waves to him. The biggest boys are now rid of him, of their principal torturer throughout their years of growth – ah, it was for their own good; he was arming them for life, arming them for agriculture, the fishing industry, cattle breeding, commerce, industry, art, family life, dreams, and worship, but now they are rid of him, they have passed their exams and are ready to wear their armour in battle. Here they come, dutifully storing away in their little brains the area of Switzerland and the dates of the Carthaginian wars, assaulting mountains with the following item of natural history in their hearts: fish are vertebrates! and limping home again with their first experience of a weakened circulation of the blood. The headmaster meets them, meets these children when perhaps he should rather have been meeting with hardships and adventures; he himself is an old man with the mind of an adolescent, he is half-starved and threadbare, his coat hangs on him as on a coathanger, the loop shows above his collar, but here he comes, the headmaster of the school, of the great stone building.

'How did the trip go?'

'So-so, bulls, farmers . . .'

'You must rise above that sort of thing, soar above it. Do you want to hear some good news?'

'Yes, yes.'

'Frank is to go to college!'

Some of the children are shrewd enough to pretend that this is the best news they could hear, others are indifferent, one or two are envious. Look at Reinert in his knee breeches – easy for him to show pleasure, for he too knows the fact about fishes and possesses marked linguistic abilities! Young Frank himself is not without an interest in the news; his scorched face turns even darker for a moment, but he doesn't buckle at the knees. No, for he has received gifts before now, had been helped and lifted by others all these years, has never had to shift for himself, something will turn up, everything work out right! And is a special surge of joy now to course through his veins? Through Frank? Why, the lad has never known joy, never a day of joy. He has worked hard at school, has felt a satisfaction in being esteemed for his industry and vanity, and that is all. Not for him the knowledge of red explosions; he has never soared aloft and plummeted to earth, never gone down into the pit and floated up again, he has risked nothing and averted nothing. Instead of fighting his way out of trouble, he has avoided getting into it. Shrewdly done, poorly done. God has equipped him for a philologist.

He takes his leave and wanders off home; he is to have fresh fish for supper, something he can well do with. Father is home, Abel too is sitting for once in the family circle; the useless old tomcat prowls round and round, miaowing at the smell of fish.

It is as if a strange element has entered the house: Frank, become even more of an oddity. Now he is to be confirmed and leave home. Granny is speechless about it, and is already treating him as a minister is treated by an erring member of his flock. Perhaps she thinks this will one day stand her in good stead, in the confessional.

Oliver sits at the table with the smallest girl on his lap, Petra with the next smallest (the one with blue eyes), and they all eat. Truth to tell, Oliver is a little uncomfortable; he prattles to the little one to make the atmosphere somewhat less solemn. 'She's so small,' he says, 'and she's Daddy's very own girl; she's not big or dangerous, she's just nice and good. Whose very own girl are you? Yes, Daddy's own, I thought as much.' Occasionally he pops a morsel in the child's mouth; the rest of the time he looks after himself. He's a formidable eater, is Oliver, or would be if Petra wasn't firm with him. 'Well, well, it's young Abel we have to thank for the fish tonight,' he says.

As if that were more than a matter of complete indifference!

Petra, full of the event that has befallen the household, makes Frank answer her questions.

Oliver nods and says with dignity: 'College – yes, that's the way!' But alas, his intellect does not permit him to discuss the matter further, and as soon as he has finished eating he returns to playing with the child, to which he offers the white angel as a doll. By now there is not much left of the ornaments on the chest of drawers, they have been used too freely as children's toys; and as for the little pocket mirror in the brass frame, no, it has not been lost, but Oliver has scrounged it for the purpose of gazing in the mirror while he is at the warehouse. This ruin of manhood, this sample of womanhood, has taken to gazing in the mirror!

He waits for a chance of being heard, sits there poised for an announcement. Of what news is he the bearer? That Johnsen of the Wharf is now a double consul? Well, that too, that is the first item. But then suddenly he says to Petra: 'They were talking about a great party there's to be at old man Johnsen's.'

From time to time Oliver would come home with a message for his wife: it might be that they wanted her for something at the Johnsens' – Mrs Johnsen had hinted at it, Scheldrup had dropped a word – or it might be that the consul himself had a job for her. Occasionally there was nothing in it: there had been a 'misunderstanding' on Oliver's part, or it might even be that he had invented the whole story. But whenever Petra got one of these messages, she put on her best clothes and went out; it did no harm to anyone, and at the very least it give her some leisure time.

'Oh, so they're having another party?' she asks.

'I gather so. Seeing he's been made a double consul. You'll be hearing about it.'

'So it may be that I'm to help?'

'Yes. Or it may have been that you're to go and clean the office this evening. I didn't hear too precisely.'

Petra goes. Granny stays behind with the little girls; otherwise the house is deserted. Oliver sneaks out after his wife, watching jealously to make sure it is really the Johnsens that she is making for. She is used to this, knows he is behind her at every street corner, and averts all scandal by diverging neither to the left nor to the right.

Nor is Abel sitting at home. He has found a choice whip, handle and all, and hidden it under the doorstep; now he takes it out and inspects it: a braided whip, very tough, very suitable – he sees its possibilities straightaway, and at the very least he can carry it around and crack it. At the butt is a handsome brass cap. He knows every driver in the town, and has a shrewd idea which of them has lost his whip, but unfortunately Abel's circumstances do not allow him to do the honest thing and go with it to the owner. Instead he goes to fisherman Jørgen's.

Oh, if only he could have stopped haunting that house, that

Eden from which he had been expelled! If only Edevart had lived somewhere else!

But isn't that Edevart just crossing the street a block ahead? On the other hand, isn't this the municipal engineer coming straight towards him – can Abel run past him in order to overtake his friend?

'Hullo, Abel!' says the municipal engineer. 'Look, I've an idea it's you who has hung a string of fish on my back door a couple of times. I want to pay you for the fish,' he says, taking out his purse.

'It – er – no,' stammers Abel.

'What? My wife is certain it was you.'

'It was only a few,' says Abel.

The municipal engineer thrusts a krone at him; he has no great reserves to pay from. 'It was very good of you,' he says.

They part company, and Abel continues on his way to Jørgen's, his eyes a little moist at the municipal engineer's words.

The hens have gone to roost, the backyard is silent. But as Abel peers in and sees Little Lydia, he calls out on impulse: 'Edevart!'

Little Lydia answers: 'Bah, you gave me quite a fright, you little crow!'

'I was only looking for Edevart.'

'Come here! Edevart's just gone out again. What have you got in your hand? Edevart's been home and had a bite and gone out again. Come here, I tell you!'

'Little crow yourself!' Abel suddenly and unmistakably hears himself say.

Until this moment Little Lydia has been kneeling before a chair with her writing things in front of her; now she gets up, the malice drained out of her, leaving only regret for her hasty words. 'You mustn't be angry,' she says, and show signs of resorting to tears as usual.

Who could bear it? Abel hesitates to comfort her directly, but goes as far as to ask: 'What have you been writing?'

'Letters. Just look at my fingers!' she says, holding out her inky hands. 'And good grief, what a state I'm in!' she cries, shaking sand from her dress.

Harmony is restored between them, and Little Lydia lets her tongue run on. 'You can count yourself lucky that you don't have all these letters to write. Can you write letters?'

'I don't know.'

'I made so many friends among the other girls at the dancing school, and I have to write to them all. Is that a stick you've got there?'

'Can't you see what it is? It's for beating carpets. It's a carpet beater.'

Little Lydia bends it, tries it out on the air, and nods: it's terrific.

'You can have it,' he says.

Done.

They chat about this and that, with Little Lydia in the role of mature young woman: she has so much to do in the daytime, by the evening she's exhausted with all the sewing and ironing and housework she has to do. 'Do you know what I'm sitting here thinking?' she asks.

'No.'

'Oh well, forget it. Only, Mama will be calling me any moment, and then it'll be too late if you want to say something to me.'

Caught completely off guard, he shrinks to nothing. What is he to say? What can she mean?

All of a sudden, 'Yes!' comes from Little Lydia in a piercing squeal towards the house, and in she rushes.

But Abel hasn't heard a soul calling her.

Another ruined evening, an evening of utter misery. A day or two later the driver in question got wind of his beautiful whip and came to recover it. Which, of course, just about polished off Abel for life.

12

The years went by. The youngsters were confirmed, they grew rapidly, they became tall and grown-up – even more grown-up than usual, the fashion just then being for shoes with extremely high heels.

And so, behold Fia Johnsen as tall as her mother, brown-eyed and pale, a nice creature; her freckles had nearly worked their way out, and she wore her hair in a long plait at the back. People had watched her throughout the years of growth, they remembered her being born, they performed prodigious feats of memory; why, they knew what she wore for her confirmation, the women would stand around the pump expatiating on all the crêpe. It was good to be Fia Johnsen.

Her brother, Scheldrup Johnsen, was in one country after another in the pursuit of learning, disappearing every now and then from his fellow townsmen's view; but Fia stayed mostly at home. She learned to dance and play the piano and dust and be a comfort. She enjoyed drawing and painting; it was she who perused the illustrated papers and magazines in the consul's house, she likewise who had painted the decorative plates which still hang all the way around the dining-room walls. 'My daughter's work!' the consul is in the habit of saying to his guests.

Her talent had blossomed first under the school drawing master, who was also the town drawing master; later she travelled to bigger towns and to capital cities. She learned more, and every time she came home she was able to smile at the decorative plates with greater expertise. Now she had reached the stage of being able, unaided, to paint the view from her window and parts of the garden. Good. But Fia was very young and pitifully thin, by no means underfed, but undeveloped, short on muscle, short on work. What was she to do with herself, this talented girl? Her parents could afford to keep her at home or to keep her abroad, whichever she preferred, and whether she was here or there she was nice, she was charming, and she never went upstairs two steps at a time, no, never. But that was all. She needed no career. Her talent was superfluous. For her, life was neither real nor earnest.

'She could do with a bit of regular work,' said the doctor.

He had been saying this for years, to the vexation of her parents. Work? What work could their daughter do?

'Perhaps you'd like to have her as a servant?' asked the consul.

'She'd be no good at that.'

'Not even that!'

'No. But try removing her diamond rings and putting her to work in the garden.'

'I have a regular man for that. You know, poor Fia works all right in her own line, and now she means to buckle down to it for a while and have an exhibition.'

'Good God!' exclaimed the doctor.

The two gentlemen were sitting in C. A. Johnsen's office, in the double consulate, so that the consul was debarred from simply walking out. 'Well,' he said, 'my daughter has hardly troubled you very much with her art. Certain critics, on the other hand, have been decidedly complimentary about it.'

'Don't we know it. All right, but what bloody good is art going to do the child if she goes around looking a picture of misery?'

'She'll doubtless grow out of that.'

'It's by no means certain.'

Strange how much Consul Johnsen put up with from the doctor – that in all these years he had never once had the guts to show him the door! The mystique of medicine? Why should that concern the consul more than the next man? Then again, the doctor's social standing in the town was of course immense, no question of that; but was it remotely comparable to that of the consul himself? It was a real mystery to one and all that the doctor dared to speak to such a mighty personage with so little ceremony.

Just now, moreover, Consul Johnsen had reason to put up with vexations less well than usual; he had enough of them. Making a great effort to avoid being offensive, he said: 'Fia's parents can only hope that Providence is more charitable to her than you are, Doctor. Won't you light another cigar before you go?'

'Thanks, I will, when I go. If you set about things in the right way with Fia, she wouldn't be so dependent on the charity of Providence. Tell me now, won't she sooner or later be marrying in any case?'

'And if so, would she be unfit for it?'

'A man wants to marry a woman, not a painter.'

The consul said with a smile: 'All I can say is, she can pick up the qualities of a married woman later on. Not that the question will arise for several years. For the time being she's devoting herself to art.'

'I put it to you,' said the doctor, 'that if she had not been able to afford this amusement, she would have had to become a more efficient female. Alternatively, I put it to you that she may not always be able to afford it.'

The consul smiled again. 'Then *you* will have to provide for her.'

'Look, I'm only putting it to you.'

The doctor's importunity was insufferable, and if the consul had known the real reason for this importunity on this particular day he might after all – after all – have shown his visitor the door. It was none other than the new diamond ring Fia had been given, a diamond ring that denied the doctor's wife all blessed peace. What did that child, that chit of a girl, want with such a thing? She should still be in shorts skirts, for heaven's sake. And what had become of the poor little diamond ring that the doctor's wife herself had been led to expect years ago? How weary, flat, stale, and unprofitable seemed to her all the uses of this world, boo hoo!

The consul, however, was unaware of the battles between the doctor and his wife; and he sat there as if he had discovered a certain amount of sense in his visitor's words – indeed, he became positively pensive. He was fond of Fia, and her well-being meant more to him than anything; no doubt he showed her rather too much indulgence, her stays in towns grew costlier and costlier, but that was a necessary part of her development – he could hardly pull her up short and shame her before her new friends and acquaintances. In her goodness she had taken to helping her fellow artists by purchasing their paintings, but over this her father felt obliged to remonstrate: it made no sense, his expenses were high enough already, his purse was not bottomless. Good: Fia bowed her head and corrected this fault of hers, though she secretly retained certain others – venial sins, be it understood, mere bagatelles by comparison with all the good qualities and graces she possessed. In public she was well-behaved and ladylike, though perhaps a shade too tall. She liked to be taken for a fledgling from a traditionally cultured and well-feathered nest – a mixture this, perhaps, of deception and self-deception. When she missed the mail boat she would say to the bystanders: 'If only I had our own steamship here.' Alas, their own steamship could scarcely afford to go cruising at Miss Fia's behest; moreover, she was a tub incapable of doing more than eight knots, a tub whose normal earnings were a bare five per cent, and occasionally minus two.

And just now she was on the minus side again.

The good consul had not always been the good shipowner, and

it was the true art of shipowning that Scheldrup had gone out into the world to learn. There was evidently a difference between managing a tramp steamer and sending a schooner laden with whale oil across the North Sea to fetch coal. The *Fia* failed to show a profit every trip; she by no means lumbered at her eight knots from triumph to triumph. But it was not only the loss; the *Fia* had other ways of proving a trial. Just now the crew were bellyaching, complaining about the food, deserting; it was beyond the consul's understanding why the same food should be any less good this year than in previous years. It vexed him as he sat there now.

And then an incredible piece of news had assaulted his ears: that even that trading fellow Davidsen had been made a consul – only a single consul, admittedly, but still a consul. It seemed there were no limits – Davidsen, who had moved here from the next town twenty years ago and was still regarded as a newcomer by the real natives; who time and again stood serving behind his own counter; who sold toy fishing tackle to children and thick, heavy ropes and canvas to ships, all common or garden stuff, with no dry goods or gleaming hardware. At Johnsen of the Wharf's the clerks wore collar and tie; at Davidsen's they had to go around in shirt sleeves and be prepared to handle a hawser. Fair enough, there is no shame in work; but this was no work for the consular service or the diplomatic corps.

Was this the sum total of the consul's vexations? There was one more: a spot of bother with Oliver, the warehouseman. How so? He had been fiddling with the weights. To his own advantage? Not a scrap; to the consul's advantage. Fair enough, there is no shame in faithful service; but fiddling is not allowed. What had happened was that Mattis the carpenter had brought a note for forty pounds of pollard, and when Oliver went to weigh out the bran, he had apparently forgotten his fat little finger somewhere on the balance. There must have been an appreciable weight in that little finger, since Mattis became suspicious and went off to Grits-and-Groats Olsen for a reweigh. Just as he thought: grossly underweight!

Now of course, leaving the building with his sack of bran was the worst thing Mattis could have done; he ought to have struck his brow at having 'stupidly' left his purse back at the shop, and then lured one of the clerks round to the warehouse to check the weight. But Mattis, who was genuinely stupid, followed his big nose and began forthwith to emit lightning and thunder; and what was the good of that? He ran around the town from one set of scales to another, getting his sack of bran weighed, and not forgetting to tell the why and the wherefore. Finally he came back to Johnsen of the Wharf's, by now oozing flour and in a rare old rage. As it happened, Olaus was in the shop at the time, and Olaus was in tremendous form today, having had brandy for breakfast and brandy for lunch. At first he was listless and preoccupied, but on hearing the carpenter's story he suddenly emerged into a newly based consciousness and raised his voice in turn: 'What's that? Short weight?'

'Short weight!' said the carpenter. 'Enough's enough!'

The chief clerk, Berntsen, tried to hush them. 'You mustn't make such a noise, the consul's in the office.'

'I'd be glad if he came out,' said Mattis.

'Come on, let's have the consul!' bawled Olaus.

'Look, Olaus, put this tobacco in your pipe and be off with you!' said the clerk. 'Come along, Mattis, you come with me.'

They went round to the warehouse.

Oliver took it in excellent part, and spoke condescendingly to the enraged carpenter. Why should they be getting at each other with malice and fraud? He had to laugh. Did Mattis suppose that he – Oliver – bore him a grudge for some reason? Again, he had to laugh. If a mistake had occurred, it had occurred by accident, as might happen to anyone.

'It's not the first time I've become aware of it,' said Mattis.

Oliver gave him a sidelong glance and answered: 'As for that you'd better guard your tongue a bit. You may have to produce witnesses.'

Berntsen weighed the sack, then made up what was wanting and a fraction more. 'That's how you should weigh out for Mattis,' he said, to end the dispute. 'That wasn't nice of you, Mattis, running around the town with your sack – you should have claimed your rights here on the spot.'

'Yes, but it put me in a rage; it's not the first time.'

'You hear that, Berntsen!' said Oliver, calling him to witness.

But Berntsen was an old hand and proceeded cautiously. Mattis the carpenter was no bad customer, and a master craftsman to boot, with a journeyman and an apprentice. He owned a house, though not a home, having only Maren Salt, to be sure; still, Mattis was no Tom, Dick, or Harry, and now he had been elected to the Town Council. 'Well, you must take it easy, Oliver,' Bertsen warned him. 'The mistake is yours, as I understand, and I think I can speak for the consul in saying that you mustn't make mistakes with the weights.'

So ended the affair.

The consul had been notified of the incident, and although of course he personally was above suspicion, he was greatly vexed. So people ran about the town checking up on his weights, did they? And to think that anyone should dare to stand in his shop and bawl, 'Come on, let's have the consul!' It was all of a piece with the crew of the *Fia* complaining about the food. No, the good spirit had departed from the earth. Everything was being levelled nowadays, boundary lines were being blurred, people were starting to rub up against him, trying to mix with him; a doctor imagined he could say what he liked in his presence. And then these consuls springing up in every street!

In short, the doctor might have found a more suitable time and moment for testing the consul's forbearance.

There is a knock at the office door, and when the consul doesn't answer, the doctor calls: 'Come in!' The doctor actually does that. It is not so many years since Consul Johnsen would have cried 'Stop!' at this point, he has not always been so defenceless; now he seems in some secret way cowed. What in the world has he to fear? Does the doctor know something about him? Has this small-town physician and quack whetted his sword against the double consul?

Enter the pharmacist: a nervous little man, pale, with the merest hint of a beard, well-to-do, married, but childless and bachelor-like, stains on his clothes, smelling of medicines and tobacco.

'Good morning!' he says.

'Do you think so?' says the doctor. 'I think it's a miserable morning.'

The pharmacist exchanges courtesies with the consul. Then he extends a hand to the doctor, saying: 'Allow me.'

'I'm not sure that I will.'

This must be the man's idea of a joke; and he rejects the pharmacist's proffered hand.

The consul offers the pharmacist a cigar. After which sheer necessity demands that he set to work on some large sheets of paper on his desk, glance cursorily at them, arrange them in order, and then scatter them again.

'I can see you're busy,' says the pharmacist. 'I'll go directly.'

'It's these consulates I'm saddled with,' says the consul.

'Yes, I suppose it's not all a case of "pleasure at the helm".'

'Right now I'm busy with reports to my governments; there's quite a bit of work in it, I assure you.'

It may well be that the consul has said this half in jest, but his dignified manner suggests that his honorary posts are hightly burdensome.

'Your governments?' asks the doctor. 'That's tough, do you have several governments? Surely you only have one government, like myself – the Norwegian.'

The consul can at least go so far as to ignore the doctor and ask the pharmacist if he needs some really good wine, a Madeira, vintage so-and-so.

'What's the price? No, then it's too dear for the store. But I can take fifty bottles for the house.'

He doesn't offer it to *me*! the doctor is doubtless thinking. 'The huckster, the Jew!' is doubtless on the tip of his tongue. 'Where's Scheldrup at present?' he says aloud.

'At Le Havre. Why do you ask?'

'When's he coming home?'

'I don't know. He may be away some time yet.'

'It's nine months since he was here last.'

The consul casts his mind back and says: 'Yes, that's right.'

'That's right, yes,' the doctor echoes. Then he yawns blatantly, and gets up for the purpose of knocking off cigar ash onto the polished surface of the stove.

'Here, there *is* an ashtray, if you don't mind,' says the consul.

'Beg pardon!' The doctor crosses to the window and looks out into the street. What colossal, deliberate impertinence, to turn his back on a double consulate!

'Can I be of any service to you gentlemen today?' asks the consul.

The pharmacist thanks him, declines, and calls out: 'Come along now, Doctor! We mustn't detain the consul any longer.'

'I'm looking at the children out there,' says the doctor, without hurrying or turning around. 'Including a little girl with brown eyes that must be one of Oliver's.' Then he turns and asks the pharmacist point-blank: 'Does it not strike you how many brown-eyed children we're starting to get in this town?'

The pharmacist is evasive. 'Really? Oh, I don't know.'

'And a new specimen arrived only yesterday.'

The pharmacist (still evasive, but nervously eager): 'Another new specimen? Well, what is one to say?'

'At Henriksen of the Shipyard's again. That's to say, Mrs Henriksen's. This is brown eyes number two for her.'

The pharmacist (agog for the doctor to say more): 'What do you say? It's a case of Jacob's rods. Wasn't there something about white rods and black rods?'

The doctor buttons up his coat and with a great show of indifference prepares to leave. 'You ask, what is one to say? Well, one can hold one's tongue. There's no miracle about it, either in the one house or in the other, it's plain nature. These blue-eyed couples get brown-eyed children from a brown-eyed father, whoever he may be.'

'You don't say!'

'Don't I, though! And this isn't a case of throwback. I've made a few inquiries, and there are no brown eyes in the family, at least not for a fair number of generations.'

'Well, I'm damned – if you'll excuse my language.'

The consul contributes an occasional little laugh or a 'Hm!' to the conversation. Otherwise he stands quietly waiting for the gentlemen to take their leave.

'Well, you must excuse me, Consul,' says the doctor at last. 'By the way, Pharmacist, how tiresome that your Madeira hasn't been delivered yet – I could have gone home with you and sampled it.'

'I'll send it up this afternoon,' says the consul.

From the threshold the doctor has a parting shot: 'Bear in mind what I said about Mademoiselle Fia, Consul. Let's get her strong and healthy. I have something of a secret soft spot for the charming lady.'

The consul finds himself alone, and sits staring at his large sheets of paper, arranging them in order and scattering them again. What was the purpose of these gentlemen's visits? Is there not something suspicious about their casual encounter here? Had they arranged a rendezvous for the purpose of instigating a manoeuvre against the double consul?

His jaw sets more and more firmly. When the pharmacist knocked at the door it was the doctor who called 'Come in!' lest his egregious associate go away again. A plot! A conspiracy!

Suddenly the consul opens the door into the shop and says to Berntsen, his chief clerk: 'Make out the doctor's bill – he was asking for it.'

But even after giving this order Consul Johnsen is still not finished with the business; unauthorized thoughts have entered his head. Ah, he is no longer able to take everything lightly, as once he could; troublesome reflections keep rearing their heads now and blunting his appetite for work. The reports can wait; for that matter, Berntsen can write them.

He goes to the mirror, puts on his hat, imitates his carefree air of former days, and goes with a batch of letters to the post office.

13

In leaving his office in working hours he was, of course, giving way to a feeling of perplexity, he was seeking refuge. Taking his own letters to the post office was a mere pretext; normally this was done by one of his clerks. Studying the steamship schedules on the post-office wall was likewise a pretext, a device for giving the staff time to warn the inner office that Consul Johnsen was there in person.

The postmaster emerged with astonished, questioning eyes: could he be of any assistance to the consul?

No, thanks. Wait – if the postmaster had time to check his records for a certain registered letter containing a cheque; the consul had had no word of it since.

They went into the inner office to sort the matter out straight-away; afterwards they sat and talked. It was chilly in there, with a faint smell of sealing wax and stamp-pad ink; the walls were hung with tinted drawings of houses for God and man, free-standing towers and gates, friezes, carvings, handsome doors, stoves, all works of the untrammelled imagination. Outside the window onto the garden, blossom-laden lilacs swayed to and fro.

Here the consul, seated in a wooden chair, listened to a singular flow of chatter, utterly different from the kind that buzzed about him daily. Was this the sort of thing he had come to hear? In the ordinary course of events the postmaster bored everyone to death; the doctor would flee from him, and was in the habit of saying: 'God has not granted me the patience to listen to all that innocuous stuff.' But Consul Johnsen had seated himself in that chair; he must have been tired or at his wits' end.

Oh, that windbag of a postmaster! – a man infinitely well-meaning, tediously kindhearted, and really not a whit better than Carlsen the blacksmith, with indeed the difference that the blacksmith hardly ever spoke or worried other people but kept his idiotic contentment to himself. Contentment in a world like this! The pair of them were perhaps little better than the women at the pump – no, they themselves *were* two women at the pump, exactly, except that their gossip was religious; still, they had the same feminine simplicity of soul. They had achieved an understanding of life with which they made do; the postmaster had even arrived at his standpoint by the path of philosophy. From time to time, of course, events might give them a good slap in the face, but this hardly seemed to affect their outlook; thus the blacksmith, despite his delinquent children, still clung to his religious tenets and continued to thank God for good and evil. Was not this the faith of Israel? It was thought quite possible that the two men were right; that they were models and paragons of virtue; but for all that, the town declined to change its ways, the town remained the little crawling anthill it was – a proof indeed that life took its course despite all theories, especially perhaps religious ones. Was not then the outlook hopeless for the two righteous men in all the town? And how came they not to join with the rest?

Perhaps the postmaster had had some pleasant experience that day; God knows, but it may have been so. At all events, he was in wonderful spirits. It didn't take much to cheer him up, he was an unassuming man; the mere fact of his oldest son's obtaining his mate's certificate recently and getting a ship at once had been enough to make the father foolishly happy. Was a mate's position something so tremendous? 'There's depth to that boy,' said the postmaster; 'the letters he writes us! Not that I know which of our children can rightly be called the best – take the one who's working on the land. He sets aside part of his wages and sends his sisters enough to buy themselves some nice boots. What a lad! I daren't shake hands with him any more, he squeezes mine to pulp, ha-ha, the bear! And you should see him untie a knot in a rope, he has nails like pincers, only sometimes he uses his teeth. You can afford to with teeth like that . . . So Scheldrup is still at Le Havre?'

'Yes.'

'I saw it on his mail. The doctor was writing to him yesterday.'

'The doctor was writing to him?'

'Yes. And Fia, how pretty she is, so very pretty and polite! My wife was standing at the window looking at her one day and called to me to come. I beg your pardon, you were about to say something?'

'No, not really.'

'I went for a long walk in the country early this morning – you must drive that way, Consul, when you go to your country residence. You know how suddenly it plunges into the forest and another world begins, an extraordinary, kindly disposed world, saturated with stillness, but also full of tiny sounds. I left the road to avoid meeting anyone, but would you believe it, there was a man sitting there, deep in the forest. He'd seen me, there was no turning back; there he sat, playing a mouth organ. A strange man, a labourer, a vagabond. I had a long conversation with him. He was none too bright, his talk was all about food and money, but there he sat playing his mouth organ, poor fellow. "Why are you sitting there?" I asked. "I'm allowed to, aren't I?" he answered back. "Certainly." "What business is it of yours, then?" he asks. "None at all. But play a bit more." "What'll I get for it?" he asks. "A few coppers. I'm the postmaster in this town and I handle a lot of money in the course of a year, but none of it's mine." "I bet you swipe a letter from time to time," he says. "How could I do that? I'd be put inside straightaway." "No," he says, "the gentry all stick together. It's only us on the road who have to pay for it." He talked a lot of rubbish, and I explained to him that I had my salary, and provided it went far enough, I had just about all I needed. No, that was beyond him, he could never make things go far enough; if he earned the price of a pair of shoes he had nothing left for trousers, and vice versa. With these farmers it was one long grind, he said. If he came and asked for food, they made him work first, heavy work, woodcutting, the heaviest work going in the summer. In the evening they gave him porridge and milk, no bread and butter, no curdled milk with sugar and crumbs, which they could easily afford, the earthworms! A discontented creature he was – the morose, listless type. If we assume that the human race is governed by some evolutionary principle, this man hasn't got very far as yet; maybe he's already been on earth countless times, but has hardly made the tiniest progress. So he departs into the darkness again every time, virtually unchanged; then returns to life and starts again from scratch.'

'Is that the way it goes, do you think?' asked Consul Johnsen with a smile.

'What is one to believe? We can hardly assume an unjust First Cause – there are too many difficulties involved; we must assume a just one. And we can't assume that a just First Cause has condemned this vagabond to eternal misery from the outset. Originally, therefore, we're all on an equal footing and enjoy the same chances; some use them, others misuse them. The work we do on ourselves in this earthly life stands us in good stead in the next; but if we work our way downward we're set back accordingly. That must be the reason for the sad fact that there's been no observing change in mankind within historical times: we've neglected our chances.'

'So you think we die and return to earth many times?'

'What is one to believe? We're given chance after chance. The First Cause has time in plenty, it contains eternity within itself, and since we're part of the First Cause we never perish. But this is the point: we don't come back here in the same state every time, it lies in our power to improve our lot for our next life.'

'So your man will get his curdled milk?'

The postmaster smiled. 'Things like that are only important to him now, from his present standpoint – whereas I'm talking about his disposition, his spiritual make-up. And here we come to a point of some significance: this man sat there playing his mouth organ.

And yet he must have done some work on himself in his previous lives. He played songs and dances for me, played them superbly – I never heard anything like it. It's not his skill I'm talking about, but his doing it at all, sitting in a wood, playing away. And now just listen: he told me about a kind of aeolian harp he'd seen at a Jew's house; it had strings of varying thickness and various metals – steel, copper, brass, silver – and there were little balls hanging from it, which the wind carried against the strings in a series of gentle blows. That was how the aeolian harp played. It was strange, hearing such words in the mouth of this man. No, he hasn't been standing still throughout his earthly lives, he's cultivated a little plot of garden in himself, with just one flower in it. So it all depends on whether he'll conduct himself this time in such a way that the plot of garden will be bigger in his next life.'

'Surely the whole of this theory must begin with the question of whether there is or isn't a personal First Cause?'

'Where are we to begin? you ask. Does not even the First Cause have a first cause? We come to a halt in time and assume this personal First Cause. It's even more impossible to manage without it. The question eludes our apprehension, of course, but we need a power, a necessity behind everything; we know nothing positive about it, but it exists for us by virtue of our need for it, and this need in turn exists as part of the First Cause to which we belong. We're endowed with it; if it didn't exist we wouldn't possess it. Do you regard these conclusions as unreasonable?'

'It's not my line; I don't know.'

'I don't know anything either; no one knows anything. But we possess one light which never goes out. Otherwise we'd be in total darkness.'

'What light is that?'

'The light of *human thought.* It goes astray, it makes mistakes, but we can be certain of its existence. And it's part of our endowment, it comes from the Godhead.'

Silence. The two gentlemen sat and pondered.

The consul asked: 'Godhead – which one? If this human thought of ours was any good, it should ultimately be able to find the right Godhead, shouldn't it?'

'It has been found. In and by our need of it.'

'But you see, men keep swapping one godhead for another. The

Greeks swapped godheads, the Egyptians swapped, we Scandinavians have swapped. Nowadays we name our fishing boats after the old gods.'

'Excuse me,' said the postmaster, 'now you're talking about gods, whereas I spoke of the Godhead. You're talking about theology.'

Another silence.

Really, this was a pretty tedious conversation, and the consul would doubtless have taken his leave – except that for the moment he had nowhere to go, least of all home. And then there was this strange contentment that the postmaster carried around with him day after day, year in, year out. Who else was contented? Young and old, great and small, everyone was anxious, under pressure, weighed down by some burden, with the almost solitary exception of this academic dropout turned small-town postmaster. Was he a bit dim, a good-natured dolt? Perhaps. But that was not the whole story – far from it. He was, for example, by no means invariably meek and accommodating; the consul had heard him defend himself with confidence. Peace was what he wanted, and if he didn't find it, he would grab it. No, he was not to be trampled on. The tiresome thing about him was his philosophical speculations, an endless punishment to his fellows, and to those who understood such things a terror.

Why would he not keep his mouth shut? Presumably because he thought he had something worth saying. But it was a voice crying in the wilderness of his native town. His home was so quiet – for his wife had little to say for herself, answering when a question was asked her and otherwise attending to her domestic duties – that all kinds of ruminations were dammed up in the postmaster's brain, and though he muttered and talked to himself, this did not always suffice; from time to time some innocent citizen had to pay for it by listening to an elucidation of matters that far transcended freights and timber prices.

If Consul Johnsen had been in his usual energetic frame of mind, if the recent shock to his system had not set him searching for an unfamiliar peace, he would most certainly have taken his leave. Instead, he continued to sit there, while giving the impression that he hadn't really the time but stayed purely and simply from courtesy towards a kindly man – looking at his watch, abruptly opening his briefcase, to see if perchance a letter had been overlooked. Then he remarked casually: 'Ah, human thought – how it seeks and seeks and never finds! There can't be much to it, eh, Postmaster?'

'Why, it's the one thing we can be certain of – the light that goes on burning and is only extinguished when life on this planet ends. Really, that means a great deal to us. What this light achieves, how much darkness it dispels – that's another matter; even if we only revolve in endless circles or error, maybe that in itself is movement, life; a smooth forward course, lacking friction, would inevitably paralyse movement. If it served any purpose we ought to kneel before human thought, before the light; ah yes, if we were religious, if we had any mercy on ourselves, we'd regard human thought with veneration. But we're too "intelligent", we decline to bow our heads, crammed as they are with worldly mechanics. How we seek and seek and never find! you say. There I disagree. I agree that we never find, but as to our seeking – no. But why should we seek if we never find? Well, supposing the search itself represents movement towards a goal. However, we do very little seeking, there are not many who seek; instead we go and "learn", we develop our intellects. What poverty, what sterility! Look at these "intelligent" people who've learned only their own subject; they know that, all right – that's what school is for, study, the art of memorizing.'

The consul smiled. 'Speaking for myself, I'm absolutely unlearned. That's to say, I've had other things to learn, and I'm not even fully qualified in them.'

'Really? You mean we're not capable enough, not sufficiently clever in a worldly sense? But of course we are. That's not where mankind's deficiencies lie. Throughout historical times we've made a fetish of such things and pursued them to a dangerous degree; but we've omitted to bow our heads. Now we've got ourselves in a jam and no mistake, and the way out won't be via more knowledge, more external skills, but via introspection and meditation.'

'Surely we can't all be philosophers?'

'No, and neither should we all be men of one-sided mechanical learning. But that's exactly what everyone makes a fetish of – it's become our highest aim. In the last few centuries nothing has enjoyed so much esteem as the culture of learning – the upper classes have infected the lower classes with this esteem, until every man longs to have a share in it. Oh, the importance attached the world over to the mechanics of reading and writing! Not to acquire them is a disgrace; to possess them is a blessing. No great founder of a religion has ever practised these arts, but nowadays they're indispensable for young and old alike. No one makes a fetish of bowing his head in meditation, everyone reads and writes his way to the stock of ideas required by contemporary man. It's nobler to read and write than to do anything with one's hands, said the upper classes. The lower classes listened. My son shall not till the soil off which all creatures live, said the upper classes; he shall live off others' labour! And the lower classes listened. Then one day the roar began, the roar of the masses; by now the masses had learned enough of the arts of the upper classes, they could read and write. "Here, bring us the good things of this world, they're ours; to hell with working for the next life – you don't catch the upper classes doing that kind of work!" '

'Do you think it would be better if the art of reading and writing was the property of the few?'

'That's not a new idea. No, the best of all would be to get rid of all this superficiality, for every class to lose its faith, its superstitious faith, in rote learning. It's alleged that the roar would cease if there was still more learning, and so people work away at acquiring more and more arts, and more and more skill in those arts. And their heads are held higher and higher but emptier and emptier, and no grave meditation bows them down. No, that's not the path that leads forward; even in a worldly sense it comes up against a sheer precipice. When my children were small I sometimes used to look at their textbooks – I have to admit, I knew precious little of all these arts. Just go on giving them more, don't stint them, make them sick and tired of learning, all well and good. But the roar will continue, the roar will increase. A bowl of curdled milk? Several bowls of curdled milk, lots of them, they're ours! Next life? Why, we read that the next life is just something dreamed up by pious women, it doesn't concern us! – Oh, how little mercy they have on themselves!' said the postmaster, shaking his head. 'They have this little plot of garden with its flowers in, but they're liable to return for their next earthly life in totally different worldly circumstances but with their spiritual make-up unaltered.'

Here the consul tried to look even less interested; he carried his performance to great lengths, casting his eyes over the drawings on the walls, paying sudden attention to one in particular, getting up, putting on his pince-nez, gazing at a handsome gateway. For, of course, Consul Johnsen wanted people to pay respect to his – Johnsen's – judgement; he couldn't at the drop of a hat let himself be converted to several lives upon earth – damnably palatable and attractive doctrine though it was. He might return and create further havoc, vanquish the enemies who had upset him, give parties, do some wenching, manage steamships, make money, play the coastal-town tycoon a few more times – he could ask for nothing better. Then Consul Johnsen remembered that tiresome appendix to the postmaster's speculation, to the effect that one might come back in totally different worldly circumstances, and again felt utterly at sea. Come back as a sailor, as a vagabond? Come back as nothing after having been so much? He sat down again and hastened to excuse his inattention. 'It was that superb gateway, a positively celestial gateway! What was I going to say? We don't seek, you say? But many people think they've found the answer. Some people find it reasonable to suppose that when a man dies there's an end of him.'

The postmaster (still in fine fettle, still on his toes): 'Except for his final scream, his scream at the darkness confronting him. In that case, what have we been on earth for? For the sake of meaningless movement? Why?'

But the consul, fearing a long exposition of this equally unattractive doctrine in turn, hastily interposed: 'Christians believe in salvation after death.'

'True,' answered the postmaster. 'In itself salvation is not a bad idea, it has conforted many a dweller on earth during the night. Though, mind you, even this salvation has to be earned, isn't that so? Indeed, they say that only a few will attain it, so what chance do the others have? No one is exempted by Christianity from working on himself. On the contrary, it is harsh in its demands: no man shall attain salvation gratis and unearned, it says. Those are the requirements of the law. The Gospel is in its way even harsher: one must believe in the First Cause's policy of bloody atonement, believe in it blindly, believe in it senselessly. "My heart leaps up on

121

Christmas Eve, for then was Jesus born." Not everyone can sing. But everyone can work on himself according to his capacity. There's nothing unreasonable in that.'

The consul's next remark was: 'I was just thinking that in your view I must have done a disservice to a certain boy whom I've helped to acquire some learning.'

'That depends,' answered the postmaster. 'Maybe the boy was not too well endowed this time, and was incapable of rising to a higher level. That we don't know. But certainly your intervention can't have made it any easier for him to bow his head. You don't imagine that, surely? Why, your intention was precisely to take this child out of the masses and make him hold his head high. Now he's sitting there on his bench, getting himself taught till he's fully qualified; then he'll arise, a brilliant ethical vacuum, and go out into the world to teach the same vacuity to others. Who on earth can teach us what is in question here? We ourselves – nobody else. The only thing others can teach us is a mechanics that is worthless except for purposes of worldly wisdom. That's just what we see in the masses: they've learned about as much mechanics as the upper classes themselves used to in the old day – all right, but their spiritual life has been at a standstill. That roar of theirs? As if it expressed anything but peronal worldly avarice! The masses do nothing for the inward well-being of others, they haven't managed to work up any ethical solidarity among themselves. They profess social instinct without even possessing it. They want to roar and turn everything topsyturvy, and when the crunch comes, even their own leaders are incapable of restraining them. The whole caboodle's crashing – let it crash!'

Consul Johnsen nodded. He was following better, now that the subject was no longer ethics and the higher nonsense; the last bit was right-wing politics, business – that postmaster was not so mad. The consul said apologetically: 'You see, the boy was highly recommended to me by the headmaster and others.'

'Well, then,' said the postmaster, 'take the boy, send him to higher and higher schools, make him perfect in outward skills. He'll return to gladden the hearts of his own people and train them even more thoroughly in spiritual emaciation. He won't, of course, muffle their roar, not a scrap, and he'll remove them even further from any introspection. But perhaps this was the very thing, the only thing, he was fitted for; who can say? Perhaps he's had a series of earlier lives on earth and fixed himself up in such a way that he was incapable of rising higher in this one. In that case, the First Cause will have to wait for him and his ilk until a change occurs – the patient First Cause with time to spare, eternity to spare.'

The traces were being kicked over again; the consul would have to put an end to this. What, after all, had he come for? On account of a random anxiety, not about the next life, but about this one. A bit more politics, and he would have been enthralled – he, the mighty pillar of society whom envy sought to overthrow, whom upstarts aped, whom the *Fia*'s crew had just caused fresh vexation and more work – what remedy should he apply to all this? Work on himself indeed! The postmaster was an ass.

'Well,' said the consul, rising, 'we're completely in the dark, both about this life and about the next – especially the next. If we knew anything about the hereafter for certain we'd doubtless behave more appropriately in the here and now.'

'We may be excused,' answered the postmaster with a smile, 'for harbouring a little worldly curiosity on this score. But as far as our previous existence is concerned, the Cosmic Principle doubtless has its reason for keeping us in the dark. This existence may have been so black with misdeeds that remembering them now would overwhelm and crush us. That could well be – in which case we have an incentive in the uncertain hope that we didn't behave too badly.'

'But in that case was it necessary to endow us with so much frailty from the very outset?'

'If we assume that life consists of movement made for a purpose, then it's illogical to suppose that we weren't endowed with hope from the outset. That is certainly not the case. But we may well have been endowed with frailty as you put it – so that our long course should have a modest beginning, so go speak. However, our being as full of frailty as we are today may well be our own fault, for neglecting our chances—'

'Yes, yes, yes,' interrupted the consul. 'What I mean is that we'd have some encouragement to improve in this life if we knew for certain what we could expect in the next.'

'As long as it didn't make us worse, Herr Consul; things are bad enough as it is. Do you suppose man would lay up a store of good deeds if it was known for certain that this wasn't strictly necessary, and above all, that there was no hurry? On the contrary, he'd have a fling, sin on credit, sin to the last farthing, and set himself back by many existences. It would be harder than ever for him to work his way upward, easier than ever to let himself slide. For that matter, he might have to start his next life at rock bottom. All would be lost, no garden, no flower, though movement would remain . . .'

When Consul Johnsen returned to his office, it was to avoid being talked into anything. The postmaster might dismiss theology with a snort, but his own doctrine was theology all right! The consul was vexed over the entire visit – he was no Nicodemus coming to the Teacher at night; he had gone out for a little diversion, not to be converted. The only real piece of information he returned with was that the doctor had written to Scheldrup at Le Havre. What about? Malicious gossip, perhaps; intrigues; a five-krone visit to a woman in confinement at the shipyard – damn that doctor!

The consul did not forget to instruct his chief clerk, Bernsten, to send fifty bottles of Madeira up to the pharmacist. Then suddenly his thoughts jumped back to the postmaster – God, the drivel that man's wife must have to endure! Supposing he were to send the postmaster also fifty bottles of Madeira, as a gift? But they would probably come back with the messenger.

Beyond a doubt, the wine would come back with the messenger; and the consul gave an involuntary smile at the fantastic frugality of these people. Work on himself – how? Who had ever seen anyone being thanked by Providence for that? The town boasted a blacksmith named Carlsen, a man of God, who toiled and held his peace, injured no one, bored the pants off no one over the number of lives on earth – yet he was chastened by adversity, by domestic sorrows, delinquent children, a son reputed to be a common tramp; where was the justice of this? Blacksmith Carlsen had a brother, Police Constable Carlsen, a sly old dog, a fox rather, with a wealthy piano-owning wife, a son in the Ministry of Ecclesiastical Affairs, a daughter in the Missionary Society – all this perhaps because Police Constable Carlsen had *not* worked on himself?

Let us work *for* ourselves!

14

Henriksen of the Shipyard trusted in God that his wife would survive on this as on previous occasions, even though she was very ill. The hope proved vain. A message reached him just before he was due to go home for his dinner, as he stood among his workmen driving in a rivet; without even driving it home, he threw down the hammer and ran off, crying: 'Is she much worse?' 'Yes, she's lying still now.'

She lay still now. In the morning the doctor had left full of hope; towards noon the minister had been sent for; he arrived too late.

Such things can happen.

Now it was a matter of the funeral, standing treat for the mourners, flowers, black clothes, flag at half-mast. Henriksen got help from both fisherman Jørgen's Lydia and Oliver's Petra; even so, he had to fall back on strong drink to get through it all. He wept much, and at night gave way to despair. What made it all the harder for Henriksen was his wife's refusal to send for him throughout that terrible morning when she lay dying; she had wanted to spare him, she was always so good. 'But fetch the minister!' she had whispered. And he had not arrived in time.

She lay there now, brought down in full flight, in full health and youth, a year or two over thirty. It was dreadfully sad, and although the Henriksens were just ordinary people who had worked their way up, all the town dignitaries wished to attend her burial. That was their wish. Mrs Consul Johnsen put up a little resistance. 'We didn't go to that trading fellow Davidsen's when he was made consul,' she said. 'No, but he wasn't being buried,' answered Johnsen. 'These Henriksens,' she continued, 'we don't mix with them, you know – so why should we attend the burial?' 'To prevent gossip,' answered Johnsen. His wife gave way, but made a great point of her kindness in doing so. Poor Mrs Consul Johnsen, in the ordinary course of events she stirred abroad as little as possible. In recent years her weight had gone up and up, and all in all her build was not designed for physical exercise; emphatically not. Whereas the consul, whose belly remained at a constant and reasonable size, and whose hair took its time over thinning and greying, walked in the procession with a silk hat on his head and his chest thrown out.

This multitude of mourners gave Henriksen a certain consolation, and in bowing to the Johnsens, to the doctor and his wife, to the world at large, he may have beamed with excessive radiance; his little girls he had trained to curtsy in gratitude. The coffin was borne by workers from the shipyard, and followed by the entire town. Flags mourned on every mast, the church bells tolled. Even Olaus joined the procession, explaining to all and sundry why: all right, this was the bleeding shipyard where he'd got his hand torn off; still, Mrs Henriksen had always been a good sort through and through, a bloody good sort, all honour to her memory – you haven't got a screw of tobacco, have you?

And there by the pump stood a group of women with their hands under their aprons, watching the procession and discussing in hushed voices all this floral display and pomp. God help me if Olaus isn't there, too – he's beyond shame. Oh, he knows what he's doing, it's the drop of something and the bite of food he's after, that blue nose of his has caught wind of it. Yes, Henriksen could be counted on for that, for providing refreshment in style; he was no skinflint. His workmen had the day off, and any townsfolk who chose could come to the long tables erected in his garden.

Oliver hobbled along with the rest. He didn't drink and had no need for a bite of cake, being accustomed to buy for himself any titbits or goodies he fancied. He joined in because all the respectable folk of the town joined in. Besides, there was no business at the warehouse that morning, a wind seemed to have blown everyone away. Oliver brushed his clothes, scrutinized himself in the mirror, locked the door, and joined in.

A cortège of four consuls and a whole town was no ordinary matter, and even a Swedish brig that lay discharging flour for Grits-and-Groats Olsen proceeded to lower her flag.

As well she might, since the stevedores had knocked off, unloading was suspended, and the quay lay desolate. Now this same brig had a sick man on board, and the doctor had been sent for. But the doctor couldn't come till after the funeral, when he wouldn't waste a moment.

Now, however, seeing from the churchyard the brig's flag of condolence, the doctor was struck by an idea: what if the sick sailor was dead? After his misfortune with Mrs Henriksen, he was now duly alarmed; so as soon as decency permitted, he whispered his apologies to Henriksen and deserted the band of mourners.

Making a beeline for Grits-and-Groats Olsen's quay, he went on board the brig. It seemed as dead as the grave, but eventually he found a man lying in the forecastle and went up to him. 'I'm the doctor,' he said. 'Can I take your pulse?'

The Swede extended a hand.

'Now let's see your tongue.'

The Swede opened wide.

'Are you eating?'

Well, yes, he was.

'Sleeping?'

Well, yes.

The doctor listened to his chest, tapped it, got him to turn over, and tapped his back, too. 'You're sweating a lot. How are your bowel movements?'

Well, you see, they weren't exactly all they should be; they'd given him a lot of trouble the last day or two, but it seemed to be clearing up, he was on the mend now.

'Ah, this is something you mustn't neglect,' said the doctor.

'Come again?'

'You mustn't be casual about this. Now, I'm going to write something out for you, and you can get it fetched from the pharmacy.'

'Why?' asked the man in surprise.

'Why?' echoed the doctor, looking at him idiotically.

That damned Swede, that rogue and madman, was he pulling the doctor's leg? He now explained in a few brief words that it was not he who was sick but one of his shipmates.

What? Then where was the sick man?

Well, you see, he wasn't really sick, either; he'd cut himself on a bottle just now and bled a lot, but since the doctor hadn't come straightaway, they'd managed to bandage him up themselves.

The doctor was evidently beginning to take offence. He said sharply: 'Then where is the sick man, may I ask, the one who cut himself?'

He had gone to the doctor's surgery, he must be sitting there waiting.

Before leaving the forecastle, the doctor could not refrain from asking savagely: 'But why the devil did you let me examine you, may I ask?'

But to this, too, the man had a most plausible answer: he mentioned the word quarantine, he thought the examination had to do with the general state of health on board, nothing else.

Well, so perhaps he was not a scamp of a leg puller after all but a harmless fellow. And if at this point the doctor had burst out laughing and said a few jovial words, he would have taken the sting out of his mistake; instead of which he made matters worse by showing his irritation, buttering and waxing bitter, so that the incident acquired significance. Not surprisingly, the Swede started answering back; he also laughed most disrespectfully, and suddenly he stood up on his bunk. Whereupon the doctor left.

Needless to say, the story leaked out into the town, into the little town, and the doctor did not escape some malicious litle improvements to a story which was already quite ludicrous enough. Among those who had it in for him there was much slapping of thighs; Consul Johnsen, for example, had his first good laugh for several days.

'What a fellow that doctor is!' said the consul to lawyer Fredriksen. '*He* doesn't need to question a patient about how he feels, he can tell that for himself, the doctor can, at a single glance – the fool! And so he found the Swede had puerperal fever, too, did he?'

'God knows if it wasn't something like that!'

'Ha-ha, that's priceless! Come along in, Lawyer, and let's drink a glass to a good election.'

The gentlemen went in.

By a good election they probably meant two different things, but Consul Johnsen was no fanatic – come to that, no politician, even. He was simply a pillar of society. He a fanatic, he a politician? Good gracious, a few years back he could have been elected to Parliament, to the Storting, with the greatest of ease, but he had turned it down – he hadn't the time, and besides, he was a double consul and a great man already. Later the wind had started to change, and this year he would scarcely have got enough votes even if he had wanted them, so diligently had lawyer Fredriksen canvassed the constituency. In any case, it was a matter of complete indifference who was elected; nothing would change for C.

A. Johnsen, double consul. This Fredriksen was very far from being in his circle, but let him be elected, fair enough. That being so, it was not entirely imprudent to give him a glass of wine in private; an upstart like that might take it into his head to make a great to-do about that spot of bother on the *Fia*. Again, fair enough, carry on; the double consul would remain the man he was; well, why not – 'Have another glass of wine, Lawyer. You're a rare visitor to my house!'

Lawyer Fredriksen, however, certainly had no wish to be a rare visitor to that house, no wish at all. Had he not, for the last couple of years, cherished the youthful idea of being able to come and go as a member of the household, not to say of the family? The secret had been well guarded from the world and would not emerge into the light of day while he remained a cipher, a mere coastal-town lawyer; but the election – maybe the election would open his mouth. It all depended.

'Miss Fia brought some visitors home, I think I saw?'

'Oh, that goes without saying!' answered the consul indulgently. 'More painters, colleagues, two of 'em. If we hadn't been so well off for food and accommodation, we'd have been in a fix, ha-ha!'

'Young lads, weren't they? Are they any good?'

'I've no idea. Or rather, I think so. Much talked about and written about. And they bring plenty of life with them.'

'Oh?'

'They do their art thing all over the house; one's painting my wife, the other myself, we dance to their tune. The worst of it is, my wife's being done in all her finery, and she's got so keen that she has sittings both morning and afternoon; so for the moment she lives in a low-necked silk dress. Don't ever get married, Lawyer!'

'Really?'

'It'll bring you a wife and children, nothing but expense, ha-ha!'

Really now, this was a piece of ostentation; the lawyer disliked the tone. It was an impertinence to suggest that he should remain a permanent bachelor – why so? Nothing but expense? The lawyer must have thought to himself that the consul for one had not exactly lost by his marriage: it was Mrs Johnsen who by bringing a substantial dowry had been able to give her husband a flying start. What else had he taken Johanna Holm for? She was no beauty and no genius. Oh no, Mr Double Consul, but for your wife you would have been a small shopkeeper and a Johnsen of the Wharf to this day, remember that! But it was precisely this that the consul remembered with reluctance; the doctor in his usual needling way had once reminded him of it, and the enmity between the two gentlemen dated from that moment. Mrs Johnsen, on the other hand, never forgot it, though she was far from harping on it or using it as a stick to beat him with. In the early days, when she had caught her husband in one or two incautious bits of wenching and wanted a separation, she had demanded all her property back; and since his business was entirely dependent on her support, he had had no choice but to learn more caution.

Thus the lawyer could at this point have answered slyly and perhaps rendered the consul a bit more compliant; but he lacked the courage, and there was no occasion to do so if he could gain his ends by fair means. So he said: 'As Socrates puts it, "Marry, and you'll regret it."* But I suppose it's like death: we shall all go the same way.'

'You too, Lawyer? Well, it's not too late, of course. Cheers!'

The lawyer drank in silence. Too late? At least he was considerably younger than the consul, who still strove to make conquests all over the place. Perhaps the consul failed to realize that he was sitting face to face with a man who might be elected to the Storting; his tone was a shade too lordly. 'Should the question arise, I have no intention of waiting till it's too late,' he said. 'We all have to keep within our age, don't we?' – one in the eye for the consul.

Exit the lawyer. Once again, fair enough, carry on. So he was to be elected to the Storting, join the rabble, the national talking shop, was he? Thank you, but the consul would rather be the man he was. He had recovered his energy and his good humour, sent off his reports to those foreign governments, decided on his attitude in the seamen's affair, resolved to take a firm line with the doctor, made the transition from fear to anger, worked himself into a quasi-belligerent mood – all right then, come what may!

* A misleadingly incomplete version of a saying attributed to Socrates by Diogenes Laertius: 'Marry or don't marry, either way you'll regret it.' Trans.

This surely, was quite something.

On top of which he was a most amiable host to his daughter's guests, talking with them, sitting for them, supplying them with wines and goodies from the store for their picnics, taking care of their comfort, and presenting them each with a yellow silk scarf when they mooned about the garden till late at night.

The consul understood very well that if Fia brought home guests of this kind it was only in order to help them without actually buying their pictures. She was no inexpensive young lady: he would have to keep these portraits of himself and his wife, and he couldn't even ask the price but must hand out an arbitrary sum. What else could he decently do?

Well, no matter, the consul did no elaborate sums; indeed, he was rather proud of the whole transaction. For the purpose of these young gentlemen's visit had become known in the town, and not only in his own little town but in the capital, where it was in the papers that the two young artists were at present staying with Consul Johnsen, the coastal magnate, in order to paint portraits of his family.

'Have you been putting me in the papers?' he said to them with the air of a playful god. 'I'm not having any scandal,' he said. 'And by the way, you're staying here on the quiet, remember that! If it gets about that you're painting my wife and me, I'll find myself paying higher taxes!'

How good he was a talking to the youngsters and smiling his superior smile as he heard about their pranks! It was nothing very serious they got up to, they were decent lads as far as he could see, though he'd be damned if he'd trust them too far, hee-hee! And indeed they drove out to his country residence and got up to high jinks there; one night, for example, they painted the black horse grey. Next morning, whether from genuine consternation or good acting, the stable lad lost his reason for a considerable while, and only recovered it on receipt of a five-krone piece for washing the watercolour off the horse.

But Fia now – had she taken a fancy to either of these young bucks, was she so to speak in love with them? If so, it can only have been in a calm and correct manner. She was friendly and informal with them, but always with a certain guardedness; she never forgot that she was a nice girl. The painters used to call her the Countess, a nickname to which she had no objection. It was a reasonable nickname, with some positive advantages attached; but did she not deserve it? Her father's daughter, almost her hometown's daughter, scion of its most respected house, artist, poetess, lady of many talents – what talents had the others to show if it came to that? Alice Heiberg, a consul's daughter like herself, but with no particular ability, trained only in the daily round, the common household tasks; Grits-and-Groats Olsen's daughters, who might possibly grow up into capable girls but were being spoiled by foolish parents bent on turning them into ladies. Who else was there? The two little Henriksens of the Shipyard were still such new arrivals, mere children, who in any case would now never get anywhere.

Fia was the Countess, tall and lissom, distinguished in her bearing, entirely correct and proper. During the last year or two she had affected large hats and colours that were a trifle daring without being reckless – just as much as she could carry off. Thus it was not surprising, when she walked along the street in her painter's rig, that another artist, the postmaster, should stand stock-still at a window and rejoice over her.

No, the consul could not believe that Fia harboured intentions; if she had, he as her father would have had to speak seriously to her. These boys were not for her: one was the son of a district magistrate (and to that extent had a background of education and breeding), the other was the son of a house painter; both were equally poor. Far be it from Consul Johnsen to look down on any class of humanity, but he had only this one daughter, she was his beloved child, and he intended to shield her as best he could. A businessman's son from an old and important house would suit him better.

The consul, therefore, raised no objection when the two young artists sat down to dinner one day and announced that they had both received commissions – 'For which we may thank the consul,' they added.

'Congratulations!' said the consul. 'What are you going to do?'

'Portraits of Consul Olsen and his wife.'

'Not the Grits-and-Groats Olsens!' shrieked Mrs Johnsen. 'Well, would you believe it!'

This set the whole table laughing, and the consul said mildly: 'A commission's a commission. Surely you see that, Johanna.'

'Haven't Heiberg and Davidsen ordered their portraits yet?' asked his wife. 'Ah, well, give them time!'

Another round of laughter.

Turning to the two artists, the consul vouchsafed a brief explanation; the town was so full of consuls nowadays, and all the younger ones had to ape the oldest. You had to laugh about it, Johanna! At the same time, it could also be distinctly irritating that in this household they could scarcely stir a muscle without the others stirring the same muscle, in tempo. Still, it simply wasn't worth taking such things seriously, Johanna!

His wife did *not* take them seriously; he hadn't understood. If anyone smiled at the sight of the other consuls, it was she. Her exclamation had been intended as a shout of pure joy.

'As for Davidsen,' said the consul, 'he's quite a different kettle of fish: no pretensions, no culture, but no antics, either. He's a workingman who stands behind his counter and sells green soap. I've got a soft spot for Davidsen.'

'Hee-hee!' laughed Mrs Johnsen, deep in thought. 'I'm just wondering, since I've been painted in a silk dress, what Mrs Olsen will wear to go one better?'

This occupied them for a while; they discussed clothes, colours, a simple gold chain versus jewellery. In bygone centuries persons of rank had no inhibitions about being painted in all their finery, with lace, buckles, chains, precious stones; nowadays people sat in a frock coat – the consul, for example – and one might get an excellent picture of the frock coat.

'Well,' said the consul, raising his glass, 'I hereby express the wish that the gentlemen may be just as successful, just as brilliantly inspired, with Consul Olsen and his wife as they have been with us. We are both of us highly satisfied and deeply grateful.'

They drank to that.

Fia asked: 'When are you starting at the Olsens'?'

The artists replied: 'Any time, straightaway!' Then they mentioned that there were two young daughters in the family, and that there was a possibility of their being painted, too.

'So that's it, they're going at least one better!' cried Mrs Johnsen. 'And now I know what Mrs Olsen will wear: she'll be painted in *two* silk dresses!'

More laughter, laughter that filled the room. It was very seldom that Mrs Johnsen made a witticism; she must have had her reasons for doing something so unexpected. The consul said straight out that she was terrific, she was brilliant!

But then the lady, who evidently had great difficulty in coping with praise, ruined the effect by wondering what Mrs Olsen would have on her feet – two pairs of shoes?

Naturally they all laughed once again – but why can't she pipe down? thought the painters.

To stay at Consul Olsen's and paint proved an excellent paying proposition; the two artists had never had it so good, with cakes and wine in the morning, and coffee and cream waffles in the afternoon. Then there were the 'little girls', the two young daughters, buxom, healthy, jolly, and altogether succulent. The house painter's son fell in love with both of them, but made no progress whatever – it was not *that* easy to gain a footing at Consul Olsen's; though had it been the magistrate's son ... The girls were tolerable; maybe they gave themselves a few airs, and spoke rather more genteelly than they had learned at school; still, they were damned nice girls, young girls, nothing was lacking. Indeed, it was rather the case that they had too much of everything, vital statistics included, not to mention a great crop of ash-blonde hair and lips a trifle too full; their flaws consisted in superabundance; also, they swayed their hips too much when they walked.

Mrs Olsen had evidently been maligned: an amiable lady, kind-hearted to the point of being tearful and emotional, motherly, with gentle eyes and a receding forehead. Her sole concern was her daughters, that they should be genteel and happy. How she loved these daughters and let them do as they liked, growing up to no purpose and with no manners, into frippery and inanity! It was certainly not Mrs Olsen who had asked to be painted; she protested against it every day and wanted to make way for her daughters, both of them in one picture, a double portrait. Time and again Consul Olsen had to prevail upon his wife to sit still – 'Do you hear, Henrietta, once you've been started! The double portrait will come later!'

So the victim sat there in silk, watch chain, and rings galore, in order to please her husband.

Olsen himself was more given to cutting a dash and making a splash, a man bulbous with small-town opulence, an upstart, a lucky speculator. It amused him to sit singing music-hall songs and grimacing, then suddenly to plunge into a long, stately silence, communicating only by nods and shakes of the head, and pretending to have big business to think about. 'Sh!' his wife would say, 'leave Papa in peace now, little girls!' And Papa was good-natured and kindly and very vain; he loved to see the company fall silent while he sat and thought big business.

'That's it!' said the painter. 'Now we've got just the right expression, that's terrific, the firm mouth, the shrewdness. Hold it now,' he said, as if he were taking a photograph.

And Consul Olsen's vanity forced him to busy himself with a big Argentinian corn deal lest he sing and grimace away the firmness of his mouth.

The portrait promised to be outstandingly good, and the painter, the son of a painter, asked if he might exhibit it in the capital, in Christiana. Go ahead, go right ahead! Not that the consul fancied being exhibited, far from it, but if it would help the painter, so be it! He was happy to oblige the young artist, the whole family wanted to oblige him, even the daughters, though they were not in love with him. In this respect his colleague, who was painting Madame, seemed to have better chances; yes, the magistrate's son seemed to have better chances. Ah, but he too was well and truly swindled one fine day. Peculiar ladies they must be, but they came from a mercantile family and evidently preferred the mercantile life, to judge by their frequent allusions to Scheldrup Johnsen. Strange girls indeed, and perhaps none too bright. Or what? One day when the magistrate's son had already started on their portrait, damned if they didn't play hooky from a sitting. Their excuse was that they had unexpectedly bumped into Scheldrup Johnsen in the street and had stopped to talk to him, he was only home on a flying visit.

As if that was any excuse! The painter regarded it as a swindle and an insult.

15

Scheldrup Johnsen had indeed come home unexpectedly, and was to leave again equally unexpectedly.

Taking with him his father's chief clerk, Berntsen, he went to the doctor's surgery, greeted him curtly, and put this question to him: 'What's the meaning of those letters you sent me? I've come home to find out.'

The doctor (caught off guard, attempting a smile): 'Letters? Oh, those!'

'In one you wrote that a new specimen of a brown-eyed child had come into the world, a day or two later that the mother had died.'

'Yes.'

'Yes. Well, I want to know your reason for telling me all this.'

'Can't we be alone?' asks the doctor in a subdued voice.

'No, I want a witness against you,' answers Scheldrup.

'The thing is, what I want to say is unsuitable for strangers' ears.'

'Then I know what's suitable for yours!' says Scheldrup, advancing a couple of paces. The doctor retreats, his mouth trembles, he says: 'No, wait a bit, I can see I've made a mistake, I do beg your pardon. That's what I did, made a mistake, I mean, between you and someone else, please pardon me! Really and truly, I didn't mean any harm.'

'Really and truly, I ought to give you a good thrashing,' says Scheldrup, his voice trembling, 'you slanderer, you—'

'Wait a bit, let me—'

'You shit, you loathsome old bitch. Yes. I ought to box your ears.'

The doctor has rallied a little. 'Wait a bit, I put a question mark, you remember. Really and truly I wanted to ask you something in the name of science, ask you something in the name of my own science. Have you got the letters with you?'

'If I'd had them with me, I'd have made you chew them up and swallow them.'

'No no no, let's talk it over, talk it over calmly, shan't we? I do beg your pardon, it was in the name of science. I thought I might do it; after all we did know each other. Don't you remember, I *asked* you, put a question mark. You see, it's a point on which science is uncertain—'

Scheldrup's fury knows no bounds, he storms on and on; his performance suffers from his lack of moderation, goes right off. 'Balls to you and your science! On top of everything else, you're a coward, a craven cur. So now you're trying to jabber your letters away — I could spit on you.'

The doctor has rallied still further. 'Don't be so angry, the whole thing's not worth it, simply not worth it. What's more, it's unwise, when I'm offering my apologies.'

'What do you mean, unwise?'

'If we were alone I'd tell you. It's unwise, it may bring retribution.'

'I wish you and your retribution to the devil, understand?' yells Scheldrup.

The doctor repeats: 'I do beg your pardon.'

But these raised voices in the normally quiet surgery have attracted attention in the house; they conjure up the doctor's wife and oblige Scheldrup to bow in silence and depart with his escort.

Thus, the sole result of a journey from Le Havre was an apology, a few empty words! That evening Scheldrup contemplated a second visit to the doctor and got as far as talking about it to Berntsen, but was dissuaded in time: the doctor had had enough, had had more than enough!

What an excellent chief clerk Consul Johnsen possessed! His advice was good, he knew what he was doing, he looked at the question from more than one angle; nor was it impossible that as he stood there in the surgery he had realized what the doctor kept hinting at. Though what was there to realize? Nothing, mere gossip; still, for his own sake and that of his whole family, Scheldrup had best keep his mouth shut.

'No, leave him alone now,' said Berntsen. 'You've scared him as much as he can take.'

Scheldrup gave in. So be it. His anger had drained away, he would be content with the apology. Besides, a box on the ear was an awkward business; many years ago he himself had received one which had done him no good at all — that scandalous slap from

Petra – and he couldn't allow boxed ears to cling to his name for all time.

Early next morning Scheldrup went on board again to begin his journey back to Le Havre.

And now the doctor got himself into another lovely scrape.

For he, too, like many another, had gone down to the mailboat in the early morning; he had had a rough time and wanted to freshen himself up – and one hell of a freshening up was what he got! How was he to imagine that Scheldrup would leave again so soon – Scheldrup, who used to come home on holiday for weeks on end? There he came, walking along the quay, accompanied by father, mother, sister, and two extraneous painters. Should the doctor bow? Bow first? Better do so, there were ladies in the party. So he bowed, even though he was standing well to one side, and having done so, he moved even farther to one side.

But suddenly Scheldrup's anger seemed to boil up again and he went for the doctor; perhaps he took his presence here at this particular moment as a piece of defiance or impertinence. What now? He strode ahead as if to trample the doctor under his very eyes, yet without looking at him, no, never a glance. Did he mean to walk him down, walk him into the sea? Only four paces were left between them.

Then it was that that remarkable chief clerk, Berntsen, bobbed up between the two gentlemen and, saying to Scheldrup, 'Look, you've forgotten this!' drew him a little to one side and handed him something, God knows what, perhaps only some rubbish. But from now on Berntsen was extremely busy on the quay; he was here, there, and everywhere, yet always at Scheldrup's side. 'I've come to keep an eye on some goods,' he said; 'we're expecting some goods.' And even when Scheldrup went up the gangway, Berntsen followed him in order to keep an eye on some goods on board.

Scheldrup stood by the rail talking in muffled tones to his family down on the quay. And his family stood there in a state of utter bewilderment, first at his coming and now at his leaving again. His father had not pressed him in any way, and to his mother and sister he had vouchsafed only one answer: 'Business!' They were all completely in the dark.

Suddenly he pointed towards the doctor down on the quay and

called to Berntsen, loud and clear: 'I say, Berntsen, I ought to have given that fellow over there a pasting after all – he's had the nerve to show up!'

Silence. A solitary voice was heard from the quay: 'What the devil – what's he on about?' It was Olaus, scenting a brawl.

'And when you get back to Le Havre, perhaps you could remember to send us some more fabrics, same as before,' responded Bertsen instantly, 'cotton fabrics in suitable patterns, perferably about fifty pieces.'

'Right.'

'Hadn't you better write it down?'

Scheldrup was obliged to take out his pocket notebook and write it down.

Then the ship shoved off and Berntsen jumped ashore.

The doctor stood there swaying like a man who has just been struck, his face vacant. This lasted for a moment; then he drew himself up, threw out his chest, and sauntered away. Really, it would have been unreasonable to expect him to stand for this, to stand for an insult from a young shopkeeper on a public quay.

All in all, the doctor had suffered many vexations of late, but he left the quay with the air of a man resolved to endure them. Olaus followed him with his eyes, then unburdened himself on the subject of the doctor's stuck-up ways.

At this moment the two Miss Olsens arrived at a canter; such nice girls, and so young and so breathless. 'Oh dear, we've come too late!' they said. 'Was there anything interesting on board today? Why are you all down here, why are you waving at the boat, Fia?'

Oh, they knew all right. The Miss Olsens must have heard the news while they were still in bed, and jumped straight into their clothes; but even so they had arrived too late.

'It's Scheldrup going away again,' answered Fia.

'No – you don't say so! Already! Well, I never!'

More than that they could scarcely venture to say. They stopped to talk to lawyer Fredriksen. 'Well,' called the doctor, 'were you too late for the leave-taking?' Ah yes, the doctor's salvation had been achieved, he was out of danger now and had recaptured his superior touch.

'Leave-taking? What leave-taking?' asked the Miss Olsens as they walked past.

The doctor gazed after them ironically before turning back to the lawyer. 'We were interrupted. Can't you answer my question?'

'No, not off the cuff.'

'Really? Surely it's a social issue?'

'I suppose so. But it's also a very personal issue.'

The doctor gave a sardonic smile. 'I thought that as a lawyer, and now – with the help of God and of right-minded people – as a possible future legislator, you might know the remedy for a social evil.'

'A rise in the national birthrate is today not usually counted among the social evils.'

'Here we go again – the postmaster's elegy on offspring.'

'No, that's something from which I dissociate myself.'

'*I* count it among the evils. But in any case, what we're discussing at the moment is the case of a certain man filling the town with his brown-eyed illegitimate progeny.'

'Do you mean that?'

'And know it.'

'These things are very difficult to prove.'

'Fairly difficult, yes; especially when your witnesses die. But perhaps this is the moment for science to step forward. Professional science is an incontrovertible witness.'

'Do you mean that, too?'

Really, this was a little bit too offhand of the lawyer; he was ill-advised to tease the lion. The doctor asked in astonishment: 'Do you doubt science, then? Are you still stuck with that viewpoint?'

The lawyer, the platform orator, doubtless thought to himself: He says I'm *stuck* with my viewpoint – that was deliberate, that was cunningly put. His only resource was to lighten the tone of this ponderous, solemn conversation. 'No, there you misunderstand me. Science, naturally! But listen, Doctor: brown-eyed children are pretty children, after all. And if what you say is true, the father must be a man of experience and ability, and consequently a good progenitor. In these liberal times—'

'Are you trying to make fun of me?' asked the doctor. 'Good day, Lawyer!'

Really, he could have screamed or smashed something! Everyone and everything was against him! And a lawyer like that – unkempt and unshaven, how democratic can you be, and now he had stuck a feather in his cap like an Alpine tourist, the prettified kid!

The doctor's various vexations were beginning to make him impatient; ought he not to stand up and teach them a lesson, teach the riffraff a lesson? His position was still reasonably secure, of course, but right now people showed him no respect, absolutely no respect. But for the lofty contempt which he felt for the hoi polloi, he would have turned around from time to time and asked them what the devil they were smirking about as he passed.

And then last week he had received a lengthy bill from Consul Johnsen, Johnsen of the Wharf, the doyen of the shopkeepers. Yes, he should get his money, at the first opportunity he should get his coppers, please, here they are – one of these days. Ha-ha, the doctor had to laugh – he would send the money by post, that was what he would do, in such a way that everyone should see. Wouldn't that be a laugh? And from that day and hour, no more business from him in that shop, that dive. Why, that was the place where a certain respected citizen hadn't even received honest weight in bran.

He had a sudden impulse to exchange a few words with Mattis the carpenter and learn a little more about his famous purchase of pollard. He consulted his watch. Yes.

A visit of such grandeur and distinction was more than Mattis the carpenter had ever expected at his workshop, and he at once invited the doctor into the parlour, where they seated themselves among chairs and rocking chairs and whatnots and tables with thick plush covers. The central hanging lamp dangled down almost to the surface of the central table, the walls were hung with photographs of relatives who had emigrated and a picture of the Storting of 1884; the sprays of foliage in the garland on the stove were dry as paper. The overfurnished little room was cramped and stuffy, and the conversation never got off the ground; Mattis seemed so changed, so out of sorts.

The doctor had a folding screen that needed gluing together.

The carpenter would send his apprentice for it.

'The door and the window were both left open the other day, and of course the wind came and blew it over and smashed it.'

'Yes. That can easily happen.'

'But it oughtn't to happen, ought it? There shouldn't have been a through draft. It's those stupid maids. How about you, Mattis, maybe your house is well looked after, but maids are maids.'

Mattis sprang to life and agitation; he shook his head rapidly several times, which could mean anything, except yes. 'It *was* well looked after,' he replied, 'but she's leaving.'

'Leaving? Why?'

'I don't wish to talk about it. They're mad.'

'What's her name again?'

'Maren Salt. Not all that old, fifty perhaps, but mad like the rest. Really, at her time of life! They go around panting at the nostrils like young fillies!'

'I expect you'll sort it out between you,' said the doctor.

'Sort it out? I'd sooner the devil sorted it out!' proclaimed the carpenter in a fury. 'Enough's enough, and too much is too much!' he added.

The doctor wanted to go. These domestic details of an artisan's home were of no interest to an academic mind, and he was displeased by the carpenter's unconstraint; they were not equals. However, he had come on a mission. 'Listen, Mattis,' he said, 'weren't you given short weight once at old man Johnsen's?'

'What?'

'I ask because other people may have been exposed to this or that in the same quarter.'

'No,' answered Mattis curtly, shaking his head.

'You say no?'

'It wasn't at the consul's, it was at the warehouse.'

'So you think Johnsen didn't know about it?'

'The consul? How could he know about it? He's not at the warehouse.'

'Were you really given short weight in that outfit?'

'It was that Oliver. No one else, just that Oliver. I can't imagine why you're asking me this, if you'll excuse me, Doctor.'

'When will you collect the screen?' asked the doctor, rising.

'Straightaway. This instant. And it'll be dry by tomorrow. It's a pleasure, of course. This way, Doctor, if you please!'

Wasted effort. Back he went the same way he had come, the town doctor, a person of consequence, an authority; back he went, his face registering disappointment over a bagatelle, over nothing. Doubtless he too had once had his youthful dreams, had seen himself rising in his career, seen himself reaching the heights; his skin was soft in those days, his blood red, he was in love, he could smile – where was it all today? Life – life had fallen upon it and consumed it! He had become more and more engrossed in petty vexations and petty interests; year by year he had grown more wrinkled and more malignant. Alone with his wife for every meal, in an empty house, without family, without children, alone with his learning and his unsuccess, inquisitive, calumnious, and small. Doubtless he too had once had his youthful dreams, but that was long ago; now he was stripped, all that remained to him from of old was student-hostel jargon, student-hostel radicalism, free-thinking and flippancy, with never a trace of the youthful beauty and sincerity that are found even in youthful faults. He had degenerated, his mind had been transmuted; yes, things had gone wrong for him, he was no longer a person. Listen, he would save up and get Johnsen's bill paid, then he would strike up a connection with some other tradesman and open an account with him, perhaps with Davidsen; yes, excellent, with Davidsen, who as a new consul positively needed the patronage of respectable folk. A plan, a purpose, worthy of a housewife in a fix!

He went home, found his wife out, went to the bedroom, found the screen intact. Well, well, it must have survived being blown over! what had he made such a fuss about? He was again seized by disappointment, a disappointment so poignant and bitter, an anger so extreme, that he struck the screen to the ground and trampled on it. All right, let the carpenter's boy come! No, not one satisfaction remained in his life, not one glittering joy. In twenty years, in ten years, he would be dead, and in that moment he would be forgotten.

He went out again; the surgery could look after itself. Needless to say, here came the wretched postmaster, walking towards him, muttering to himself as usual; the doctor could scarcely bring himself to touch his hat as they passed.

Next he encountered Henriksen of the Shipyard – oh, the smallness of that town, and of its people, too; they liked to keep their distance, to read each other's backs as they passed in the street. Well, he would have to exchange a few words with Henriksen, the widower would expect it of him, and in other circumstances the doctor could have thrown out hints about payment, about his fee. Truth to tell, it was this fee that should have covered most of his bill from Johnsen of the Wharf. But now Mrs Henriksen was dead, his patient was dead – an outrageous misfortune, a stunning blow.

'Are the others all right? Is the baby well?'

'Yes, thank God, he's well, he's terrific.'

The doctor perceives that this child helps to soften Henriksen's sorrow; he is now a widower, true, but this splendid little boy has been left for his consolation. Henriksen is not completely prostrated, not utterly crushed, and the doctor may even cherish a hope about his fee.

'I'll go home with you and look at the child,' he says.

Henriksen (happy, grateful): 'Oh yes, if you will, Doctor.'

'I certainly will, I'll steal this half hour from the surgery and come with you. And you yourself, Henriksen, you're in the best of health?'

'Yes, thank you, Doctor. As far as I'm aware.'

'Of course. Sound as a bell. Did your wife not say anything before she died? Some intimate confidence or other for your ear? They generally do.'

'No,' answers Henriksen, shaking his head. 'You mean, like her asking me to look after the children, look after the baby? No.'

'When they're dying, they feel the need to ask forgiveness for one thing or another, something wrong they may have done in secret, you know, some *faux pas* or whatever. The dying have sometimes asked me to convey their requests.'

'Oh no. Indeed not. And besides, she had nothing to ask my forgiveness for, not a bit of it. I wasn't with her either, alas.'

'Did I hear she wanted to see the minister?'

Without a shadow of suspicion Henriksen answers: 'Yes, I imagine she wanted to receive the sacrament.'

The boy is big and bouncing, a real prospect for the future; moreover, he has grown despite his bottle feeding, a screaming, squalling spitfire.

'But he has brown eyes,' says the doctor.

'Yes, isn't that extraordinary?' Henriksen replies. 'There she was, all those months, wishing for brown eyes for this child, like the last. "If only God will grant it brown eyes, it's such an exquisitely pretty colour," she used to say. And now her wish has been granted.'

'Well, that at least is a good thing,' says the doctor with a crooked smile.

But Henriksen takes it at face value. 'Yes, isn't it? Ah, it must have been Providence. A glass of wine, Doctor? A whisky-and-soda, perhaps?'

They go into the living room and sit down with their whisky-and-sodas, and Henriksen at once moves on to his second glass. He talks about his wife, about his loneliness, how unbearable it is. In the daytime his work keeps him going, but when the night comes – night! He is all friendliness and attention towards his honoured guest; by and by he is even expressing gratitude for his help – yes, for all the help he has given.

'Unfortunately it was not in my power to help you more effectively,' answers the doctor.

'No, but I have no hesitation in saying that you did what you could. Why, you were here time and time again, looking after her and writing out prescriptions. We all did what we could, we have that consolation – that she wanted for nothing that we could supply. But it seems her time had come. Have some more whisky Doctor.'

'Shall I? Well, if you say so.'

Henriksen beams. 'It's an honour, a real honour to my house; my wife should have lived to see it. And now I'd be glad if you'd send me a bill, Doctor, a proper bill. Yes, do that. Or if you'd like to tell me now, just the total, that would do.'

'Oh, that can wait till another time.'

'Yes, everything that could be done was done, we have that consolation,' mutters Henriksen, lost in thought. 'Yes, I really want – let me, while I think of it—'

Henriksen gets up, opens his bureau, returns with a banknote, a thick red banknote, and hands it to the Doctor. 'Here, if you're happy about it. Is that about right, is it enough?'

The doctor is not in the least avaricious or grasping; what he has earned he has spent and more, spent it on food and drink, on 'enjoyment', and he has the decency to be embarrassed by this fat banknote, this gift in effect. He answers: 'That's too much, I can't take so much – half that!'

Henriksen shakes his head; he is in an expansive and kindly mood, and eager to show himself worthy of the doctor's thanks. 'Take it, Doctor, it's from her and me. Not another word on the subject!'

'I'll come here at any time, Henriksen. To see the little one. Day or night.'

The doctor walked home as if rejuvenated. What had happened? Why, he had felt defenceless, and now suddenly he was possessed of a weapon. 'At your service, Mr Johnsen of the Wharf! You sent me a bill, a trifling matter which I had overlooked; here now is a yellow form from the post office apropos a registered letter awaiting your collection.'

Yes, he was happy, but not to the point of conversion, of an upsurge and crisis of thankfulness. Life was unchanged, his enemies were the same as before, chance had offered him a stupid, idle triumph over them which he did not intent to forgo. He could have walked straight into Johnsen's store and settled his debt with Berntsen, but he refrained; instead, he rubbed his hands over a suitably malicious letter which he intended to enclose when he sent the money.

Forgo his triumph, indeed! Why, there was another of the brown-eyed brood, the town was crawling with them! He stopped the boy and questioned him: 'Isn't it you who comes to my house with fish?'

'Yes, at one time.'

'Have you given up fishing?'

'Yes.'

'What are you doing now?'

'I – I'm going to sea.'

'But what are you doing now? You need a good wash.'

'I'm with the blacksmith right now, but—'

'But you don't care for it? No, you go to sea! What was your name now?'

'Abel.'

'Tell your father – your father at home – to come to my surgery some time. I've got something to discuss with him.'

16

Well, a good wash was something Abel had needed all his days, though, of course, being at the blacksmith's had hardly made him whiter.

How absurd it was for him of all people to stand in a smithy, to be anchored to a mud floor, to work the bellows and hammer iron at the command of a tiny dancing sledgehammer! But Abel had to do something; he had long since been confirmed and had grown into a big, strong fellow. And one day the blacksmith, Carlsen, called him into the smithy: 'Here, couldn't you take this sledge-hammer and do some hammering for me?'

Abel hammered away, and on the whole he rather enjoyed standing there using his strength, beating stars out of the red-hot iron. He hammered till dinner-time, when the blacksmith took him in and gave him a meal.

'I've go this urgent job to do now,' said the blacksmith. 'Could you help me again this afternoon?'

'I could do that all right,' said Abel.

In the evening he was given another meal, and a krone before he left. 'You've done a good job,' said the blacksmith; 'you couldn't come again tomorrow, could you?'

'Sure,' said Abel.

It was his own decision. All his decisions were his own – whether this trait was inherited from his father, from Oliver, or acquired through having to fend for himself throughout his formative years.

He stayed at the blacksmith's for a week.

'Where are you staying these days?' asked his father.

'At the blacksmith's. I get my board and a krone a day.'

'Well, well, Abel. Well, well!' said his father, and there was an undeniable touch of pride in the cripple's heart. 'Are you going to stay with the blacksmith for good?'

'For good? No. Only while he's got all this work on.'

But the blacksmith was kept busy for weeks, for months – what quantities of forging and repairing and finishing off! – and Abel had to stay on. Not that he bound himself as an apprentice or forgot the sea, but all in all he had a good time at the blacksmith's, and earned some decent food and clothing, both of which he needed.

The relationship between the blacksmith and his boy was a friendly one; occasionally they would sit and smoke a pipe in the middle of a job, the blacksmith's excuse being that he felt poorly and couldn't go all out. Abel's general impression was that there was no real hurry about the work still waiting to be done; true, fresh jobs came in from time to time, but not more than the master could have coped with single-handed. One evening Abel asked if he need come again. The blacksmith had never heard such a silly question; why, there had never been such an urgent job as the one coming up in the morning!

Blacksmith Carlsen was a widower whose children were grown-up and married; Police Constable Carlsen was his brother. A steady worker who scraped a living from day to day and aspired to nothing more, he had run his little smithy along these lines for a generation an a half. A widowed daughter kept house for him. Sometimes he would recount his experiences, all of them trivial, everyday happenings, but to a man who had never left his smithy or his hometown, every trifling matter had an exaggerated importance. Why had he never launched out with journeymen and apprentices? He had never bothered to do so; he hadn't the resources or the house or even the forge for the purpose. Moreover, the large flock of children that he had acquired over the years prevented him from making a splash. 'Think of it,' he would say, 'five girls, five of that sort alone! And then two boys into the bargain!' And then of course there was another blacksmith out in the country, right on the road into town, who did all the farmers' work, horse-shoes and ploughs and scythes. Carlsen was a town blacksmith who made little domestic articles for the inhabitants, and occasionally – as now, and for which he needed Abel's help – larger items for marine purposes.

'Well, what's the object of life?' asked Carlsen. 'I've always fought my way through – with this fellow here!' he added with a smile, pointing at his hammer. 'More than that I don't need or deserve. My children will die. And then, however much I'd had, I'd have had to leave it all behind. Adolf now, he's a sailor, he's got a wife in England and writes that he earns barely enough to support his family and can't afford to send anything home; I write back every time that I'd rather send him a bit if he needs it. So he sails and sails, and in so and so many years he'll die, too. Ah yes, Abel, my boy, that's the way we shall all go. You see, Adolf now, he's the youngest, it's eighteen years since he first went to sea, and he's never been home since. Eighteen years is a long time, before you were ever born, and as a matter of fact he bought his sea chest from your father. Sails and sails, until the day when he has to lay up! It's strange to think how tiny he was when he used to mess about in this smithy – it doesn't seem all that long ago.'

There was a catch in the blacksmith's voice; he got up, went over to the bench, and gazed at the opaque window. 'Hm!' He cleared his throat and assumed a fierce expression. 'I suppose really I ought to clean this window one of these days,' he joked. 'What's your opinion, Abel? It must be forty years since it was daylight!'

Then he laughed and sat down again. 'Well, well, to be sure! And my oldest boy's roaming the country, doing all sorts of work. He was the kind who never wanted to do anything regular, he'd rather go from place to place. I dare say that's all right, too; I don't really know. He never comes home, no, he's a real oddity; he's taken it into his head that he won't come home until he's made a lot of money and can build onto the house and help us to take off. The boy must have become more and more disturbed while he was abroad. Take off – does he mean we're to fly? If only I could have talked to him for an hour or so! Still, his sister meets him occasionally, the one that lives at home with me; she meets him occasionally, they're real good pals, and he plays the mouth organ to her. He was an expert on the mouth organ when he was still quite small, and now he's even better, I hear. Isn't it strange to think of us all? His sister met him recently, and he was playing the mouth organ, but he'd grown such a beard that she hardly recognized him, and he'd already got several grey hairs. But no, he wouldn't come home until he'd become a capitalist, we weren't to see him! It's some kind of disturbance, that's all. And yet there was a time when he, too, used to potter about in the forge here, hammering and carrying iron bars and chattering away to himself. It doesn't seem all that long ago, not to me it doesn't, just a few years. And wherever you saw him in the streets here he'd take the mouth organ out of his pocket and play for a while. And as long as his mother was alive she'd often give him an extra helping of food because he was growing so fast, and whenever he got some new clothes he'd come and hold out his little hand and thank us. Hm!'

The blacksmith jumped up and started bustling about. 'No, this won't do; are you crazy, Abel? Hee-hee, a fine pair we are! Get cracking with those bellows again!'

He could joke and make a great pretence of merriment, but in truth he was anything but merry: old and tired, over emotional, worn out. He had no strength; Abel, young as he was, could lift twice as heavy a weight and keep going all day. On the old man's side were manual dexterity, practice, the knack of minimizing effort; but often he would gaze with his lack-lustre eyes at a tough assignment and shrink from tackling it.

No, he was certainly not merry. Nor was his joy in his children unconfined; not in all of them. One of his daughters had in her time been the talk of the town, the one married to Kasper, Kasper, who had been driven by her escapades into abandoning the sea and taking a job in the shipyard. By now both she and the gossip about her had eased off; but many years ago, when her husband was a sailor, she had abandoned her home and turned sailor herself, a heedless, cheery sailor. Oh, she was a young filly and no mistake. In those days her husband, and perhaps even more her father, had enjoyed universal sympathy.

And yet ... it was a far from comfortless existence, that of Carlsen the blacksmith, he had enough for his needs and something to spare, he was content with his lot. Every evening he would thank God for the day that was past, marvelling that it had gone off so extremely well, that nothing had gone wrong. They could easily have had an accident! Afterwards he would exchange quiet, low-keyed banter with his daughter: 'Yes indeed, we two men have got through a lot of work today, but what about you? I can't see that you've touched a thing – the chairs are still all in one piece.'

They laugh at this, and the daughter replies: 'Ah, but unfortunately I've broken two plates today.'

'Is that all?' says her father. 'In that time I could have broken a dozen!'

Seeing them in such good humour, Abel ventures to ask again if perhaps he can stay away tomorrow, if he really needs to come any more. But at this the old blacksmith turns serious, looking at the boy as if he feels this is about the worst thing he has ever heard him say: why this hurry to leave in the middle of the biggest rush of work, and where was he off to?

Abel wanted to sign on for a voyage.

Sign on? What, as late in the summer as this, getting on for winter? In the spring was the proper time. Surely he could stay another month at least? Because right now they had all these big jobs on hand, picks and drills to sharpen for the municipal engineer, two door locks to mend at Consul Heiberg's, a new steel spring for the baby carriage at Henriksen of the Shipyard's, a new shaft for the churn at Consul Johnsen's country residence, and all sorts of clamps for the painter who was to paint the church. Work for many hands for a long time ahead.

Abel stayed.

Ah, but the sea – catch him forgetting that! There was his friend Edevart, in South America according to latest reports, having already been at sea a couple of years, and here was Abel still on dry land, working in a smithy! No, thank you! That is not to say his job was entirely without its attractions: it made him nice and sooty, people could see what it was, and it gave him a certain prestige among his peers when he strode through the town with clattering iron rods over his shoulders, like any grown-up man. And how the small boys had to keep on their toes and jump aside to avoid being impaled on these same iron rods!

So it wasn't all that bad. What was more, Abel got nourishing food at regular hours, order was established in his sleep, he settled into a better mode of life. And was it not extremely snug in this artisan's home, where everything was in its place, the floor was clean, and the fuchsia stood bleeding in the window? On Sundays the blacksmith put on his best clothes and went for a quiet walk about the town and its environs. He was not a churchgoer, but he was an honest and religious man, with a thousand sins of which he repented, and a thousand of God's blessings which gladdened his heart. Everything was good beyond his deserts.

One Sunday Abel ran into him in the street. 'Keep me company for a bit!' said his master. 'Where are you off to?'

Abel was off to nowhere, he was just walking, he was lonely. Little Lydia had completely outgrown him, good luck to her, serve her right, he wasn't looking her way! Edevart, her brother, had once been a good friend, but now he too seemed to have grown too big for his boots, he never wrote him a word, and now he was in South America. So where should Abel be off to on a Sunday? Whatever happened, he couldn't sit at home in his new clothes, scrubbed clean all over, with the gleaming new sheath knife and sheath that he had bought. His brother, Frank, was away at this or that college and never at home, while Oliver, his father, had rowed out to the skerries as he constantly did on Sundays, still looking for adventure. No, Abel was off to nowhere. However, he knew a good place for adders out in the country, and perhaps he was on his way there for a hunt. He was not too old for that, he was still a boy.

Or had he been waiting for the blacksmith? If so, it would have been in order that certain people should see him in reputable company. It would do no harm if she should be sitting at the window of the cottage as he and his master went by. Though as to that, she could please herself entirely – what was her name, now? Little Lydia? Be that as it may, he walked past in the exclusive capacity of indispensable assistant to Carlsen the blacksmith . . .

After passing fisherman Jørgen's cottage, the blacksmith begins to be aware that he is doing all the talking, that Abel never answers. The blacksmith, of course, is not in the position of having discovered at a lightning glance something in a certain window to set the heart aflutter; he realizes he is too old a companion for Abel, acknowledges the fact with a smile, and says: 'Well, thank you for your company, Abel, I'm going this way.'

Off goes Abel after the adders. Their haunt is a rock-strewn slope, where they like to bask lazily in the sun, usually in large numbers; Abel and others have hunted them more than once over the years. There is danger and glory in this sport, in their school-days it even brought them fame.

As he approaches the place he hears shouts and racketing from other boys who are there before him, and stops in his tracks. Of course they must be mere kids, eight-year-olds, to be so stupid. No sensible person makes a racket on an adder hunt; one holds one's breath and walks as if on a nettlebed.

What now? On the other side of the heath he knows of a good echo; thither he goes now to do a little shouting. He is still a boy.

Here it is peaceful and secluded; not a soul in sight. He shouts;

yes, the echo is there. But the fact of the matter is, he has much more important matters on his mind than testing echoes; he throws himself down in the heather and relives the passing of a certain window, Well, taking it by and large, what has he achieved by this caprice? The knife and its nickel sheath were facing the right way and sparkling nicely, but did she see them? And besides, the figure behind the windowpanes might well have been one of her sisters and not herself. Nothing is certain.

He lies there for a long time, reliving the incident again and again, and weighing all its possibilities; at times an exquisite pang sends shivers through his breast and he hugs himself in rapture; at other times he abandons hope, throws himself defiantly into the air, and shouts aloud: 'Good luck to her!'

'To her!' mimics the echo.

He shouts: 'All right, good luck to her!'

'Luck to her!' answers the echo.

He shouts increasingly loud and clear, he spells it out for the echo and gets it to say every word. This occupies him for a while, but he cannot sit forever entertaining himself with this mountain parrot; instead, he falls to musing on this selfsame echo, this speech without a mouth, this sound of voicelessness, this ventriloquism of a blindfolded being that sits perhaps beyond the frontiers of life. He had acquired the habit of holding up to the requisite scrutiny both himself and what he meets with on his way; no one has taught him this, no one else has unfurled him, he had done it all himself. How many a pleasant hour he has spent with himself! In earlier days he would turn to his father and ask him astonishing questions, and Oliver, we know, was not the man to miss a discussion of profound issues, he who had knocked about the world so much. Latterly, however, and especially since his unfortunate addiction to Little Lydia really gathered momentum, Abel had tended to seek solitude, and to grapple with these issues by himself. Blacksmith Carlsen has also influenced him; the old man's wise and gentle simplicity has done him good, his gaiety had cheered him up.

'Boum!' he shouts, like a gun.

'Boum!' answers the echo.

An answer so curt and resounding, it sounds like an invisible leap. It is weird, he struggles painfully with the problem, it fools around with him, damned if he understands it. He is surrounded by riddles and mysteries; he has gone out in the vague hope of stumbling on an adder, and quite right, he hears, let us say, an echo. And this topsy-turvydom is itself inconceivable and mysterious; on this, too, he could ruminate from morn till night. Yes, he could ruminate! It is not some kind of appetite, or a black man's sport, or earning money, damned if it is. And whatever it is, Little Lydia at all events understands nothing about it; she may be sitting there at home, looking out of the window, but really she should know how stupid she is! He sees great plains with animals on them; he sees towns, forests, oceans, infinity, epochs—

Has he been asleep?

He sits up and clears his throat, yawns, flings out his arms, and stretches. Instantly, something dangles from his sleeve, a dark, gaping rope end, a long beast that twists like lightning into the heather. Ha – but here one does *not* scream and clutch at one's skirts and cry Mouse; one is up in a flash and after the fugitive, finds him, tramples him down, crushes his head. Done.

Ah, but who saw it? Heaven and earth, no one. The deed was wasted.

He lifts the beast by the tail and carries it with him; he will present it to an anthill on the way. It's a really splendid fellow, spotted, striped in zigzags, a beauty, and utterly repulsive. He finds no anthill and continues to drag the dead reptile along; he meets no human beings either, not even a child.

This is growing tedious, he is still a long way from the town. Suddenly he feels a stab of pain in the hand, in the right hand which is carrying the snake, and when he looks at it the hand is dark and swollen; he must have been bitten after all. And here again one is not a girl who shrieks and dissolves in tears; even though nobody in the whole wide world is there to see, one behaves like the man of iron one is. Abel drops the dead snake, locates the wound, and starts sucking the poison out. He knows how to do this, he had done it before; at the same time he removes his suspenders and winds them tight around his wrist. Strange that he didn't feel the actual bite; now he has had the poison in him for several minutes, and it gets harder all the time to catch up with it merely by sucking. When he gets going he takes the dead snake with him.

And now he feels more and more stabs of pain in the hand; well, at least he is having a Sunday without monotony. From time to time he looks at this hand, which refuses to get any whiter; at the wound, a ridiculous little cut, nothing whatever to write home about. But as he walks and the hand becomes no better, he looks at it impatiently once more, scrutinizes it, as if to investigate whether it really is a wound and whether the wound is his. Yes, an error is out of the question. Now he is showing more signs of interest in it, and the sight of a man a short distance ahead is not unwelcome. He sucks and walks on.

He puts the hand holding the snake behind his back, to avoid frightening this person; it's Carlsen the blacksmith sitting there. Hither he has come, here on a stone he sits in solitude, with folded hands and a pipe that has gone out. 'Is that you again, Abel?' he asks. 'I'm just sitting here uselessly, looking at this whole world of mountains and valleys and marvelling; I can't stop marvelling. Do you see that fell there, that peak, hee-hee, a sturdy fellow that, just look at all that rock he's draped around himself! Ah, the world's a good place! Were you thinking of going home?'

'Home, that's right.' Abel nods. But then he's got this snake, you see, and he's been bitten slightly—

The blacksmith jumps up, old, flustered, and trembling. 'No no no—'

'Oh, it's not dangerous,' Abel explains.

But this sympathy does him a power of good, one is not too old for that when one is still a boy; this fluster, this terror in another human being for one's own benefit, is positively sweet. It makes one swell with pride and laugh like a man and say Pooh, it can't possibly by anything; still, if Master will kindly tie this tremendously tight around the wrist, a bit higher up, that's it . . .

They set out for home. 'I've never seen such a tough fellow as you,' says the blacksmith. 'Doesn't it hurt?'

'No, not a scrap, only a little.'

Abel makes a detour in order to find an anthill that he remembers from his vagabond days; the blacksmith shakes his head, but goes with him. And from the anthill they proceed home together, the old man actually a little bit proud of the young one, exhibiting him to one or two people they meet, and spreading top-grade terror.

They enter the town; fisherman Jørgen is standing at his door. 'Just come and look at this boy and this hand of his!' says the blacksmith avidly. Abel is bursting with glory; he is not stopping at this door, least of all at this door. He merely smiles and passes on, while the blacksmith calls after him to hurry: 'Yes, go on now! Straight to the doctor! This instant!'

In point of fact, Abel is in a cold sweat and sick as a dog, but in his seventh heaven. Aha, Master is still standing there telling them all about him; certain people can well afford to learn how a man of iron behaves after a snake bite.

'Wasn't it you I gave a message for your father?' asks the doctor. 'Why doesn't he come?'

'I don't know.'

'Tell him to come at once. Or else he'll be fetched. Tell him that! Now let's have a look at that hand. Ugh, what a sight!'

The doctor knows his stuff; every summer he has adder bites to cure, and never a death. 'But this is a particularly virulent case,' he says each time; it makes the patient so proud, he can tell all and sundry that he had been face to face with death. But this time the doctor says more than once that it's a very dangerous case.

17

Oliver was not the man to be at a doctor's beck and call, not he; he was of more consequence than that. His position as warehouseman put him on an equal footing with the upper classes, with Johnsen of the Wharf's shop people, even with chief clerk Berntsen. Indeed, Oliver was if anything a degree more select: he didn't go running upstairs and downstairs for customers, he remained stationary. The perfect position for a man like Oliver.

He had found his niche: it was a splendid business administering a warehouse, being good-morninged and good-dayed, earning your food and your clothes, with time to look in the mirror and make yourself attractive. On top of which he was able to cultivate his personal interests, rowing out to the skerries every Sunday, nosing about and dreaming and yearning, God knows for what –

perhaps for a better life, a new Jerusalem – and always returning from these expeditions with some *trouvaille*: a piece of driftwood, some contraband seagulls' eggs, or the most precious and contraband of all: a handful of eiderdown. Not once was he caught in possession: one doesn't strip a cripple naked in the hope of finding a bag of eiderdown about his person. By now Oliver had collected a fine old crop of eiderdown over the years; the problem was how to get rid of it. But even if he could never convert it into cash, he meant to continue collecting it just the same – with this line of goods, whatever he saw he had to possess.

At home, too, things were going better; his wife had evidently grown more submissive with the years, she had settled down increasingly to home life and coffee, coffee which he could come by relatively cheap; the occasions were fewer when he needed to creep after her with a fish knife up his sleeve. She continued, however, to be frequently truculent, she continued to snort through those mobile nostrils of hers and to sniff the air; for Petra nothing was ever quite good enough or quite enough; she was an unhappy creature, born hard to satisfy, born greedy, in contrast to Oliver, who could find satisfaction in the smaller portion, could find satisfaction even in her. No doubt about it, Petra was some kind of Satan-spawn. Still, as long as she never played around – and of course playing around was something she never did, she never went too far, unauthorized persons got no further than staring at her, and only once had she had a blue-eyed child. All in all, Oliver could rest content, he had her every day to go home to, he warmed himself at her, ate at her table, and lay in her bed; she wafted her breath over him as they slept. That, after all, was no small thing. And in any case, she was his wife and no one else's, as far as anyone knew.

And attractive, surely? Yes indeed: a pleasing figure, winning ways, a certain natural luxuriance, a certain rankness of appetite – or he would never have taken her, kindly note! But her allure was not something scattered to the four winds, and if only Mattis the carpenter had been well out of the way Oliver's mind would have been at rest. Scattered to the four winds, she? Petra, who was capable of boxing even Scheldrup Johnsen's ears? As who should invite any Tom, Dick, or Harry and say, 'Come, let us spread ourselves a little, let us plunge into bottomless depravity'? No, no, not a bit of it. She was more like an altarpiece, so help me God – on Sundays she wore a gold cross that she had picked up and wore on a velvet band around her neck. And no one imagined anything so stark, staring mad as that she was available over the counter. Not a bit of it.

In her way Petra was the right wife for Oliver; many a time he wished for nobody better. The blue-eyed child? Certainly, this little girl had upset his apple cart; yes, for several months she kept his suspicions ablaze. But so effeminate, so feminine had he grown that he could not in the long run hold out against the child; daily life brought the little girl into too frequent contact with him – when no one else was at home he was obliged to rock her cradle. Moreover, his suspicions were, you might say, cheated; he had been expecting a horse's nose in the little face, but as the girl grew, she developed a nose that was unusually attractive. Damned if he could understand it. At one time he discussed the matter with one or two people: how he had suddenly become the father of a blue-eyed child, whereas the other children had brown eyes, and what was one to make of that? He received evasive answers; fisherman Jørgen was not in the least surprised, there were stranger things to be seen – for that matter, nature was full of mysteries.

Under the circumstances, Oliver was a reasonably happy father. Such children were bound to make their mark, few fathers could boast of better; and by the time he was old and had worn himself out at the warehouse, his children would be grown up and would help him in their turn. Of Abel perhaps he had no great expectations, but Frank – ah, Frank was at this or that college becoming learned, and in time would obtain some splendid position. He was already a university student, studying his way forward and upward.

One final point: Johnsen of the Wharf's being a double consul did not come amiss, it was a source of pride to Oliver. There was talk of Grits-and-Groats Olsen following suit and taking on a warehouseman as a status symbol; and old Martin, the veteran fisherman, was rumoured to be after the post. Carry on, take it, Grits-and-Groats Olsen, too, was a consul and a man of means, perhaps even a good employer. But was he twice a consul? Hee-hee, old Martin, you'll be covering just half the ground, but carry on!

So the days and the years went by, and Oliver lived as best he could, making his way as though only moderately one-legged. For eighteen years he had played the human being according to his capacity, which was as great as some people's, and greater than others'.

One Saturday evening he was brushing his clothes and his shoe in preparation for going home. Of late he had shown a mysterious wariness; whatever the reason, he peered out into the street and, on seeing the doctor blocking his path, drew back in and waited. Why did he avoid the doctor, whom anyone else would feel honoured at being stopped in the street by?

The doctor was strolling up and down with the postmaster, from whom on all normal occasions he fled; they strolled up to Davidsen's store and back again, several times; Oliver was incarcerated. Was the doctor actually lying in wait for the cripple? Being reluctant, perhaps, to pay him a personal call at a warehouse? Oliver heard snatches of the postmaster's conversation, without understanding a word; the doctor could understand it all, no doubt, only he didn't seem to be paying much attention – indeed, he seemed rather to be using the postmaster as a mere pretext for lying in wait around here. A disagreeable performance.

Now Oliver had had this remarkable experience of twice being sent for by the doctor; and maybe he was baffled by what it could mean. Or was he? He had acquired the curiosity and cunning of a woman; he wondered whether perchance it had something to do with Consul Johnsen. He had felt his way cautiously, mentioning the matter in all humility to the consul; how he was a poor unlearned man, how the doctor wanted him to go to his surgery, and what should he do about it?

The consul had at first dismissed the matter, saying with a laugh of surprise: 'How should I know?' But a sudden thought struck him, and he asked: 'You say he's sent for you?'

'Twice.'

'Really. What does he want you for?'

'I don't know.'

'Don't you take any notice!'

Whereupon Oliver had acted accordingly and taken no notice.

But here outside was the doctor, apparently keeping him under observation.

The doctor could hardly have been having much fun; his rare contributions to the conversation usually occurred when they met someone he wished to impress; then he would give the postmaster a shrewd question to answer. If Oliver had understood a word of it, he might have profited from the following discussion:

'There was this question of offspring. You didn't answer me on that point.'

'Perhaps I failed to make myself clear,' says the postmaster. 'Is it not the case that when parents see their children grown up, their concern is no longer so much for them as for *their* children in turn, the grandchildren? Surely this suggests a line implanted in mankind, that of perpetuation without end.'

'On the other hand: is it not rather careless of this implanted line to let children be incessantly born into the most wretched existence, into hunger and cold and a bad upbringing, into shame and ruin? If at least they were all born into good homes . . .'

'I don't know if the question can be put like that,' answers the postmaster. 'After all, it may be that we are born to the destiny we have earned in previous existences. Again, there are indications that suggest this: some children may be brought up in excellent homes and become delinquents, while others may be born in abject poverty and turn into splendid human beings – they bring themselves up. You can be sure there's no lack of such cases in this very town. Life is a mixture, one vast welter of such cases, which our logic is apparently incapable of explaining.'

'By all means, let us use logic, since the alternative is a load of nonsense, if you'll forgive me. You were saying just now that children from excellent homes may become delinquents. True. But at the same time they had earned their destiny in previous existences. Had they in that case deserved to be born into good homes?'

'Why not? That doesn't necessarily mean that good homes and worldly comfort are the supreme good, that a life free from torment is the supreme good. Look at it from the other angle: some people may actually be sustained and nourished by suffering, may find their happiness in suffering.'

The doctor is unable to restrain a groan. It is heavy going, this politeness towards the antithesis of his own cherished beliefs. He looks at his watch, turns on his heel, and sets off for Davidsen's again at a furious pace; but the postmaster still hangs on. By the time they return, they have changed the subject, the postmaster's speech has taken a social turn.

'Naturally it's the working middle class that prevents life from dying out, I don't see how anyone can deny that. It's emphatically not the masses, though they're the ones who talk about "we workers". Oh, the masses have learned the tricks, they can read their screaming tabloids, they've acquired the stock of ideas that they require. "We workers." Does that mean the farmer, the fisherman? Not so, it means the industrial worker and no one else. He's the one who roars. Do you remember, Doctor – that you and I have known a time when there were no industrial workers in our country but every cottage had its own industry? In those days life was not too busy to allow us time for keeping the sabbath, it was no poorer in food, no richer in sorrows, the way of life was simpler, contentment greater. Then machinery gained control, mass production started, the industrial worker arose – and to whose profit and pleasure? The manufacturer's, the employer's, no one else's. He wanted to make more money, he and his family were to enjoy greater worldly luxury, he couldn't believe he would ever die—'

'No, listen,' says the doctor, smiling, 'did he not find work for many people, did he not provide bread for hungry mouths?'

'Bread? You mean money for bread. He found work for them in factories – while the soil of Norway remains untilled. That's what he did. He lured young men away from their natural place in life and exploited their strength to his own financial advantage. That's what he did. He established a fourth grade in a world that had too many grades already, a whole class of industrials, life's most unnecessary workers. And then we see what a human travesty such an industrial worker becomes when he's learned the tricks of the upper classes: he leaves his boat, he leaves the land, he leaves his home, parents, brothers and sisters, animals, trees, flowers, the sea, God's high heaven – and in exchange he gets the Tivoli, the Working Man's Club, the saloon, bread and circuses. These are the benefits for which he chooses the proletarian life. And then he roars: "We workers".'

'Absolutely no industry then?'

'What? Was there no industry before?'

'Absolutely no factory industry then?'

'What is one to answer? We can think of one or two exceptions.'

'There, you see!'

'For example, the manufacture of windowpanes.'

'Ha-ha-ha!'

'In warm countries they're an unnecessary commodity, but in our climate we need them. That was what I meant.'

'My word, yes,' says the doctor. 'You don't need to apologize for the fact that we human beings need windowpanes among other things.'

The postmaster is so gormless at times, so lacking in native wit, that he runs the risk of walking into a trap. He happens to quote the saying 'The last shall be first,' just as a young graduate, the deputy district magistrate, is passing, whereupon the doctor asks maliciously, as if unable to make head or tail of it: 'But in that case, what on earth are the first to be?' The postmaster, however, answers in good faith: 'The first shall be last.'

'Ha-ha-ha!' laughs the doctor again. 'Well, I'm damned,' he says. 'Tell me, Postmaster, how do you always manage to be so happy about everything?'

The postmaster, by now probably aware that his leg is being pulled, answers: 'Not always and not about everything.' Then he falls silent.

'It must be habit,' says the doctor. 'You can't do without happiness. The rest of us who are of this world have to manage without. Of course it's habit.'

The postmaster remains silent, and the doctor has to resort once again to the question of offspring in order to get him going. At which point the postmaster refuses to let himself be trampled on, and unexpectedly calls a halt. 'Was it you, Doctor, who mentioned love? What do you understand by that? You should have said sex life, animal functions, you should have said lechery – ah, but even that must be all prudence and prevention, and as childless as possible.'

'What on earth!' exclaims the doctor in amazement. Then he resumes his role of superior being, and feels disinclined to argue. He looks at his watch, and suddenly the postmaster ceases to exist for him. He calls into the warehouse: 'Come on out, Oliver, I want to talk to you.'

As if Oliver was at a doctor's beck and call! He sits in his hideaway in his warehouse until the doctor has gone; then locks the door and leaves.

However, there is no escaping this encounter: the doctor waylays him at the first crossing. Changing his whole tone, and even raising a finger to his hat, he says: 'Good evening, Oliver, it was lucky I met you – can you come with me to the surgery for a moment?'

Oliver goes with him; perhaps his curiosity has got the better of him, perhaps he wants to have done with it.

'Have you any objection to my examining your hip?' asks the doctor.

'What?'

'It's in the name of science. You're a good specimen. Take your clothes off.'

Oliver hesitates.

'It won't take long; five minutes will be enough, two minutes. I want to look at your hip; do you never have any pain there?'

'No.'

'Well, let me see now.'

No, Oliver won't. It's Saturday evening, he has to be getting home.

What's all this nonsense? Two minutes.

Oliver refuses. Oh no, so far and no further. All right, the doctor may enjoy a high esteem in the town, but then that story about the Swedish seaman has hardly increased it; on the contrary. Nevertheless, Oliver would probably have obeyed and taken his clothes off, only he seems afraid to do so; he must have some special reason for declining. What's biting him? He puts on his sly, malignant expression before focusing slowly on the doctor and saying: 'No, I'm not going to.'

'You're a fool,' says the doctor. 'What's more, your beard's not growing so well – how come? You're getting as fat and hairless as a woman.'

'There's nothing wrong with me,' says Oliver.

'That's exactly what I wanted to look into. You shan't be the loser by it. There's something I'd like to clear up, about the abdomen; one minute and it's over.'

'No, I'm not going to.'

The doctor refuses to give up. 'What happened in that accident of yours?'

'I got a barrel of whale oil in my lap.'

'I don't understand.'

'It knocked me down and broke my leg. So it had to be amputated.'

'Let me see how high up it was amputated.'

Oliver demonstrates with his hand.

'No, I mean take off your trousers.'

'No,' replies Oliver for the third time, 'I'm not going to.'

Speaking as if his words are worth their weight in gold, the doctor says: 'As you please. I was only trying to help you.'

Oliver sets off for home. It is getting late, already he can hear the Saturday-evening music from a dance hall. It occurs to him that perhaps he is not sufficiently attractive to pass the smartly dressed boys and girls who usually gather outside, and to avoid doing so, he makes a detour. What a coincidence – why, there's Petra talking with who but Mattis the carpenter! They are extremely animated, the carpenter indeed looks flagrantly passionate, and once again Oliver has to endure that gimlet through his heart; he starts chewing as he walks. Then Mattis catches sight of him and retires into his workshop. And he is wise to retire like this, to disappear at the very moment when Oliver is coming towards him, chewing. Petra, for her part, is wise to wait for her husband; if for an instant she had thought of flying like a deer, he would have called her back in a voice of thunder, would that husband of hers.

They walk side by side, Oliver chewing in silence.

Petra, doubtless aware that a storm is in the air, takes the offensive and mutters: 'Hm. This is a fine state of affairs.'

'Yes,' says Oliver in turn; 'this is a fine state of affairs.' And with these words he rolls his eyes in her direction.

'About Mattis, I mean. You've heard, I suppose?' she asks.

Heard what? He has heard nothing. Totally engrossed in his own concerns, he answers: 'You're the one who's going to hear.'

'What are you muttering about?' she asks, innocent and carefree. 'You mean, you *haven't* heard?'

It must be something special, curiosity gets the better of him, the gimlet stab in his heart becomes less excruciating, and he asks: 'What's all this you're trying to bamboozle me with?'

This is precisely the moment for Petra to put up her price; she is even a trifle hurt. She says: 'I'm certainly not trying to bamboozle you with anything. I shall keep my mouth shut.'

Oliver is obliged to veer right around and start begging before Petra will give in. Ah, but the news is far too good for her to miss being the first to tell it; she had reached her limit. 'It's Maren,' she says.

'What about her?'

'Maren Salt.'

'Yes, of course.'

'She's been brought to bed. She's had a baby.'

Oliver seems at a loss how to take this news, which in any case has cheated him of another violent scene with his wife. He answers with some irritation: 'So that's the kind of thing you were standing there yakking with him about.'

'Yakking? He simply came out of his workshop and told me. He's terribly upset.'

'It serves him right.'

'You surely don't suppose it's that Mattis who's the father?'

'And what do you know about it?'

They quarrel over it, fall out over it. If Mattis is not the father, Oliver is still more at a loss how to take it. But in any case it is Saturday evening, it is late, Oliver is hungry and ungracious, all he can think of is getting home. When at last he has got some food inside him, and plenty of it, life takes on a rosier hue; he laughs and questions Petra more closely about Mattis, what he had said, how he had taken it.

Petra tells her story. She is content that the storm has passed over, she too is in a good humour now. There's no denying it, she mimics Mattis and makes fun of him. Mattis had insisted all along that Maren should leave the house before she was brought to bed, but Maren had kept putting it off and cramming his ears full of lies, how she was still a long way from her time. Then one night he heard a baby's cry in the house, jumped out of bed, ran for the midwife, ran for the doctor. The doctor had his doubts and said: 'Isn't she a woman of forty, fifty? It's not possible, surely?' To which Mattis replied: 'Do you think it's me who's had the baby, then?' 'Are you sure there *is* a baby?' asked the doctor. 'Whatever it is, it's lying there howling. Come and see.'

Petra laughs, Oliver and Granny laugh, even the two little girls appreciate fully the absurdity of Mattis the carpenter and cannot keep a straight face. 'You ought to have seen that Mattis,' says Petra. 'There he was, hopping about, sniffing with that nose of his, out of his wits because he hadn't shown the old woman the door in time. "They say she's between forty and fifty," he was shouting, "but she's sixty if she's a day, and is that sort of thing decent? Going around waggling her nostrils like a rabbit's ears when her days are practically numbered!" '

Then Petra had been sly and said: 'Well, reckon the best thing you can do is to take her, Mattis.' 'Take her?' he had yelled. 'Why should I take her? To hell with that! If ever the day should dawn for me to change my circumstances, you can bet your boots it won't be with a fallen old maid. Enough's enough!'

The entire household laughs.

But as if to restore a modicum of dignity Oliver pulls himself together and says: 'But was all this a matter to be standing and jabbering about with a strange man in the middle of the street?'

Petra feels secure by now. 'No, I could have gone in with him,' she replies, 'but I didn't want to do that.'

'I'd have liked to see you try.'

'Why not? He's so quaint and simple, I doubt if you could find anyone quainter than that Mattis. I'll wager that anyone married to him could have had child after child the wrong side of the blanket. He wouldn't have understood the first thing.'

'Yes, you'd have liked that ... Go to bed, children!' he yells without warning at the little girls, and off they go. Even Granny leaves the room. 'Yes, you'd have liked that,' he repeats.

'Me?' retorts Petra; 'why drag me in?'

'I suppose you think you're on too short a tether, you can't go grazing far enough afield.'

'Me?' laughs Petra. 'Hee-hee-hee!' she laughs. 'No, I've got a husband who keeps the field glasses on me. I'm well aware of that.'

Oliver looks at her distrustfully – is she by any chance making fun of him? He prepares for an angry surveillance.

Petra twists him around her little finger. 'Though come to that,' she says ingratiatingly, 'come to that, you might have a heart and leave me a little more free to go where I like. You really might, Oliver. Because you know I never do anything I shouldn't; I just look around and walk about and see what's in the shop windows.'

'That's not the proper thing for a married woman who's reckoned as belonging to the upper classes,' Oliver answers. 'Where were you wanting to go – to the dance hall? I wouldn't put it past you.'

'And what if I did go to the dance hall? If I just looked in very briefly?'

'Yes, and took the little girls with you,' sneers Oliver. 'No, as long as my name is Oliver Andersen, and as long as I hold the position I hold, it's not going to happen. That's my answer.'

'Well, well,' says Petra, giving in. 'It's for you to decide, and if you say no, then it's no.'

'That's very true,' says Oliver, puffing out his feathers.

'But surely I could go and see Maren Salt?'

Oliver flares up: 'I'd have you understand that you can't go visiting people like that, do you hear, and that you're not to set foot in that house. Out of the question. Because when a man is made a manager, you can't just go where you like, you have to keep to your own class. I'm not standing for it, and you'd better just get it into your head that I won't have it.'

'Well, well,' sighs Petra, and allows him to have the last word.

But at heart Oliver was flattered that his wife had asked him for a little more rope, he really was. For it wasn't every wife who asked; many of them had their fling and never said a word about it.

18

One event succeeds another: Mrs Consul Johnsen and her daughter were walking in the street one day, content with themselves and the world, when they saw in a side street the painter who had painted Mrs Johnsen's portrait, the district magistrate's son, saw him with one of Consul Olsen's daughters on his arm. Mrs Johnsen, who was stout and heavy, would gladly have sunk to the ground for a breather. Fia merely said: 'Yes, they're engaged, I hear.'

This was just about the biggest piece of impudence Mrs Johnsen had ever encountered; it might at least have been the other painter, the house painter's son. Not that either of them would have won Fia – perish the thought! – but how could anyone go off and do such a thing under Fia's very nose? And what did Fia say to it? Calmly said, 'Yes, they're engaged, I hear.' What the devil was Fia made of – was she plain cold? Now it only needed the other young starveling, the painter's son, to come and fall on his knees for Fia – whereupon, of course, Mrs Johnsen would show him the door, and the garden gate for good measure!

Oh, what a world it was to live in!

Consul Johnsen took it much less to heart, scarcely gave it a thought, saying, much as Fia had said, 'Engaged, are they? Don't disturb me now,' before returning to his newspaper.

'Just imagine, those youngsters we did everything in our power to help!' said his wife.

'Yes. But don't disturb me, do you hear?'

The consul had other things to think about: lawyer Fredriksen, Representative Fredriksen, had apparently put a question to the government about what steps it intended to take in respect of repeated complaints on the part of the crews on board our ships. He did not specifically mention the case of the steamship *Fia*; no, but neither did he attempt to conceal the fact that even in his own little town there were rumours of widespread dissatisfaction with the shipowners. The situation demanded an official inquiry.

A storm had burst over the head of Consul Johnsen. This pettifogger, this unshaven upstart, who had received wine and patronage in his house, and who now repaid it by attacking him! A double consul and a great man had many a cross to bear.

If Consul Johnsen had been aware of earlier events, his surprise would have been less. He had his daughter to thank for this vile trick on the part of their representative. Look at the lady now, look at Mademoiselle Fia, dainty, mild, and innocent; and yet she had occasioned a question in the Storting! Such is life. For not only had lawyer Fredriksen had his proposal rejected, but she had offended him, forsooth, into the bargain. She hadn't done so intentionally, of course, but by pure misfortune. Such is life. And nowadays it took less than ever to upset Mr Fredriksen's feelings.

Naturally he was somewhat surprised at being rejected out of hand. Here he was, having at last succeeded in being elected to the Storting, no longer therefore merely lawyer Fredriksen; but this seemed to make no impression on her, she had not even asked for a period of grace. 'No,' she had said with a smile and a shake of the head.

He had, of course, taken it nicely and said: 'Will you not allow me to hope, Miss Fia?'

No, he must excuse her.

And he had continued to take it nicely, like a gentleman. 'Then you are not free, Miss Fia?'

Yes, she was.

'We-ell,' he said, and fell silent.

She was a riddle to him, the entire girl was a riddle to him; he could not but feel she was acting against her own best interests. He drew away from her.

The Countess, who found this unusual situation rather trying, was induced to say more, to say foolish things, insulting things. No doubt she did so to be kind, to smooth over her harsh decision, but she hinted that she came from a good home and could not think of leaving it.

'You could have a good home all over again.'

It wouldn't be the same. She was bound to her home by every tie; she was surrounded by cultivated society, refinement, illustrated magazines, traditional culture—

The lawyer looked at her. Then he stopped taking it nicely, and started to laugh. She let him laugh, she was not embarrassed. When he was serious again, he said: 'But, my dear Miss Fia, all these things you've listed – surely you could have them all over again, couldn't you?'

'Where?' she asked.

'We-ell—' But here the lawyer reached an impasse. He fell silent again, this time for good.

For some time after this he was seldom to be seen in the streets, never stopped for a chat; he grew reserved and sat brooding at home, brooding over goodness knows what – perhaps over the splendid dowry he had missed. It could well be that.

In the Storting, likewise, for the first few weeks he was notably withdrawn; he voted correctly each time, he never put a foot wrong, but he remained silent. Until, that is, he spoke his mind on the question of the seamen and revealed at last the inward fervour that possessed him.

Yes, he made an excellent speech that moved the assembly, the country, and the people, so heartfelt was his feeling for the downtrodden, so humane his temper. It had been pointed out that there were two sides to the question; quite so, that was precisely what there were. And now it would do no harm if the refined shipowners, if these representatives of cultivated society and ostensible culture, were to begin looking at the other side. These ships might make the most prodigious voyages and earn money hand over fist, while the crew languished on the same food, and under the same treatment, as had prevailed in the old days, when men were hardier than they are today. And was the work they performed entirely safe; was it a game, perhaps? The government should go on board our merchant vessels and see the state in which the crews so often returned. Those who were not worn out came limping on one leg, with one arm; the service had mutilated them. In this condition they came home to their dear ones; the speaker had seen examples in his own town. But whenever there was a possibility of ameliorating the deplorable conditions under which these men lived, it foundered on the opposition of their high-and-mighty masters. What if considerations of humanity, what if right and justice, were allowed to prevail! If the government was incapable of bringing about a change in this lamentable state of affairs, then the Storting could enforce such a change – if it had the will.

Inevitably, a Conservative, a shadow from the past, spoke in reply to this speech, taking exception to its exaggerations: there were, unfortunately, instances of a seaman being injured, but very few occupations were entirely free from danger; he himself had been a seaman in his younger days – the only option open to a lad in his town – and he had no such dismal memories of the food and treatment he had received ...

Old man's chatter, old-time chatter; indeed, lawyer Fredriksen did not bother to listen. Nor, perhaps, did he listen much more carefully to the Cabinet Minister who followed. This man could think of nothing safe to say, he hovered upon the surface of the waters, his attention would be brought to bear on the situation ...

Well, that was at least a beginning, declared Mr Fredriksen, and to that extent he was able to thank the Minister for his courtesy. On this cool note he appeared to have sat down; he may have wished it to be understood that he was not impressed.

The report continued:

The President glances up at the clock, assuming, mistakenly, that this question has now been disposed of. The Representative for Telemark, 'the Bleater', gets up to oppose the closure and to announce that he too has been intending to take the floor.

'Well, that kills any hope of our finishing just yet,' says the Conservative with a faint smile.

A telling remark. However, it served only to goad the majority: was the Representative from the dales to be debarred from supporting the lawyer from the coastal town, a newcomer who stood so exactly on the right side in the question of the downtrodden seamen?

And in the afternoon, indeed, lawyer Fredriksen won a complete victory and got his Commission of Inquiry appointed. A promising debut, one might say, his constituency could be proud of him . . .

Consul Johnsen read the newspaper, flung it away, picked it up again. It was a long time since he had been so roused to indignation. Finally he took the paper out to Berntsen, saying: 'Read this drivel!' He was outraged. Here he sat enthroned in his town, giving lavish help left and right, taking cripples into his employment, paying for their children to go to college, exercising charity, doing good – and what did he get in return? Attacks! If only Scheldrup had been at home to take over the defence; C. A. Johnsen was tired, this life of conflict meant starting from scratch every day, he was at the end of his tether.

If only he had one single blessed place to go! To the postmaster again? Yes, if he was absolutely set on being overpowered by religious chitchat! No, he would rather take a turn up to his garden and make out that he was taking an hour off before returning to the office and starting work with renewed vigour. Who could tell, it was a resourceful idea, a temporary expedient, a sudden impulse, perhaps a gift from heaven; that could well be.

And the consul actually did find a little peace in his garden; his daughter sat there in all innocence, painting lilacs, exchanging small talk with him. It was pleasant to see her hit if off so well, hit off the likeness so exactly, and it did him good to see her so content with her existence.

'So you're sitting here being industrious, Fia?'

'Yes. It's for that blessed exhibition. Don't you think, Papa, I can be rather proud of this picture?'

'Most certainly.'

'I think so, too. And what's more, this is only a beginning.'

A strange creature, Mademoiselle Fia – she lived her life with superb guardedness. But let her be as she was; she herself regarded that as the right way to be. Her happiest hours were surely those she spent sitting in the National Gallery, copying and getting the copy exact. And if anyone took an interest in her painting and wrote something about it in the papers, she couldn't have wished for greater happiness. She was good-natured, without bitterness, she submitted to patronage, her ambition caused her no agony.

Yes, a strange creature; she may have been deficient in certain respects, but these deficiencies seemed always to prove advantages and blessings. Did she possess a sense of guilt? Apparently not. She was quietly content with herself, did nothing she shouldn't, felt no regrets, showed no trace of melancholy. What change could she wish for? She painted and travelled, and that was all; in the town she had good friends, she had had many experiences, but no great ones. Some people found her overgrown with expertise, with affectation. 'Listen, child,' they would say, 'were you born moderate? All the same, Countess, permitted and permissible audacities do exist; for instance, you can safely fall in love, my girl!' 'Why should I?' she would answer.

What change could she wish for? Could not all the endless years wasted on artistic toil and moil have been put to other uses? Why should they? They were cherished years, a poetic mission, a vocation; she stored these years like silver heirlooms. She toiled and moiled, she got nowhere, absolutely nowhere, but she kept on, it was a kind of obstinacy; to stop or turn back was unthinkable, she required no deliverance from her *idée fixe*, it was what she was suited for. No, she had no sense of guilt and no melancholy.

And now, as he sat there listening to her and seeing himself in the mirror of her mild well-being, her ageing father may have thought to himself: God knows if Fia isn't the wisest of us all! She's escaped all the persecutions and punishments of fate, while the rest of us toss and tumble in everlasting conflict!

'They've got their knives into us shipowners in the Storting,' he said. 'They say we starve and mutilate our seamen.'

She didn't flare up, she took it nicely, she put down her brush and turned it over in her mind. 'Really?' she said.

'But of course! Evidently that's how it strikes outsiders.'

'Does it distress you?'

'Not exactly distress. But it's no fun for me, either, I'm getting old and worn, and Scheldrup's away. Well, Fia, thank God I have you!' he concluded.

'If only I could be any use! Papa, they haven't got their knives into *you*, have they?'

'They don't mention me by name. But I've been singled out clearly enough by our own representative.'

'By—?'

'By Fredriksen, you know, the lawyer.'

'Really?' she said, and turned this over, too.

'I can't imagine what I've done to him to make him go for me like that.'

'It's simply lack of culture,' she said mildly.

Was it a look of disappointment or of meditation that crossed his face at this comment? He was in no hurry to agree with her. 'Culture? I've no idea how much culture he has. It's not exactly in demand these days. We're all simply people nowadays.'

She didn't answer. Her face had a stubborn expression which he recognized: she was not going to give in.

'I think this is one of the very best paintings you've ever done,' he said. 'So you think it's lack of culture? You may well be right. Tell me, by the way – you don't care for the lawyer, do you?'

'Me?'

'No, you don't, not a scrap, I knew that. He's an able man, of course, who's going to make his mark, still – still, if neither you nor your mother nor I care for him, then there's simply no point in the fellow coming to the house. That's what I had in mind. We won't invite him in the future; speak to your mother about it, she's been inclined to favour him.'

Well, that was off his chest; now he was really free to go.

'So it's true, is it, that he's got engaged here – the painter, I mean, what was his name? Is it the older girl or the younger he's engaged to? You've heard about it, haven't you, Fia?'

She chuckled: 'I'll guarantee I was the first to hear about it. Between you and me, Papa, I was the go-between for both parties.'

'Really? Well, well, Fia! Go-between!'

So that was how she took it.

When the consul walked back to his office, he had neither sorted out the lawyer nor made a few thousand on a deal, but he pretended to himself that he had achieved something and rubbed his hands together like the picture of zeal. This, however, was merely a piece of spurious energy. He bowed to one or two people he met; he bowed nicely to the ladies – good, they responded as one does respond to a great man, they had not yet read about the affair in the Storting. All the same, the ladies did not respond as in the old days, their eyes no longer swooned a little as they used to when they met him; he had aged, young ladies now kept their eyes for ungrizzled hair, he must try his luck further down the ranks, he was at a low ebb. So what? He was the man he was.

He walked into his office, looked at his watch, and sat down in his chair. 'It's remarkable how a break like that bucks you up!' he might have said as if he believed it himself. Ah, but it had hardly bucked him up for long: lawyer Fredriksen's question in the Storting continued to haunt his mind. Lack of culture. Perhaps Fia was right. Certainly she was the wisest of them if she took only a go-between's interest in necking – she was damnably wise, that girl! He would have no objection if she kept off all billing and cooing for a while yet; he knew from experience what an ungovernable force there is in love, and she would discover it soon enough.

Mutilated seamen? Whom in consequence one maintained, whom in consequence one just about took in one's lap and fed with milk from a bottle! If only Scheldrup was at home. But Scheldrup was the hard, modern type who thought of nobody but himself, and was now talking of spending a year in New Orleans.

And look, here was the office overflowing with work not done, his desk one mass of letters, telegrams, bills of lading – surely Berntsen could come and dip into the mounds and take a few things off his hands. Was the consul old? A little worn, fagged out; was it to be wondered at? But old? And even if he was old, he was the man he was. If his hair was getting thin, he would have himself photographed in a hat, in a tall hat . . .

He got up and called Berntsen in from the shop.

'Who was the lad in a student's cap standing out there?'

'Frank.'

'Frank?'

'Whom the consul supports. Oliver's son.'

'Oh, him.'

'He's come to claim his new suit. His annual new suit.'

'I see. Listen, Berntsen, couldn't you lend me a hand and tackle some of this? Look, it's piling right up over my head. You're such a quick worker.'

Berntsen promised to find time that evening.

'Thank you. First and foremost, send off the insurance premium for the *Fia*. It's utter chaos in here and I've too much on my mind. Did you read the paper? What are we going to do about the lawyer?'

'Are we going to do anything?'

'I don't know. No, perhaps you're right, we'll just let sleeping dogs lie. But maybe one of these commissions will come asking questions?'

'Then we'll answer them.'

'Right! Answer point by point. Oh, and, Berntsen, if the need should arise, could you take on this matter of answering the commission?'

'All right.'

The matter was now in the best of hands, and the consul felt as if a great burden had been lifted from his shoulders. His relief restored his sense of being the master, and by way of showing off a little, he said: 'That student, Berntsen – send him in for a moment.'

Frank came in and stood before the great man.

'I'm glad to see you're not spending too much time at home, young man,' said the consul. 'Because that means you're wrapped up in your studies, I imagine? I didn't recognize you – I had to ask Berntsen – you've grown so much in the last few years. You're at the university now; are you getting on all right?'

'Yes, thank you.'

'I'm glad to hear it. We all have to make our mark, you in your line and I in mine. What was I going to say? – As a young man, you will, I hope, be on your guard against dissipation?' said the consul suddenly. 'Against irresponsibility of every kind?' he added.

Oh, that Consul Johnsen, he was enough to make a tombstone smile. He continued: 'Yes, seriously, you must; you're to be a sensible lad and resist temptation. I expect that of you.'

Frank didn't smile; he stood there, tall and thin, bending low as if in church, answering yes or no, nicely and correctly, in the right places, and leaving the consul with an excellent impression of him. Was it the consul's intention that this young man should take with him a favourable memory of this meeting with his benefactor? Who knows, it might at some future date benefit the benefactor, if further attacks were threatened. In any case, a little talk never did any harm.

In perfect good faith, the consul seized this opportunity of showing his moral side. 'There are noble pleasures,' he said, 'and there are empty pleasures. In recent years I have come to the conclusion that the pleasures of home and family are the right ones. One can forgo the other pleasures if one sets one's mind to it. That is my experience.'

Oh, that Consul Johnsen! He had presumably reached the cooling-down age, and now that his desires were gradually deserting him, he did not intend, shopkeeper that he was, to be short-changed on the credit of having 'conquered' them.

Not, of course, that Consul Johnsen was utterly and entirely hollow; he did in fact have a kindly heart. Thus, he thought for a moment of offering the young student a chair, an idea which he abandoned in favour of a better one: he went to the safe and returned with a banknote – a great fat red banknote – which he presented with the words: 'Here you are, a bit of pocket money!'

And Frank bowed the deep bow that he had once learned from the dancing lady.

'You needn't go proclaiming it from the rooftops,' said the consul. 'We're told not to let our left hand know what our right hand's doing, isn't that so!'

'Yes.'

'Well, we're only human. But we must try to do the best we can. I assume it's the church you're going into?'

'No, I'm not sure—'

'You're not sure?'

'I'm better at languages.'

'Languages?'

'Philology.'

'Hm. Is there any future in that? Hm.'

But the consul seemed a little disconcerted, whether because he was thinking that he might have spared himself his moral lecture, or because he feared that a linguist would hardly be as useful to him in the future as a parson.

He dismissed the boy without more ado. 'Well, now I must do some work!' However, he didn't turn him out but continued talking amiably. 'Think it over now, whether you shouldn't rather go into the church. Really, you know, I haven't treated your father or you badly, I don't treat anyone badly. But what you make of your life is something you must decide for yourself, I can only advise you a little. Goodbye, young man.'

19

The young man returned to the store and resumed his search among the ready-mades. Being slim and narrow-shouldered, he had no difficulty in finding a jacket that would go on, but the height to which he had shot up meant that the matching trousers were too short. There was a frock coat and trousers which fitted in every respect, but these Berntsen regarded as too expensive.

The worthy Berntsen was not entirely the man he appeared: for all his mild goodwill towards men, he was far from being a lamb. His vigilance, his unremitting care for the firm's best interests, sometimes made him tiresome even to his boss, and Mrs Johnsen herself would go to one of the assistants in preference to Berntsen whenever she wanted something delivered from the store. She found no pleasure in looking at dress materials and finery with Berntsen at her elbow. Still, he was a fiendishly able businessman.

'In my opinion you're too young to wear a frock coat,' he said to Frank. 'We might think of that in a year or two.'

Frank objected that Reinert already wore a frock coat, and he was younger.

It was no use. What Reinert, the sexton's son, wore was not universal writ and mandate; at one time he had even sported an outlandish pair of knee breeches. Besides, said Berntsen very mildly, it was all right for Reinert: his father paid.

Young Frank had long been accustomed to recognizing a rebuff and submitting to it; such rebuffs gave him no great offence, they merely kept him in his place, so that he seldom ventured too far above it; if ever he did, he very soon retreated. He knew, of course, that somehow he would find a way around. On this occasion he took the allotted clothes with thanks. After all, what were clothes to him? His mind was on higher things.

Reinert had been waiting for him outside, and the two students sauntered through the streets together, not because they were bosom friends, but because they were students. No, they were not bosom friends. Both were bright, at languages positively brilliant, but Frank was reputed to be a good lap ahead. It was this lap that Reinert couldn't stomach, he couldn't endure being the under-drudge; often it gave rise to bitterness, and made him hanker after such revenge as lay within his power. However, there was one field in which he excelled despite his lack of years: with the girls, the ladies. Could Little Lydia, or the young shipyard girls, resist him? Here he had the advantage of a flair for dressing fashionably and well, with starched linen shirts and pointed shoes, plus the additional advantages of a stout heart and an absence of bashfulness – he was the last person in the world to be cowed by a rebuff. So when they chanced to meet the Heiberg girl, Alice, it never occurred to him to turn into a side street; he raised his cap and stopped. That was what he did.

And now it was Frank's turn to be the drudge: he got not one word out of the lady, scarcely a glance. He had to be on his guard against casting an eye up at the church tower to see the time, for Reinert had acquired a trick of taking out his watch and flaunting a new locket containing a lock of hair; and immediately, of course, the ladies, fools that they were, had to ask if they could see the lock of hair. Frank, who had a new suit under his arm and a fat bank-note in his breast pocket, must for once have felt he was sitting pretty, for he asked the lady: 'And how have you been since the last time I saw you?' 'Yes, thank you,' she answered Reinert. Really, Alice Heiberg was just as big a fool as the rest.

'I'm just popping home with this parcel,' said Frank cunningly. 'I'll be right back.'

This gave Reinert no chance to say: 'Going home already? It's not late, let me see!' But wait! Reinert, that insensitive soul, that far from delicate soul, simply said, 'I'll give you half an hour!' and took out his watch. Catch Frank turning up again in half an hour, just catch him!

At home he came much more into his own; he was the master of the house, the others walked on tiptoe in his presence. 'Let me see what clothes you've got this year,' said his mother. 'Go and put them on!' When Frank told how he had been sent for by the consul, his mother and grandmother were agog with curiosity and began questioning him: 'What did he want? Aha, the consul!' Frank feigned indifference, sometimes answering, sometimes not, for sometimes silence is the best answer. They were greatly disappointed at his not wanting to become a parson; his grandmother couldn't understand it, seeing as how he had the brains for it. Whereupon Frank smiled, oh, such a sad little smile, hardly a smile at all, the merest soupçon. The little girls ran their hands over his clothes – what lovely buttons! A small triangle of red silk projected from the breast pocket; it was sewn in, a permanent fixture of a handkerchief. The trousers were too short, and his mother wanted to put this right by letting them down; she set to work forthwith, for Frank need to go and pay his respects to the headmaster. But Granny was lost in thought, shaking her head and muttering discontentedly.

'That's what they'll be able to say now,' she muttered.

'What is?'

'That you weren't up to becoming a parson.' She was presumably thinking of the women at the pump.

Frank said nothing. Which was a good answer.

'You must let our Frank think it over,' said Petra, who had not yet given up hope.

Ah, but Frank had no intention of being talked into it; his intentions were firm, firm as bone or cartilage, irreversible, for days and nights he had mulled it over – be quiet, he knew his vocation.

He went to see the headmaster. His trousers were and would always be too short; his jacket hung on him casually, as if cut in accordance with some grammar that allowed alternative forms. He strutted along, a curious sight in his cap that denoted the mandarin class. The road to the school had been rebuilt since he was last at home, and in some confusion he pulled up short in front of a house, saying to himself and to a woman who was standing in the doorway: 'I must have been thinking of something else . . .'

'Well, where do you want to go, sonny boy?' asked the woman.

'To the school,' he answered curtly, turning on his heel.

'Well then, you should go *that* way,' the woman called after him.

Huh, fancy her not knowing who he was! Or did she know? At all events, she didn't know him too well to be familiar and 'sonny-boy' him and show him the way without being asked.

The headmaster, exhausted after the annual examinations, was sitting at his ease in a dressing gown and slippers, refreshing himself with a grammar. There is nothing in the world quite so mild and peaceful as a foreign grammar, nothing quite so pure, so incapable of disturbing or deceiving!

'Come in! Is that you, Frank? How nice! Do you know this, Frank, old man? Just bought it – brilliant! I ought to have had this grammar before the exam, but here I've been, grinding away at the old one, preparing myself. You see, my daughter's been taking French for me for most of the year, so I had to brush it up for the exam. Yes, that's the way it is in our subject: if we get out of practice for a while, we find we've forgotten what we knew. Ah, but then, thank the Lord, isn't it a pleasure to immerse oneself in it again? To kneel in the shaded temple and quench one's thirst with the pure waters of learning!'

The headmaster had grown old in recent years, a grey-haired child with withered eyes behind his glasses. He was pleased with Frank, had heard only good of him, wished him more good things in the future, had the highest hopes for him. Why, with the industry he showed he was sure of an honourable future; it was by no means impossible that he might one day become headmaster of this very school from which he had gone forth . . .

The old philologist was humble; his life, his very vocation, had subdued him to modest habits of thought; no one could have boasted less of his philology. He never mentioned the great scholars, the high priests of linguistics; probably he understood nothing of their work, scarcely even knew their names – what had he to do with men of genius? His vocation lay not in making discoveries but in teaching, only teaching. Teaching so as just to survive, teaching so as just to guide others through the curriculum to the examination. The headmaster, then, had done his bit. A meagre, pitiful existence: poverty and cultural darkness, decline, wear and tear, blindness. If only it had been madness, fate, some divine folly; but the folly was human, simian.

The headmaster went on to talk about other promising pupils, one or two brilliant embryo teachers like himself, tremendous fellows; Frank by now had reached a point at which the headmaster could afford to take greater interest in fresh examples of infant prodigies. 'Goodbye, Frank, old man, and God be with you!'

Frank went home; he too was pleased, exhilarated. He had had no occasion to declare allegiance to any particular course of studies, and the veteran linguist would doubtless assume he intended to major in philology – what else? And basically it was all the same, provided he read a lot and learned a lot: that was the object of the exercise. Frank left the headmaster, the man in charge of the great stone building, and went home.

In the evening his father returned from the warehouse and Abel from the smithy; their arrival made no difference to Frank, who had the little room in the original cottage as his home and his lair. It was intended that even in the vacation he should read and learn, study, remember, immerse himself in languages; and he did what was intended. By the time he was told to come and eat, he had found something out – he had become even more learned and otherwordly. But all these meals wasted a lot of his time.

He would make his entry holding an empty can that he had brought in from outside and ask: 'What do you think it says on this can?' No, not one of them knew. But his mother, doubtless recalling the label from her serving days at Consul Johnsen's, hazarded: '*Laks, kanskje?*' – salmon, perhaps? 'But that's not what is says in English,' answered Frank in injured tones – his mother was ruining his wisdom with her practical knowledge: 'it says *Alaska Salmon.*' Whereupon his father, who had been a sailor and knew many things, chipped in: 'Alaska's a country; do you think I don't know what Alaska is?'

So the can heralded no triumph.

They came to him with other incomprehensibilities. His mother proffered a spool of thread: here you are, *Brook Brothers, 50 yards.*

Once again his father chipped in – he couldn't afford to spare his son – and swelling with pride proclaimed his interpretation. 'Seaman's English!' said Frank. One way and another, the pater-familias, Oliver, made himself thoroughly disagreeable by re-membering his English; he impaired still further the mystical grandeur of the occasion by deciphering his wife's packet of needles: *Silver Eye. Cast Steel.* 'It should have been in small letters,' said Frank. This was beyond his father. 'Why should it have been in smaller letters?' he asked. To which Frank gave the only correct answer: he kept his mouth shut – and suddenly he enjoyed a well-deserved rehabilitation. His mother produced a box from some store, saying *Toilet Soap. Superior.* Aha, this brought Oliver up short, every word was Greek to him, and Frank had to come portentously to the rescue.

Meanwhile, his brother, Abel, sat there, not understanding a word of the performance and saying nothing. What a difference between the brothers! For one moment a faint pity for Abel seemed to stir in his learned brother's breast; after all, he had only just come home, and had no wish to neglect him. 'Well, well, Abel,' he said, 'there's no witchcraft in it – you'd certainly have known just as much as I do if you'd studied.' Abel gave a some-what exhausted smile and shook his head.

Thus on numerous occasions Frank's relatives derived great benefit from his linguistic mastery. Learning had made its entry into Oliver's home. Strange that none of the neighbours dropped in for interpretations of foreign or enigmatic words in newspapers or on packets of tea. They had no feeling for culture or intellectual conundrums, they were lethargic and shiftless. Such was Frank's environment.

One evening Oliver comes home and says: 'Well, when you've eaten, Frank, when you've got some food inside you, I've got a question for you!' At supper there is an air of excitement; only Frank remains calm, not doubting his ability to answer.

The moment arrives: Oliver puts something on the table. The old sinner puts a deck of cards on the table and asks Frank what is says on the wrapper. Playing cards! The womenfolk wax indig-nant, but Oliver allays the storm. 'Hold your tongues!' he says. 'I know all that, and I wouldn't handle such things or bring them into this house, if that fellow Olaus hadn't asked me to.'

Far from taking it amiss, Frank takes it very nicely. He has had no chance to display any very extensive linguistic knowledge of late, and is presumably not averse to giving another performance. 'Whist à 52 Blatt, Verzierte Asse. Well, Abel, what do you think that means?' asks Frank, benevolent as ever. Abel gives another exhausted smile and has to let his opinion remain unspoken. Frank begins: 'Actually this is in three different languages,' then proceeds to explain the meaning from the first letter to the last; not for an instant is he in any doubt, not even over the ornamental aces. Fanastic! Meanwhile, Abel has got hold of the grubby cards and demonstrates that they are perfectly ordinary aces – what is one to make of this? Frank now becomes very pensive, and declines to discuss the matter. 'But I can vouch for the original text,' he says.

At this point Oliver, who has been listening in silence, exclaims: 'Marvellous!'

Everyone looks at him, and indeed he has put if fairly strongly: Frank's performance has not seemed particularly brilliant. But then on previous occasions Oliver has cramped his son's style, has poached on his preserves with his own English, and now he wants to set him up again; he has a way with children. He assumes an ecstatic expression: what a head his son has on his shoulders!

Is Petra jealous? At Oliver's pronouncement she tosses her head and says with a sneer: 'Your son?'

A door closes in Oliver's mind; his face goes vacant, his mouth droops, his fat fingers lie listlessly on the table.

Petra explains herself: 'He's not only your son, he's mine too, isn't he?'

Oliver slowly comes to. 'Well, who said he wasn't? Of course he is, of course he's your son, too!' And now he comes to in superb style, oozing righteousness again and refusing to make any distinction between the sons. Abel is included in this speech: 'Well, once I've got you two boys nicely off my hands and set you on the path of useful knowledge and learning, then I shall have done my bit. More than that is beyond my means.'

The following evening Oliver was able to put the aces in their context: that scoundrel Olaus had, out of pure mischief, put a different deck of cards in the wrapper, in the hope of fooling Frank. But Frank had been as right as rain! 'And you were right too, Abel, because the aces were no different from what they are all over the world as far as I've been. And it's just as I say: what you've both got is learning, praise the Lord!'

For all that, Frank had been none too brilliant; whatever the reason, these domestic sessions could hardly have brought him an adequate return. Or could they? Did they offer him any scope? Length and breadth were wanting, the framework lacked spaciousness: father, mother, brother and two sisters, grandmother. He hit on the idea of taking out learned textbooks: mathematics, he explained, sky-high calculations; yes, he took to reading aloud about geometry, algebra, rules for establishing the derivative of a function, integrations, a circle whose curvature is equal to the curvature of an arc at a given point is called the arc's circle of curvature at that point; its radius is called the radius of curvature.

Oliver said brokenly: 'It's almost as if it wasn't a human being speaking! Do you have to learn things like that?'

'We have to learn everything.'

He had risen far above his station, and now he talked like a savage. He could make himself understood to no one but himself; he couldn't even, like a magpie, make himself understood to magpies. Where would it end? He asked Abel: 'I don't suppose there's a single foreign newspaper to be had in this town, is there?'

'I don't know. But the municipal engineer keeps newspapers.'

'Foreign ones? In foreign languages?'

'I don't know. How about Norwegian ones?'

'Norwegian ones!' Frank sniffed.

In this little seaman's town everyone knew 'Engels' – who didn't know 'Engels'? But young Frank knew too much of everything; he was obliged to take himself into his own confidence, asking questions and answering them, nodding and shaking his head, believing and doubting in silence. From time to time a groan would reach Granny in the old living room; it came from the little bedroom, from the rock to which he was chained.

Abel was an unbelievably simple soul; he would pick up a book and ask: 'What sort of book is this?'

'Latin. You wouldn't understand it.'

'Oh, is it printed in Latin, then?'

No answer from Frank.

'Would you like to come sailing with us on Sunday?'

A sceptical shake of the head from Frank. 'Who else is going?'

'There'll be several of us.'

'Anyone from the shipyard?'

'From the shipyard? No, they're too small. Little Lydia's coming.'

'Little Lydia!' Another sniff.

An unbelievably simple soul, Abel. No ecstasy was his from reading books, he talked like a blacksmith. 'Little Lydia,' he had said. Frank had never cared for sailing, now he cared for it even less; he had grown accustomed to keeping himself to himself. He no longer associated even with Reinert; the two students now functioned independently. The fact was, the egregious Reinert was putting on almost too many airs in public, with his frock coat and locket and his flow of grown-up talk. One day he greeted Fia Johnsen and complimented her on her hat; this was going too far, and Mademoiselle Fia passed by in silence. Frank, to be sure, had stood well to one side during this encounter, but Reinert had the impudence to drag him into the scandal by laughing loudly and saying: 'Did you see that, Frank?' Frank took a shortcut home.

No, and besides, he had other things to do than loiter around with Reinert, raising his cap to the girls, the ladies, and joining forces with them. Empty pleasures. He did, however, go down to the shipyard from time to time; he had found favour with Henriksen, who showed due respect for the educated man, and he would take an occasional stroll with the oldest of the little girls, Constance, and tell her of things from a wider world than hers. Mind you, Constance was still only a little girl; that is to say, she had not quite finished growing; still, she was well forward and listened gratefully to his news of the wide world. They were pleasant walks. Frank behaved nicely at the Henriksens', saying 'I beg your pardon?' and 'I beg your pardon!', accepting a cigarette, taking it out of his mouth before speaking, and drinking coffee with his little finger elegantly extended. There was no question of a major infatuation, just a small pleasure in the heart, a nice taste. Anyone could see what Reinert's vehemence might lead to: his heart would give a great jump, even in broad daylight, and in public, he would be seized by a frivolous urge to whistle, to sing. Frank kept infatuation at arm's length.

When Sunday came and Abel called at his home to take his

sisters sailing, he asked Frank once again if he wouldn't like to join them.

'No.'

'We're taking food with us, we shall go ashore and dance. The Thumbtack's taking his accordion.'

'No.'

Nevertheless, Frank's gaze followed them for quite a while as they set off; he may have felt a faint glimmer pass through him, a reflection of life outside. The poor boy had been led astray from the start. He watched a blue pulse beating beneath the surface of his wrist, his chest was growing hollow; at eighteen his child's brain had reached a weird old age.

Out in the living room his grandmother was rejoicing in his refusal to join the sailing party – ah, this was a small step in the direction of the prospective parson! Granny had orders not to disturb the student. Now, however, she timidly opened the door, carrying a cup of coffee which she begged him not to refuse.

It came just at the right moment.

'And you were right to stay at home,' she said.

'Well, what was there to go for?'

He entertained no doubts, he made no mistakes; in staying at home he was keeping prudently to the straight and narrow. He failed to realize that only he who does nothing is immune from making mistakes.

Then he buried his nose in his books again. And meals wasted a lot of his time. Indeed, a summons to come and eat merely informed him that he wasn't hungry, which he knew already.

20

And indeed it may well be that Abel made a mistake in arranging that sailing trip. Little Lydia never turned up, and the day was wasted. He stuck it out till the evening, leaping and dancing around a green island, shouting and playing the goat, but the moment he was home he set off to ferret her out and discover what her game was. He failed to find her in; it was Sunday, Little Lydia was at Police Constable Carlsen's, putting in some practice on the piano.

Right.

The following evening he again went to look for her and failed to find her. She was out; her sisters were at home.

By now Little Lydia must have heard that he wanted to talk to her, but she made no effort to meet him; she avoided him. Well, there was doubtless some perfectly natural reason for her absence; she was sure to be at home on the third evening.

But no.

Abel's spirits died down. Evidently he still regarded the world as a possible place of residence, but it wasn't an interesting world, and life was brutish and unnecessary. That day he had seen Little Lydia in the company of two other girls and Reinert – Reinert, that sexton's son who was perpetually chasing the girls – yes, it was in his company that Abel had seen Little Lydia. A fine state of affairs. That same Reinert could do with an enforced halt in his rake's progress, and Little Lydia needed sorting out. Abel would see to that, he would sort her out. But such things are not done with a sledgehammer, they are done with patience and tremendous finesse. You can't always sail into harbour, sometimes you have to kedge. He resolved not to go visiting the girl any more – far be it from him; he would meet her by accident in the street. A day or two later, however, not having seen her in the meanwhile, he was off at a canter to the old familiar backyard.

During this interval he had several times died down and blazed up, died away and blazed up again. For the moment, to be sure, he was in a flaming rage; but when he found the girl at home, all he could say was: 'Well, have you given up playing around at last? When we're married you'll dance to a different tune! Why didn't you come sailing on Sunday?'

Whether perhaps Little Lydia had been expecting him this evening, whether perhaps she had even made up her mind to a great show of friendliness, Little Lydia smiled and nodded as though returning a greeting, and said: 'Is that you, Abel?'

Abel was disarmed. By rights he should now be settling accounts with a certain person, but as the director of this proposed undertaking, he ground to a singularly crestfallen halt, mouth slightly agape.

It was Little Lydia, rather, who refused to shirk realities. 'No, the reason why I didn't come on Sunday was because I was going to play the piano. I couldn't do two things at the same time.'

'No,' he said. And yet he knew perfectly well that she hadn't been playing the piano all day, but only in the evening. Besides, she had promised his sisters to come, and then left them in the lurch. Ah well, damned if he could make it out.

She sat there on the rickety little wooden steps, sewing, effecting some repairs on minor alterations to a dress; she was handy with her hands. Then things went the way such things so often go: it must have dawned on her that she had been under attack, and why should she stand for it? This blacksmith's boy and his sisters seemed to think they were her equals, but they would have to think again. 'I've got rather more to learn than you have,' she said. 'Perhaps you imagine playing the piano's easy?'

'No.'

'The notes alone are so terribly difficult. And then there's all the practising.'

'But why do you have to learn it?'

What a simple soul he was – why did she have to learn it? Because all respectable folk learned it. She had learned to dance, she had to learn to play the piano, to do embroidery, to crochet borders for her slips; oh, the things she had to learn! Even carrying a parasol in the sun was not something she was born with, she had to practise doing it in a certain way, in the grand manner. Her sisters too had learned and learned, they weren't just anybody either, they had no intention of throwing themselves away; they sat at home, sat waiting for a ship's officer or a shop assistant. That is how respectable folk behave.

Little Lydia, then, was not unduly offended by Abel's question; she simply neglected to answer it.

Abel remained standing there.

She had put aside her thimble for a moment. Abel picked it up and started improvising: 'It's sort of veined – what can it be made of?'

'That? Ivory.'

His feeling for ivory was somewhat undeveloped. The ultimate in splendour that he had heard of was the Temple of Solomon; not thimbles. Inspired perhaps by the devil, he put the precious thimble down, ran his hand over the blue washable dress she was working on, and said: 'As far as I can make out, this must be brocade.'

She at once interpreted this as the gibe which perhaps it was, and retorted: 'A lot you know about it!'

Silence.

'You don't happen to have a spare step, do you?' he asked.

'A step? Oh, do you want to sit down? It's all yours.'

She got up and stood aside.

'No, that's not what I meant,' he said deprecatingly. 'If there isn't room on the step for both of us, I can stand.' But now, having gathered a bit of speed, he continued: 'What was I going to say? No, it's a load of nonsense, that piano playing of yours. What good will it do you when we're married?'

She literally collapsed on the step, she shrank to a dot, and it was some time before she could find words. 'What? Married to you?'

He gave her a searching look, as though trying to be objective. He was unaware that she had in effect led him up the garden path, only a little way of course, but led him up the garden path before turning him around towards the gate again and letting him go.

'I shall never marry you,' said Little Lydia.

These words, Abel concluded, amounted to a refusal. Nevertheless, he stood looking at her, looking at her as of unavoidable necessity and blinking a little from time to time. What a strange way of talking she had, just as if she meant to have none of him! She could do as she pleased, good luck to her! For the moment he was in a ferocious state of mind.

Little Lydia looked up, nodded, smiled, and said: 'I mean what I say.' Ah, but then it became clear to her beyond doubt that she had been exceedingly sharp; this was uncalled for, she could afford to relent a little. 'You could help me by holding this,' she said, handing him a pleat to hold.

No, he didn't move.

'Do you hear?' she asked, and jabbed him in the calf with her needle.

He jumped a foot, then flew into an insane rage – the devil only knows why. Without uttering a syllable beyond a single yelp of 'Ow!' he stood for a moment biting his lip, pale, ready to burst into a torrent of words. Nor did it help to appease him when Little Lydia burst out laughing. What on earth – a man who took adder bites in his stride and often raised blood blisters on his hands at the forge, and now he becomes airborne at the prick of a needle! But it was true. Now, however, she must have realized the necessity for a little correct behavior. 'Goodness, what a jackass that Reinert is!' she said.

This recalled Abel to his wits and reminded him of his mission to save her, to save Little Lydia. 'Yes,' he agreed.

'A show-off!'

'Yes. Have you only just discovered that?'

'Still, he's a smart guy. And his hair curls a little.'

'Oh, so perhaps you fancy him?'

'Me? Mama says he's improved greatly. And of course he's learned masses of things.'

'Ha-ha-ha,' said Abel. 'Baloney,' he added. 'Has he learned such a lot? I know a hundred times as much as he does, let me tell you. I'm not as good at books exactly, but I'm a hundred times better at other things.'

'Oh yes, other things!' she snorted.

'A hundred times better, and don't you forget it! You wait and see, he'll never be a parson. And the same goes for Frank, he'll never be a parson, either. A sexton's boy like him! And if you go trusting someone who looks so much more than what he is, then you're acting dumb, if you don't mind my saying so.'

'Me? It never entered my head to care for him.'

This altered the case: Abel must have felt easier at once, he could kiss her now, by golly, kiss her on the mouth. There she sat. But kissing a girl by surprise is not easy, it demands technical proficiency – you have to hit the target. No, instead he seized the grindstone standing by the wall, mustered the friskiness or the ungodly strength to lift it from its casing, and deposited it in her lap.

What next! People talk about being struck dumb, but he had never heard such an ear-splitting dumbness. Then she screamed, Little Lydia screamed and bellowed, indignation made her alien and mean. There was nothing for it but to lift the grindstone from her lap and replace it.

'You pig!' she snarled. 'How dare you—!'

'Hee-hee-hee,' he laughed, shamefaced and unhappy. 'Fancy my doing a thing like that!' Though for the matter it was remarkable how little it sometimes took to put Little Lydia in a rage. He was not like that. She must have got it from her mother.

'Look how you've messed up my needlework,' she said. 'A clean dress!'

'I'll put it under the pump,' he offered.

'Idiot!'

He tried to talk her back into a good temper, hinted darkly at his feelings for her, said he loved her, he didn't care what she thought of him, he meant to have her, he would go to every pump in the town for her sake, she must excuse his goofing with the grindstone . . .

She stood up, shook out her dress savagely, brushed off the sand, flopped down on the creaking step again, and set her jaw.

'And by the way,' he said, 'I wish I hadn't done it. Not that it's anything to worry about.'

'Indeed!' she retorted, glowering up at him, goring him with her eyes.

'I wonder where your brother Edevart is, right now?' he ventured.

'Be quiet!'

'When's he coming home, do you know?'

'Be quiet, do you hear, shut your trap!'

'Shall do!' he said and nodded. 'Just tell me which way you want it,' he said. Then he withdrew into his shell.

Needless to say, it couldn't go on like this. After a while she got up abruptly and again began knocking sand off her dress as if she was not yet presentable. But she had almost recovered her temper; she even smiled a little.

Mind you, they were not all that old, as people go. Suppose he was nineteen, that would make her a mere seventeen or so. Or if we were to tell the truth and say he was only sixteen, that would make her still less – what age would that be? And there they stood.

'What did you mean by it, you madman?' she asked, laughing.

'Mean? I don't know.'

'Look, why don't you sit down?' And she sat down herself.

Now it was his turn to be silent for a while as he stood there leaning against the rail. But when she again offered him a pleat of her dress to hold while she sewed, he took it and held it. At which she said, pointing at his hand: 'That's a funny growth of hair you've got on your hands.'

'Funny? There's nothing wrong with it.'

That hair! It had germinated in the heat from the forge, a black outer skin of which he had been proud; no one in his age group had one; he had outgrown them, left them far behind. One way and another, what a manly pair of hands he had grown!

'I'm thinking of staying out my apprenticeship with Carlsen,' he said. 'What do you say to that?'

'I don't know. How long will it take?'

'It won't take long. And after that I'm to have the forge cheap, Carlsen says. He's going to help me.'

'The forge? What will you do with that? Oh, I see, forge in it. But are you going to be there all your life?'

'Other jobs are not much better. I don't think the other fellows are anything much, either.'

'But you'll get so black.'

'And when the time comes and we get married—'

She didn't fly off the handle this time – no, but she cut him short very decidedly: 'Which isn't going to happen.'

'—Then we'll be able to afford a house,' he concluded.

'Never!'

'How do you mean?' he asked, puzzled.

'I don't love you,' she replied.

He looked at her hands, looked at her face, thought it all over. 'Oh, that will sort itself out,' he said in a tone which suggested she could regard the matter as settled.

But once again Little Lydia showed herself her quick-tempered mother's daughter; she was not going to take this lying down. 'Let go!' she ordered, tugging at the dress.

But of course it takes more than a tug before fingers like those let go.

'Did you hear me? I said let go!'

'Indeed. Just tell me which way you want it.'

With that he let go, and with that they were at loggerheads again.

'You ought to be ashamed!' said Little Lydia.

He answered with a grown-up air: 'All right then, so I'm only twenty, if that's what you mean. Or perhaps not quite twenty yet.'

'Lord, the fibs you do tell!' she exclaimed. 'Why, you're hardly anything, you were only confirmed – no, not last year, but the year before. Do you think I don't know when you were born?'

Abel had to laugh. 'Oh no, Little Lydia, you must excuse me there – considering I was born before you were even thought of. Oh no, I'm not so far short of twenty, whatever they may say. I ought to know, after all.'

'Well' – Little Lydia waved him impatiently away and said: '*I'm* being confirmed in the spring.'

'Well, that's a good thing.'

'A good thing, is it, what do you mean by that?'

Silence. He may have thought it a good thing to get it over and done with, then she would be free and ready; but he dared not provoke her any more.

'There now, I've finished my sewing,' she said, rising.

'Well, goodbye,' he said. But then he asked brazenly for a glass of water.

'If there's any here,' she answered, looking all around. 'Why don't you go in and have a drink?'

'No, I can go home and have a drink. It comes to the same thing.'

'Not at all!' cried Little Lydia. 'I'll go in and get you some water,' she said, as if to her he were the only person in the world.

When he had drunk they continued talking for a while, and by the time he left, he had succeeded after all in getting his arms around her and kissing her a good many times. Alarmingly supple and dangerous arms the blacksmith's apprentice possessed.

He was swinging them as he walked home, one of the lords of creation, the object of the girl's choice, prospective owner of a smithy. Yes, everything was sorting itself out! He would have liked to tuck himself away and avoid company, but they had a visitor at home: Maren Salt was sitting in the front room.

They were all there except the student, and they managed to get a lot of talking done in a short time; Maren Salt was busy, she had only gone into town to buy a few things, and had felt like dropping in on these old acquaintances. Oliver himself put in an occasional weighty word while their guest drank a few cups of coffee and ate buns from the baker.

'How is it you're able to get away?' asks Petra. 'Is the baby asleep?'

'Don't ask me. That Mattis is looking after him.'

'Mattis?'

'I feel the child's quite safe with that Mattis.'

'You don't mean to say that fellow Mattis looks after your child?'

'Oh, don't I? How else could I manage?' demands Maren Salt. 'I had to go out this evening and buy some things for the house, and that Mattis is sitting at home. He looks after him every time, that's the way it is.'

Oliver pronounces with digntiy: 'In my opinion, that fellow Mattis will take you, Maren, when the day comes for him to change his circumstances.'

Maren Salt is not averse to hearing this, but Petra seems almost to feel a twinge of jealousy. 'I think not,' she says. 'Well, well, it's all the same to me.'

'He could do sillier things than that,' asserts Oliver, taking Maren's side. 'Then when the time comes, he'll have the boy to train and hand the workshop over to.'

'The boy – why, he's scarce been properly born yet,' Maren objects. 'So that may not be for a long time.'

Petra says: 'I wanted to come and see him. He's a big baby, isn't he?'

'There's no denying it. The doctor says he's a thoroughbred.'

Petra sits up and takes notice. 'Did the doctor say that?'

'Yes, is there anything odd in that?'

Silence. Petra ponders. 'No,' she says at last. 'It's just something the doctor says. He's said it about mine, too: that they're thoroughbreds. I don't know what he means.'

Oliver speaks again: 'As far as I understand, he means the child is big and strong and healthy, for example. Yes, praise the Lord, ours have all been bonny.'

Petra asks: 'What sort of eyes has he got?'

'Brown eyes,' answers Maren.

At this Petra, who has again turned very strange, for all the world as if she was jealous, can't help blurting out: 'Where have you been and got brown eyes for him?'

'Hee-hee, that's what you'd like to know!' answers Maren Salt with a coquettish laugh.

'I've a pretty good idea,' says Petra, severely and bitterly. 'He's everywhere!'

Maren stares at her. 'The way you do talk! Who do you mean?'

'Oh, nobody. I mean nobody.'

'No, you needn't bother, either,' says Maren, 'because you'll never guess,' and she looks sly and mysterious and says no more. Devil take the old girl; who was the father, then? She sits there as if debating the question herself; yes, as if she has a choice and is being fastidious.

'Isn't there a drop more in the pot for Maren?' asks Oliver.

A fourth cup is poured and drunk, while they continue talking twenty to the dozen. Petra ought surely to have recovered most of her good humour as Maren Salt sits there, her own eyes visibly brown – is it to be marvelled at if her child has the same? But Petra seems for the moment to have fastened her suspicions on a particular man and to be incapable of disengaging them. 'It's him all the same,' she insists. 'He's crafty enough, he took someone with brown eyes this time, to be safe.'

'I don't understand what you're blathering about, Petra. But I may as well tell you straight out that you're blathering,' declares Maren, though still with a friendly laugh.

In her indignation Petra fails to observe decorum towards her guest. 'Do you suppose he took you for anything else but your brown eyes? Really, Maren, you can't help knowing that you're not exactly a chicken!'

At this stage Oliver appears to feel the need for him to intervene, which he does by taking his hat and limping out, accompanied by Abel. This leaves the womenfolk, five in number, young and old, sitting there. But Petra is too exasperated to be much of a hostess, and Maren Salt is in danger of breaking her coffee cup. Though cut to the raw, she restrains herself and merely says: 'True, I'm no chicken. But you, Petra, are no heifer either, remember that. And as to that, I guess you've had plenty from that man you sit there suspecting me of.'

Petra, very much aware by now that the little girls are sitting there listening, tries to laugh it off. 'I've had? Not a farthing have

I had from any man but my own husband, I'd have you know. What should anyone else give me money for? Praise the Lord, we get by on what Oliver earns.'

This is a way of diverting the conversation, but a bridge had been built, and over it they all proceed; gradually the two warring mothers come to a truce. They switch to gossip about the town and its inhabitants, the fifth cup of coffee is poured, all the womenfolk sprawl over the table and stare into each other's face. There's just been another shindy out at that Kasper's place; the fellow who works out at the shipyard, he's been beating his wife. Maren had heard the news this evening.

Petra is furious with Kasper. 'What had his wife done?'

'Something to do with another shipyard worker, of course.'

'Just let him dare try raising his hand to me!' threatens Petra.

'Well, yes – but that wife of his!' says Granny, who is old and burned out. 'Was there anything she didn't get up to that year her husband was at sea? Shipped aboard a foreign vessel as a stewardess and spent a long time in foreign parts.'

Maren Salt comments: 'It's strange she didn't have a child.'

'How do you know what she had?'

'Ah, but then she'd have had more children afterwards.'

'No,' says Petra, 'she's not the type who has children; she can do anything she likes.'

Granny falls into a reverie over this ancient episode of the young sailor's wife and her outing in foreign parts; there was talk enough about it at the time. 'And with that excellent father she, has, blacksmith Carlsen, a good, respected family, and in spite of all that . . .!'

'Such things can happen,' says Maren Salt. And she has more news from the town: the younger Olsen girl was married in Christiania halfway through the month.

'In Christiania, why was that?'

It has been in the paper; Maren has heard it read out in Davidsen's store.

'Who did she get?'

'A painter, it said.'

The little girls know all about it. 'The painter who painted paintings at Johnsen of the Wharf's and at Grits-and-Groats

Olsen's,' say the little girls; they have it all figured out, the spawn do, there's nothing wrong with their wits.

'Seems like his people are big shots, from what Davidsen was saying.'

'Strange, its being kept so quiet, no one hearing about it.'

To which Maren Salt replies: 'They say the bride was in a bit of a hurry.'

'So *that* was it!' comes a knowing whisper from the entire company. Then they all mull it over for a while.

'Yes, they get married and they struggle along, there's no end to it,' Petra pronounces. And she ventures once more onto dangerous ground: 'You can count yourself lucky, Maren, not to have got yourself entangled in all that!'

'Perhaps it isn't too late yet,' says Granny.

'That Petra of yours thinks it is,' replies Maren, taking fresh umbrage.

Petra refuses to give in. 'If I'm to speak the truth, then I should think you've put any such idea out of your head once and for all. How old are you?'

'Old enough not to remember,' replied Maren as she gets up. 'Well, I mustn't stop here all night. Thank you all very much for the refreshments and so on, and make sure you drop in on me when you're passing, Petra.'

All right, Maren Salt was no chicken; but as she walked home carrying heavy parcels from the shops as if they were nothing, her feet twinkling like a dancer's, no one could accuse her of old age. Nor had she any looks to speak of, the brown eyes were pallid and entirely devoid of any glow, but it showed the woman she was when at her age she was able to have a child. Just keep quiet about Maren Salt; she was good enough. Were fisherman Jørgen's daughters, were Lydia's daughters, any better – they who sat at home and played at being respectable folk – were they any better? And even Fia Johnsen herself, was she so very much better, she who painted lilacs, and looked at a man and a milestone with the same eye?

'I've been a long time,' said Maren Salt as she entered.

Mattis made no reply; all in all, he was not friends with her. Moreover, he was singing to the child and in the middle of a verse.

Shall I try him with a bit of town gossip? Maren may have

wondered; a bit about Kasper and his wife, a bit about the wedding in Christiania? But Mattis was not the type to be bothered with news. 'Has he been awake?'

Mattis sang the verse out and replied: 'No. But you'll very likely jabber him awake now.'

'It doesn't matter, he's due for the breast.'

A remarkable sight: Mattis the carpenter singing beside a child's cot.

He had been snorting mad, hopping mad. He had had to put up with an appalling, an insane trick of fate, and had failed to get Maren Salt out of his house before she was brought to bed; it told severely on him, it perplexed him beyond measure. What the devil, in his own house! But it wouldn't be for long; oh well, it would take two days, three days, then she'd be out on the street — come along, get a move on, and don't forget to take the brat with you! But more than a few days went by, and then day after day went by, it was an awkward business having to take a snow shovel and shovel her out, and where was she to go? And a brand-new baby, a powerful chap, it seemed, with some outrageous lungs, still, all the same ...

Mattis the carpenter was a forgiving man: he forgave a pair of doors he'd once been diddled out of, he forgave a young woman who cheated him over a gold ring, and so on. He flared up and snorted, but he forgave. What else could he do?

And of course Maren Salt was soon on her feet again and attending to her work. The baby made no great difference either way. It demanded no food, only breast and sleep; it lay in Maren's little room, in her own bed, and took up no space. Mattis found all sorts of reasons for not going sternly to work. Still, in six months' time, at midsummer, when neither of them would freeze to death, then they'd be shown the door; enough was enough! Or at most in a couple of years, when the boy was able to walk unaided.

Next he swore that he would never set eyes on the child; but this proved impossible to carry through. Maren Salt, the mother, might have gone running to the pump; the baby would decline to organize its howls accordingly but would unceremoniously summon the carpenter. This happened two or three times. Mattis ground his teeth and was the picture of an angry man, but he was not made of stone; he noticed that the baby fell silent when he spoke to it, that it grew calmer at the sound of a human voice; consequently he spoke to it more and more, and the end of it was that he took to singing. When the baby started opening its eyes and recognizing him, he lifted it up and carried it around. This monster, this droll little fellow, so light to hold in his hands – be quiet, none of this screaming for the journeyman and the boy to hear out in the workshop, shut your trap! Though no wonder you're crying, poor mite, you're cold, you've had no breast; by God, I'm going to give her a talking to! It wouldn't surprise me if she smothered you one fine night in that narrow bed. Listen, we'll take that eiderdown of yours and carry you in it. There, you see, you're warmer straightaway, and by the Lord God, I'm going to give her a talking to . . .

'He's lying here getting cold!' he calls to the mother.

'Cold, is he?'

'I don't know and I don't want to know. It's not my business. Only you're not going to let him lie here and starve.'

'He's not starving.'

'Do you think he's crying about sweet nothing, damn-all? Call yourself a mother, indeed!'

Maren Salt has found that it pays to humour the carpenter. 'I'll give him the breast,' she says.

'And make a proper job of it!' demands the carpenter. 'I can't remember a time when he's howled worse.'

Mattis goes back to the workshop, to the journeyman and the boy. He is angry and shamefaced; at the door he turns and addresses Maren: 'I'm not coming in to him every time, you needn't think that; I don't care if he screams himself to death. But we must have peace from screaming babies in the workshop, in my own house. Yes. He can't lie here screaming himself into a frazzle!'

And so Mattis goes into the workshop; the journeyman and the boy are about to leave. He fulminates against Maren and the baby: 'The things one has to put up with! But it won't be long now. I know someone who won't have them in the house any more. If it wasn't for the fact that there's a penalty for turning them out; but there's a heavy penalty for that, one of the heaviest penalties going. You know that, don't you?' he asks the journeyman.

The journeyman doesn't know too much about that, but it strikes him as not unreasonable.

'A terrible penalty, years and years. And I'm not going to risk that.'

Just now he was working on a little bed, a child's cot, for a family in another town, he said, and he had had the measurements given him, so it was a straightforward job. It was to be a handsome cot, with bars and even a bit of carving on the end pieces; furthermore, his orders were to have it painted white before sending it off. So there he was, working away at it. But deuce take that song, that little nursery rhyme, he couldn't get it out of his head for days on end, he caught himself humming at work and making himself ridiculous. A man with a nose like that, humming nursery rhymes as he planed! He suspected his journeyman of not always keeping a straight face.

He was certainly a very happy man the day he was able to send his apprentice to the painter's with the cot.

And he might have been an even happier man the day he got it back, gleaming and white as snow, and could pack it up and send it off. But Mattis had to endure yet another trick: the order for the little cot had been cancelled; the family had bought one ready-made, Mattis had received a letter to that effect. This latest misfortune, however, he took with remarkable calm, saying: 'It can't be helped, I can always get rid of the cot. But it's as I was saying: the things one has to put up with! No, one should never bother oneself with these orders from other towns.'

In short, he was saddled with the cot.

Meanwhile, the youngster in there, Maren Salt's child, might just as well borrow the cot; he could use it for a week or so until it was sold. That wouldn't do it any harm.

21

Ideally speaking, of course, a wedding should take place at the bride's home. As for Consul Olsen, he celebrated his younger daughter's wedding in the capital, in a palm court at the biggest hotel. His head was not innocent of plans, God knows if he hadn't toyed with the idea of an overseas wedding, in the Argentine, say, or Australia. To this man with his expansive outlook, it was an attractive proposition to make a splash and hit the headlines on such an occasion; a big hotel was fine, you had only to ring for five waiters. It was smart in more senses than one, for his wife would escape being overwhelmed with the effort of providing the refreshments.

Thus was the painter, the district magistrate's son, wedded to his model. There were a few whisperings in the bride's hometown at the haste and lack of warning; all things considered at every pump, there was something odd about it. But at all events, the young lady had abandoned the mercantile life and abandoned Scheldrup Johnsen; it was no longer a case of preferably him, but of preferably another.

To this wedding lawyer Fredriksen was invited; as a member of the Storting and chairman of his commission of inquiry he was, of course, already established in the capital. There was no avoiding his presence: a person of consequence, with by now an office *je ne sais quoi* about him, almost the sign of the Norwegian lion. 'Welcome!' said Grits-and-Groats Olsen, and showed his guest to a place of honour.

And it was on this occasion that lawyer Fredriksen intended to lay the foundation of his happiness and arrive at a provisional understanding with the Olsen's other daughter, the older one. It was to be a secret, they were to wait a bit, God knows why, but it formed part of his plans for the future, said the lawyer; presumably he had no intention of always remaining a member of the Storting, period. But the provisional understanding was to be gloriously binding.

Thus the Olsen's other daughter seemed likewise destined to abandon the mercantile life and the dashing men of business. She was buxom and healthy, with a luscious mouth and a superabundant crop of ash-blonde hair, while for his part the lawyer was getting on in years, no athlete, a bit of a slattern, with no Grecian nose, but a devil of a fellow; short on hair, but rich in folds of flesh at the nape of the neck – in brief, there was a shade of difference between the two. The lawyer was good enough.

He visited his hometown. Yes indeed, he had at once been made chairman of the commission of the maltreated seamen, and he held his head high. What a career! Not that he trampled anyone underfoot, but his voice seemed more powerful than ever, a thunderous pair of lungs Doubtless it came of his practice in the Storting, when he put his famous question to the government.

In the afternoon he went for a stroll around the town; all sorts of people might be wanting a word with him on his homecoming: the doctor, who wished the double consul joy of the question in the Storting; the customs officer, who was a man of the Left; the young deputy district magistrate, who was himself a lawyer in the making; and many more from the rank and file. And the Storting member denied no one a word or two in passing. For some reason or other, it was the doctor whom he least cared to be buttonholed by just now, but this there was no preventing; the others went on their way, but the doctor continued to cling to him, he was his usual self.

Yes, the doctor was the same citizen of his town. He didn't change; he visited the sick, wrote out Latin prescriptions, believed in his learning and his science, earned his daily bread. Sufficient unto him was the evil of each day. On rare occasions some small joy might befall him, as when Henriksen of the Shipyard handed him a fat banknote after the death of his wife; but by and large the doctor was a joyless man. Some time ago he had transferred his custom from one tradesman, from Johnsen, with whom he was dissatisfied, to another, to Davidsen, whom he wished to try out; but they were both alike, Davidsen too sent in his bill. The poor fellow was a consul, but he was not rich and was obliged to be small-minded; they were all shopkeepers. At present the doctor had no regular tradesman.

He earned no envy, there was nothing showy about his existence. Naturally he never grieved at himself, at his having been denied the ability to change or improve, at his being a failure in life, a lost sheep, a sourpuss, a fool, self-important despite his dubious character. It was other people, the town, and in part Providence that were at fault. Of course. He himself was as he should be.

Alas, how he might have grieved at himself!

The doctor had no taste for a genuine risk, for danger, but he never shrank from controversy; on the contrary, he stung, he needled, whenever the opening offered, and had made himself not a little feared with his tongue. A gadfly for persistence, a wasp for readiness to sting. He found it gratifying to be a man whom not everyone dared answer back. It was his daily, his hourly triumph, it made him snigger and laugh. He was not malicious by nature, far from it; his qualities were acquired, school and schematic presentation in books had made him what he was. Nor did he even attain to anything respectable in the line of malice, he had started too late; as an elderly castaway he attained only to sour dissatisfaction, to bitterness, rancour, petty vindictiveness, slander. When anyone died, this physician with the dangerous tongue would say: 'Ah well, another pair of shoes has become vacant!' And if his hearer looked a little askance, this too he found gratifying.

He couldn't leave the Storting member alone either, but stung him merrily from various directions. Thus, the doctor felt obliged to disapprove a man like lawyer Fredriksen decking himself out in high-heeled shoes even if he *had* been elected to the Storting – he walked badly enough before. That new frock coat might pass muster, but shoes like those on feet like his!

The lawyer was not aware that there was anything wrong with his feet.

'That's because you don't know anatomy.'

'I know all the anatomy I require.'

'There we have it: people go off to the Storting and don't require to know more than they know already.'

'People occasionally come back to the district physician in their constituency and supplement their knowledge.'

'Huh, it's not just a question of supplementing – people need to begin at the beginning, old man.'

The lawyer had no desire for a quarrel; on the other hand, he couldn't allow this disrespectful fellow the triumph of seeing him quit in anger. He therefore stayed and held his tongue; ah, but all the time he was at pains to show how little this doctor meant to him. 'Hullo, there's our barber, Holte. Good evening, Holte!' he said, stopping in the hope that the doctor would go. No, he didn't go. 'What time of the day are you least full, Holte? I need a haircut.'

'What, do you give yourself the bother of going to the barber's and sitting and waiting?' inquired the doctor. 'Why don't you get him to come to you?'

'We democrats are not so grand,' answered the lawyer.

'Grand, did you say? No, God knows you're not!'

They met Mattis the carpenter, and again the lawyer bade him good evening, exchanged a few words with him, and left him.

The doctor said: 'Yes, the good Mattis; if you can believe it, he's another with brown-eyed progeny in his home. He was not exactly pleased when it happened!' But here the doctor's mind switched, perhaps by some association of ideas, to another topic, and he said abruptly: 'That question of yours in the Storting was magnificent. That's the way to give it him, the filthy swine!'

The lawyer replied deprecatingly: 'No, that question is the thing I'm least happy about of what I've done in that place.'

An immediate sting from the doctor: 'What else have you done there?'

'Well, nothing,' said the lawyer, determined not to quarrel.

Having rendered the great man sufficiently small, the doctor had attained his object and could afford to make a show of friendliness. 'Naturally a lot of things go on in the Storting that we outsiders know nothing about – committee work, for example, not to mention the work of commission. It's good that you're stirring things up over the relationship between sailors and shipowners; mind you leave no stone unturned – why on earth should these shipowners make a mint? Ignorant and uneducated people who've only ever learned to stand behind a counter, but they smoke cigars with gilt bands, drink old vintage Madeira, lavish diamond rings on their wives and daughters – it makes one want to throw up. Damnation, here comes the postmaster! Well, now you'll have to excuse me, I'm off. He's decided to give his belief in multiple existences another airing. Can you imagine anything more awful than that man? The fact that his life is consciously and unremittingly directed towards the good – that alone, hee-hee. "Offspring!" he says, and rejoices in his children. He's an idiot. I hope you'll excuse my making a getaway, I don't want to do myself the injury of listening to him. Good evening, Postmaster! Keeping an eye open for God as usual? We were just talking about you.'

'I am grateful for all the good you gentlemen have spoken of me.'

'And for the evil, perhaps?'

'You at least, Doctor, haven't listened to any.'

'Really? But I too think of myself first.'

'Precisely for that reason,' said the postmaster.

The doctor gave a start and said: 'Well, well, so you think it's in my own best interests to speak well of you?'

'Yes, I do. To speak well of everyone. Mr Fredriksen, welcome home again!'

The doctor should really have been on his way, but there was something about the postmaster's mild rebuke that invited him to linger a moment and at all events to show his sting. 'Postmaster, you simply aren't of this world. You believe in the good and say: "What are we to believe?" This world demands logic and reality, not sentimentality.'

The postmaster had the advantage that these controversies invariably took place on his own territory, with which he was thoroughly familiar, and where his cogitations had at least brought him to a certain standpoint. It may have been this that so often put him in high feather, ready to defend his opinions, at times positively witty. Moreover, the postmaster was no lamb; on occasion he could wound, with downcast eyes and a faint smile. His actual words might amount to very little and be polite enough, but they were not always lacking in guile.

'I don't know what this world demands,' he said. 'For that matter, we need to consider not only what it demands but also what it ought to demand. Logic being as flimsy as it is, perhaps the world needs something more. I don't know. Logic doesn't get us anywhere.'

'Ah yes, in science.'

'Do you think so?'

'Don't I indeed! Science has no use for metaphysics and superstition; that is its logic.'

The postmaster shook his head. 'Science dances around metaphysics, and stabs and stabs at it with its spear without getting anywhere. Does it get anywhere? No. Because this fundamental life force is invulnerable and eternal. You can't stab an ocean.'

'Were you at a so-called folk high school?'* asked the doctor.

'No. Unlike you, I never attended any high school.'

This gibe tempted the doctor to rudeness: 'It would have done you no harm if you had. Then you might not have ended up in this delightful place as postmaster.'

'That's no great shakes, you think?'

'What do *you* think?'

'I'm content. Certain other people are incapable of denying themselves the pleasure of appearing great, even if they really are great. That is a fault in certain other people.'

'We were talking about science—'

The postmaster interrupted: 'No, there you'll have to excuse me! Unlike you, I'm not a scientist; I can't discuss scientific questions.'

So much the worse for you,' retorted the doctor. He continued: 'Scientific truths are one or both of two things: self-evident or logically demonstrable. Well then, metaphysics is neither.'

'But, my dear doctor, I neither claim nor believe that metaphysics is science. Surely it's almost the exact opposite.'

'Then it's poppycock, my dear postmaster, pure unadulterated poppycock! If we didn't have science, what *would* we have? Moses and the Prophets – let's hear what they've got to say!'

'Metaphysics takes over where science ends.'

'Science is never-ending. It fumbles, it doesn't always quite reach its goal, but it keeps going and keeps going, it's always advancing.'

'Yes, so they say,' answered the postmaster. 'I expressed myself badly, of course. What I meant to say was that metaphysics sets to work just where science doesn't quite reach its goal – at the two or three points, minor points, details, where science has not exactly reached the absolute apex. There's only a hair's breadth in it. Let's have it at that.'

'Attempting a bit of sarcasm, are you? Hee-hee, and you believe

* From the mid-nineteenth century, folk high schools, originating in Denmark, were a widespread form of adult education in the Scandinavian countries. They led to no degree or diploma, were cultural rather than vocational, and were attended largely by agricultural workers and others with little previous formal education. Trans.

in a whole system of existences as the explanation of life's mystery. That's what lights you on your way.'

'What is one to believe? At times the light it gives out is indeed faint, like the stars at night. It isn't a strong light; it isn't the sun and broad daylight, it's only the stars at night. Enough to distinguish things by, very faintly.'

'Wouldn't it be better to take the light of science as far as it will reach?'

'I have that, too. It's when it stops that I have to make do without. Then science is left far behind – that's to say, a hair's breadth behind – and peers after me as I go on.'

'No, on that point you must excuse me – science has something other to do than peer after you. But in so far as it falls behind, it does wisely enough, it requires solid ground under its feet.'

'A ground that shifts every second generation.'

'That's what the simpletons say, those who know least about it. Does mathematics, for example, shift its foundations?'

'Mathematics – to give you a little more amusement rather than to answer your question – mathematics has from the very beginning to "assume" something. It searched by the light of my stars and found a rickety X to stand on. An honour for X, in the absence of anything better.'

'Briefly and to the point: so mathematics is no use?'

'Do you think so? It's certainly a great deal of use to people who like brain work pure and simple for its own sake. Mathematics stands by itself and is what it is. But it's completely irrelevant to our spiritual life.'

The doctor clapped both hands to his ears as if to block them, an involuntary gesture of perplexity. Why had he sought this pointless altercation, which bored and exhausted him? He stopped short of blocking his ears, perhaps he wavered for a moment between screaming aloud and taking to his heels; then he checked himself, yes, he even impelled his resolution to the point of raising his hat and saying: 'Well, thank you, I've had enough now. I have a sickbed to visit with my poor science!' And he cut across into a side street.

When the postmaster in turn made as if to go, the lawyer detained him; they were about to pass C. A. Johnsen's store, the double consulate, and the lawyer wanted someone to talk to past the windows. Oh, he knew what he was doing when he chose this route: he meant to walk right out to the double consul's residence and beyond, up the hill known as the Prospect. He had his reasons.

The lawyer raised his voice to the pitch of a certain question in the Storting: 'Everything you've said, Postmaster, may be all right up to a point, I have a lot of sympathy with it. But won't all this metaphysics and spirituality make us unfitted for life here below? Won't it inhibit our dynamism?'

'Since you ask, and with no intention of instructing you – yes, I hope it will curb us a little. We *need* to shrink from fleecing each other too blatantly. You don't disagree with that, do you?'

'No.'

'At present we labour senselessly at shoving each other aside in order to get a chance for ourselves; we have to compete, we're told, and do more than compete. What if we were to work a little more *on* ourselves instead of *for* ourselves?'

'But supposing it's precisely this working on ourselves that makes us, in worldly terms, less dynamic? Then, surely, we shan't get on in the world?'

'But we shall go *up* in life. Just think if from time to time we bore it in mind that we shan't live here below for hundreds of years at a stretch! We come into the world, stare at everything for a little while, and go out again. Really now, Mr Fredriksen, we can get *on* without having to get on *top* of others.'

'We're born with different endowments, perhaps to different destinies. Napoleon's activity was of this world; he wanted to get on, even if that meant getting on top of others.'

'But that wasn't the side of him that conferred the most blessings on himself and the world.'

'That may have been his destiny. He and others – we all act as we're impelled to act.'

'Yes, we assert the superior force of destiny. That gives us a delightful excuse for our own behaviour.'

Really now, the postmaster was becoming a bit too free and easy, perhaps even personally offensive; the lawyer would have none of this, this was not what he had brought him along for. 'I'm going right up to the Prospect,' he said. 'I hardly imagine you're going that far?'

'No,' said the postmaster, and turned back.

Lawyer Fredriksen heaved a sigh of relief and looked at his watch; everything was going according to calculation. The crowning mercy was that he had got rid of the doctor, for he was aware of the man's stained relations with Consul Johnsen, and was reluctant to be seen in his company just now. To hell with spirituality and metaphysics, to hell with anything of that kind which gets in the way of our life here below; are we not to get on in the world? Not that he intended to trample anyone underfoot exactly, lawyer Fredriksen had no intention of doing that, but neither did he intend to be curbed. Herein he showed a healthy dynamism. But run a man down, stick a knife in him? Not a bit of it! Consul Johnsen's chief clerk, Berntsen, was very likely expecting a police search and interrogation, but nothing was going to happen; his master the shipowner could go in peace.

Perish the thought that he should make himself more disagreeable to Consul Johnsen than he already had! The lawyer had shown his claws, but he did not wish to use them; the chairman of the commission had humane reasons, and lawyer Fredriksen intimate ones, for acting thus.

He walked past the double consul's house with its ornamental carving and veranda and balcony; a large house, a garden full of lilacs and jasmine, an aroma of riches and culture, a fountain, concrete urns, butterflies, flagpole, all the trappings. He turned off up the hill – correct, Fia was out for her evening walk; Mademoiselle Fia was relaxing after the labours of the day. He had not forgotten her, he had not given her up; he looked upon her as before, as the pauper looks at the millionaire. His prospects with her could only be regarded as having improved; perhaps the lady would now desist from standing in her own way and getting her sums all wrong. Surely she and her family must by now have acquired a respect for his performance in the Storting?

At this point she caught sight of him behind her and lengthened her stride.

Oh, the lady didn't get her sums right at all; she was quite unversed in sums, had no use for sums. How she was shaped and made, God alone knew.

She continued to increase her pace, but in vain; he overtook her, and what's more, during that rose-red evening hour he received her final answer. How she forged ahead, how she tried to give him the slip! How she must have yearned for the sunset and for beauty, to strive so hard! But lawyer Fredriksen was not the man to throw in the sponge.

He doffed his hat to her back and said breathlessly: 'You've nearly walked me to death, Miss Fia.'

She (elegant and pale, with many perfections, slightly over-dressed as usual, cool, every inch the Countess): 'I'm sorry about that. My thoughts were far away; I always come up here when I want to be alone.'

'Is it good to be alone so much?' he asked. 'What do you think about when you come up here like this?'

'About all this!' she answered, pointing at the whole wide world, at the clouds, the sea, Nirvana. 'Yes, it does me good.' And she seemed scarcely to understand this man, this animal, who stood there, devoid of all noble delight in nature. What a deficiency in a man!

'I've just come home from the Storting, I wanted very much to call on you.'

'That was kind.'

'You too have been away for a while?'

'I come and go, you know. I'm just off to Paris.'

He must have thought: The devil she is! Big, big, it has to be big, Notre Dame, the Eiffel Tower, Rothschild. And at this moment he may have felt a certain fear that he was beneath her, since he said: 'What are we Storting members and lawyers to say about the really big things? That they are unattainable. But we can attain quite a bit, we also, Miss Fia.'

A black speech for the lady to hear.

'I mean we can rise, we also, step by step, reach higher and higher positions. That is the good thing about a democratic society, that one and all can attain the highest offices.'

Silence. The lady seemed not to be weighing his chances.

Right, so lawyer Fredriksen proceeded to business, gave her to understand what she meant to him, that she meant absolutely everything to him, and so perhaps she could give him some hope, a little more hope than last time?

'No,' said the lady.

Did he hear correctly; would she not think it over this time, either?

'No,' she said, shaking her head. 'And now look at that sunset,' she said, 'that's what you should be doing. Look at those colours! How magnificent the world is from here!'

He refused to give up: 'Yes, the prospect is pretty enough,' he said, 'but what about the prospects?'

She looked questioningly at him.

'My prospects? My future?'

And now she really did grow rather annoyed: he could very well have used somewhat different words when she was showing him colours. Was there no poetry or culture in this person? 'No, excuse me,' she said, 'your future is something you must discuss elsewhere.'

22

It all recoiled on Oliver, an innocent man who had done nothing to upset lawyer Fredriksen's plans. Why should he have to suffer for it?

Oliver was slinking home from the warehouse when the lawyer overtook him and proceeded directly to business. 'Well, Oliver, you have a permanent position, and it's time you paid off the mortgage on the house.'

Anything could have caused it, but the lawyer had just come down from the Prospect, from a business transaction which he had lost, and perhaps he was keen to win the next one. Had he no very great faith in the binding nature of the understanding with Consul Olsen's daughter? Or was he suspicious about the dowry? At all events, he spoke now briefly and to the point, like a man forced to save what could be saved; no, there was nothing faltering or foot-loose about his words.

Oliver's answer was simply, how could he pay off the mortgage on the house out of his wages at the warehouse, which were barely enough to live on?

'And what precisely has that got to do with me?' demanded the lawyer. 'Sell the house and pay me my money; then we shall be quits.'

Then what were Oliver and his family to do with themselves?

'Here we go again!' exclaimed the lawyer. 'Is it some sort of obligation on my side that you're counting on? Think again – the house is depreciating in value year by year; you don't even keep it painted, it's rotting away.'

'I'd thought of having it painted this summer.'

'No, I won't have this sort of thing going on any longer. You know where my office is – either you or your wife will come.' And with that the lawyer left him.

Naturally Oliver had to send his wife; she managed it once before and was more cut out for it. Moreover, it so happened that Petra was just now looking particularly good and particularly cheerful, and she had got some attractive new underwear, so that she must have been feeling in remarkably fine fettle throughout her being. No one could blame her for that. And she wanted to get going right away, that very evening. Oliver objected that the office would be closed at that hour. 'Then I'll knock at his other door,' Petra answered. Oliver could not but admire this enthusiasm and exhorted her: 'Well now, see that you make him realize what it is he means to do to a cripple.'

When Petra had gone, Oliver took from his pocket some goodies and buns that he had brought with him for himself and the little girls. He made no distinction between them, he divided tolerably well, and the one with the blue eyes, Bluebell, got if anything the largest share, since she was the nicest and really the sweetest, when all was said and done. Funny it should turn out this way. The father had long expected to see a horse's nose on that blue-eyed face, but was blessedly fooled. In his joy over this he now made quite as much fuss over the blue-eyed child as over her with the 'family eyes.' On one occasion he had beaten Bluebell, when she flopped into the sea off his own quay. No limping then; he flew to save her, he drew her up from the deep with his crutch. When she opened her eyes, he gave a sudden cry and smashed his clenched fist a couple of times into her wet bottom. His joy was transformed into momentary fury. Otherwise, he never beat his children. That was the mother's jobs. Oliver was the one who had the better way with the little ones, and who had their entire hearts in return.

And now the three of them are sitting there enjoying each other's company, and sharing this little secret about the candy. It's as if they're dividing up and devouring stolen goods; they have fun pretending that Mama's coming, Granny's coming; they set some aside for their brothers, for the student and the blacksmith's boy. Truly, there never was such a father for throwing a children's party. Then he tells them about his voyages on the seven seas, how he has knocked about the world and seen people who could eat burning hurds and dogs that drew milk carts. 'Great suffering snakes!' say the little girls. Huh, that was nothing to what he's seen: monkeys, peacocks, camels (like what Abraham, Isaac, and Jacob had), savages with rings in their noses, tropical cloudbursts, active volcanoes. Once he had seen a pirate chaser, a clipper, three-master, with thirty-one sails set; another time a murder in a café in broad daylight. 'Goodness!' shudder the little girls, 'weren't you ever attacked by horrid people yourself?' It would have taken some doing to attack *him,* he replies; to attack a man such as he was in those days, he replies. Alas, it was his destiny to be disabled and paralysed. The little girls pity him, and the three sit there like three women.

Suddenly they think they hear someone coming; Dad hastily clears the table, cramming two whole buns into his mouth at the last moment, and sitting there with immovable jaws. Screamingly funny he looks, like a stuffed animal, with his solemn face and his mouth full of buns. False alarm, no one coming, the conspirators are safe. And now the little girls are overcome with boisterous merriment; they ask Dad questions to make him talk, they tickle him in the ribs, pinch his cheeks, laugh till they choke. Dad has to climb on a chair to chew his way out. Three children.

After a while there enters Frank, the student, worn and grey from his day's work, as though weakened by debauchery. He eats his food and his buns in silence; he is still struggling with the meagre memorizing fare he has come from. There is something pitiful about the boy, with his off-the-peg charity clothes and hands that have no grip, so good at languages and so immature.

His father, Oliver, evidently thinks there can be no harm in addressing a few words to him with fatherly effect: 'You mustn't study so terribly hard, Frank, it'll make you poorly. And as I see it and as I understand it, you know more than any man in the town, for what that's worth.'

Frank says nothing.

'Come, tell us a bit about what you've been reading and looking into today.'

Well, they don't understand it, but Frank drops a hint or two, to give them some faint idea of the thing. He mentions verbal forms, suffixes, dissimilatory substitutions; he lowers himself almost to the dust and explains case and gender. The delirious orator has it in his head, he expels it via the mouth, noises, a laboriously acquired figment of the imagination which occupies him night and day, birds' chatter, a gigantic mess-up. He treats it all as something choice and precious; when the little girls repeat a word wrongly, he corrects them; the little man becomes a great man thereby; in his learned ignorance he has attained the cocksureness of the schoolboy. No one has taught him to think; under the pressure of his task he has merely trudged and drudged ahead. There can be no question of his having misused his time and his strength – he has reduced life to linguistic knowledge without ever feeling cheated. Thus, he walks and walks in his wilderness, a futile, follish trek made not in order to arrive somewhere but simply and solely in order to be one of those who walk in the wilderness. And this work of his is a life sentence.

He is boring his audience; Dad yawns, the little girls go further and rise from the table. Frank observes their defection; somewhat chagrined, he says fretfully: 'Yes, that will be the day, when I sit here and actually teach you something!'

The little girls flop quickly back into their chairs, and Dad makes excuses for them. 'They'll never learn it in any case, it's too deep for them. But we all think it's one of the most extraordinary things we've ever heard. And I've heard darkies talking, while knocking about the world.'

But Frank has been put out of humour, he is fagged out and impatient; he prepares to go out, to get away from them.

'Are you going out?' asks Dad.

'Yes.'

'Well, all right, and thanks for what you've just been telling us. But that German words should have sexes – because after all, I've heard more Germans than most people – still, if you say so—'

'Your tie ain't on proper,' Bluebell informs him.

As a stickler for accuracy, Frank corrects this speech, pulls it to pieces, shows the full extent of its wretchedness. Really, it's hopeless struggling with them, they haven't been learning languages from the age of eight. So he goes out and forgets about his tie.

The three of them are on their own again. Their good humour, too, has been destroyed; they seem unable to recover their gaiety, and the Brunette is angry with Frank. Dad makes excuses for him. 'Yes, but he's not going to be a parson, so what does he have to learn all that for?' 'Be quiet. The headmaster isn't a parson either, he's a scholar. What are you talking about?'

Now Abel comes home, and since he has already had supper at the blacksmith's, he is given only two small goodies. But Abel is a bit of an oddity, and when he has dispatched the candy, he produces from his pocket a fresh supply of titbits that he himself has brought with him for the others. You see, Abel gets regular daily meals at the blacksmith's house, whereas at home their way of life is highly erratic, and it's not every evening that his sisters, or perhaps even Dad, go to bed as satisfied customers. As Abel puts the two little bags on the table, he yells at them that they are not to touch the sweets – he has bought them for himself, don't you dare taste them, he's going to smack his lips over them himself, in bed. Whereupon his sisters and his dad fling themselves on the bags and stuff themselves with sweets. 'Robbers!' roars Abel. 'Have you got any more?' asks the Brunette. 'I'll give you more!' 'Ha-ha!' But suddenly Dad whispers: 'What about young Frank?' It turns out that Abel's pocket contains two Danish pastries especially for Frank.

They stuff themselves, they have a good time. Mother and Granny are left out of the reckoning; those two drink coffee galore and have their own good times, they often have a blowout on their own. It is Oliver, Dad in person, who has introduced these secret mini-banquets. They probably began with his desire to do well by the little ones, but they have degenerated as time goes by, as this man finds less and less need for openness; it is easiest to meet the children in the passage and slip them a titbit which they can swallow on the spot. Ah, they all have their memories of these blessed deceptions, of this daddy who does good by stealth. Do you remember when ... Do you remember when? they say to each other. All things considered, there is no one quite like Daddy.

There they sit.

'Look at his hands and wrists,' says Dad of Abel. 'Just like mine were when I had the use of my limbs.'

'Let me see, Abel,' says the Brunette, plucking at the beard on his hand. He yells, he complains to Dad: 'You're the oldest, can't you speak to her?'

The evening wears on, the cottage is filled with family life. The world outside is an irrelevancy. They have no yearnings for anything better; what better could there be? Hullo, Bluebell had even got a bit of colour in her cheeks from stuffing herself with Danish pastries. Here we have a father surrounded by his children. In outward appearance he is fat and gentle, and if not examined too closely will pass as innocent. What children he has! The little girls are bright, bright as buttons; they are fiendishly quick-witted, real smart; they figure out a lot. Frank is already a scholar, and Abel already a man. Nothing could be better; with sweets thrown in, it is paradise.

Now it is time for Abel to go across to the old cottage, to Granny's part, where he lodges. His lair is a bench that turns into a bed at night. It serves admirably; Abel is tired and sleeps like a log. Off he goes, for of course he has to be at the smithy early in the morning.

Shortly afterwards the girls too retire to bed, and Frank comes home to his little room; Oliver sits by himself at the table. Petra seems to be taking a long time, heaven knows what she's up to. He yawns, takes out his pocket mirror, and examines himself in it. When Petra comes in he means to ask her what she's got to show for this long absence; without fail, he will pose her this question.

When Petra at last comes in, she has a piece of news for him; she averts all disapproval by getting in first with: 'There's a foreign steamer in.'

The former sailor rises at once to the bait and asks: 'Where?'

'She came into the quay.'

At this news Oliver forgets everything and hobbles out to have a look. He is gone a fair while, and when he comes in again, he is able to show off his expertise: 'To judge by her flag, she's an Engelsman.'

'An Engelsman!' cries Petra.

'She has the same kind of portholes as the grain carriers, so she must be bound for Grits-and-Groats Olsen.'

To keep him happy, she continues to affect an exaggerated interest and exclaims: 'For Grits-and-Groats Olsen – trust you to find that out!'

'Well,' he says, 'you don't suppose I've knocked about the world for nothing, do you?'

Here she takes the opportunity of interpolating: 'I know I was a long time at the lawyer's, but you see, I had to talk to him.'

'Yes,' Oliver acknowledges. 'What did he say?'

'He grumbled.'

'The Scrooge! If only I had the full use of my limbs! But what agreement did you come to?'

'Well, he softened up a bit after a while. He's willing to take his time. But getting him to that pitch wasn't the work of five minutes.'

'No.'

'He said I was to come again next week.'

Well, at least that gives a respite. Oliver says: 'Let me see that you handle it properly – that you pay him back for all he hands out to you, the monster.'

With which he goes out again. It's that Englishman that excites him. His sailor's heart yearns after that foreign steamer at the quay; he wants to see her at close quarters, inhale her smell, a vessel from foreign seas and ports, English language, half-naked stokers, the skipper up in the clouds on his bridge. He stumbles into many inquisitive townsfolk on the quay; he meets fisherman Jørgen and the inevitable Olaus, with his pipe in his mouth.

'I'm glad you came,' says Olaus. 'Now you can help me to get some tobacco in my pipe. They don't understand what I'm shouting about.'

Oliver is nothing loath to be the English-speaker, and when a gangway is let down, he goes on board. But Olaus is so immutably the old Olaus that he pulls a face at the tobacco they give him: there's no more than will go on his thumbnail, and he's tasted better, ugh. 'Isn't there someone else with good strong tobacco – where's the mate?'

The English sailor appears to understand the Norwegian words, or perhaps he has merely read Olaus's discontented face; but to cut a long story short, he puts away his tobacco and goes off.

Oliver follows him with his eyes, and a far-off memory flickers through his mind. Has he met this foreign seaman before, or at the very least someone he reminds him of? He might have seen him in a seaport, in a street, in a hiring hall, but where? The world is so wide, and Oliver has knocked about it.

He encounters another member of the crew, and tries out his almost long-forgotten English on him, learns where the ship is from and to whom in the town she is consigned; everything is of interest and takes him back to his former life at sea. He learns how much cargo the boat carries, how many hands are aboard, how old the captain is, how long they have taken getting here from the Baltic. In return Oliver describes himself, an old seaman, started as a nipper, was A.B. at the time of his accident, when the barrel of whale oil came and smashed him up. Well, that was a tidy while back, and a few years ago he had salvaged a large derelict, single-handed, you might say – that wasn't bad for a cripple. For example, it had got him into the papers. For many years now he had been manager of Consul Johnsen's warehouse over yonder. He was married, and he and his wife had four children; one of the boys was a student.

Olaus is frankly fed up with listening to all this chitter-chatter in an unintelligible language, and goes ashore. The Englishman is more patient; incidentally, he turns out to be the mate, the second mate, but not hoity-toity and dressed up; on the contrary, a splendid fellow. He even takes a bit of interest in this funny little town he's about to discharge in. Oliver forms an excellent impression of him.

By the time he goes ashore he is full of knowledge, and competent to gather his acquaintances around him for his report. Fisherman Jørgen is a loyal listener, old and slow-witted; he stands where he stands, listens, says little, hangs on the speaker's words, and doesn't abscond, no racehorse is he. There is something submissive about the worn old fisherman; his wife must have bowed his will in the course of half a century. Ah, but he is too solid to be the jumpy type. Mind you, old Lydia is hot-tempered and capable; to this day she is the town's handiest washerwoman, to this day she has a tongue like a grater; but she has never got her husband to hurry or hustle, he is heavy and guileless, with a stoop.

God knows, perhaps he has rather too many daughters-of-the-house surrounding him, occupying chairs in his cottage. His son, Edevart, is at sea.

Although the foreign vessel is an ordinary cargo boat, Oliver boasts about her as though she were his own: he has gone about on board and had a look around. The saloon was in mahogany, with gilding—

'You weren't in the saloon,' interrupts Olaus.

'What, I wasn't in the saloon?'

Olaus lets out a yell: 'Do you mean to tell us you were in the captain's saloon? The captain's ashore.'

Oliver gives way: 'But I went past the saloon and saw it all. I can't think why you never manage to keep your trap shut.' He turns to the others and continues: 'The captain must be a rich man.'

'Did he tell you so himself?' asks Olaus.

At this point Oliver stops short, the warehouse manager stops short – he is too good to stand there bickering with someone so far beneath him. The cripple has his pride.

But Olaus had his, too. He too stood where he stood; had anyone ever seen him give way? When Oliver and the others left the quay, Olaus remained behind, for no other purpose in the world than to be the one who didn't go. A stiff-necked, crazy creature, with no malice in him, only a tongue that was lamentably loose. Permanent boozer that he was, he never bowed his head or begged for anything but tobacco. He had no manners, and refused to touch his forelock to the town dignitaries. His formidable health allowed him to sleep anywhere, indoors or out.

Neither a skipper nor a doctor nor a consul nor any of the little town's stock-in-trades, but a dock-walloper with a tobacco pipe, a wreck containing valuable iron; there was something of a man in the poor bastard.

He too might be thought to have one or two things to complain about; he too was a cripple, knocked flat by an accident, facially disfigured, a man with one hand, but thank God still a hand left; he didn't take to tears, he just reared a bit, whoa. Then he diluted his sorrows in brandy and put up with them. A bit of an oddity – it never occurred to him to steal outright, you could trust him with your goods on the quay; but he was a mighty expensive beast of burden who would fleece you if given half a chance. His rudeness was that of a straightforward, genuine man. He never slunk away into hiding; he stepped forward like the man he was, rough and irresponsible, full of assurance. All in all, a mixture of good and bad qualities. Was he known to go on jaunts to the neighbouring towns for the sole and exclusive purpose of fighting? Don't you believe it, Olaus undertook these jaunts in order to do a little desperate drinking and bolster himself up. The missing hand didn't bother him; it couldn't grip, but it could lift and carry. One-handedness is the good fortune of not being without hands – that's the good fortune it is. Olaus escaped despair, he had a hand. He looked most decidedly down on the fat Oliver, who hobbled along the quay and hadn't even got legs, poor bastard.

Between the two cripples there was mutual contempt. Beyond a doubt, Olaus was the superior. Oliver knew this and could not curb his envy, which manifested itself in an obtrusive compassion for his brother in misfortune; he pitied him because misfortune had turned him into a drunkard who raved and beat his wife. 'I don't beat her,' bawled Olaus. 'It was only when she started keeping company with other men. You look to your own wife.' At which Oliver's compassion knew no bounds and he said: 'It's a great pity the way your face looks, but it's even worse about your hands. There's just no way you can help yourself, you can't even thread a needle. I do feel sorry for you.'

Well, no, Olaus couldn't thread a needle; that was just one of the things he couldn't do. But neither was he delicate and hairless and womanish about the face; on the contrary, he was bony and sharp-featured, dark-bearded and dark-complexioned; the charge of gunpowder that exploded into his cheeks had stayed there forever and refused to grow lighter. Whereas Oliver's face was smooth and round as a baby's bottom, with hanging cheeks and a moist mouth. There was very little attractive in Olaus; in Oliver there was something repulsive. Ah, but in the last resort it was he who was top dog, he who had the wilier head, greater gumption. Was he not at this very moment, as he walked home in the evening twilight, in the grip of a bright idea – that here was a chance to dispose of his eiderdown, to ship it quietly out of the town and out of the country?

You see, he had this eiderdown up in his loft, tied-up capital, the untying of which would hurt nobody, would on the contrary benefit a whole family, Oliver's family, threatened as it was with eviction. As an offence, the whole affair dissolved into nothing; it was spread over a hundred petty pilferings of a handful of eiderdown, spread over half a generation – had the town dignitaries a cleaner slate for this same period of time? And be that as it may, the thefts were already committed, and disposing of the goods and preserving them against moth and rust could hardly increase his guilt. Might not eiderdown spoil from lying too long in a loft?

Other people were not a hair's breadth better than he; they merely lacked the initiative to bring off a coup, or else they had never been forced to it. They would have liked to, all right, not doing so bothered them greatly, but they were fettered; they were the prisoners of their own honesty, prisoners who fretted at their inability to let themselves go. That was it. So what demands could one make of a man like him, like Oliver, a poor unfortunate cripple with a large family? Was he not equally capable of noble and upright conduct, when he could afford it? But when had he ever been able to afford it? He lived his life like a mushroom in the dark, manager of a warehouse with temptations in every corner, in winter so cold as to give him chilblains, in summer reeking so ineluctably of liver and whale oil as to take his breath away and send him staggering back when he opened the warehouse door in the morning. Small wonder, then, that he did not remain entirely innocent and velvety of soul. So much of what he did was darkened by a shadow; darkness and he seemed to have some tacit understanding – really, the marvel was that he hadn't murdered the double consul and stolen his warehouse.

But he had more wit than to do that; he perpetrated no lunacies that came to light. His methods of weighing and measuring goods were impossible to supervise and varied somewhat according to the customer, while his Sunday outings with the boat were consistently veiled in mystery; it was at night that he came home bringing some item or other with him, such as this eiderdown hidden in his armpit. In the course of the years it had grown to a handsome chunk of eiderdown; it would all go into a sack, but when loose was enough to fill a small room. The English steamer might provide a market for it.

Oliver takes his time; his sagacity prescribes caution. Entirely as a joke, and as if to test him, he asks his learned son Frank the English for *ederdun,* and of course Frank turns over a few pages in a dictionary, the work of a moment, and finds the word: eiderdown. Starting that evening, Oliver takes to making regular trips to the quay when he has finished at the warehouse, showing himself down there, talking to the Englishmen, taking little turns. It leaks out of him that he has some eiderdown – anything doing? Yes, very likely, says the mate, the second mate. He has some eiderdown, has he – how much? 'Well, only a little, enough for a bed or so.' A sailor standing by says: 'You mean, not enough for another bed as well?' Yes, there might well be, Oliver has been buying small wads over the years; he must certainly have enough for two beds or so ...

They talk it over. Oliver hasn't exactly got a licence to deal in eiderdown, he has no shop, but he can bring a sample that night. An agreement is reached.

The sample is fine, incomparable, superterrestrial; a fleck escapes and floats up into the clouds. To lie on eiderdown is to soar aloft, to swing in the air. A fresh agreement is made concerning price and time of delivery; the gentlemen do not haggle. They calculate in pounds, but Oliver can't accept pounds, they would look too suspicious in his hands. *All right,* they consider the matter; he's to be paid in Norwegian currency – if not before, then just as they're sailing, depend upon it! Oliver has the generous nautical heart; besides, he likes the gentlemen and has faith in them. He will fetch the down bit by bit and they can settle up at the end. Not worried about the payment, not in the least, *gentlemen*!

They invite him to join them in corners and behind bulkheads in order to keep him to themselves, they hand him various edibles, they treat him like a brother; a different story this, from the crew of the *Fia,* who scarcely had eyes for a cripple. Ah, there's no one like the English; Oliver is virtually sat down on their collective lap, is chatted up and quizzed. It's all right for him to answer with a Norwegian word or two when stuck, they don't mind, they'll be sure to *make it out.* By now they have seen just about everyone in the town, but they haven't seen the postmaster – does that man simply squat there day and night in the inner office, sitting on the registered mail? Mate and sailor take an interest even in such irrelevancies as whether the postmaster had an apartment for his family over the office. They also discuss Oliver's personal affairs: so he has a student son? Great. Oliver has a pretty wife, they know that, very good figure, they have seen her on the quay; why doesn't he bring her down to see them? They won't eat her …

They offer him drinks, but for these Oliver has no taste; whereas they have noticed his fondness for food and have scrounged from the steward one or two delicacies for him, which he eats on his own. Peerless *gentlemen*!

Finally, the unloading is completed and Oliver brings the last instalment of eiderdown. This evening he finds only the sailor; it is blowing a gale and raining. The captain and first mate are at a farewell party given by Consul Olsen; the second mate has toothache and sends his apologies, he's decided, weather or no weather, to go for a walk along the country road and work up a sweat; his mates are ashore.

Everything is in order, Oliver is to get the money during the evening, Norwegian money – indeed, that's what the second mate has gone for.

As the only people on board, they don't need to confine themselves to corners and bulkheads. The sailor invites his guest to beefsteak and fried potatoes in the forecastle. It proves a memorable meal, Oliver golden and hazy within from satiety and well-being. His eye falls on a chest, and another old memory flashes through him. He looks at the sailor and is on the point of shouting 'Adolf!'

'What's your name?' he asks.

'Xander,' answers the sailor.

Silence.

'It's strange,' says Oliver, 'how like my old chest that one is.'

The sailor answers casually: 'Really? It's not mine. It belongs to one of the others.'

'It's not yours?'

'No. If you've had enough, I'll take your plate out. Come, let's go up on deck.'

'Exactly like my old sea chest. Same kind of handles, green; we used to shred tobacco on it, there's the mark—'

'Really?'

'What did you say your name was?'

223

'Xander. Let's go on deck. They may come on board again any moment.'

They go up. It's blowing and raining, darkness is falling fast, the sky is utterly cheerless. They stand by the rail looking out, they talk about the weather and shake their heads. By now the ship has been cleared, the pilot is waiting in the hotel, but they will hardly be sailing before morning.

Something moves over by some crates on the quay; a tarpaulin is lifted, and a head sticks out and listens – the head of Olaus, who has turned in for the night.

Oliver, who is perhaps still plain fuddled, in some degree, after his mighty meal, suddenly asks: 'Where did you get it?'

The sailor doesn't understand.

'That chest. I sold it to a boy named Adolf.'

'It's not my chest, I tell you!'

'No, excuse me, it's not yours, but—'

The sailor says: 'If you're going home now, look in first thing tomorrow morning. We shan't sail tonight.'

It was then about eleven o'clock.

23

Oliver starts off home in a state of some confusion. Does it take no more than a good meal and an old sea chest to set his mind reeling? Does Oliver in fact possess all that wilier a head, all that greater gumption, than the man under the tarpaulin?

He meets some of the Englishman's crew as they go back on board; the lads have come from the hotel and are tolerably merry. Oliver recognizes the situation from of old.

Outside Grits-and-Groats Olsen's house he sees some people holding umbrellas and lanterns; it is the gentlemen of the farewell party who are saying goodbye before going home. The double consul is not among them, nor is Consul Heiberg, who likewise gives himself airs and doesn't mix with the Olsens. Oliver sees lawyer Fredriksen and hears his thunderous voice; he sees and recognizes the two Englishmen, the captain and the first mate;

recognizes Davidsen, the postmaster, the municipal engineer, the customs officer. This makes up the party. It occurs to Oliver that he can to some extent safeguard his eiderdown money by getting some official information about the ship's departure, so he decides to follow the two ship's officers. His gumption has returned.

'Good night, good night!'

The postmaster has no umbrella to lend, but asks the group at large: 'Won't anyone borrow my lantern? I live so near. You, Captain?'

'No, thanks. God bless!'

The postmaster shares an umbrella with Mr Davidsen, who is going the same way; the lantern he carries so that most of the light from it falls on his companion. In the high wind they talk little, and that little is only of commonplace matters. Davidsen, who is a small-tradesman-cum-consul, has nevertheless noticed something this evening, and when they stop outside his door he asks mysteriously: 'Did you see how taken up the lawyer was at the party?'

'Taken up?'

'With the lady, the daughter, what's her name, Olsen's daughter, the older.'

No, the postmaster has not seen that.

'That could mean something perhaps,' opines Davidsen.

'Perhaps it could. He has nice children, Consul Olsen has, nice girls, the one who married the painter and this one who's left, charming ladies. I'm thinking of what you said – no, what could it mean? She's so young and nice-looking; the lawyer must be twice her age.'

'Crazier things have happened before now.'

'Yes indeed. Yes, we labour and travail and take wives and struggle and strive and arrange to die at a great age! I beg your pardon, you were going to say something.'

Small-tradesman-cum-consul Davidsen was not exactly going to say anything, but he has made some movement, given a little start, fearing perhaps that the postmaster is about to launch into another of his tedious disquisitions, and therefore answers: 'I was only going to say you could take my umbrella.'

The postmaster declines. No, thanks, it's only a few steps, he has an umbrella at home. What was he going to say? Ah yes, by contrast with the forest hare and the seagull—

'The lawyer, why, he's only thinking of the dowry,' says David-sen hastily.

The postmaster continues: 'Oh, the endless turmoil in which we mortals spend our nights and days! We never rest. Our object is not to have enough but to have more than enough. Our souls climb up and tumble down again, crawl on all fours, make fresh attempts to rise, and tumble down again. Then one day we die. The English captain wanted to try and weigh anchor tonight; it's no weather for it, but he wants to weigh anchor tonight. He has to get to a port seventy-five miles from here and load, he wants to be ready to take in wood pulp by seven o'clock tomorrow morning. Then he's crossing the North Sea and making a fresh attempt to rise. By weighing anchor tonight he gains a day. Does he gain a day for life? No, no, he fags himself out, but he gains a day's earnings. The beasts and the birds, they will be sleeping tonight.'

'Won't you have my umbrella?'

'No, thanks, it's almost stopped raining. Well now, I mustn't detain you any longer. The English captain talked about God—'

'Yes, he was religious, I heard. But now we must turn in, Post-master.'

'Religious, yes. I may not have understood everything, because the English have a religion which is unique in this world, and justify it in an entirely English manner. The Englishman enslaves one people after another, takes their independence from them, castrates them, makes them fat and placid. Then one day the Englishman says: Let us now be righteous according to the Scrip-tures! And so he gives the eunuchs something he calls self-government.'

'It's exactly as you say. Well, good night, Postmaster!'

'Good night! Oh, are you wanting to turn in? Otherwise there was something else. Could it be that the English have their own God, an English God, just as they have their own monetary unit? Can you explain otherwise their incessantly waging wars of conquest all over the world, and afterwards, when they've won them, thinking they've done something noble and high-minded? They exhort all men to understand it thus, they thank their Eng-lish God for the success of their misdeeds, they wax religious over it. And then there's that remarkable English characteristic of assum-ing that other people will share their delight in what they have done; *now* mankind must really turn over a new leaf, they say, now let righteousness prevail, now let's all be religious! To other people it may seem extraordinary that the English don't hang their heads; they must surely have their own God, whom they have appeased and who has given them dispensation. They write in their newspapers that now the moment is ripe, now mankind is to change its ways; they turn it into a programme. Come now, let us set about being religious, they say; what else is there left for us to do? Ah yes, mankind must change its ways with a vengeance, everything must be different from what it was before: we must have different pictures on the walls, different books on the shelves, different sermons in the churches; we must have different social relations, different furniture, different science, a different love, a different piety – in short, a different kettle of fish. Why? Because the English themselves have changed their ways? The English will never change their ways. Because mankind has suddenly become different from what it was before? It will be an immensely slow process; it will take many, many earthly lives before mankind becomes different from what it was before—'

The postmaster looks up; there is no one with him, Davidsen has gone. Davidsen must have stood there for as long as he could endure before making his getaway. It is not the first time that someone has made a getaway from this lay preacher; his congregation deserts him all too often. A congregation prefers the gospel it expects. The postmaster preaches one they don't expect; he is one against the congregation.

The postmaster walks home, head bowed; the back door is open as usual and he enters the passage. Something moves over by the opposite wall; he lifts the lantern and sees a man.

A man. A stranger, in his thirties, an unknown man with a sparse dark beard, wearing a waterproof raincoat with leather belt around the waist.

For a few seconds they stare at each other, each apparently taken aback by the encounter. Then the man clutches at the expedient of looking at an umbrella that is hanging there on the wall; he looks at the postmaster again and back at the umbrella. He seems quite pitifully confused. This umbrella – he seems unable to remember when he hung it there.

Does he not get any help from the postmaster? What – from the postmaster, who can't even help himself, who has collapsed with his back against the wall and stands there holding the lantern aloft?

But then the stranger takes down the umbrella and in something like desperation starts explaining himself; it all sounds sinister and odd – is he mad, is he drunk? He speaks in English, the words are there, but the man is crazy; now he is seeing if the umbrella will open and talking to it. 'The dentist!' he says. 'I should think so! Who can tell me where this will end? Understand?'

The postmaster is as stiff and white as a corpse. At first his face had lit up with happiness, as though he knew the man and would speak to him, then he paused and reflected; he must have realized his mistake; he went rigid.

Does he not know the language? Indeed he does, he has been stammering away in it with the English captain and mate earlier in the evening. Has he nothing to say? But perhaps he has too much. As the stranger glides across to the door, the postmaster whispers: 'Wait a bit!'

'The dentist!' says the man. 'Don't you understand anything? I'm mad with toothache. Doesn't he live here? I saw a name-plate—'

The postmaster whispers: 'I had a son—'

'It's not me,' answers the man, trying to pass.

'Where have you come from?'

'Keep away!' orders the man.

The postmaster says with downcast eyes: 'Did you have that umbrella when you came?'

The man appears to turn the question over. 'Didn't I? Er—'

But suddenly the postmaster remembers the door leading to the inner office, to the registered mail, the most important of all – the door is unlocked now, standing ajar now. The postmaster rushes in there, and a moment of two later a groan is heard.

Once out in the backyard, the stranger stops abruptly, pauses for a moment, then retraces his steps. He re-enters the passage and hangs the umbrella in its place. Through the open door he sees the postmaster in the inner office, slumped back in his chair. The lantern is burning away beside him.

The stranger emerges into the street once more and starts to run. It is blowing and raining. Oliver, on his way up from the quay, sees this man hurtle past him. Why, it's the second mate – he must be having a rough old time with his toothache! 'Hullo there!' he calls, intending a reminder about his money. The man merely continued to hurtle.

What – this arouses Oliver's suspicions. Besides, why should the second mate be heading for open country at his hour? At high tide tonight the wind will very likely change, the storm die down, and his boat sail – doesn't he know that? Oliver shouts after him once more, but in vain. Then, by Jove, he sets off along the country road in the second mate's wake, making incredible leaps with his crutch. Given an incentive, Oliver is a highly competitive long-distance man. And now the incentive is his money.

He is gaining on the runner when he sees him stop, hears him give a kind of signal; this happens just beyond where the open ground ends and the road goes straight into the forest, plunges violently into the forest; right, it's from here that the signal is given. What's more, Oliver hears a signal in reply. It's not the weather for wenching, is Oliver's thought; there must be something else going on – the question is, what? He bounds along to the first trees and positions himself in hiding.

He sees a pair of figures emerge onto the road, go up to the second mate, and stand there with him, three heads in a huddle. Very mysterious, very strange. Being to leeward of them, he might have expected to hear the sound of their voices, but he hears nothing; evidently they are not talking, or they are talking in whispers. They are like spectres; they move, look at each other perhaps, do business, but speak never a word. Oliver finds it all quite eerie, and would gladly have quit but for his business in hand.

Time passes, creeping on till it is past midnight and high tide; the wind drops. All at once the group starts to hustle and bustle, the spectres approach, Oliver can even hear that they are talking. There are two of them in addition to the second mate: a woman and a man with a long beard. As they draw level with him, Oliver hops out into the road, to be greeted by an exclamation from the group. The second mate seems to want to push ahead, but Oliver addresses him and asks for his money. 'Come on board!' the second mate replies. But immediately he thinks better of it, thrusts his hand impatiently into his raincoat, and hauls out money, notes, quantities of notes; the man with the long beard keeps striking matches to give him light.

Then three short blasts on a siren are heard from sea – the English vessel piping for her crew. The second mate breaks into a run.

Curiously enough, at this moment Oliver's mind is less on his money than on his companions. Naturally he doesn't lose his head, he stows the money safely in his pocket, but having done so, he expresses great surprise over the female member of the party. 'Are *you* out on a night like this?' he asks, addressing her by name.

'Yes,' she says in confusion.

Oho, she must have fancied herself safe in the dark, but a match has betrayed her. Now she wavers, sore perplexed, and yields up this yes under pressure.

What happens next? Oliver is Oliver. His brain goes gradually to work; the occasion is so absolutely right for a man like him: dead of night, the mystery of all this money in a raincoat, the remote rendezvous, and finally the woman – yes, it's her, Carlsen the blacksmith's daughter, the widow who keeps house for her father. As far as that goes, Oliver has heard no ill of her up to now, but maybe she takes after her sister and her vagabond brother – Carlson the blacksmith has been unlucky with his children. And what is his daughter up to this evening?

'I saw you,' says Oliver.

To this he gets no answer. And if Oliver has thought to obtain some advantage by rumbling a secret about her tonight, he is doomed to disappointment.

'What have you been doing here?' he asks.

The long-bearded man joins in: 'We've been singing duets. What were you doing here yourself?'

'Me? You saw for yourself. I was getting my money.'

'Your money, indeed. For eiderdown, wasn't it?'

'Oh, you know that, do you?'

'Yes, I know that.'

Oliver turns to the widow. 'Who have you got mixed up with? Is he your boy-friend?'

'What if I am?' the man retorts, in a quite unmistakable manner and taking a pace forward.

Oliver vacillates and says: 'I only wanted to hear where you come from. I don't know you, do I, or what? Do I know you?'

'Where I come from? Not a thousand miles from where you get your eiderdown, ha-ha!'

It is clear enough to Oliver that he is getting nowhere, and he switches to being a lamb. 'I don't own any bird islands. All I've done is buy up these bits of down from one person or another in the course of twenty years, I may say. No, I'm not the man to own any bird islands, worse luck; I'm a cripple, as you see.'

Either the long-bearded man is extremely sure of himself, or he is merely pretending to be so; either way, he takes no further notice of Oliver whatsoever but turns to the widow and chats carelessly to her: 'It couldn't have gone better, and now the rain's stopped. He's bound to catch his boat all right.'

'Yes.'

'They can't sail without him and make themselves shorthanded. No, it couldn't possibly have gone better. He'd have been on board by now if he hadn't been held up counting out that money. Would you believe it – eiderdown, stolen goods! But it couldn't have gone better. Are you cold?'

'No.'

'You don't need to be so downhearted; what's the matter with you? He's sailing and we're left behind, that's all. A stout fellow!'

'He was having a rough old time with his toothache tonight,' says Oliver, in an attempt to ingratiate himself.

The man takes no notice of him and continues: 'Still, it was a swine of a night for us to be meeting him here in all innocence. Why wouldn't you accept his raincoat when he offered it to you?'

'I didn't want to have it.'

'No, you didn't want to have it. All the same, he meant it innocently enough.'

'I didn't want to accept anything from him.'

Silence. Suddenly the man says with a laugh: 'Isn't he your boy-friend? Well, stop talking nonsense!'

'Shut up!'

'I'd have thought you were allowed to meet your boy-friend. Though for that matter neither of us has anything to answer for, we were out for an innocent walk and bumped into him. That's all there is to it. But are we going to stand here in the middle of the road all night?'

'If I'd known everything—!'

At this point the long-bearded man does something unexpectedly jovial: he produces a mouth organ from his pocket and starts playing a dance. Perhaps he does it to cheer her up, perhaps also to emphasize his own unconcern, to emphasize the innocence of his presence on this road tonight. It is inconceivable that he should play now, but there is no mistaking it: Oliver hears the music with his own ears. And in another attempt to ingratiate himself and make friends with the man, Oliver calls out: 'That's terrific, so help me God!' He leans forward towards the widow and declares: 'I've knocked around all over the world in my time, but playing like *that*—'

The man breaks off, turns to Oliver, and says: 'What are you waiting for?'

The cripple sees clearly that he is not a favourite with this man and answers accordingly: 'No, I'm not waiting for anything. I think I'll go down and see the boat weigh anchor.'

The man resumes his playing.

Ah, but here he made a mistake, he was too brazen; his playing at once aroused Oliver's suspicions. Of course he knew this vagabond; come to think of it, he recalled hearing him play as a boy. Besides, he remembered the legend of this musician, a local lad, Carlsen the blacksmith's son, the artist on the mouth organ, the hobo of a thousand road and railroad construction jobs. What was he up to now? His sister was with him, his brother Adolf was on board the Englishman, the fellow with the sea chest – a whole band of brothers and sisters at one fell swoop. It vexed Oliver that he hadn't managed to let them know to their faces what he knew about them.

He went home musing on many things. It was a mighty tangle to unravel, and God alone knew if there was any net gain to be had by worrying over it any more. The second mate was a complete stranger to him, and perhaps the most important person of all. Besides, Oliver had his own bit of business to regale himself with: a pocket bulging with money, the reward for his diligence in rowing out to the bird islands year after year.

He was almost home when the English vessel blew a long blast on her siren and pushed off from the quay.

All in all, a memorable evening, almost up to the standard of the memorable day when he came in from sea with the derelict. And Oliver would not have been averse to cutting a bit of a well-earned dash when he entered his cottage; for here he was, the man who could hold his own, the sleuthhound with a hell of a brain – here he came with money and secrets and knowledge. Here, however, there was nothing doing; the household was asleep, Petra was asleep. Not that they were normally hand in glove, it wouldn't normally have occurred to him; but at this particular moment he could have bulked himself out a little with mystery in her presence and dropped tiny hints for her to lie racking her brains over till she was blue in the face. Yes, but Petra was asleep. She must have been tired, poor old girl, it was one of those evenings she had had to go to lawyer Fredriksen for further negotiations about the house; it wasn't all that long since she had come home, she had just had time to be sleeping so nice and soundly.

Oliver deliberately woke her by dropping his crutch on the floor. And at the thought of all that he stood for at that moment, he said in a voice of displeasure: 'You might have had something warm for me when I come home from an important bit of business, I'm drenched.'

Petra, who must have been sick of his boasting and bluster about important bits of business, answered irritably: 'Warm? I didn't find anything warm when I came home.'

'Oh, you've been out, have you?'

'Didn't I have to go to the lawyer again?'

'Are you never going to be finished with that lawyer?' he exploded.

No answer.

'And what in heaven's name do you keep finding to talk about? One week follows another, and there's never an end to it. I mean, bloody hell! Well, just let him wait till the day he gets me steamed up and I stuff the money down that throat of his! You don't believe me? I couldn't care less what you believe, but you don't know me properly, I'm not so broke as the pair of you think I am ...'

No answer.

Oliver was getting nowhere. All the same, he determined to try again, in a slightly more friendly spirit: 'Well, well, the Englishman's sailed by now' was his opening gambit.

Petra was asleep.

No, the moment was totally ruined, its grandeur and solemnity reduced to nothing. A nice way to come home to your family with a fortune in your pocket!

He pulled off his wet clothes, unhitched his wooden leg from his hip, and lay down beside his wife – an island and an adjacent island. He had run out of ideas. There was no chink in her armour, her breathing was heavy and peaceful, her body was in repose. It was too dark for him to see her, but she smelled comfortable and she was warm; she lay cooperatively on her side to give him room. The adventures of the evening continued to engross Oliver, the hours went by; when there was just enough daylight to see by, he reached for his wad of notes and counted them again, furtively, with his back to the bed.

In the morning, so affronted did he feel, he declined to drop a single hint to Petra; a woman who slept away a golden opportunity of hearing some news deserved no better. But he got no joy out of this, for what should happen but that Petra herself was able to announce an unheard-of event in the town: she came straight from the pump, and without even waiting to put down the pail informed him that the post office had been robbed in the night and that the postmaster had been found on some steps in a remote part of the town. He was sitting here without a hat, and was beside himself.

At any other time Oliver would instantly have seized his crutch and bounded into town, but now he was held back by his vexation over Petra's having cheated him of his triumph last night. Nor was he prepared to show the slightest surprise at this tale of hers, this cock-and-bull story of hers; on the contrary, he finished eating his breakfast and tormented Petra in the most priceless manner by not questioning her. How her anger mounted! She had apparently pledged herself not to pour him any more coffee, however empty his cup might be; he could jolly well look after himself. Finally, she said: 'What! Have you been struck dumb overnight?'

'Struck dumb?' he echoed in astonishment.

'Well, do as you please!'

'What am I supposed to talk about?' he asked. 'What are you getting at?'

'Oh, so you didn't hear what I told you?'

'What – that crap? I know a bit more than that!'

She shot him a glance; a thought struck her. 'Why, *you* haven't gone and mixed yourself up in it, have you?'

Charming! To sit here with clean hands, as innocent as a new-born babe, and then to be suspected of something like that! Clearing his throat with some dignity, he said: 'Maybe you'll watch that tongue of yours!'

'I was only asking. No harm meant.'

'Well, watch that tongue of yours!' he repeated, rising.

Petra was indeed furious at his disrespect for her great news, her colossal news, but as he had the crutch within reach, she judged it somewhat safer to go than to stay, and with a toss of the head she went to the old living room to share the news with Granny.

Oliver finished his meal and went out. The town was so pre-occupied with the events of the last few hours that there were no customers at the warehouse, and Oliver had ample opportunity for reflection. It was a stroke of luck that he hadn't let any cats out of the bag last night, an example of God's providence; from sheer self-importance Petra would have run around repeating every word, got him implicated in the mail robbery, perhaps even jeop-ardized his eiderdown money, despite his innocence. His watch-word now must be caution: no major disbursements in the first instance, no unduly good clothes, absolutely no finery – which meant that the pink tie in the haberdasher's window was not to adorn his neck.

Oliver thought it all out with some care. Beyond question, he was walking around with some of the stolen money in his pocket; but *he* hadn't stolen it, God was his witness. Blacksmith Carlsen's children, if reported, might possibly shed a little light on the case, but Oliver had no intention of reporting them – perish the thought! Every consideration pointed the other way. For a start, Abel was apprenticed to the blacksmith, and the widow cooked his food. And was not the blacksmith himself Abel's master? Oliver had too much paternal feeling to plunge his son into ruin. Come to that, the blacksmith's children might well be innocent, who could say? The one who knew most about the case was perhaps the second mate, a stranger whom nobody knew.

Oh, that second mate and that Adolf with the sea chest, those likely archcriminals! Had they not even asked Oliver to bring his wife aboard the Englishman, saying they wouldn't eat her? It was lucky that Oliver hadn't taken Petra and exposed her to goodness knows what, that he wasn't the sort to take his wife to someone. And now it appeared that his sense of propriety had guided him aright; she might have ended up in a regular nest of criminals . . .

The town buzzed with sensation: the newspaper carried an article written by a veritable master of the printed word; Police Constable Carlsen was conducting investigations here, there, and everywhere; the postmaster was incapable of making any coherent statement, he sat dejectedly gazing at the floor, overwhelmed by it all. He began by describing after a fashion a stranger he had stumbled on in the post-office passage around midnight: the man was old, with a long grey beard, and may have worn a mask; he spoke English. During a subsequent interrogation the postmaster altered his statement: the stranger might not have been old, but on the contrary young; the postmaster would have had no chance of overpowering him. The man had no umbrella. In short, the postmaster talked nothing but rubbish and confused everyone; he had gone crackers, had a stroke; the doctor visited him and diagnosed softening of the brain and mental lethargy. Good grief, a man once capable of designing towers and houses with columns!

And the town buzzed. It would be wrong to say that people withheld their assistance from Police Constable Carlsen and the authorities in their investigation; for the first few days they devoted themselves to it body and soul, and let almost everything else lie fallow. Thus, it came about that amid the hullabaloo another news item was entirely swamped, one that might well have repaid attention, namely, that Consul C. A. Johnsen had received a Danish decoration, the Cross of the Order of the Dannebrog. Was anyone breathless at this honour, did anyone mention it? A two-line notice in the paper, casual congratulations from the few townspeople who remembered to offer them. Mrs Consul Johnsen, of course, put a higher price on the distinction, which she made the subject of telegrams both to Scheldrup, who had now arrived at New Orleans, and to Fia in Paris.

24

In the big cities it is assumed that people in the small towns have almost no share in God's plenty where great events are concerned. This is a mistaken and insulting habit of thought – most certainly they have bankruptcies, frauds, murders, and scandals just as in the great world. Admittedly the local newspaper prints no special handbills, but news spreads surely and speedily from the pumps and penetrates into the tiniest nooks and crannies. Was there anyone in the entire coastal town who didn't know about the mail robbery by breakfast time next morning? Unless it was the Grits-and-Groats Olsens, who were late risers and often had breakfast in bed.

And no more than the small towns lack sensations do they lack variety therein; small-town folk have all the diversity of events they could require. Perhaps you thought they would be reduced to living and dying on a mail robbery? In that case the *cause célèbre* would have lost its news value less rapidly. The doctor did his utmost to keep it alive – in a sense it enabled him to stand victoriously over a broken postmaster – but people very soon got sick of discussing it.

What then was the outcome? There was no outcome, things never even got started. The old or young man who spoke English and perhaps wore a mask but definitely had no umbrella – this presumptive criminal was nowhere to be found. Telegraph messages were sent in pursuit of the English ship, but by then she had finished loading in Norway and was on her way to some home port. Telegraph messages were sent there, too, but although on the ship's arrival some sort of judicial inquiry was presumably held, it led to nothing. Naturally it came to light that Adolf was Adolf, a blacksmith's son, a Norwegian seaman, but he was married and resident in England, and on a British vessel he was adequately protected by the British flag. Besides, his captain was religious.

The second mate likewise proved to be a Norwegian, son of the postmaster in a specified small town, unmarried, with excellent certificates of good conduct; no suspicion rested on him – and in any case the father would surely have recognized his own son in the stranger in the passage, which he had not done. Oh, and again there was this business about the British flag: that the British flag would not have protected a criminal for a single day, no, not for a moment, as the whole world knew. In other words, the second mate and Adolf were at present in British service under a religious British captain, and any kind of extradition was out of the question.

Why had these two men not visited their parents while their ship lay discharging at their hometown? Well, you know, that was one of the more delicate questions put to them, but even to this they had a satisfactory answer. They were reluctant to present themselves before father, mother, brothers, and sisters with empty hands, and they had not yet managed to save up a decent sum out of their wages. That was the reason. But God knew – the second mate testified – that he had been ashore and circled his home many an evening, looking up at the windows, trembling when he heard a door open or close, folding his hands when he saw his mother's shadow on a blind. It was touching, the court itself was touched, and that is quite something, for a court to be touched.

One peculiar feature of the seaman Adolf cropped up: when his clothes and his person were searched, it came to light that his entire body was heavily and lewdly tattooed. It was quite strikingly obscene, and when asked where he had had it done, he answered: 'In Japan.' These pictures damaged Adolf severely in the examining magistrate's eyes, though as proof of mail robbery they failed to satisfy. The second mate had no tattoo marks, and his body was notably spick-and-span, so that he acquitted himself much better, and indeed this fact was of benefit to both suspects.

No, nothing more came of the mail robbery; nor indeed was it an inordinate sum the thief or thieves had got away with: some seven or eight thousand kroner worth of registered mail. If this had then to be divided among several people, no single portion would amount to very much. One was tempted to say: 'Much good may it do them!'

The affair no longer bulked large, and Police Constable Carlsen showed little zeal in his investigations, which indeed was hardly surprising, since the case had brought much unpleasantness on his own nephew, and by that token also on himself. But neither were Police Constable Carlsen's superiors eager to go to extremes: it was foolish to pick a quarrel with England over a trifle; besides which, the town at large wished to see Carlsen the blacksmith spared – a man who deserved better children than he had.

But the postmaster, now? He had taken the catastrophe so much to heart as to be unrecognizable, a bowed and broken figure with shifty eyes and constantly mumbling lips. The shame and injury that had befallen his office had proved too much for his high self-respect, for naturally he had no other cause for sorrow – his son had done nothing wrong. The postmaster was the object of universal sympathy. True, for as long as he had lived in the town he had bored the pants off sensible people with his everlasting religiosity and his metaphysical twaddle up hill and down dale, but now that fate had struck him down, virtues far predominated over blemishes in their memories of this haunted soul. Was it not he who had designed the senior school, that colonnaded building that caught the traveller's eye while he was still out at sea and stayed in his memory until his dying day? Now he sat here with his understanding clouded, less than a child.

'He's benighted and dead, poor old chap,' said the doctor. 'I've seen it coming on; his eyes were beginning to pierce, he'd gone off his rocker, and only needed a trifling misfortune to make him go under. His faith has finished him.'

In contrast to everyone else, the doctor found it difficult to forget the mail robbery; he even clung to his suspicion that the money had sailed away on the English ship. What was to prevent the second mate, with his local knowledge, from letting himself into his home and stealing the registered mail? 'Offspring!' the postmaster was always saying. Alas, offspring were capable of anything! Offspring Adolf was the same kind; those ghastly drawings he went around with on his body spoke volumes about his character. Some joy those two fathers got from their children, indeed!

The doctor was, in fact, incapable of letting up on his triumph. Never had he trod the town's sandy street with less effort, never had the soundness of his philosophy been so clearly vindicated. To that religious wreck of a believer, the postmaster, he would regularly make his way, observe him for a while, and then leave him; detecting in his patient no sign of any relapse into light and lucidity, he consigned him to eternal darkness. Was it not *human thought* this boastful child was always mouthing about in his homilies? That human thought never ceased, that human thought was the light that never went out? In *his* case at least it had gone out, leaving a black wick! Weak heads like his should never start ruminating on their own account; they should design schools and churches and stay wedded to the catechism.

The doctor may have had nothing to boast or get in a golden glow of joy about, but he felt some satisfaction of a kind. His materialism proved right, the circumstance of the postmaster turning imbecile overnight strengthened the doctor's position, it was as if he had prophesied the disaster; no one came near him in authority, any decision he made had to stand. When he said that the postmaster's faith had finished him, one or two people asked: 'His faith?' To which the doctor replied: 'Certainly, his superstitious faith.' And that, too, had to stand.

But the doctor was as far as ever from any golden glow of joy; life was and remained infamous. But for the occasional pleasure of being able to bait a fellow creature it would have been unendurable. Do you suppose, for example, that he had gained anything by changing tradesmen? He had, you remember, broken off his long-standing connection with Consul Johnsen and gone over to Consul Davidsen – and incidentally, he had done this not to injure Davidsen but to give his little store a lift. And what was the outcome? The scantest possible appreciation: Davidsen too sent in his bill. They were all alike, Davidsen was merely one more consul. And into the bargain Consul Davidsen wasn't even a man the doctor could have a decent talk with; he never answered, he always acted as if overwhelmed, the sly little devil, and submitted with a smile to the grossest taunts.

So the double consul was better, after all, though he too was only a tradesman and a shipowner.

There were rumours of priceless goings-on when the doctor came and congratulated the double consul on the Order of the Dannebrog. He had brought the pharmacist with him on this visit, and the pair had been extremely servile. Contrary to their normal practice, they had approached the consulate by way of the shop, and sent in their cards by one of the assistants; after which they had deposited their hats, sticks, and galoshes, and run pocket combs through their hair and beards. Both gentlemen wore gloves.

The consul appeared in the doorway, somewhat surprised, with their cards in his hand, and asked jokingly if they desired an audience. They bowed their assent. 'Well then, pray come in!' said the consul, still treating it lightly.

But when on entering the office they remained as solemn as ever while offering their congratulations, even the consul may have begun to find it quite in order that they should behave so ceremoniously; this was perhaps how congratulations on an order of knighthood ought rightly to be tendered, how should he know? True, he protested a little and said: 'Come now, these forms are hardly worth clinging to!' But no, they were resolute, and declined to be seduced into a lighter tone.

The consul offered the gentlemen cigars; they rose, bowed, took a cigar each, but refrained from lighting up. Wishing to make himself agreeable, the consul now began talking of the recent mail robbery; the gentlemen bowed at everything he said and fairly hung on his words. So far, so good. Consul Johnsen was exquisitely polite; as the town's leading citizen he could not afford to be a stranger to good tone. One of the clerks came in and delivered the mail into the consul's own hands; the consul slung it across to his desk without even glancing at it. His chief clerk, Berntsen, entered and asked a question; the consul answered over his shoulder: 'Later! I'm engaged now.'

During all this the gentlemen sat quiet as mice, as if awaiting a further display of aristocratic tone. But when no more appeared to be forthcoming, the doctor, possessed perhaps by the devil, determined to get his satisfaction in a more heavy-handed manner. Accordingly he turned to the pharmacist and said a few words; out of respect for the knight he pitched his voice low, but he said: 'I really believe we should have left our shoes out there as well.'

Light dawned on the consul; inside he may have contracted in a grimace, but he never batted an eyelid as he answered the doctor: 'No doubt you were afraid you had holes in your socks.'

Consul Johnsen was still the man he was! His riposte went home; for a moment the doctor was an abject sight, as he smiled and said: 'I dare say, it's possible. ' But almost at once his powder ignited and he added: 'By the way, I've paid for the socks and for everything else I've had from this store.'

'Yes?' queried the consul.

'I've kept the receipt.'

'Really?' As the doctor remained silent, the consul continued: 'So what? I don't see what you're getting at.'

'I'm not getting at anything,' replied the doctor. 'I was just stating a fact.'

Here, the consul should probably have stopped and not gone any further, but he was doubtless offended at being made a fool of, and unable to deny himself a touch of superciliousness. 'Your and other people's little purchases out in the shop are something I really know very little about; it's Berntsen who looks after that. I sit in here and occupy myself with more important matters.'

'Yes, there's no doubt about that,' the pharmacist concurred. He was losing his courage, and wanted to pour some oil on the waters.

But the doctor only sneered. 'Naturally!' he said coldly. 'We are great men, we sit here and make our dispositions, we talk and write about our *one* little cargo boat, we're above standing at the counter and selling green soap and thimbles.' Here the doctor drew breath through his teeth as if he were shivering with cold – or rather, perhaps, as if he were furious.

The consul replied: 'It's precisely as you describe it, I don't interfere in minor matters.'

'How great *are* we, by the way?' the doctor burst out. 'How great *are* we, you and I?'

The pharmacist put in hastily: 'No, this was not the intention. Forgive me if I don't see it like that; what's got into you, Doctor?'

The doctor rose. 'Do you know what, you pharmacist's soul, you?'

'Sh! It's like this, Consul, we wanted to come here today in order to – We thought, the doctor and I, that as good acquaintances we could make a little joke of – I mean, naturally it never occurred to us to make fun of you personally, but that we could pull your leg a little about the Order, about the knighthood, which I suppose neither you nor we think all that highly of. Perhaps we've set about it in the wrong way, but we thought we might come and give both you and ourselves a little amusement.'

'And in that you were not mistaken,' answered the consul. 'As you saw, I joined in the joke from the word go.'

'Can you really be bothered spelling out to him anything so obvious?' exclaimed the doctor. 'I'm surprised at you, Pharmacist. Come, let's be off. Adieu!'

Well, the pharmacist got up – yes, but he allowed the doctor to go before embarking on another explanation to the consul, all couched in the politest possible terms. He hoped there would be no hard feelings between good acquaintances, the doctor had gone too far, there was no sense in taking off one's shoes, and the business of directing a big steamship from one port somewhere in the world to another, from Genoa one day to Zurich the next – it was almost beyond human understanding—'

'Zurich isn't a seaport, you know,' said the consul with a condescending smile.

'Oh, isn't it? I'm afraid I don't understand much about shipping matters, I only know I get pills from Zurich. But what was I going to say? In any case, it's a gigantic labour, sitting here as the director of oceangoing ships and at the same time running the town's biggest general store. For that matter, the doctor and I might well have taken off our shoes out there, I tell you candidly; but if I know you aright, you wouldn't have liked it. The doctor has perhaps gone far enough off the rails without that, and I will ask the consul to bear with both of us.'

'I've already forgotten the matter, please say no more. I wouldn't dream of taking offence at the doctor; really, I have other things to do,' answered the good-natured Consul Johnsen. 'Let's call it a day!'

'Finally, as regards the decoration: you're the town's first knight, of course, and I'm sure there's no one who grudges you this well-deserved honour. Perhaps it's in appreciation of your brilliant handling of that derelict some twenty years ago?'

The consul (smiling): 'Well, there may have been one or two other trifling matters since then.'

'Naturally. Masses of important things, not least your valuable reports. Now I suppose the other government will very soon follow suit – wasn't it Bolivia?'

'What? I'm not the Bolivian consul.'

'I beg your pardon!'

'It must be Olsen or Heiberg who's the Bolivian consul.'

'I see. But then aren't you a double—'

'—Consul? Yes,' replied Consul Johnsen, laughing heartily at the other's embarrassment. 'Yes, of course, double consul, ha-ha-

ha! But really it must be one of the others who's the Bolivian double consul, ha-ha-ha!'

'Ah yes, it's Holland I'm thinking of,' said the pharmacist, crushed. 'Just my luck to get it wrong! In any case, your cross of knighthood is an honour, not only for you, but for our whole town. We are all honoured by it. And no doubt the Dutch government, too, will express its appreciation soon.'

'What? No, there's no special grounds for that. Won't you light your cigar before you leave? Well, it's up to you.'

'Well, they must be feeling pretty shamefaced by now' may have passed through the consul's mind when the two gentlemen had left. And he must certainly have reflected that in any case it wasn't the doctor who had gained anything by this whole silly visit. The gentlemen themselves may have thought otherwise, God knows; the pharmacist may have gone out of the door sniggering to himself, and when he told the doctor about his exit line in the double consulate, the two gentlemen may have had a good snigger together. Oh, that bit about directing ships on all the oceans of the world – when it was a well-known fact that in this respect Consul Johnsen's grasp was shaky, and that the cargo boat *Fia* was managed mainly through his son, Scheldrup.

The doctor, however, still seemed dissatisfied, saying: 'When all's said and done, he didn't even begin to understand we were being malicious. He's probably sitting there at this moment trying on his Dannebrog.'

The pharmacist thought the consul had understood.

'Understood? What does he understand? Did you say "gigantic labour"?'

'I said "gigantic labour".'

'And Bolivia, and Zurich? And he didn't throw you out?'

'He's a bit slow in the uptake. But he'll get there in the end.'

'Not a bit of it. No, that idea of ours misfired.'

The doctor went to the Olsens'. He often went there, almost every day of late, in his professional capacity. The son-in-law, the artist, was there on a summer holiday with his wife and child. There was nothing wrong with the child, but the young mother, like all young mothers, was anxious and insisted on having a doctor.

The doctor had no objection to calling at the Olsens', it meant an extra good fee; he was even beginning to acquire a taste for it. Here there was no undue grandeur or formality, but neither was there any parsimony – all was fullness and abundance, a little prodigal, a little wasteful. On entering the hall you might find unmatched ladies' gloves lying about, or expensive umbrellas, now broken. The actual rooms were marked, not by disorder, but by symptoms of too much money, money spent on picture frames, carpets, chair covers; the curtains hung right down to the floor, where they trailed. No, there was nothing niggardly here, but the furniture and fittings denoted the self-made man, the *nouveau riche*.

So what? the doctor may have thought as he drank the vintage wines and smoked the good cigars; here was kindliness at least, and hospitality, and for good measure the greatest readiness to acknowledge him. He sank into the sofa while everyone hung on his lips – if the riches were new, so what? Riches are riches, a million is no worse than a thousand. And there the doctor sat. He was not, of course, a man who was easily impressed, but in these surroundings he undoubtedly cut an indifferent figure: his dickey grated irritatingly against his chest, and his shirt cuffs needed constant pushing back with his little fingers, or they would have slid down over his knuckles.

'No,' he said, 'there's nothing wrong with the child today, either. All she needs is a few more teeth to complete the resemblance to her handsome mother.'

The young wife (with a deep blush): 'Oh, that's good! We were so anxious about her again. And the funny thing is that it wasn't me who was the most anxious.'

Consul Olsen asked: 'Who was the most anxious, then?'

'You, Papa. Oh no, you can't deny it!'

The consul made excuses. 'I wasn't anxious, but I saw no point in her lying there and suffering if we could help it. She's named after me, Doctor.'

'That explains a lot,' said the doctor.

In this house the doctor was a different man: he relaxed his guard and forgot his pinpricks; they respected him without them. He behaved in a friendly, protective manner, he positively enjoyed himself. Conscious that he was these people's superior, he refrained from widening the gulf between himself and them. Here, too, he found a good humour that tasted none too badly for a change (the doctor was hardly pampered with it at home), along with laughter, health, and of course a certain childish gentility.

Here people came and went perpetually. In addition to the son-in-law and his family, the visitors included the other artist, the painter's son; yes, they had brought him along. To be sure, he was not married into the family like his colleague, but he too was made welcome, in an attic room with a carpet and curtains down to the floor.

And now this painter's son wanted to do a portrait of the doctor. 'What will you do with it?' asked the doctor, adding candidly: 'I can't afford it, and nobody else will buy it.'

'It's your face I'm keen to paint,' replied the artist. 'Payment immaterial!' he added gaily. You know, that painter's son wasn't at all a bad fellow, he had a line in repartee, he was inflammable and constantly in love, and he had an honest face; but his hands were large and coarse– the doctor looked at those hands with aversion.

'Well, paint away!' said the doctor, with an air of indifference.

'Thanks. But I wanted to paint you in your study, surrounded by medicine bottles and fat volumes, absorbed in your science.'

The doctor started perceptibly. A remarkable artist this, such understanding of a learned man and his work! The doctor was evidently touched: a faint flush spread over his meagre cheeks, and to conceal it he took a sip at his glass.

Yes, he liked it here at the home of the Grits-and-Groats Olsens.

He had come in the first place without too many expectations. He had wished to ennoble this house as he had ennobled the houses of others – of Henriksen of the Shipyard, Heiberg, David-sen and his store, Johnsen of the Wharf; now he had come to feel a sense of well-being here, for as long as it might last. Besides which, he had another idea: he might simply ignore the Johnsens for a while in favour of Consul Olsen's – try that, see how it tastes! He intended to get things into balance, to create an equal power beyond the pale; why, he could rule the town on a basis of dis-sension, with two cocks of the walk!

This might have worked well, but it all foundered on the Olsen family's languid good nature. No, the Olsen family was quite un-teachable, they had no brains for skulduggery or guile. Food and money and furniture bought wholesale they could understand; but they had no culture or illustrated magazines or plates painted by daughters of the house. The Olsen family kept both feet on the ground.

'Johnsen of the Wharf has been made a knight,' said the doctor. 'Your turn next?'

Grits-and-Groats Olsen shook his head mournfully and answered: 'No such luck.'

'It's not beyond your reach. It just takes a little working.'

Grits-and-Groats Olsen shook his head mournfully again and answered: 'I'm consular agent for a country that has no orders.'

'So. But listen to me, Consul: you could at any rate have a country residence.'

'A country residence? I see. Yes.'

'But of course! Why should there only be one country residence here? And why should he have it? You're certainly a richer man than he is.'

Grits-and-Groats Olsen smiled and shook his head. 'Come now, you mustn't exaggerate.'

'A country residence, then. And you could drive out to it with a pair of horses.'

'A pair of horses? No.'

'You can afford it.'

'I can indeed,' answered the consul with a swagger. 'But a pair of horses – no, you must let me off that. I can't even drive one horse.'

'You'll have a coachman for that. Why, good lord, you're a man who knows the meaning of the word dignity. A coachman with gleaming buttons and gold on his cap.'

'No, no, no, the very coachman would split himself laughing,' declared Olsen. 'And I couldn't bring myself to sit behind a pair of horses.'

The doctor suggested: 'I'll sit with you the first few times, or rather, Mrs Olsen and I will. Isn't that so, Mrs Olsen?'

Mrs Olsen (completely overcome): 'Me? God bless us all, no. The doctor's wife might, the doctor's wife herself might . . .'

No way around that one.

25

Well, after that, everything went on as usual again in the town – only the postmaster remained a broken man. He had been dismissed with a scanty pension, and had moved with his family to a little house opposite the shipyard, while a new postmaster moved into the post office.

The summer was over, and the two tasselled student's caps were travelling back to their studies. They were not exactly bosom friends, but they were travelling back on the same boat. Bosom friends? You see, Frank had worked throughout the vacation and had gone another lap ahead of Reinert, and how could that make for a relaxed or harmonious relationship? My word, how Frank had studied during these weeks! It showed, too. He had managed to weave into his consciousness so much recondite knowledge of languages, bit by bit, without grossness, without violence, simply by devoting his time and his vital forces to it, that standing there on deck he looked decidedly skinny and yellow, without density in any dimension, and thus superbly equipped for learning still more. To the life around him he gave no more attention than it deserved; for hands he had no use, the doings of the crew he regarded with an apathetic eye; the engine-room people were abominably greasy. Frank could not stow barrels and crates in the hold, no, that was not what he existed for; but he could look up words in dictionaries, he sat possessed of rarified and sacred linguistic values; no comparison was possible. Refinement is gained by grinding away at books and lost by manual labour.

On board the boat he met a slight acquaintance from the school bench, the Thumbtack, who bobbed up from the stokehold like a pale Negro, half clad, with a sweaty face and a wide-open shirt front. 'Hullo!' he said, nodding.

'Hullo?' returned Frank, trying to recall the Negro. 'Are you here?'

'Yes. Didn't you know?'

'No,' replied Frank, rather distantly.

'I'm a fireman. How's Abel – fine?'

'Abel? Yes, as far as I know.'

The Thumbtack was disposed to renew memories of school: Do

you remember this, have you forgotten that? He laughed, revealing white teeth, and quite unaware that the rest of him was dirty; he stood right in the draft, of which he was quite unconscious. Frank shifted his ground twice, three times, and said: 'There's a terrible draft here!'

'All right at home? Sisters all right?'

'Yes, as far as I've heard.'

'Ha-ha-ha, anyone would think you hadn't just come from home,' said the Thumbtack. 'And fancy your not knowing I was here. Your sisters know.'

Frank (looking away): 'I have so many other things to think about.'

'But surely you remember the time we broke the window? When the headmaster caught us?'

Frank (more and more distant, almost on the horizon): 'No, it's so long ago.'

The Thumbtack perceived that his classmate was a learned man and decided to try questioning him a bit about himself. 'Going back to the university?'

'Yes, of course.'

'Well, I never! And how far have you got? I suppose you'll soon be a parson?'

Frank pulled a face. 'Parson? No, no.'

'Oh.'

'It's languages I'm studying.'

'Oh, all the different languages. Well, that's no joke, either. All the different tongues, same as the headmaster. I suppose that old Reinert's going to be a parson?'

'That I don't know.'

'What, you don't know?'

Frank said reluctantly: 'No, I don't know what he's going to be.'

'I saw that old Reinert come on board this morning, but he didn't seem to know me.'

'No, that could well be. You're so grimy, you see.'

'Yes, but I called hullo to him,' said the Thumbtack as he started hoisting ashes from the stokehold and heaving them overboard.

'It's terribly dusty here!' said Frank.

No, Reinert only knew those whom he wanted to know; indeed,

he scarcely knew Frank, who was his fellow student and was even a lap or two ahead of him. Frank hardly saw him on board: he was travelling second class and mostly drifting over to first – while Frank stood there on his third-class deck with the consciousness that he knew more languages.

Reinert had done no work worth mentioning during the vacation, only a little revision to please his father the sexton; he had been much more occupied out of doors. Here he had been far from idle: he had made a complete conquest of Little Lydia and the shipyard girls, and young as he was, he had even made great progress with the Heiberg girl, Alice. Really, the boy looked bloody good with his curls and his smart clothes; added to which he was so intrepid a campaigner that he might well have passed for an adult. He went to such lengths that he was actually on the verge of eclipsing the deputy district magistrate with the ladies, even though his competitor was a man who had completed his studies.

Frank wandered about the deck, blue with cold, trying to find sheltered corners as the ship turned. The first thing he meant to do when he got to Christiania was to buy himself an overcoat with a velvet collar.

He passed the smoking saloon; the door was hooked back. He peered in and stopped. Then he raised his cap and would have liked to pass on, but he had stood there a little too long, and the people sitting directly opposite were known to him: lawyer Fredriksen from his hometown, a great man, but nonetheless chatting with a lesser one, with Reinert; there they sat chatting and smoking, while the lawyer trimmed his nails with a mother-of-pearl knife.

Frank did not go in, but he was well enough known and acknowledged to have no reason for slinking away, either. So he addressed Reinert through the doorway and said: 'I met the Thumbtack on board; he was asking after you.'

Reinert made no reply, and sat blinking as if lost in thought.

'He's a fireman on this ship.'

'Really?' said Reinert absently.

'Who's the Thumbtack?' asked lawyer Fredriksen, as if he didn't know.

'A schoolmate of ours,' answered Reinert. 'Yes, I'm looking forward to seeing *Les Cloches de Corneville* again.'

'I haven't seen it.'

'Klausen's sublime. Everyone says so.'

'I have so little time for theatres and circuses,' lawyer Fredriksen thundered. 'You see, I have my work in the Storting, and on top of that I'm chairman of a parliamentary commission . . .'

Frank saw he had no business to be there and wandered off. Come to that, he needed to find another sheltered corner and indulge a smile: he knew more languages than the pair of them put together, and Fredriksen probably had no more than a few scraps of German left – scraps of everything!

So what, could not lawyer Fredriksen smile in turn? It was with his languages as with his anatomy: he knew all he needed to know. Now he was on his way back to his commission, fully rested and ready to pick up the threads where he had dropped them. These meetings of the commission were a good thing, his attendances were reported in the press; he could draw fresh travelling and subsistence allowances from the treasury; in the evenings he met his colleagues and peers over a toddy and a long pipe. It brought him prestige, and a little backwoods paper included his name in a list of future ministers of state. Who said we lacked men? There was, for example, Attorney-at-Law Fredriksen! It did the lawyer no harm to be singled out, he gained something by it, gained a little by it; yes, he had the future at his feet. Already he was a man who in the course of a conversation could take out his pocket knife and start probing his nails.

So these three local lads went off to Christiania: Frank, Reinert, and the lawyer, each with his object, his ambition, his future. The Thumbtack stoked the boilers.

And the coastal town remained when they had gone.

They left a gap, each in his own way; Frank's was perhaps the easiest to fill. The little room became vacant, but his grandmother escaped having to tiptoe in the cottage and could clatter the rings on the stove to her heart's content. This was no small change for the better. Abel now inherited the little room from his brother, but that was neither here nor there, he occupied it only at night; and besides, Abel was no scholar.

So probably the lawyer made a deeper dent by his departure. Not that his office suffered particularly from his absence, his business was not too extensive to be forwarded to him by post and dispatched from his desk in the Storting. But then the lawyer now had a certain provisional understanding; Miss Olsen may have missed him, or at least have found it quiet without his voice. What was to come of it all? Just wait, the time was not yet ripe, but it was ripening: a backwoods paper had named the coming men, among them he of the understanding. Miss Olsen must surely have missed, if nothing else, a certain heavy step on the stairs, a puffing gentleman making his entrance, a neck with folds of flesh, a fumbling hand: 'Good evening, good evening!' If she had any memory, she must also have recalled the cigar ends in the ashtray, the chatter, the businesslike way of discussing love and Norwegian politics: 'What is it, fundamentally, that we strive for in this life? To be well off, what else? We rise continually from one position to another, become better and better off, eat well, dress well, put money aside, grow rich, own houses in the town and shares in ships in the harbour, have a country residence, sail if we feel like it, drive if we feel like it. We do nothing foreign to our nature, we do not aspire to inconsistency, we leave that to others, every man to his taste! Later on – later on we can start up businesses and provide jobs, we can also do good round about us, extend a helping hand. We hear of a homeless family and allow them to live in one of our houses. Welcome, come and live here, you and yours! We hear of misfortunes and take a sympathetic interest, we are the reverse of hardhearted; sailors are mutilated in their perilous calling, we step in and secure them their rights. In this way we engender solidarity, we resolve on progress and democracy; only let us combine it with service, the flag, and the fatherland—'

'Yes,' Miss Olsen might possibly put in at this point.

'You agree? Yes, that's the way it goes, and what's more, that's the way it ought to go. But then, you see, it's not good for mankind to be alone, the individual and the office alike demand a helpmate, Miss Olsen—'

'Won't you light another cigar?'

'Thank you. As I was saying, a helpmate. She is necessary for several reasons: the house needs a mistress, she must see to the rooms and their furnishings, the housekeeping purchases go through her. Somebody comes to see the husband, he's at work, at a cabinet meeting, but the wife represents him. The management committee of an old people's home or a lunatic asylum desires her valuable support; well then, the wife signs an appeal. Ah, now she is raised to a higher plane, to new honours, but also to new duties. She cannot always be refusing; the public has its eye on her, society makes its demands. Could you then satisfy these demands, Miss Olsen?'

'Me?' Miss Olsen might say with a laugh. 'No, I'm not sure. Yes, I suppose I'd have to if it came to the point. What do you think?'

'I take it for granted. And now it remains to clear up the question of whether you're willing. It's several months now since our first understanding, so you've had time to think it over again and again. However, I myself am waiting for certain contingent developments, so there's no hurry, you can have longer still.'

Whereupon Miss Olsen might well ask in some surprise: 'Our first understanding, you said – what understanding?'

'Why, our provisional understanding. Don't you remember, at your sister's wedding? I thought we agreed—'

'We certainly didn't disagree.'

'There, you see!'

'But it was you who did the understanding.'

'Well, we won't argue about that; it was I who did most of the talking, you're right there. I gave you my promise . . .'

This is just a bit of affectation on her part, lawyer Fredriksen must have thought. But for safety's sake he decided to mention a certain matter, hint at a certain matter that had occurred to him. These artists and painters who had got into the house might turn the girl against him. It was inconceivable that such a thing should happen; still, he would drop a hint: 'In short, I laid my offer at your feet, and there it lies. Hm. Who's that singing away in the attic?'

'It's the painters. They have a studio up there.'

The lawyer smiled. 'Ah yes, these young fellows, carefree souls, singing and painting on canvas! The other I don't intend to discuss, but your brother-in-law does at least come from a cultured home; his father and I were contemporaries at the university. How's the boy getting on! A young man like that has nothing to fall back on; he's learned nothing solid, hasn't studied. The other I won't even mention, but your brother-in-law was at least born with good chances. Mind you, it may turn out all right, he may sell a picture now and then; later on I intend to buy one from him myself and to delegate the choice to you.'

'What—!'

'That is what I intend,' said Mr Fredriksen, nodding as if from an eminence. 'Buy a picture and ask you to choose it. Will you do that?'

'Do you dare to entrust me with that?'

'I dare to entrust you with far more important things, naturally. As for his paintings, we'll buy not one but two. That's what we'll do. Now I'm travelling back to Christiania in the service of my country. For the moment our understanding can rest; when the time comes, I hope we shall feel the same way . . .'

This, then, was the position over the provisional understanding. The lawyer had gone it virtually alone! You see, he had settled this matter several months ago, and settled it to his own satisfaction, but today it had occurred to him that he would like to be less completely alone in the understanding, he would like for good measure to bring the other party in on it. Naturally Miss Olsen would close with the offer; he had only to ask her, pop the question. It went as we have seen: she tried a few little tricks, but these did not signify; the long and the short of it was that she would buy pictures for their walls.

And so lawyer Fredriksen sailed.

But now, by the same token, Miss Olsen remained behind in the town, thinking her solitary thoughts. How much had she promised this man? Nothing. Not one damn thing. But had she flatly refused him from the word go? Some women refuse nobody, not one; even the most impossible man will serve as food for thought. Miss Olsen was certainly not the grasping or designing type, but she had this man coming to the place, had him up her sleeve; one was better than none, she was getting on in years, her sister was married – God knows, a future is a future, a Minister of State is no mean man when he becomes a Minister of State. Come, no harm in thinking about it at least! But grasping? She was not knee-deep in calculations; she was a natural girl like the rest, Nature herself directed her tactics. She had never suffered want – why should she want for a suitor? She had plenty of everything else, and now into the bargain she had a Minister of State, when once he made it! There was nothing incomprehensible in this, any more than a hen among the flower beds is incomprehensible.

It was natural and inevitable that Miss Olsen should miss the lawyer now he had gone.

Did others miss him? The house of Oliver? Hardly. Oliver himself was presumably more than glad when his clamorous creditor left the town again, while Petra must have been tired of constantly scuttling off to the lawyer's. Their negotiations had at last come to an end. She could not possibly have acquired a soft spot for this man who tormented her so, there was certainly no question of a partiality – perish the thought! Was there talk of a miracle and an inexorable love; did they say at the pump that both parties were on fire, did they say sparks flew? The lawyer owned the roof over Petra's head, she talked to the man in order to keep this roof – that was all. Admittedly, she had to go and discuss the matter rather often, and Oliver, her husband, may have grumbled at times that she never managed to wrap it up; but did she dress for these visits in any more drastic or provocative a way than by wearing a new slip under her dress? Not as far as Oliver knew. She had these new slips and evidently liked wearing them. Petra was a married woman, she was proof against any man's advances. Many years ago, while still young, she had boxed Scheldrup Johnsen's ears for a mere nothing; what wouldn't she do now that she was greying at the temples and her children were almost grown up?

Oliver had no grounds for suspicion. He said: 'Well, so he's gone?'

'Yes,' answered Petra. 'And I'd be glad if he never came back.'

'What – do you think he's gone for good?'

'I don't know. I'd be glad if he got lost!'

Oliver looked at his wife and saw that she meant it: she made a grimace of repugnance and spat to one side. She could not have spoken more plainly, she detested the lawyer.

'No, he is not a man of God,' he said. 'But lawyers – when were they ever any different, for example?'

'And what I say,' continued Petra, 'is that next time you can go to him yourself. I'm not stirring another inch.'

Could anyone speak more plainly? Oliver was by no means put out, quite the reverse; next time he himself would take a turn along to lawyer Fredriksen's, he said; a short, sharp turn, he said, and nodded. And he proposed to settle up with the man once and for all; he would tell him his name, Oliver Andersen, and demand a receipt for a certain heap of money that he'd fling down on the bloodsucker's desk. The cripple and coward enlarged on how he would go about it.

Come to think of it, Oliver had definitely grown bolder of late; the consciousness of having money in his pocket made his carriage more erect; his character improved. During the first few days after the mail robbery he had still been unsure of himself and had asked Petra to sew an inside pocket on his waistcoat. Petra took this as braggadocio and laughed scornfully. 'A strong pocket!' said Oliver. 'Yes, made of sailcloth!' said Petra. So Oliver had to fall back on his mother to get the work done.

But now that he had his inside pocket and his wad of notes in it, Oliver felt safe; no one would think of searching a cripple who had done no harm. The eiderdown money was his.

It was tiresome that his money could not properly be allowed to see the light of day. It would have gladdened Oliver's heart to be able to walk into the shops, order this and that, and then extract from his pocket his entire bank to pay with; but this pleasure was denied him, the money had to be spent with a certain degree of furtiveness. One good thing was that it was mostly in notes of low value; at cautious intervals he might take one such note out of the bundle and trade it in for goods. In this way he had provided himself with candy to suck daily, plus a little finery, a new tie, and a stiff collar; for the little girls he had bought shoes that tied over the instep. No one suspected him on the grounds of excessive disbursements; a couple of larger notes lay untouched in his inside pocket.

This worked well; Oliver's requirements were not excessive, he was easily satisfied. He was certainly no glutton, even if he had a bit of a sweet tooth. Petra was just the opposite: born covetous and greedy. Right now Oliver needed his new and better character; he had to make constant allowances for Petra and give her frequent mild warnings. Damned if he could understand her, she had grown more contrary and unaccommodating than ever, as if by some sudden affliction; at present neither food nor drink was good enough for her, she couldn't stomach either one or the other; the last lot of coffee tasted frankly rotten – 'What sort of coffee's this you're bringing me?' she asked. She had seen a piece of Emmentaler cheese in Davidsen's store, and if she had still been the parlourmaid at Consul Johnsen's she would have had cheese like that. Furthermore, she had seen a cake of yellow soap in the window of Holte the barber, and how nice it must smell!

But Oliver, who had money in his inside pocket, Oliver was able to answer: 'Now, don't be so greedy for everything you see, Petra! Think instead for a moment of what you and I earn! Come to mention it, we don't do so badly.'

Here Petra revealed her ungovernable contrariness by starting to bicker with her husband. This time, instead of being afraid of the crutch, which lay within his reach, she ridiculed both it and him, saying that she lived with a crutch and talked to a crutch and slept with a crutch and would have to die with a crutch – what a life! And at the last words she spat to one side, as if she were about to throw up.

With his powerful shoulders, Oliver might have stood up and cleft the table with an axe, or demolished the stove, or issued some other little warning; instead, he did something quite unexpected – he went out into the town, returned with both the cheese and the cake of soap, and said, 'Here you are!' What an experience! For a moment Petra was dumbfounded by the incomprehensibility of it; then she resorted to tears: she didn't want the things, she refused to have them! How could he be such an idiot as to get into debt over these nonsenses? Take them back!

'Well, now you've got what you wanted,' he said.

Wanted? Was she never allowed to make a little joke? On top of everything else, was she to be tongue-tied for life? Bah!

Now it must surely have hurt Oliver's feelings that he, in common with the lawyer, had caused her to spit; but he held his peace on the subject. What a change came over a man when he acquired a new character! Oliver persuaded his wife to taste the cheese, and yes, she tasted the cheese and spat it out. It was a different cheese – just don't try pulling any fast ones on her! Petra turned pale with ungovernableness and gave the little girls a sharp reprimand for smiling. When she smelled the soap, she had to hold her nose.

There was no pleasing her.

Not that either Oliver or the little girls had anything against keeping these luxury purchases for themselves.

So it went on, day by day, good days and bad, with friction, little incidents, an occasional sumptuous meal of fish when Oliver had rowed out of an evening, an occasional plateful of buns with the coffee when he had changed a note. Things went by no means badly; the family's existence was more tolerable than that of most of the town's small fry. How many others had a permanent post and an inside pocket for their money?

Of those worse off, take for example the unhappy postmaster and his family. The doctor was still unable to discover any improvement in his afflicted patient; he sat where he was put, silent and broken hearted, already partly dead. Nor could anyone suppose that he enjoyed any inward satisfaction, that he chuckled and laughed in private, or slapped his thigh with merriment. Far from it. He gave no indication of consoling himself with his former philosophy, his joy in his children, those children who were to be so much more than he himself, who, praise God, were already working for a better earthly life next time. The postmaster seemed to have given up thinking, given up seeking, given up believing. He had searched for many a long year and eventually found a path that offered a little light; he had followed this path for a long way – until fate reared up against him, erect and terrible, and stopped him. His ruminations had swept him away.

His wife and daughters were capable women; one of the daughters was to work in Consul Johnsen's store, while the son who was on the land gave all the support he could, and the scanty pension went almost further than expected, though it could not provide for so many grown-up people. Things would have looked black had not the son in England, the gifted second mate, come forward. When he heard about the mail robbery and his father's misfortune, he came forward like a man. In an admirable letter he exhorted his parents and sisters to trust in God in their trial; he too had suffered evil over the affair and been interrogated and suspected, though no stain attached to him, of course. He forgave the world for having suspected him and informed against him; praise God, justice had prevailed; in England justice always prevailed. Finally, he intimated that this was clearly a call to the town to repentance and soul-searching; such an unheard-of event concerned not only him and his family but everyone. In short, he was religious. What a son! He never even mentioned the crux of the matter, but the crux of the matter was that overnight, as it were, he must have found himself better off; whether his pay had gone up or he had found a new coal mine on English soil, he sent home a tidy sum of money and promised more later. This was a regular act of rescue, and his laudable conduct furnished his mother and sisters with an unexpected happiness. They went to the pater-familias and told him the news; they had agreed to do so rather abruptly in order to give a jolt to his deadened brain, hoping that joy would bring back his wits in a trice, just think if it did! But it didn't, they were disappointed. The postmaster listened to them; yes, he even seemed well-disposed to try to understand their babel of voices, but he remained none the wiser. It was just as if he had heard the news before or had imagined it for himself. If there was any change in his face, it can only have been that it turned a little paler. His wife burst into tears.

'No,' said the doctor, 'your son the second mate can't be ex-pected to cure your husband.'

The postmaster's wife seldom had much to say for herself, but now, riled by the doctor's continual cocksureness, she asked: 'Why not?'

'Why not?' echoed the doctor. 'Because I could more easily be-lieve that the postmaster himself will eventually get tired of sitting looking at his own navel.'

Such language towards a stricken family – not to mention God! But it was one of the doctor's routine decisions. It had to stand.

The doctor went home to his surgery. He was currently sitting for the painter, and was therefore decked out in his ageing frock coat and the striped trousers he had bought for Fia Johnsen's confirmation. That was an eternity ago.

He passed Johnsen's double consulate, and since he always kept a watchful eye on this establishment, he soon discovered that it had hung out yet another new sign: FASHION DEPARTMENT. BLOUSES. KNITWEAR. HATS TRIMMED. The sign had appeared above the door overnight.

The doctor stopped, read it through carefully, and to avoid talking entirely to himself, he nodded to a small girl who was curtseying as she passed and said: 'Our knight has a passion for new shields.'

Ah yes, Consul Johnsen had cleared the extension to his store, where the stoves and a couple of harrows had stood for years, and turned it into a fashion department. Just that.

The doctor went on his way smiling, came to his own front door, and found the painter pacing up and down, waiting for him. 'A discovery, young man!' he shouted from a distance, 'a big thrill!' And with this he was launched.

The doctor did not ordinarily hold conversations with the sons of house painters, but this young man was another story, an artist and no insignificant person, pitifully short on book learning but with sense enough to listen when erudition spoke. During these sessions the entire town had to run the gauntlet, from the unfortunate postmaster to the Johnsens of the Wharf and the Grits-and-Groats Olsens, from Davidsen and Heiberg to lawyer Fredriksen and the cripple Oliver – the fellow with all the brown-eyed progeny in his home. The painter received much entertaining information about the town's affairs. The doctor was both witty and malicious, nor was he altogether untrained in archery, but sometimes, you know, he tried to be too clever, so that his arrows fell quivering just beside the mark. Even a doctor could sometimes miss the target.

'Young man, you're a stranger here,' he might say. 'The whole town is a den, a hole, and without me it would be a swamp. I give people a little medicine!' Thus they sat in the small-town surgery while the painter painted and the doctor let his tongue run away with him. There was nothing very professional about the room, despite the painter's wishes and the proposed title for the portrait, namely, 'The Physician'. The doctor had dug out some books and set up some medicine bottles; on the table stood a stethoscope, on the wall hung an alphabet used for testing people's eyesight for spectacles, in a corner there may have been a little sublimate standing in a cup; and that was all. Where was the operating table, where the glass shelf supporting a vast variety of instruments? The only chairs in the room were a couple of Windsor chairs. No microscope, no skeleton, not even a skull, that symbol of a medical man's unflinching courage in his communion with the dead.

This was the frame for the doctor's portrait. They were agreeable sessions, interrupted only by an occasional man with a poisoned finger or a newly married woman with a peculiar toothache. The doctor made a splendid model, full of life, full of nonsense, bitterness, disbelief, and cantankerousness; his face was constantly changing, its only constant feature an expression of unshakable superiority. How obvious he made it appear to the young man that the town was a den and a hole!

Finding the painter here now by his own front door, he didn't even wait to get inside before pitching into his big thrill: 'Young man, it's not only lawyer Fredriksen who links fat profits with the fatherland!' How he shot off his arrows, what a hit-and-miss performance it was! Johnsen of the Wharf had opened a fashion department overnight. Mind you, this must be the work of the chief clerk, Berntsen, a man of great ability; he made so little on stoves and harrows, the turnover was so slow – forget it, let's have fashion! Not that it didn't fit in very nicely with the rest of the business: Johnsen of the Wharf supplied household managements with their day-to-day purchases; now he would supply servant girls with their finery as well. Fashion department! Who was to run this new section? Eureka, the down-and-out postmaster had two daughters, and the older was to take it on. It was a stroke of luck for Johnsen of the Wharf that the postmaster was a broken man and that one of his daughters needed to go out and earn her living. She was an able girl and a good-natured girl, but now she was to set out from her little cottage door near the shipyard and go and manage a fashion department. She hadn't learned the business, but this didn't matter, there was nothing much to it; Johnsen got her cheap, and was even able to bask in the philanthropic glow of having given her work. 'Young man, this town's a hole ...'

The mill was in motion. The painter couldn't get a word in. At long last the doctor said: 'Well, let's go in and paint!'

'I'd prefer to skip it today,' said the painter.

'Really, skip it? Very well. Have you something else to do?'

The painter answered: 'Somehow I don't feel quite in form.'

'Really? Oh, very well. Good day!'

But as he watched the painter's retreating figure, the doctor may have become suspicious of this lack of form; why, the young man had his paint box with him as usual – was he perhaps going somewhere else?

Exactly, the painter was going somewhere else. He had been asked by Mrs Consul Johnsen to add the Cross of the Dannebrog to the portrait of her husband he had painted a few years ago. Oh, these coastal-town consuls and consuls' wives! Anyhow, she had explained it all in the little note she sent to the painter. The portrait was, of course, a good likeness as it was, wrote Mrs Consul Johnsen; but Fia was just home from Paris and had suggested that a touch or two more of colour would sit well on it. After all, Pasteur wore the Legion of Honour on his black frock coat.

26

Autumn and winter came, the days drew in. There was pleasure to be had from standing in the smithy, with a roof over one's head, hammering iron that glowed and gave off light, and eating and drinking properly as one did in the blacksmith's house; yes, by Jove, there was many a worse lot than Abel's. And he himself thought it was all right. Why, for a start you could do your work without needing gloves or a cap. His most important garment was a leather apron.

His master, Carlsen, had declined sadly in recent months; he talked more and more despondently about his loss of strength, hinted at giving up the smithy, mumbled about death: how death may enter in or pass by till next time, but we must all die! The autumn had been hard on him, thinning and whitening his hair, his thoughts were now few and unworldly, he took long rests while Abel worked. Of course the mail robbery must have made an impression on him; his brother, Police Constable Carlsen, had been unable to resist telling him of the judicial inquiry in England and of the filthy pictures tattooed on Adolf's body. The old blacksmith answered: 'It's not our Adolf.' Police Constable Carlsen went on: 'And just think, here he was all that time the boat was discharging, and never once came to see you!' 'Yes,' answered the blacksmith, 'he certainly met his sister if he was here; I seem to remember that. Both the boys see their sister, why should they see me? You mustn't be unjust to them.' 'Oh, so Adolf did come here?' asked Police Constable Carlsen. 'No,' answered the blacksmith.

Idle talk. However, Carlsen the blacksmith took it differently from the postmaster; he was a simple, unlettered man who looked at things more with the eye of habit. There was nothing hysterical in his habits of thought, which centred on his craft, that of a blacksmith, a member of his class. It is good to be a member of one's class; otherwise one becomes an upstart, one's primitiveness gets eroded. And was not the blacksmith a father? Knowing far more good than evil of Adolf, he did not despair. Why, only a few years ago the boy was padding about here in the smithy and asking questions and hammering little bits of iron and hitting his fingers and crying and being comforted; wasn't that so? That Adolf in England must be a completely different Adolf – and even he might have hit his fingers, might even still be young. 'People are all right,' the blacksmith would say; 'all of them except the scoundrels.' But in any case, he must have given up all hope of seeing either of his sons succeed him at the smithy; so who was to take his place?

He said to Abel: 'In a year's time you'll have learned more than I knew when I started on my own.'

He must have meant something by this pronouncement, or was it merely praise and appreciation? At all events, it sent a long golden shaft of light into Abel's soul; his thoughts flew to Little Lydia and the future! That extraordinary boy! He was as you saw him, muscular and straightforward, grimy, guileless, bubbling with life; he had developed a powerful chest, and although his bearded hands seemed roughly and readily formed, they had strength in them and no mistake. His shoes he had personally mounted with iron all around, and to connoisseurs in soles Abel's were something rather special.

On his way home that evening, he sought out his father and put him in the picture. Oliver – although he himself had for weeks been pondering deeply something that had happened at home – Oliver now set aside his own thoughts and listened attentively to his son. 'He must mean it's you who's to take over and plain manage the smithy,' he said.

'Well,' said Abel.

'I don't regard it as impossible. What's your own opinion?'

'I don't know.'

Nodding his head as though the matter was settled, Dad declared: 'I can't see it in any other light.'

Yes, Oliver was the children's friend, they came to him with their doubts and their sorrows, he had the right sympathetic touch, he was made for the kind of father who let his children bring themselves up. Abel, that impossible madcap, had once hinted at marrying and setting up house; he had his reasons for it, he said, things would never be right till he got her. Well, even at that Dad had not burst out laughing; on the contrary, he nodded: it was not all that crazy, not at all, in certain ways, and it didn't come to him entirely as a surprise. For Abel would shortly be the town blacksmith and a craftsman, and big and broad-shouldered, and then he'd be able to do practically anything he wanted, for example. All he needed was a little more time to think it over and get himself organized with a stove and accommodation and so on, but a couple of years would soon be gone, he'd see! Abel protested that he couldn't possibly hold out like this for another two years. 'No, that I can quite believe,' conceded Dad. Abel went on: 'Because every vacation that Reinert comes home and cuts me out.' 'Reinert!' exclaimed Dad with a scorn that consoled Abel greatly. 'That young pup, he can't be more than eighteen or so!' Abel, who can't have been more than sixteen, hastened to say: 'I'm not more than eighteen, either.' 'Yes, but it's different in your case, you're a craftsman and a skilled hand; when you're qualified you can be your own journeyman and master any day of the week. That's what I say: is there anything in the world that goes quicker than a year or two? Just look how first one man gets married, and then the other gets married, and they're not so much as bricklayer's assistants! But what are you?' What all this talk of Oliver's doubtless meant was that time would help the crazy kid to get over his fancies.

And today once again he had a cheering effect on his son as he expounded his view of the matter in a string of well-meant platitudes: Blacksmith Carlsen would set Abel over all the smithy – as Pharaoh set Joseph. 'I tell you, Abel,' he said, 'that the way you've mastered your trade, and the way you've performed what he's put you to do and God has appointed, he can't mean anything else.'

No, thought Abel likewise.

'You will be set over all his goods; we'll go home and tell your sisters, this is great news! A year is less than anyone imagines; because what is a year? It's just God giving a single blink of his eyes, and that's a year. And managing a thing is exactly the same as owning it. There's a world of difference between a good manager and a bad manager, and when I manage the consul's stores and his great warehouse, it's just the same . . .'

Claptrap and bunkum, sentimentality and bombast. But then Dad said: 'You boys have got what it takes, both you and young Frank! Now if you'll stay for coffee, I've got some buns with me here,' he said, eager for a festive occasion. 'It's Saturday night tonight and you don't have to go to the smithy tomorrow.'

Ah, but Abel was busy, Abel had an engagement; he lost no time in sprucing himself up and going out again. He was like a fisherman who gets a nibble and hauls away. You see, that Reinert had been back home for an eternity of a summer and spoiled life for him; now he was gone again, but still Little Lydia had not been as she ought; many an evening Abel had parted from her with a heavy heart. Tonight it was a good deal lighter as he set off to see her.

He found her in, he enticed her out; she must have read in his face that something had happened.

He began by extending his hand, and when in her surprise she hesitated to take it, he took hers by force.

But ever since Little Lydia had started doing work for Consul Johnsen's new fashion department – making slips and blouses – she invariably had a needle in her hand and several more in her bosom; she was not to be approached.

'Oh, I've pricked you, I see,' she remarked, unmoved.

Yes, that seemed at least as clear to him as it was to her; he pulled a sour face and sucked the blood.

This little incident was perhaps not so unfortunate after all, it acted as a curb; otherwise he might at once have come out with the direst impossibilities.

'Have you something to say to me?' she asked.

'In the first place,' he began, 'I'm to take over the smithy one of these days!' And with that he went straight to the point, exaggerating repeatedly and brushing aside a number of little questions she tried to put. Yes, he was a journeyman, he'd be qualified soon, this year as like as next, and could do anything he wanted. His father had advised him to get himself organized, with a stove and accommodation and – 'It's nothing to stand there like a goose and laugh at!' he said indignantly.

'No,' she said, to humour him. But by the way, was he quite all there – only just confirmed, wasn't he – or *was* he confirmed?

'I won't even answer you,' he said.

Yes, but goodness, the nonsense he talked! And her mama laughed at him every time she saw him. How old was he?

'Twenty-three years and three months,' he answered, looking as if he believed in his own exactitude.

At this Little Lydia laughed aloud and asked again: 'How old did you say? Lord preserve me from you, Abel!'

'You're only making fun!' he exclaimed angrily. 'How old are *you*? You never think of that.'

Little Lydia cared no more for being little than he did; indeed, she liked to be regarded as a dressmaker, and had gone into long skirts ages ago. 'Me?' she said. 'How old am I? Why do you ask? I'm not going to stand here listening to you any longer.'

Abel shifted his ground. 'No, you'll only listen to that Reinert. But that's going to come to an end. I can't believe you care for that Reinert, Little Lydia.'

'Me? Mama says he's a smart gentleman.'

'He's a bastard!' cried Abel, absurdly agitated. 'If he comes here again, I'll pick him up between my nails. Understand?'

'It's time I went in,' she said.

'Between these nails!' he yelled, raising his first to heaven. 'I'm capable of that, just you see!'

It must have dawned on her that he was suffering; and when he went on to declare that he must have her and couldn't wait any longer, she humoured him to the extent of saying no, very likely he couldn't. He continued to talk; his voice took on strange tones, it trembled, he meant every word; and finally she answered in earnest, more like a grown woman than the little girl she was: 'Well, but I can't say that I love you.'

He smiled incredulously. 'Oh yes,' he said. And then he spoke again: how they might be able to live upstairs at the blacksmith's. There was a little room, painted blue, with nice shelves; the blacksmith had certainly meant him to take over his accommodation as well, what else could he have meant by it all? And there Abel proposed to hide her – no more playing around with that young pup, he said, with that girl in knee breeches, that bastard, he said. It would be a new life! Abel made a fair number of similar decisions and sung their praises.

Lydia took it more soberly than he, or so it seemed; she nodded when he talked about the little room, and when he announced his intention of putting an end to all her playing around in the future, she appeared to think it hard but natural perhaps that he should do so; in any case, she raised no objection. But as she listened to his talk, her eyes very gradually closed, it was as if she was losing sight of her own eyes; and suddenly she turned and went in.

Went in and stayed there!

He waited for a while; all his life he had had to put up with less than correct treatment from Little Lydia, and this vanishing act was no worse than many another instance. As when she poured hot coffee over his hands to shave off their beard! Or when she took the floor cloth and tried to wipe away a dark shadow under his eyes, even though the shadow lay beneath the skin and came from sorrow!

Just as he was about to give up and go, Little Lydia opened the door a chink and peered out. It seemed she couldn't resist doing so any longer.

'I see you,' he said. 'You might just as well come out again.' With which he unbuttoned his jacket and protruded his stomach a little; yes, in the last resort he adopted this unworthy ploy, knowing full well that she was bound to discover his watch chain which had no watch attached.

When she came out again, she asked innocently: 'What, are you still there?'

'Yes,' he replied cooly. 'I was waiting for you.'

She found it necessary to fetch an armful of wood from the shed – a cunning device, since he couldn't keep her standing with her burden while he talked to her. So he said in a jaunty tone, and with a motion towards his watch chain, 'Well, well, since that's what you want, Little Lydia, I'll come back in half an hour.'

In fact he could hardly have had much more to discuss with her, but this was not the point; he simply wanted to be where she was, what else? So he took his turn down to the quay and back, resolved to go in and see Little Lydia again. Provided he behaved in a friendly and innocuous way, she would hardly grudge him another chat, and it would do him good.

And, whether by design or good fortune, he found her all on her own in the living room; her parents had gone to bed and her sisters were out, since it was Saturday night. Little Lydia was sewing with exaggerated industry.

He must, of course, have seen at a glance that her lips were uniquely sweet, but from politeness and fear of being forward he decided against kissing her yet, indeed against any unfair or self-interested action. 'We seem to have got off on the wrong foot just now,' he said.

This was news to her. How so? 'But don't sit there fiddling with those white ribbons, Abel!'

If this was still the tone, he wouldn't get very far this evening either, and since she now had more pins in her bosom than ever, she must have fenced herself in on purpose. Small wonder, then, that he became angry and edgy when she admonished him about the white ribbons. 'Now, you're not to be like that!' he retorted. 'I've handled materials and velvet of the finest weave before now. Though for that matter my fingers have no business there,' he added, withdrawing his hands.

Even if she had no particular preference for him, surely she ought to have been moved to tears by this and thrown her arms around him; but no, not a sign of tenderness.

He had long been thinking of ways and means to measure her ring finger; it would have to be done accidentally, so to speak. He wanted this measurement for a certain purpose, and this in fact was why he had been fingering that bit of tape. 'You have such thin little fingers,' he said. 'Is your ring finger really no thicker than that? Let me see!'

If he meant that her fingers were those of a child, not an adult, then this was an insult. 'Oh, do let go!' she said. 'I haven't time!'

Would it amount to assault if he simply took her and kissed her for this piece of self-importance? She certainly looked discouraging enough, as if she might suffer a permanent injury from it; but he jumped to his feet all the same and did it, kissed her, braved all the pins and needles and kissed her for a while. She yielded; at intervals she gasped, 'You're crazy! Stop it! What do you want?' but she yielded all right. Oh, Little Lydia and he had done it before, this wasn't the first time.

Afterwards, though, it was a bit embarrassing. He tried to laugh it off, but this didn't get him very far. She hurriedly tidied her hair and her collar, which had got twisted, and scolded him well and truly for disarranging her; then she fell silent, and seemed to be finding it quite an effort to start sewing again. Could you beat it, he must have done her a serious injury. She was outraged and no mistake; she seemed to regard not only these last kisses but all the previous ones as so much waste.

There she sat, surrounded by dress materials, lace, silk, thread, buttons and ribbons; she had even put out her two sisters' fine needlework to make a show, since she herself was mostly doing linings. And all these preparations had been thrown away on Abel; a dressmaker was far beyond his comprehension.

'I just won't have you kissing me any more!' she said suddenly.

'No?'

'No, definitely not!'

'What's that, have I been kissing you? No way!' But his effrontery did him no good at all, he must have realized that appearances were against him. And now his only resort was the one she had fallen asleep over just now: he assured her again that she was to have him and no one else, and that he wouldn't let her out during the vacation.

'Be quiet!' she said.

'Tomorrow without fail I'm going to get a stove,' he decided. 'Old man Johnsen of the Wharf has thrown out a couple of stoves, I'll go and get one of them; I'll soon get the rust off it. That's it, I'll do that tomorrow without fail.'

'Yes, just you dare!' she answered menacingly.

They wrangled a bit over this; Little Lydia was the sensible one and gained the upper hand. 'You don't seem to have a scrap of shame where I'm concerned,' she said.

'All right, I can wait a few days,' suggested Abel, bending over backwards.

'A few days!' she replied in pitying tones.

'What, won't I ever have a use for it?' he asked vehemently. 'If *that's* what you mean, I'd like to know!'

She answered, as cool and condescending as could be: 'Yes, that's what I mean.'

'That you won't ever have me?'

'Well, surely you can see that,' she replied. And with this she started gathering up the finery on the table as though to draw attention to it: look at all this, it's as much as my life would be worth to give you a different answer at this moment!

She turned around; her mother was addressing the room, Old Lydia was speaking: 'Go to bed, at once, Lydia! And you, Abel, be off with you this instant! And what's more, I won't have you running here early and late, so now you know! What kind of monkey tricks are these the brat's getting up to? Are you quite all there? Go home and do some growing up!'

The bedroom door closed; then it opened again and Old Lydia spoke once more; the grater rasped out her parting shot: 'Tell your father from me to give you a good spanking on your backside!'

Abel – he just sat there. Then he got up and stood quaintly with the chair between his legs. Finally, he collected himself a little, looking first at the closed door and then at Little Lydia. He had turned a trifle blue, but he kept himself more or less in hand and said with a laugh: 'Well, I'll be damned!'

He got no help from Little Lydia; she failed to appreciate what a man of iron he was. Not that she chased him out or helped him on his way with anything remotely like 'Hurry up now, your life's at stake, say Our Father!' No, Little Lydia was used to her mother's sharp tongue and was not afraid of it. But as Abel made for the door, she definitely seemed to approve of his making himself scarce; she never said a word to detain him.

'Well, well!' he said, not wanting to appear completely at a loss. 'I'll certainly keep out of the way if that's how it is!' Oh, but that was a rash promise he had made – 'Can't you come outside so that I can talk to you?' he asked abruptly.

'Certainly not!'

Abel went home. His parents sat arguing about something, and since it was of no interest to him, he disappeared into the old living room.

And yet the argument in the new living room was by no means without interest. Oliver's weeks of pondering on a certain subject had at last found vent in a kind of judicial inquiry into his wife. You see, Petra was again with child, and how in the world had it happened?

Curiously enough, Petra herself had tried to conceal her portliness as long as possible, just as if a married woman were not allowed to put on weight, as if indeed she had been up to no good; perhaps it was this that first aroused Oliver's suspicions. But this evening, when he taxed her directly, she concealed nothing and denied nothing.

'Petra,' he said, 'I've an idea you're swollen again.'

'The way you talk!'

'And how in the devil's name have you managed it?'

'I can see it's no use denying it to you,' she said, trying flattery. 'You see everything.'

'Yes, I've seen it for many weeks.'

Petra had had time to prepare herself; she refrained from putting the blame on him or saying, for example, You know as well as I do how it happened! No, she took the blow, but deflected it, turned it aside. 'How have I managed it? Why, it's no worse for me to have a baby than for Maren Salt to have a baby.'

What was this – Maren Salt? What had she got to do with it? Oliver was at a loss for words.

'Yes, I'm telling you straight,' Petra continued, with a rather severe, aggrieved look at her husband. 'She was a lot older than what I am now, and it beats me why certain people should be so stuck on that Maren.'

'I can't make out one word you're saying.'

'Oh,' said Petra. 'Well, let me tell you that they're accusing you of being the father of Maren Salt's child.'

Oliver fairly gasped. Had everyone gone mad? He said: 'You – you must be out of your wits!'

Petra muttered and looked even more aggrieved.

'I wish I was as free from every sin!' he said.

'*You* know what you are,' she replied implacably.

But now his pride pricked Oliver, and he began to relish the situation. Forsooth, when all was said and done, he could hardly object to this accusation, he was certainly not going to find it defamatory, at most a trifle insulting. 'Who's been putting this lie into your head?' he asked.

Petra answered: 'It makes no difference who it was, but if you really want to know, it was that fellow Mattis.'

'Did Mattis say that?'

'Yes. And he must have had his reasons for it.'

Oliver thought it over, tilted his cap at an angle, and threw out his chest. 'The things one has to put up with!' he said. 'Though come to that, I don't care what you and that fellow Mattis think of me. Only he'd better not be too sure I don't summons him.'

'You won't get very far if you only summons Mattis. You'll have to summons the whole town.'

'Is the whole town talking about it?'

'For all I know, it is.'

Again he thought it over and considered it. It was a strange and utterly unexpected situation he found himself in, so help him God! There must be some way of turning it to advantage; he started to hum as he pondered. Petra gave him a searching look and seemed incapable of understanding the peculiar process now taking place in this man, this dilapidated man: was he humming? At this moment he was possibly happier than he had been for twenty years; possibly he felt something had been restored within him, a dignity, a value, felt himself rehabilitated by a fraud – set in a false light, but rehabilitated. Why did he sit there looking prosperous and exuberant? Had he received wine and bread and a blessing, had heaven opened, had a miracle taken place? You see, the poor wretch was no longer himself; once he had knocked about the world, and at this moment he may have been knocking about it again; he sat licking his lips and putting on airs, imitating himself as he had been when he was lucky enough to find nice sweethearts in the ports. Petra was used to seeing him fat and apathetic, clinging to a crutch, or capsizing into a chair at the head of the table; ugh, he was one of the jellyfishes that lay breathing in mortal stupidity and nothingness by the edge of the quay; and now he sat there, surprised by joy over something – but what?

Petra understood him less and less, and this humming bewildered her; had she not known better, she would have had a closer look at him, to see if he was Oliver Andersen and in his right mind. She brought him back to reality by resuming: 'All you do is sing!'

'What?'

'I said, all you do is sing.'

'Sing? I just thought of it. Tra-la-la. No, I wasn't singing.'

'Well, just carry on. It takes some people that way.'

But what did Oliver do now? Got up from his chair and made a grab at her. An ape imitating the antics of others, a pair of unpractised hands on the fumble. He put on an act of falling for her sweetness, her licentiousness, put his tongue out, laughed with that moist mouth of his. Oh yes, she knew her way around! And indeed, if she had sensed that his tomfoolery had the smallest foundation in fact, she would have met him halfway, guided him even; instead she started back from his idle caprice with a shudder. On seeing this he slumped back into his chair, flabby and gruesome.

For Petra, healthy and natural as she was, it must have been difficult to refrain from spitting; that jellyfish by the edge of the quay filled her with fear and shame. To smooth the whole thing over, she averted her eyes and said, as if to herself: 'No, what you could see in that Maren Salt is more than I can fathom!'

Oliver answered feebly: 'Be quiet! I didn't do it, do you hear?'

'*You* know what you did.'

'Well, believe it then, and good luck to you. I couldn't care less.'

'No, that's obvious,' retorted Petra in martyred tones. 'You're the master of the house, aren't you? The rest of us have no say in your goings-on.'

'Come, I'm not such a tyrant, am I?'

'Well, you don't care for me in any case.'

Step by step he had become the old Oliver again, and now with no mean wit he asked: 'Oh, so who *has* been caring for you, then?'

To this he received no answer, nor, perhaps, did he really want one; instead Petra, who certainly knew how to keep him at a distance, said impudently: 'If I'd been the type that goes astray, you'd have known it all right. But I'm not that type. And I'm not that anxious to go poking my nose into your doings; as for Maren Salt, she's sixty if she's a day, and you're welcome to her!'

Well, if Petra was so dead set against dropping this idiotic idea, could you blame Oliver for putting a good face on it and letting it stand? She was beginning to make him think she really suspected him, and this suspicion would bring him profit rather than loss if he exploited it properly. 'Well, well,' he said as a compromise, 'I expect I have my faults, too; I don't know anyone who doesn't have his faults and lusts and dissipations.'

It was remarkable how easily he obtained Petra's assent to this and from now on there was not the slightest disagreement between them; on the contrary, their tone was light and frivolous. His judicial inquiry into his wife, the question of how in the devil's name she had managed to get swollen again, all this was erased from the record. Oliver let the matter pass; in fact, he went further and afforded her some degree of recognition, hinted a word or two about her being infernally fertile: forty-something and as crazy as ever!

'Well,' she replied, half in jest, 'I'm not bad, am I now?'

'You?' he shouted. 'I don't know anyone like you, for example. And I must say, you have it in you. I'll give you credit for that. So help me God, you didn't need to find out what sex you are by having a peep; you have it in you!'

27

In the morning Oliver must have had his tiny doubts back again, for he asks Petra: 'No, did Mattis say that?'

'Say what?'

'That I was the father of the child?'

'Yes, I tell you!'

'I can't think where he got that idea from.'

Petra puts her hands on her hips and answers: 'No, it's not like you, is it; but I bet that Maren knows.'

'Does Maren say so, too?'

'Anyway, she's called the boy after you.'

'After me?' Oliver exclaims. 'What's he called?'

'Ole Andreas.'

Silence. Yes, it fits like a glove, there *is* something in it, but all the same – oh, these infernal women and their ideas!

Petra concludes: 'So you see, Mattis had his reasons for saying what he did.'

At this Oliver appears to stop and to think: But how could I have managed it? And when he leaves the cottage and makes his way to Mattis, it is apparently in the hope of hearing further details.

It is Sunday morning, and he finds the carpenter, half dressed, in the kitchen. The child is with him; Maren Salt is at church. The carpenter is surprised to see this man, this alien, hobbling into his house from the street.

'Good morning!'

'Good morning?'

Silence. Since Oliver is not offered a chair, he has so sit on the woodbox. They exchange a few words about the weather, about it setting in cold; Mattis is taciturn, apart from an occasional remark to the child on the floor.

'He's grown,' says Oliver.

'Yes, there's no denying that.'

'How old is he? Why, just look, he's got some teeth already! What's he called?'

The carpenter glowers and answers: 'That's neither here nor there. He's just called the child in this house.'

'I was only asking. Not that it's any business of mine.'

'His mother's given him a silly name, but she must have meant something by it.'

Since the carpenter is so hostile and so dilatory about consenting to make any definite insinuation, Oliver himself takes the lead: 'Who shall I say he's like?'

'His mother' is the curt answer.

'His mother, yes. But on the father's side?'

'Who told you to ask?' Mattis explodes. 'Perhaps you know the father?'

Oliver laughs and takes it more or less kindly, but of course he must parry the thrust. 'Ah, you're the same old Mattis! I wish I was as free from every sin!'

'That's what they all say when something serious happens.'

'What do you mean by that?'

'What I mean? That they all deny it. And the one that's most guilty, maybe he's the one who denies it worst, so I've heard tell. They use bribery and corruption and cough up money to make people keep quiet about it.'

Yes, Oliver agrees with him over this, and pities the mothers and the children. 'Poor kids!' he says.

'They all say that, too,' retorts Mattis. Then he takes the child on his lap and addresses it: 'Your mother's gone and left you, has she? Yes you're looking at the door, but she'll likely be gone another hour yet, she doesn't care. Look, here's my watch!'

Oliver says nothing; he is not listening to the carpenter's prattle, he has had an idea. Oliver has this sluggish cunning, his brain functions best in obscurity and along side roads; now one hand works its way into his inside waistcoat pocket, ever so gently, ever so thievishly, as if he just happens to be scratching himself. Then he lifts a couple of banknotes a little, squints at them to see if they are right, and then sits as quiet as a mouse. In the little that Mattis the carpenter has said there is nothing conclusive, he has not expressed himself plainly, and Oliver has again to take the lead: 'I've heard say the boy's called Ole Andreas, but surely that can't be right? I shall never believe that.'

The carpenter (furiously): 'Oh, you've heard that! Then what the devil do you mean by asking? I believe you've come to search the house. What do you want here?'

Oliver (mildly, by no means displeased at the other's exasperation): 'All right, it's no business of mine what the boy's called, and I won't ask you any more questions—'

'No, not when you know the answers already!' snorts the carpenter through his great nose.

After a well-judged silence, Oliver resumes as quietly as ever: 'Well, perhaps you're wondering why I've come to see you, Mattis?'

Mattis answers with a blunt yes.

'I can see that!' But now Oliver brings two banknotes out into the light of day and says: 'Yes, I've come for a certain purpose. What was the cost of those doors that you made for me once?'

'Doors?'

'That you let me have. I want to pay for them. It's been a long time, but it hasn't been very easy for me.'

Mattis the carpenter is completely bewildered and can only say: 'Well, there was no hurry, either—'

'I can't expect you to wait till doomsday.'

'Those doors? No, there was no hurry. Is it the doors you've come about?'

Fair-minded and dignified, Oliver speaks: 'You see, Mattis, you never sent me a bill, so I have some excuse. But now we needn't worry about the price, I'll pay every farthing. And if there's been anything wrong between us, I want to put it right.'

Mattis mutters that there may have been faults on both sides. He seems to regret his vehemence. He says: 'Won't you sit down on that chair?' However, he remains guarded and apparently un-enthusiastic about the visit; he talks mainly to the child.

'Yes, he's found a good home here with you,' Oliver pronounces. 'A great thing for him! Well, I must say, that Maren deserves a helping hand. She's not got a bad figure.'

'Oh,' says Mattis.

'Not at all a bad figure. And of course a while ago, when she had the child, she wasn't as old as she is now. So we needn't be so surprised at her.'

'No, baby, you mustn't go putting the watch in your mouth and getting it stuck in your throat! For that matter, it isn't always the age that counts,' says Mattis in matter-of-fact ones, and turning to Oliver, 'It's when they have those nostrils that keep waving and waving.'

'Ha-ha-ha, yes, you've hit the mark, Mattis! What was I going to say? He has brown eyes. I see.'

No answer.

'They're supposed to be good eyes, brown ones are. As for me, though, I've got blue eyes and I've managed all right with them. But nearly all my children have got brown eyes; it's just as if I'm only to have children with brown eyes.'

The carpenter still makes no accusation, but he doesn't exoner-ate him either, as he answers: 'His mother has brown eyes. But, by the by, you oughtn't to let the child listen to this sort of talk any longer; he understands.'

'He can't understand.'

'Him? You can't talk about a thing that he doesn't understand. Not one blessed thing. If you say "door" he looks at the door, and if you sing a little song at the bench, he knows it's for him.'

'Mine were just the same,' says Oliver.

'He passes all belief,' continues the carpenter. 'I must watch out that he doesn't learn to read the paper from end to end just by listening to me. Bedtime prayers and folding hands are nothing to him.'

'Just like it was with mine!' declares Oliver.

No, to judge by the carpenter, it seems there can't be another child like the fellow lying there.

Oliver repeats: 'Well, in any case, he's lucky to have found a home with you!' All the same, Oliver is disappointed with the way things are going, he's getting nowhere, there's nothing doing, he must worm his way a little further, nearer the abyss. What was I going to say, I'm so forgetful – ah, yes, here I am with the money, as you see, but there's one thing I thought I'd ask you and that is, you've got the child with you now and you've got fond of him; but supposing now his father came one day and owned up and confessed . . .?

The carpenter asks sharply: 'Are you proposing to fetch him?'

'Me? Fetch the father? Where should I find him? I'm only a cripple.'

'I'd believe anything of you!'

Oliver (smiling): 'I don't want to make myself out better than I am, far from it. But that wasn't what we were talking about. No, one fine day maybe you won't have the child with you any longer—'

'Oh, so they'll come and take him? Just let them try!' Mattis threatens.

'I meant that one fine day you may be changing your circumstances and getting married, and then where will the child go?'

'Go?' shrieks the carpenter. 'Do you think I'm going to throw him out? He shan't go anywhere, I'll see to that!'

'But if the father comes—'

'Who is it you're sitting there ferreting and asking questions for? What the hell is it you want to know? Are you afraid of something, are you scared for your own skin? Sitting there stuffing his ears full of indecent talk – I won't have it.'

Oliver just manages to get in: 'Me? I'm not saying anything indecent, I'm just sitting here with money for you, these two notes—'

'Did you ever hear the like, sitting down here all innocent and talking filth? Money – what's that in aid of? Ah!' he exclaims suddenly. Light dawns at last on Mattis the carpenter; he goes white with anger, and gets up with the child on his arm. 'Stow your money and get out, I'm not touching it!'

Well, Oliver gets up, he has no intention of fighting, but as he hobbles to the door he goads the carpenter by saying: 'Hee-hee, one might almost think the child was yours. Is it you who's the father?'

'Me, did you say?'

'I'm only asking.' And now beyond question he is trying to get Mattis the carpenter still more worked up. He says: 'It's a fact, isn't it, that you made a cot for him?'

Mattis defends himself. 'It wasn't for him. And do you lie on the bare floor yourself, may I ask? Have you never heard of a child having a cot before? But now you get out of this house – enough's enough!' yells Mattis, putting down the child. 'And take your bribe money with you! Ha-ha, you thought you could bribe me to keep quiet about you being the father, but it didn't work. Keep your money for someone else, you swine, you! Out of my house, I say!'

And Oliver goes.

He looks well satisfied, as if things could not have gone better; he is actually humming again. When he gets home, Petra is of course bursting with curiosity, but he offers no explanation. He contents himself with being more of a man than ever, posting himself at the front door with his hand in the V of his waistcoat as if it were not in the least cold, and from this vantage point spouting nonsense to any woman or girls among the passers-by.

Good times, a united family, *joie de vivre* – yes, we're on the upgrade, we're sitting prettier and prettier, God grant we may keep it that way! This found expression in several really nice actions: Mattis the carpenter, you remember, had that red mailbox on the front of his house, so Oliver brought a brass doorknob for his front door and said to Petra: 'Let me see that you keep it bright!' At the risk of being caught throwing his money about, he bought little presents, out of the goodness of his heart, both for his daughters and for his wife, and even came home more often than before with a bag of coffee for Granny – which incidentally can't have cost him anything.

What an exhilarating business life had become! The winter went by, the year went by, and Oliver was right: nothing goes as quickly as a year. Nothing much happened, but enough to make a change, the family was unaccustomed to more; the baby was the blue-eyed type again, and admittedly that was a damned difficult question for anyone to fathom all at once, but somehow it no longer had the enormous significance of former days. Ought he to search Petra's heart? But then what would happen if his own heart was searched; had he not also got a certain reputation in the town? On one occasion when he marvelled with a touch of bitterness over these new blue eyes among the children, Petra retorted: 'Well, haven't you and I both got blue eyes?'

In the course of a conversation with his old friend Jørgen, Oliver argued that the plants of the field were not all alike, either: that some bore fruit above ground, and others below. 'Take apples now – some are red and some yellow. But then take the potato, which grows underground; one sort of potato is yellow and another sort completely blue. It's just the same with our human eyes: they come in very different colours. I've been thinking that perhaps it depends on me: that's to say, when I'm craziest about women, then it's brown eyes – what do you think, Jørgen?'

Now fisherman Jørgen was over seventy, mind, married to Old Lydia of the tongue like a grater, father of three big lady daughters, and by now his eyes were almost the colour of milk; he didn't know, couldn't remember. 'How do you mean, crazy?' he asked. He expressed the opinion that many a woman, too, could be crazy and bad-tempered.

But it seemed to Oliver up to him to make himself properly understood. 'Now take that Maren Salt as the latest example,' he said. 'Do you know, they're accusing me of being the father of her boy, and he has brown eyes.'

'Ah,' said fisherman Jørgen.

'Or take many others in the town; there's plenty of brown eyes, and I get practically nothing else from under me. All I ask now is that you don't believe everything they accuse me of, Jørgen, that I implore you. But I'm not going to make excuses for myself either, because I have a fiery and violent nature in me, and at home we get brown eyes and blue eyes from under me as the mood takes.'

'Ay,' said fisherman Jørgen.

Thus, Oliver rose day by day, occupying a more and more secure position in his fantasy world. Say no more, he was its creator and upholder, he walked about it with his own yardstick and made it wider; after a couple of years he stood on an eminence and looked out over a great land which was his.

And did he really manage to exist in his world? Did he not burst out laughing and give it up? One is saddled with the world one creates, as all creators are.

From time to time he had vexations to swallow. He might feel in the mood for going out one evening and taking a turn in the street, flirting, making passes, chatting up the dames. He knew the language and procedures of dalliance from his sailor days, but his old luck had deserted him; whether because he had lost his marksmanship or because he failed to find the right quarry, his shots missed fire. What had gone wrong, why did the birds all laugh at him? The saplings, the spawn, were they unable, as it were, to summon up faith in his honourable intentions? Why the devil did they shudder when he started groping at them? Ruling a world had its disadvantages.

Recently he had started rowing out to sea again. Ah yes, this was a good, well-tested resource when his trials got the upper hand, when, God knows, life had grown tough again. Rumour had it that he fished to earn a bit extra, but this fishing seemed to be not entirely serious, so often did he return home without catching anything. But did he not need a little cash, was there no bottom to that remarkable inside waistcoat pocket? Alas, he saw with misgiving that the pocket was getting empty; he might have borrowed to check the shrinkage, he might have stolen; it is not good to see poverty staring one in the face. He had his long-standing position at the warehouse, he had his wages, fair enough; day-to-day life he was able to sustain. But the little extras in the way of finery and candy that he had grown accustomed to were beyond his means. What after all had become of the money from the eiderdown? It was a tidy sum of money, and the devil only knew where it had gone! He had neither paid lawyer Fredriksen one krone on the house nor seen himself or his family in clothes for two years. By going to the next town he had changed a couple of fattish banknotes, but that was a year ago now. His inside pocket was empty. He might peep into it, he might turn it inside out, but it was empty.

So was fishing not a necessity?

In itself Oliver had no objection to rocking in a boat again. He equipped himself with a pot and fishing tackle and rowed out; he would gladly stay out from Saturday evening till Monday morning, fishing first and foremost to provide the meals he needed during those thirty-six hours. They were indolent, carefree hours; he did more drifting than rowing, he poked his nose into the coves and explored the islands; naturally he began collecting eiderdown again, naturally he kept a weather eye open for wreckage and driftwood. Once he found an empty barrel, another time a bottle with a scrap of paper in it – nothing of any value. Far out, near the path of the steamers, a nesting cliff rose straight out of the sea; he had not been there for two years, it was a mighty long way, but it ought to repay the effort of getting there. The birds nested on ledges up and down the face and were not particularly shy.

The days went by, and what a good, kind boy was Abel, slipping his father a two-krone piece as occasion offered; otherwise there would have been few goodies for Oliver. How indeed could he have afforded them? He had once had a son named Frank, a learned boy and a marvel; ah, but he sent home nothing at all, no longer came in person, and never wrote letters. According to rumour, he had a teaching job somewhere and was going on with his studies, on and on. Where would it end? Little Constance Henriksen of the shipyard had received a letter from him; he had a year to go, it said, then he would be finished. Thus, Oliver could expect no help from that quarter for a year, a long year, but what came then would of course be something worth having; it wasn't everyone who had a learned son up his sleeve!

Meanwhile, he had Abel, another brick of a boy; the fair-minded Oliver made no distinction between his sons – if anything Abel was perhaps now nearer his father's heart. Oliver often wandered into the smithy on his way to the warehouse in the morning; Abel would already be at work, and it amused his father to chat with him for a while and hear how things were going. They were always going admirably. Abel had now taken over the smithy and was in charge of it all – ah, what a son to have! There were others who came to the smithy; the Thumbtack came; he was a fireman on the coastal run, and was evidently waiting till one of Abel's sisters was old enough, then she would be his – such, it seemed, were the Thumbtack's intentions. He called at the smithy and said: 'Have you bought the smithy?' 'No,' said Abel, 'I've nothing to buy a smithy with, but I'm taking the place of the master. Can you find me a hammer lad?' 'Well,' said the Thumbtack, 'the day you buy yourself a steam hammer that runs on kerosene, you'll save having a hammer lad.' 'Don't stand there talking bull!' retorted Abel. 'I'm not talking bull,' was the other's opinion. 'I've seen several hammers like that at Horten.'* Abel too knew about steam hammers that ran on kerosene, but why should he buy such a hammer for a smithy that wasn't his? Forget it! The Thumbtack suggested he might buy the hammer on his own account and pocket the hammer lad's board and wages, an arrangement that would also benefit his master, Carlsen. 'Where would I find the money for that hammer?' inquired Abel. The Thumbtack replied 'You've got some of your own put aside, I imagine; I can lend you some, and the rest you can owe.' How badly the Thumbtack must have been in love with Abel's sister Bluebell!

No, the forge was not yet Abel's but it was now in his hands and he earned good wages. Blacksmith Carlsen was not always absent from the forge, not entirely absent, but mostly he would stand by the vice, filing something or other that needed a bit more finish; in the running of the place he took less and less part. 'What do you think?' he would ask Abel on the rare occasions when he took on a job. Besides, he was not even half a man now, he came so late and went so early. This was what enabled Oliver to have his son entirely to himself when he paid his morning calls.

They exchanged small talk and discussed the events of the town. 'No, old Jørgens getting more and more of an idiot,' said Oliver. 'He doesn't know the difference between yellow potatoes and blue potatoes – why should I waste my time talking to a man like that? I take to my heels when I see him!' Father and son never disagreed, they talked amicably about everything, and fraternally, as it were, about the things nearest their hearts; when they parted, they had planned no *coup,* decided in favour of no particular *Weltanschauung,* far from it; but Oliver had been told what his son had to do that day, whose buggy he was doing this ironwork for (it was for Consul Johnsen's country residence), who owned the handsome folding screen that had come in since yesterday (it was the doctor's). Ah, that Abel, he was a son and a half, he worked for all the gentry!

* Horten is a small town on the west side of the Oslo fjord. Trans.

Abel asked: 'So what are your views about that steam hammer I told you about? You promised to think it over.'

Needless to say, Dad hadn't a clue about this fabulous hammer, as his son must have known from the start; so wasn't Abel a kind boy, wanting to hear Dad's views? But perhaps he had no one closer to him to talk to; he was never condescending to his father; he listened to him with inward sympathy. He seemed to need Dad's approval of all he undertook.

'This I will say,' answered Oliver, 'that I've knocked about the world a good deal and seen all manner of nations, and now I've thought it over abundantly. And if you can get that hammer, then you should just take it before anyone can say knife. That's my advice to you.'

'Ah.'

'Yes, I'm telling you straight. Because there's no other master in any trade who has a hammer like that, it'll be the talk of the town and of the country, too, and just you see the sparks, Abel, when that fellow hits the iron!'

'Yes.'

'It'll get you in the paper, you can take my word for that, because I've been in the paper myself. I rescued a full-rigged ship from foreign parts, brought her in from the sea through storm and tempest and laid her alongside the quay. Then I just sent ashore for the consul and the report. What do you suppose they made of it, all the millions of people who came down on the quay and saw it? And three days later I was in the paper.'

'Yes.'

An event Oliver never wearied of wearying others with. But he didn't forget the steam hammer, either; no, he let it be known that he couldn't get it out of his head. And if one of these days he could be of any help to his son, supposing, that's to say, he could lay hands on any money that *was* money, he'd come round with it that instant. 'Just give me time to look around!' he said, nodding with a pensive air, as though he might soon perceive a possibility. Oh, money would turn up somewhere; if all else failed, he'd lie out at sea every night and bring home load after load of driftwood that he could sell ...

Just idle chatter, empty patter; when Dad left, Abel was as poor as ever, a little poorer in fact, since he had lost a two-krone bet. What happened was that Abel said: 'You can't row out at night any more, you haven't the strength.' 'I've just as much strength as ever from the waist up,' Dad replied. 'You can't even lift that pig of iron there.' 'Oh, can't I? When I lifted it last year?' 'Yes, but now you're a year older. Never mind, I'll bet you this two-krone piece!' Oliver didn't even spit on his palms; he lifted the pig and won the two-krone piece. 'I won't take it!' he said. 'No, maybe you'd rather have the pig over your skull!' his son retorted, and made him take the coin.

Just pleasantry and friendship.

Neither of them mentioned Little Lydia or hinted at marriage any more; no, Abel was now a much older and steadier man. The greater part of his beard, admittedly, still grew on his hands, but being in charge of a smithy and taking the master's place was an aid to growing up and maturing. There had been other contributory causes, however: Old Lydia, for example, had played a not insignificant part in his development. He might shrink from acknowledging the fact, but on a certain evening a couple of years ago she of the tongue like a grater had certainly given him a lesson that he had not forgotten. There had been something in what she said, a whiplash over his ears, an awakening whose natural consequence had been that he started staying away from fisherman Jørgen's house. Right, he would keep out of the way as he had promised. He needed most urgently to find out when Edevart was due home from New Guinea or wherever it was; but he gave the house the go-by. Later on he had run into Old Lydia; now that it was all over, she seemed most friendly, nodding and saying, 'Hullo, Abel!' and a few more words in passing, and he had answered politely. Some weeks later he met his sweetheart herself, Little Lydia herself. Curiously enough, he would now have preferred not to meet her, at least not at that moment, as he left the smithy all grimy and unkempt. The encounter being unavoidable, he went miserable at the knees, but managed a greeting of a kind before passing on. During those weeks he had suffered the onset of bashfulness. After that he met her from time to time in the town with parcels in her arms; he might have stepped forward and carried them for her, but he did not.

No, he didn't mention marriage any more.

He called out after his father: 'You didn't lift that pig as high as you did last year!'

'What didn't I do?' Dad shouted back. 'You could have sat on top if you'd wanted!'

Surely this ability of Oliver's to joke so refreshingly argued an unusually good mood? On the contrary, today he was suffering from unusually dire misgivings. When he found himself in the privacy of the warehouse, when he had tidied himself up and looked in the mirror and started work, it became clear to him that danger loomed: he had met lawyer Fredriksen in the town again. That Scrooge, that bloodsucker, had looked at a cripple as if he owned him. And by now it was two years since the last round.

Oliver exaggerated grossly: the lawyer had walked past him in an averagely decent, preoccupied manner, but of course Oliver was no longer the man of courage: his inside pocket was empty, the improvement in his character undone. When he came home to dinner, he had a talk with Petra; what he told was no news to her – she had met the lawyer herself.

Oliver asked: 'Did he say anything?'

'Did he say anything, indeed! Is he likely to say anything to me – in the street?'

'How did he seem to you?'

'I've no idea. Seem? I don't go looking at men, least of all at him. The old pig plagued me enough last time he was home.'

'I thought he had a disagreeable look.'

After a while Oliver returned to the subject: no doubt lawyer Fredriksen would now be starting his unreasonable demands again. 'I'm not stirring another inch in his direction,' said Petra. What, would she rather they all became homeless? And Oliver expounded the position from his point of view: he had never dreaded being homeless so much as now. They could only hope that the lawyer was human; but if he was again set and bent on taking the path of murder against a cripple, then Petra would have to bring him to reason good and proper once again.

'What do you say to that?' asked Oliver.

Petra thought it over and considered it not impossible. But there were so many things against it, she hadn't even got that much in the way of clothes—

Clothes?

She'd worn out those wretched slips. And wouldn't she also need a blouse, the type that buttons down the front? And other things besides?

If that was all, Oliver could certainly get some clothes on credit. He perked up again, tilted his cap at an angle as if he had powerful protectors, and spoke as the family breadwinner: 'I'll go straight down to the fashion department and get those articles for you!'

On such an occasion, of course, he was bound to exert his powers to the utmost.

28

Upsetting Oliver and his household must, however, have been quite the least of lawyer Fredriksen's concerns just now; he had very different things to occupy him. For in these days the town was overtaken by such an affliction, so unprecedented a convulsion, that the earth appeared to stand still. What was the erstwhile mail robbery by comparison with the sinking of the steamship *Fia*? What signified anything else when the steamship *Fia* was uninsured and might drag down Double Consul Johnsen himself to ruin and destruction?

Nothing else signified.

Other portentous events had already befallen the town: it was at this time that the old headmaster died, he who knew so many different tongues and had instructed the last generation in grammar and necessary knowledge; now he was dead, and all his learning buried with him. Another matter was well and truly aired at the pump: for two months the doctor's wife had been complaining that she was with child; it was her first, and God in heaven, how she detested it and how she dreaded it and how she suffered – was there no mortal remedy for this misfortune, was there no justice in the world? Then one day the doctor's wife was suddenly no longer with child. What? shrieked the women at the pump – whereupon they neither continued pumping nor went on their way with their buckets but stayed there rooted to the spot. Had the person made a mistake about her inside and never ...? Nonsense! Get away! But how unequally Our Lord divided between women: some had to be mothers year after year, others escaped all their lives. That was what being married to a doctor meant: he had the learning, he could do what he liked, no problem ...

In short, sensation had not been wanting.

But then one morning the thunder rolled over the pump as the news reached town that the *Fia* had gone to the bottom. It came from Scheldrup Johnsen in New Orleans; his telegram, three days old, was short and to the point, specified time and place, and assumed that the insurance was in order. But the insurance was not in order. And at this point the lightning struck the pump.

In this little coastal town which lived by its shipping and by nothing else, every woman knew what insurance meant, so surely Double Consul Johnsen ought to have known! Wasn't it precisely the kind of big thing he kept in his own hands, leaving Berntsen to manage the store and the fashion department? A clash ensued between the consul and his chief clerk: the consul believed he had ordered Berntsen to renew the insurance, and sure enough Berntsen had renewed the insurance that time he was asked to do so, but not again.

But the consul had given the order once for all.

No, answered Berntsen, that had not been his impression.

The consul tore his hair and insisted that, yes, he had expressly meant for all time, for life. Besides, Berntsen must have worked it out for himself; couldn't he see all the papers floating around the consul's desk, all the things that occupied him, the enormous daily post, the reports to his governments, the books, a world, a chaos – couldn't Berntsen have worked it out for himself?

And indeed Berntsen appeared to have stepped in to some effect; otherwise the consul's desk would have looked still worse.

Yes, but the consul had put out the insurance papers for attention.

Berntsen had seen the papers, had had his eye on them for three weeks; then they had disappeared.

Certainly, the consul had finally put them away as having been attended to.

Berntsen had heard nothing about attending to them.

Yes, damn it all, the consul had told him ages ago to send off the premium. 'Don't forget the insurance' has been his instructions. And now pray God have mercy on his soul!

The consul's lady came lumbering down to the office, weeping, dabbing at her nose and eyes, yelping, trembling, raving; it was not nice for the lady, who in addition was evidently suffering from a liver complaint, her face was so yellow. The daughter came, Mademoiselle Fia; she took it very differently, she refrained from adding her stone to the family's burden. It couldn't be helped, she said, afflictions had to be borne. They must show they had culture, she said, the Countess said; for her part, she would work harder than ever, she had her art and her calling. The two reproductions she had made in the Louvre could go, she would send them straight off to be auctioned. Don't worry, Papa!

The consul neither heard nor saw.

Ah, but there was another man in the town who both heard and saw, lawyer Fredriksen, a smart fellow, a lucky winner, a real devil in fact for getting his sums right. Here he was, home again at last after almost sitting out his time in the Storting and on his commission; and now his appearance had improved, he looked less greedy than before, God knows if he hadn't had face massage – how else could he have acquired that almost spiritual mildness? Granted, his election *in absentia* as mayor must have had some effect on him; but that would hardly account for a lawyer's visiting the recesses of sorrow and poverty and sitting by the half hour in out-and-out condolence. He went to the headmaster's daughter, who had lost her father, and to the postmaster, who had lost his wits, and generally made himself agreeable. Such was now the lawyer. Why, the moment he stepped ashore from the boat, the infamous Olaus had been impertinent and called him just 'Fredriksen', but he had taken it with a smile and said: 'Carry up my trunk, then, Olaus.' Olaus answered: 'You can carry your own trunk!'

Before throwing himself anew into his onerous public duties and calling a first meeting of the Town Council, he allowed himself a little break and took the air in light clothes and a large hat; he had bought himself a stick, his boots were in good repair, he smoked cigars non-stop, he was a changed man. What was he taking the air *for*; why should this heavy man trudge all the way up to the Prospect? His solitude had a contrived, a studied look; it was not entirely unlike love and the deeper feelings. As he went past Consul Johnsen's garden with its concrete urns and its scent of lilacs and its butterflies, he raised his large hat to Mrs Johnsen, with whom he had no quarrel, to Miss Johnsen, and yes, to the consul himself if they were all sitting on the veranda. He might be chairman of a commission against the consul, but the man's home and family must be kept out of it.

'Welcome home from Paris!' he thundered over the fence to Mademoiselle Fia.

Really, she may have thought, she had been back from Paris some time by now, and it would have been equally appropriate for her to welcome him home from the Storting, but she only gave a negligent nod in token of thanks. Who could understand such a person?

Instead of continuing on his way, he leaned his plump arms on the fence and said: 'I expect you find it's good to be home again?'

'Yes.'

'I find the same.'

How rude can one be? The consul sat there on the veranda reading a newspaper; eventually he woke up and raised his hat a fraction in return; then he calmly resumed his reading.

'I do indeed. Like you I find it's good to be home again. Not that my home is anything very special.'

'Won't you come in?' asked Mrs Johnsen.

'No, thanks, it's rather late. I'm just out for a little bedtime stroll. I'm able to bring you greetings from the Prospect, Miss Fia.'

'It must have been nice up there this evening?'

'Magnificent. A sunset and some extra nice clouds. Mind you, I don't understand these things like you painters and artist, but for my money it was something unique. Couldn't you be persuaded to take a little turn up there?'

'Now? No.'

'No, I see. And of course you prefer going on your own.'

Now the consul was relighting his cigar, but even while doing so, he could scarcely tear himself away from his reading; what on earth did he find there of so much interest? And what about his wife? They said Mrs Johnsen had not always been so tongue-tied; in the old days she had chattered away happily enough whenever lawyer Fredriksen occupied himself in conversing with her. Yes indeed, she had even seemed to fancy him a little. How rich and grand these people had become, and how compulsively they flaunted the fact! Look, there sits the daughter of the house, old enough this many a year, attractive enough and to spare, and there she sits, holding tight on to herself, just because she's rolling in money and such a catch. For that matter, lawyer Fredriksen could have been of considerable service to the family; he was no longer just anybody, he was a member of the Storting, a great man who might become even greater; his prospects of becoming even greater were almost certain, and the new elections would settle the matter. Why was he standing here, paying court over a garden fence? Most unsuitable for someone like himself – let her come within his reach, let him fasten on with his little finger! He had learned a thing or two in the great capital, he would fare better next time, he would put his arm around her . . .

'Good evening!' he called, and went on his way.

By the time the consul looked up and raised his hat in return, all he could see was the lawyer's back and his folds of flesh just below the hat. How insolent can one be? And what about that reading? The consul flung the newspaper away, rose languidly to his feet, yawned aloud, and said: 'No, I'm for bed.'

'Well, good night,' said the ladies.

Everything breathed peace, nothing breathed danger. But next day the lightning struck.

Lawyer Fredriksen first heard the news at the barber's; later he ran into the pharmacist, who confirmed it. Actually the lawyer had thought of getting a good shave and strutting to the Prospect via Consul Johnsen's house for a few more days, but on hearing of the loss of the steamship *Fia*, he quickly changed his mind and took the road to the house of Grits-and-Groats Olsen. There was nothing uncertain about his walk, nothing mysterious; he had done a sum and got it right, so now of course he was going to Grits-and-Groats Olsen's, where else should he go? What self-fulfilment in his walk!

He was expected. Miss Olsen flushed at the sound of his voice; for two days she had known he was back, and for all of two days he had not called.

'No, you see, they've made me mayor while I've been away,' he explained. 'I had to make myself conversant with these new matters. I've been working. And by the evening I was so tired that I needed a solitary walk; otherside, I should have allowed myself the pleasure of calling on the young lady straightaway.'

'I heard Mama and Papa say you were home.'

She ventured no further, did Miss Olsen; but if at this moment he had given her to understand that not for one second longer could she escape his raging love, she might well have shilly-shallied. It was over two years since their last talk. Old age was that much nearer; a couple of letters in the interim had barely sustained life in her dying memory of him. With the other painter, the house painter's son, there was nothing doing – he was only a mad artist, ready enough to fall in love with one person or another, in season and out, but as for constancy, oh, dear me, no. His latest exploit had been to go down on the quay and paint Olaus! Really, not quite the thing after painting Consul Olsen and his family. Not that Consul Olsen and his family were snooty, but they had no desire to be the talk of the town. And besides, marrying a painter was a tricky business; her sister had tried it and had not always found it too much fun, there was even talk of a divorce – the latest fashion in the land. By now she had two children; in previous years she had eased the budget by going for long stays with the old people at home, and returning laden with money and cartloads of everything. During the last year, admittedly, the situation had changed – the painter had made more of a name, he exhibited in Berlin and got higher prices for his art. Consequently it was now the painter who hinted at divorce, now that he could stand on his own two feet. It was so sad and so stupid, and indeed the catastrophe had so far been averted, but beyond question the marriage had turned out badly. No, these artistic connections were not always very secure.

But what about the deputy district magistrate? Gone. Here a year, then off to the Audit Department; nobody missed him, nobody mourned. His successor, another law graduate, turned out to have a sweetheart, complete with engagement ring – What brought him to this town, and what could Miss Olsen do with him? When he called, she didn't walk right out of the house; no, but broadly speaking she stayed in her room – why should she come down? Subsequently she saw him in town, looking like an exile, so threadbare of trouser, so preoccupied and depressed, but with his sweetheart and his ring. A man like that had the right to be left in peace.

And so Miss Olsen had remained at home, growing older and nursing her memories. Her heart had not exactly yearned for the lawyer, but he was not entirely out of her thoughts; he might pass for a bird in the hand. What was the position? Was there a prospect of his becoming a Minister of State? It was still Nature herself who directed her tactics; one day she too must be a married woman.

'Won't you light a cigar?' she said to the lawyer.

He began to speak of the sinking, that unmistakable writing on the wall for the Johnsen family. Imagine, failing to insure a steamship! What *did* the consul do in his office if he could forget something so supremely important? There were limits! Mind you, one ought to feel sympathy for people's misfortunes, but God knew, maybe this chastisement would do the worthy Johnsens no harm. What a brazen set of pompous asses they had become!

'I don't know,' said Miss Olsen. 'I don't think Scheldrup's an ass.'

The lawyer answered indifferently: 'I've no idea what Scheldrup is or isn't. I'm talking about the daughter and the parents.'

'I wonder how Scheldrup will take it. What do you think he'll do?'

At this the lawyer looked at her from another planet; nor could he help frowning as he did so. 'What a curious question! I haven't gone into it, I have other things to think about. What such-and-such a boy will do? I've no idea. Presumably carry on as before. Doesn't he stand behind a counter or something of the kind?'

'Scheldrup? No, he's never stood behind a counter.'

'No? Well, it's a matter of indifference to me.'

'Perhaps he'll come home and take over the business.'

The lawyer was irritated by this chatter and tried to maintain his lordly demeanour. 'The question of who's going to take over the bankrupt estate and the little shop is one I really haven't had time to consider. Maybe Scheldrup's up to it. I've no idea. Has he learned anything?'

'Learned? Surely that's what he's been doing abroad all these years.'

'Really? Attending school, studying at foreign universities?

Strange that nobody's heard about it!' But at this point the lawyer must have realized that he was setting about it in altogether the wrong way, for he added: 'Scheldrup Johnsen is quite beside the point, which is whether it might do the rest of the family no harm to have their proud necks bowed. It was them I meant.'

Miss Olsen could afford to put in a word for Fia: 'She paints so nicely.'

'Do you think so?' Here the lawyer looked as if he might feel obliged to express a contrary opinion. And when the young lady asked, 'Why, don't you?' he answered: 'Shan't we talk about something else – you and I?'

Which brought him to his piece of business.

Ah, but he might well have been wise to keep his mouth shut; only that was not his style. Naturally Miss Olsen must have found his coolness over a period of years fairly conspicuous, and now for him to explain himself, exonerate himself, was no easy task. Where should he have learned the difficult art of wooing a heart while meaning the dowry? Added to which, his lion's roar was against him – a voice made for controversy and debate, whereas here it had to whisper sweet nothings, to sing as it were; honestly, another man would have given up. Unaware of any danger, he charged straight ahead.

Fortunately, Miss Olsen was not too particular. Not that she hadn't learned a few genteel quirks over the years, but she still knew the proper way to size things up, she was no *ingénue*. In real terms, Fia Johnsen was less advanced, for all her Countess's airs.

The lawyer, of course, began far too emphatically – the peasant, the oaf. Cooperation, he said – was there, then, a possibility of cooperation between them? Had she thought it over?

To this she made no reply; but what was cooperation? In any case, she hardly seemed to regard it as a word that gave her the choice between turning scarlet and leaving the room.

He enlarged in some detail on how he had thought and thought about her during these two years – yes, she might have forgotten him during this time, but he had forgotten nothing; witness his two letters. All the expressions he had used at their preliminary conference were repeated in his letters and remained valid. And so, young lady, the question now was this: was there a measure of understanding and inclination on both sides?

No answer. He waited for a very long time, and finally she said, as he had done: 'Let's talk about something else!'

Was this more affectation? He must have felt he was no longer on completely sure ground. Her chatter about Scheldrup Johnsen had discomposed him; she had insisted so definitely that he didn't stand behind a counter, she could imagine him coming home and taking over the business – what did all this mean at such a moment? He couldn't sing, damn it, but he continued to talk. Did she need more time for reflection? For him the time was now ripe; that very morning he had been driven by uncertainty to come on this very mission of hearing how matters stood. But perhaps the fact was that she needed still more time for reflection?

She just said: 'Yes.'

Really? He had to admit he could scarcely believe it, after a lapse of two long years and after all there had been between them. To put it bluntly, did she not feel that this town had become a sad hole? A town of sorrow and brankruptcy and misery, while in other places people laughed and enjoyed themselves. What kind of amusements were there here?

'I'm not used to amusements,' she interpolated with a smile.

But she could *get* used to them, it appeared. Ah, those other places, with their fine streets and shop windows and Tivoli and cafés – did not such things tempt her? As for one's style of living, why, that was entirely up to oneself; you couldn't name a single thing that was not to be had. All the amenities of life were offered to you on a platter: the papers came morning and evening, the band played, the Storting flew its flag; on Sundays you could lie in bed all day if you wanted, or you could go to the theatre or ride in a streetcar or stroll in the university gardens, or hear a good lecture. What was there here? If she shared his wishes she would get away from here ...

This again was not exactly singing, but it could have been a lot worse, and the young lady should have shown some interest; but no. God alone knew what could induce this lady to let her hair down a little. In two cautious stages he moved nearer to her, and finally he reached her; ah yes, he had learned a thing or two in the capital, his fumblings had grown bolder. He got his arm around her and said, 'Dear young lady,' he said, 'if we could arrive at a rather better understanding—'

She got up, she actually got up – but stopped short of dashing for the door; the lady was confronted by no inescapable fate, she merely looked at him and said: 'I hope you're a gentleman, Fredriksen?'

Naturally. Hm. But most ladies positively liked a little flirtation, he said, nodding and winking one eye as if he knew all about it. He had intended no harm, merely an approach; after all, she knew who he was, between friends—

'Yes, I know all that,' she replied, and sat down on the sofa.

Well now, naturally he had mixed with masses of ladies, there's no denying it, gone to parties and the palace, heard great singers and all – oh yes, and some were absolutely A-one and unique, for his money; they wore dresses with very low necks, they stepped back and curtsied, they wore necklaces and diamonds. But for starting a family with and embarking with them on a life's partnership – no! thundered Fredriksen, shaking his head. For that, on the other hand, he had always remembered a certain lady in his own little town, and on her he had set all his hopes—

'On Fia,' said Miss Olsen.

How pat it came! For a moment he was decidedly caught and could only ask: 'Why do you mention her?'

Miss Olsen smiled.

'Fia,' he said. 'Let her be, let her go around in her red hat, let her paint. Honestly and truly, can one imagine a more useless creature? But that's not our headache; I don't know why we're talking about her. Now don't misunderstand me, young lady. Art and nice paintings and pictures are very important in their own way. But, Lord, how different that female is from you, young lady: she's only half the woman you are, skinny and delicate, and those spindle shanks – God help me!'

Miss Olsen could hardly have been averse to being preferred for once and given pride of place, nor did the lawyer let up for a moment: if she was unaccustomed to appreciation, now was the time to give it to her! Miss Olsen actually got up and took the ashtray to him, so that he could enjoy himself, and at this token of friendliness, of domesticity, love must have carried him away, for he encircled her with his arm. She repeated her warning: 'Remember you're a gentleman, Fredriksen!' but instead of vanishing like a dream, she happened to fall into the chair alongside. There was really no danger of his eating her alive, he was only a little rough and uncultured like all men – a thing, incidentally, not unbecoming in men.

'But you must admit that you've been greatly taken up with Fia,' she said.

'With Fia! How could she say such a thing, how could she sully her lips in such a way? Listen now, a female painter, a real case of anaemia! He would travel around the world for Miss Olsen, which was more than he would for Fia's pictures. There, you see! Art by all means, but for everyday purposes he preferred Miss Olsen's legs and arms and bosom and figure in general. 'My dear young lady!' he said.

'She has nice teeth.'

Was it still Fia they were talking about? It was diabolic how persistent Miss Olsen could be when once she got going on a subject. His answer was to lean over towards her, considerably further over, get his arm around her, and make himself snug against her warm back, talking of course the while. Now he would tell her who had nice teeth. And he would tell her who was a nice handsome girl and an ornament to her wealthy home. Why, he had been to bigger places and, frankly, higher places, so he was able to make comparisons, and this he would maintain, that for a lovely figure and stature, by and large – whereas Fia – 'Take a look down at yourself, young lady, and then look at Fia; God help me if it isn't like descending from the clouds to the earth. And what's more, whatever she says or does, and however she looks, it's all tricks and dodges and lace and affectation.'

Here Miss Olsen was constrained to laugh at the lace, and the lawyer plucked up still more courage. 'If it had even been lace on her knickers!' he said.

He felt her back sliding away a little, as if she wanted to get up, but his arm held fast. Yes, he proclaimed, he just had to say that straight out. And ho-ho-ho, he laughed, it wasn't air one wanted to marry. He was not the type who hated the joys of life; on the contrary, he was a friend of fun and games and comforts in that field, and if he was not mistaken, Miss Olsen herself might have been shaped and made for that very purpose. Correct?

'Now you must let me go,' she said, and her back resumed its sliding motion.

There was no avoiding a return to gravity and business: he explained to her that the moment had arrived, the next election would of course return him once more to the national assembly, and then he was a fairly obvious choice for government office. He might seem sanguine in thinking and talking thus, but they needed someone to represent shipping, and as chairman of the Commission on Seamen he had of course acquired an exhaustive knowledge of the subject, he said.

'Fancy, then you'll be a Minister of State!' she said.

'In all human probability,' he replied. She didn't suppose he was sitting there fantasizing, did she? Not only had he been named in the papers as the coming man, but he had heard a thing or two behind the scenes. And, young lady, he asked her now in the fullness of his heart, might it not fit the bill rather nicely if she shared his destiny and became a well-known politician's wife, a Minister of State's wife?

No answer.

He talked on, though not without letting her understand that he would not be utterly at a loss without her either, he had quite a few acquaintances; but she, Miss Olsen, was his only thought. He took it for ganted that her parents, the consul and his wife, would have no objection, since he would be making her the reverse of an ordinary wife. What was her answer now? Might he hope?

And at last she answered: 'I don't know what to say.'

'You mean that at least you'll think about it?'

'Well, yes, I'll think about it.'

'How long?'

'I don't know. Don't let's talk about it any more now.'

'How about waiting till after the elections?' he asked.

'How long is that?'

'About a month, five weeks. I would like to have you with me when I return to Christiania. I need you and love you. We'll have our own little apartment and do some entertaining, people with influence, politicians. And while I remember: we'll buy two of your brother-in-law's paintings, I said we would and I'm a man of my word; but you must be the one to choose them. So shall we say that we'll wait till after the elections?'

'All right.'

She promised nothing, not a scrap. When he had gone she continued to sit there, thinking. Miss Olsen could not complain, nothing had been spoiled for her, she was not yet lost; indeed, her lot could be a great deal worse. It might even turn out that she got a husband whom the town would one day welcome home with flags; and in that case, who would be able to boast as much of her husband?

Hearing steps on the stairs, she thought: Is he coming back? A much greater surprise awaited her: in walked her father and Consul Johnsen, the double consul himself, who had never before set foot in her home – and who had now come to sell his country residence to Grits-and-Groats Olsen.

29

The double consul's situation was graver than people could have imagined. Far from concealing the fact that the *Fia* had gone to the bottom uninsured, in his initial panic he had proclaimed it far and wide. Now he was reaping the consequences, with himself and his chief clerk, Berntsen, hard put to keep their frightened creditors at bay. They deliberated, they did business, the consul had even insured the ship by telegram after she had gone down; but this he had done on his own, and Berntsen, acting on *his* own, had instantly cancelled the crazy instruction. Berntsen was a jewel.

But the jewel Berntsen was evidently human, too. While the town was in full hullabaloo, he kept his head clear and spared a human thought or two for himself.

Behold now, little clusters of people forming at street corners and discussing the catastrophe: how the mighty double consul was now bankrupt, the man who had never before been at a loss, who could afford anything, who was the focal point for the entire town's weal and woe, who gave right and left, who had the great house with veranda and balcony – now he was bankrupt. What did people know about it? Everybody knew. Had he not been visited yesterday by a dun from Christiania? And had he not been visited today by a dun from Hamburg? And would he not be visited by a third and a fourth, by a new one every day? People knew full well it was connected with the sinking.

The repercussions were wide: every citizen felt them, the doctor observed them in his practice, the shipyard closed down. Henriksen of the Shipyard lost his nerve and said: 'Go home, lads, I've reached the end of my tether!'

And now surely, with the town in convulsions, its inhabitants were due for soul-searching and repentance. Some years back they had received a solemn warning in the shape of a certain mail robbery, but of this they had taken no more heed than of a calf with two heads; people had remained their normal selves. But now? Would not a jolt of this order, an earthquake like the double consul's bankruptcy, succeed in stirring folks' hearts? Then what were folks made of? Why, the local paper had printed a call to folks to get religion, and the women at the pump discussed this programme so that is spread to every nook and cranny in the town; but people seemed unaffected by it, no progress could be detected in them from day to day, or if progress there was, it seemed to be from bad to worse. And would you believe it, by the same boat as the gentleman from Hamburg, another visitor had hit the town, an old lady and one-time celebrity, the dancing mistress! A mad world, alas. Just now, when people should have been getting religion and becoming unrecognizable for piety, back comes the dancing lady to work on a new generation. And people remained their normal selves.

What about Berntsen, though? Aha, Berntsen locked up as usual and walked with his customary tread past the clusters of people at one street corner after another, not a scrap depressed. And that is how the chief clerk of a bankrupt boss ought to behave: attend to his master's interests and look like a man with a commercial *coup* between his sights. Alongside which, he can spare a human thought or two for himself.

On this particular evening Berntsen did not go straight home to his attic room; no, he went direct to C. A. Johnsen's great house and asked to see Miss Fia. He was well aware that the consul was out; home was the last place the consul chose to go when anything hit him. Unfamiliar voices wafted in from the living room: the Heiberg girl, Alice, was there; Constance from the shipyard; even Miss Olsen, even the postmaster's daughter, she who served in the fashion department – they must have come lest Mademoiselle Fia be all alone in her sorrow.

Now Mademoiselle Fia, the Countess, was more than capable of showing that if she had sorrow she also had culture with which to bear it. At this moment she was entertaining the ladies with an Indian fairy tale she had been reading, and which she proposed to illustrate.

She admitted chief clerk Berntsen to the little adjoining room known as the cabinet, and sat down to listen. Well now, Berntsen must recently have had his bellyful of talking with the consul himself, and since Mrs Johnsen had never cared for Berntsen in her palmier days, he would scarcely turn to her now. Which left him only Fia. That must be it, what else could it be? He must just be sitting there explaining things to her, the tough spot the business was in, the bankruptcy, what else could he be sitting there explaining? All the same, it didn't take long, a matter of minutes, and when Berntsen left the house and Mademoiselle Fia rejoined the ladies, her face was as calm and unruffled as ever. The ladies gazed at her sorrowfully, Berntsen must have brought tidings of some fresh disaster; what else? But Fia showed her strength of character.

Yes, Fia now showed no mean strength of character. Vexed though she must have been by the obtrusive sympathy which these girls, so greatly her inferiors, permitted themselves, she smiled at them; yes, she smiled at them.

Seeing this, the ladies smiled back, all happiness. 'Good news?' they asked.

'Well, what do you know,' responded Fia. 'He proposed to me.'

One-minute silence.

'Who? Berntsen?'

Smiling broadly, Fia nodded. 'My father's buyer.'

It was another minute before anyone could recover. Then the Heiberg girl, Alice, who though not rich had pretensions to gentility, said: 'Servants certainly take liberties nowadays.'

To which Fia answered: 'Yes, one has a lot to put up with.'

But faced with all these countess's airs, Miss Olsen could hardly have failed to become a little pensive. Strength of character should not be overdone. There she sat, Fia Johnsen – her father had been obliged to dispose of his country residence, he was sitting none too pretty; was it really so insufferable of the shopman to come forward right now with an offer of hand and heart? 'Well, what answer did you give?' asked Miss Olsen.

Fia merely looked at her, eyebrows aloft, and said nothing.

'I don't know that it was all that impertinent, Fia. Berntsen isn't so very much older than you, I dare say he'll have his own business one day, and he's by no means bad-looking.'

Miss Olsen gave it an alluring gloss, as if she had no objection to Fia Johnsen's making a less than brilliant match. But Fia merely looked at her again; these grocery people were not quite *comme il faut*! Certainly there was nothing superfine or delicate or exquisite about Miss Olsen; no, she couldn't copy paintings, her spelling was undoubtedly shaky, she had never read an Indian fairy tale. But Miss Olsen had her own sensible opinion, namely, that even Fia Johnsen should get married sooner or later. She said: 'Well, Fia, maybe you have someone else. Because otherwise I can't see that poor Berntsen went all that much too far.'

That was one in the eye for *her*.

'No, *really*!' said the Heiberg girl, Alice, reproachfully.

'I should have to be pretty desperate,' said Fia.

'That's just what I'm saying: you must have someone else tucked away.'

To which the Countess actually retorted, with a rare touch of irritation: 'I have ten others if I choose.'

One-minute silence. The four ladies evidently thought this was a bit steep, and Miss Olsen said: 'Well, if *that's* the case . . .!'

'Yes, that is the case,' said Fia, nodding. 'But if I had no one else in the world, I would not accept Berntsen. If I had no one else in the world, I would not accept anyone from this town.'

'Really?' said Miss Olsen, pursing her full lips a little. You see, she had a bird in the hand nowadays and he was from this town, and he might turn out good enough – why, it was by no means impossible that the town would one day welcome him with flags. However, Miss Olsen must at this moment have been jealously aware that her bird had circled around Fia Johnsen before flying to her – and how she must have suffered!

'The fact is, you see,' said Fia, 'I've knocked about a bit, and seen and heard a thing or two. What interests me is my art, and the people I mix with are artists, not the gentlemen of this town.'

Now this was too much even for the Heiberg girl, Alice, who herself had someone in this town, Reinert, the sexton's son, still somewhat young, but, oh, what curly hair and elegant manners, and, oh, what a flirt! Last vacation she had fairly clung to the lively student.

Fia wagged her head pensively and said: 'Goodness, how the artists would laugh at me!'

'You mean, if you accepted Berntsen?' asked Miss Olsen. 'My brother-in-law for one wouldn't laugh at you for that.'

'Really?' said Fia with some interest. Her curiosity was aroused. Miss Olsen's brother-in-law was not just anyone: he was an artist with more and more of a name, a rising star. Come, what had he said, what was his opinion, weren't her paintings good?

'He said you were much too refined about everything, and you couldn't love or kick up your heels, he said. I don't know what he meant by that, but that was your nature, he said, and you'd never ever marry.'

Fia ignored this sloppy style of talking and merely asked: 'But what did he say about my work?'

'I don't remember. I think he said there was no fire in it.'

'No what?'

'Fire. I don't remember exactly. But you were a cold fish, and all the artists thought so, he said.'

Poor Mademoiselle Fia, this reduced her to a long, thoughtful silence. It was hard on her, and she became very subdued. 'He hasn't seen my latest copies from the Louvre,' she said at last. 'I think I can venture to say that they have fire. And for that matter, he hasn't seen the illustrations I intend doing for that Indian fairy tale. I think they're going to open one or two people's eyes.'

When the ladies had gone she went to find her mother, for the first time genuinely disturbed, sick at heart. Her mother had of course already gone to bed, weary with grief and the burdens of the day, and her daughter's visit was hardly going to revive her, was it? What did Fia come for right now?

Naturally she made a nice, well-bred entrance, asked if she was disturbing her mother, if she should rather go, it was only – it was nothing, really—

'What is it, Fia?'

'No, you're not well either, it's nothing, it can wait till another time. But isn't it true, Mama, I *am* an artist, and I shan't let myself be put off by a little criticism?'

'What are you talking about, child – you've had nothing but good criticism, surely?'

'Too true! Oh, I'll show them! You shall see what I'm going to start on tomorrow, Mama, the best thing I've ever done!'

'Was Berntsen here?'

'Yes. Do you know what he was after?'

'I think I understand.'

'You certainly don't. He proposed to me.'

To Fia's great surprise her mother did not start from her bed and demand chief clerk Berntsen's instant dismissal; no, she lay there for all the world like one lost in thought.

'I suppose you know Papa has sold the country residence?' she said.

'Which country residence?' Fia knew nothing, had never heard anything so crazy, she thought of demanding that the deal be called off. Sold their own country residence!

'To that Olsen.'

Here Fia collapsed on the bed. So that was why the four young ladies had come here this evening: that daughter of Grits-and-Groats Olsen had brought her retinue to watch a triumph! If Fia had not had her art she would have been bankrupt now, but she was rich.

'We talked it over, Papa and I,' said her mother. 'Berntsen advised us to do it, and we agreed that at any rate you ought to have something to fall back on.'

'Me?' said Fia. 'I have my art.'

Mother and daughter discussed it. Ah yes, Mrs Consul Johnsen might well have grown thoughtful, perhaps she even understood chief clerk Berntsen's manoeuvre; all in all, she had obtained a clearer glimpse of her inferiors in the town. What about Berntsen? He had simply done what her own husband, the consul, had done in his time and what so many men did. We live in the Human Age.

They discussed it and discussed it, but Fia was doubtless thinking of her own affairs and did not keep her feet too rigorously on the ground. The artists thought she was a cold fish – was this their thanks for all the help she had given them? 'But isn't it true, Mama, that I've helped them?'

'Yes. But that's all over now. Those Olsens, the Consul Olsens, are better off now than we are.'

'But they've no culture,' said Fia consolingly.

'No. But they're so rich. Do you know, they've got cut-glass finger bowls now!'

This caused mother and daughter to smile, and altogether brighten up a little. Mrs Johnsen lay there with her yellow face and her sorrow and adversity, but she said: 'Well, we'll just have to see when Scheldrup comes; perhaps he'll know a way out.'

'Of course, don't worry, Mama! No, you see, it's not that the artist found all that much to criticize. It's just that I'm a little lacking in fire, they think. But that's something I guarantee to show them; oh yes, they'll see!'

And more to the same effect.

There she sat: Mademoiselle Fia. By now she was getting on in years, the peach bloom on her cheeks was no longer fresh, she was overripe, the first signs of something passé about the lady had appeared. In all her years she had never succeeded at anything, but equally she had never failed; her mind was impervious to change, she was impassive and charmingly self-assured. If she had never run amok, this was because she had never run, period. Why should she run? She was so proper and so sealed over. With her, love and the maternal instinct found an outlet in the painting of pictures; this pursuit she had always been able to afford; she painted no more from outer than from inner necessity, but she painted. She was never visibly annoyed with herself, she never went astray, she injured no one, wasted not, spoke nicely, curtsied. She might one day have asked the heaven above her and the earth beneath her: Am I anything? But catch her asking such a question!

Mademoiselle Fia – maybe the weight of her own advantages was more than she could sustain, maybe it was a burden on her road. It is not good to be entirely free from troubles, entirely free from self-reproach.

'A cold fish, me?' she said, getting up from the bed. 'And incapable of kicking up my heels?'

By now both mother and daughter were in a good humour and able to joke, mother sat up in bed and chuckled from time to time;

they were temperamentally akin and shared the blessed ability to suppress dark memories.

Fia feigned high spirits, heigh-ho, kicking out a little behind her, as if impelled by more than a little folly, by any amount of folly, and giving little jerks with her elbow, exactly as though she were amorously nudging someone beside her. The counterfeiting was not badly done. She lifted her skirts till the whole of her white knickers was visible: the nonpareil of fine knickers, so full of lace and ribbons, so utterly paradisal, and now they were exposed to the light of day as Fia kicked up her left leg and high, with an expression as if she really felt quite hopeful that in the fullness of time she might astonish the artists with her debauchery. 'Heigh-ho!' she repeated. Yes, because in reality she was a desperate female, yes, a real slut; wasn't that true, just let them wait and see! When she had kicked up her leg for the third time, wasn't that quite something? Had she still not made the grade? Why, all she needed was to neigh and whinny.

To be honest, the whole performance was entirely proper and innocent, but also sad; these old maid's contortions might have made a stovepipe laugh.

'And where's Berntsen?' she asked suddenly. 'Has he gone? If you think so, Mama, then why not? I'm in the mood for anything. He's probably still waiting downstairs. Shall I fetch him up again?'

This act of self-sacrifice proved uncalled for, and Fia might have spared herself her generous offer; fate allowed her to continue her old life, her nice, decorative life, exactly as before, so why should she change it? What happened was that a man came to the town, ordered all their affairs, saved the business, put the members of the family back in their places, relieved the town's spasms . . .

Scheldrup Johnsen came home.

Did he order all their affairs? Some he disordered. Alas, that couldn't be helped. Human beings push against each other and trample on each other; some sink exhausted to the ground and serve as a bridge for others, some perish – they are the ones least fitted for coping with the push, and they perish. That can't be helped. But the others flourish and blossom. Such is life's immortality. All this, mind you, they knew at the pump.

Scheldrup Johnsen seemed none too meek and mild when he came tearing home from New Orleans; he had no hard words for chief clerk Berntsen, but Father was called to account.

The consul could not understand why *he* should suffer – did you ever hear the like, was he to carry the blame into the bargain? Why, he had expressly told Berntsen not to forget the insurance.

'But what did *you* have to remember about?' asked Scheldrup.

There was no point in discussing the matter with so stupid a son, so inflexible and modern a son; he came from another world, he used words like sterling and dollars. He poked his nose into Father's books as if it was necessary to find fault with them; he was business to the marrow. Hadn't the consul a mass of things to remember? Was he not a tower of strength to the town, not to mention consul for two countries. Did he not have his reports to write?

But defending himself was futile; in the encounter with his son, the consul shrank and shrank in stature. He even hinted that he would liquidate the business. Fia's future he had already secured by selling the country residence; he himself and his wife would just have to take their chance, he might well be able to get some agencies, an insurance agency—

The broad smile that spread across Scheldrup's face was seen by his father. Offended and on his dignity, he repeated that he would liquidate the business, and pay in full like an honourable man.

Scheldrup said: 'We're not liquidating.'

'Yes,' said his father, persisting in his defeatism. 'And being the man I am, I shall resign my consulates.'

'Not a bit of it!' said Scheldrup firmly. 'We're not that well off for valuable assets.' However, he had now gone through the books; they had been rather roughly kept here and there, and this was a flaw, figures were not an approximation, figures were a serious business, a strict business, no joking with figures! 'But the position isn't really too bad, Papa; a fine thing it would be for us to go losing our heads! Let these itinerant gentlemen from Christiania and Hamburg and Göteborg and Le Havre come to me from now on!'

'Do you mean that?'

'But on one condition: that you take a rest, Papa.'

So it seemed as if his filial feelings were coming out at last, he understood that Father needed to rest. And Father was far from having any objection to taking a rest; he had had too much on his plate, his hair was nothing to what it used to be, his eyes had lost their lustre, his days their peace, his nights their joy. 'But I can't just go loafing around, you know,' he said.

Scheldrup announced: 'I want the entire management. You must rest.'

Scheldrup began by wreaking wild havoc on people and things: he gave notice to Oliver Andersen at the warehouse; he discontinued the annual allowance and the annual suit of clothes to the philologist Frank, Oliver's son; he dismissed the ancient inherited woodcutter who had served in Mrs Johnsen's childhood home for honour and glory and a silver spoon as a bonus; and finally, he terminated a certain connection with Henriksen of the Shipyard.

And again little clusters of people formed at street corners and made up their minds on the situation: no doubt about it, the consul had been toppled and Scheldrup had taken over the management; the effects were everywhere to be seen, good and bad effects, all of which were discussed at the pump. What a whirring of churns! Well now, Mrs Consul Johnsen had bought herself a small hat. Previously she had always worn a large hat, with a broad brim that fluttered up and down as she walked, a hat that appeared to have hinges all around. But now she had bought herself a hat that was almost the twin of the one which little Mrs Consul Davidsen went around in, and which cost very little. It must have been Scheldrup who had stepped in; was there anywhere he didn't step in? He even settled that mysterious affair about the shipyard. You see, some little arrangement had apparently come into being between the late Mrs Henriksen and the consul at one time, a very long time ago, while the lady was still alive and kicking and only just over thirty. That was how it was, apparently. But now the shipyard stood idle. This was the hardest settlement of all; Kasper and the rest of the work force out there were idle and had nothing to do but guard their wives from their work mates.

Scheldrup stepped in. When the emissaries of foreign creditors arrived, they were shown into his office, where he sat in solitary state; the gentlemen from Göteborg and Le Havre were not in there for long; he sorted them out, bowed them out, and sat down again. What had he said to satisfy them? It wasn't what he said but what he did that made such an unforgettable impression on the gentlemen: he wrote out cheques for their claims. Here you are, sir – one miracle after another! In the firm's ledgers the steamship *Fia* must have been valued at two hundred thousand kroner; where did Mr Scheldrup Johnsen find this million to compensate for the loss of the ship? He must have had the devil's own connections in the great world outside.

He stepped still further in. It came to light that the good Scheldrup was by no means just business to the marrow – was he now? His heart could run away with him. One day at noon he went to pay a homecoming call on the Grits-and-Groats Olsens and came away an engaged man. Had he not stepped well and truly in? It was all very matter-of-fact: neither Scheldrup nor Miss Olsen looked to the right or to the left, everything was settled on the spot. The lady never once asked him to behave like a gentleman; it was simply that two childhood sweethearts were finally united, got what they wanted and needed. This happened just when lawyer Fredriksen was busy holding election meetings; he had no opportunity of appearing on other battlefields and preventing a breakthrough, so only one outcome was possible. Well, he was the chosen man all right – in one place; from the other he was rejected. Never, in all probability, had lawyer Fredriksen got his sums so wrong; the supremely important election went against him. He could have endured a political defeat – until next time; but Miss Olsen's decision spelled a loss for life. After that it didn't help to fumble his arm around her, it didn't help to thunder. Did anything help?

He moped for a while, for a week. Oh, but lawyer Fredriksen was in no way finished. His vitality was so great, he would forge ahead – out of the way there! His goal was not supreme command, his goal was parliamentary elevation and political honour, his goal was financial sufficiency, small-town opulence; for that he was fitted. How could he fail to attain such modest ends? He was no mean figure already, mayor of his town, member of the Storting, chairman of an interminable commission, soon to be Minister of Justice. What a career! Who could have imagined such great things for him a few years back when he was threadbare and unemployed, unable to keep himself in cigars, and even reduced on occasion to asking barber Holte for a shave on credit: 'I've left all my change at home, charge it up till next time!'

Miss Olsen has played him a shameful trick, but he'll manage all right; lawyer Fredriksen will always manage all right, he will find more commissions to sit on, he will find a wife with a fortune, he will pay barber Holte on the nail in future. As Minister of Justice he will do what needs doing in the department; more is not demanded, more is not expected. One of his former buddies on the benches of the Storting will ask him some question or other, refer to some administrative duty or other, and yes, the Minister of Justice promises that his attention will be brought to bear on the matter, and yes, the honourable member thanks him. Oh, the Minister of Justice is an able man, he will see that his attention is given to some matter, there's no denying it. He's a man of drive, a leader, his department attends to matters great and small. Anyone who fears that Minister of State Fredriksen will do something out of the ordinary does not know him, he will do precisely what is demanded; for that he is made. He has become a cog in the machinery of state; when the other cogs revolve, he revolves with them. He is set in low gear, he must not revolve too fast, it is enough if he keeps going.

He will be missed when he dies.

30

So Oliver has again been taken for the most God-almighty ride: he has been given notice at the warehouse. He still goes there and does his daily work, but when the time runs out he will be on his beam-ends. It's just about the last thing anyone could have expected, for example! Oliver is deeply depressed.

He goes to Abel for a talk. Who else should he go to? The philologist Frank is a tremendous linguist and a teacher of his fellow human beings, but he has not yet sent home the substantial allowance that Dad has been expecting; rumour has it, indeed, that he is formally engaged to Constance Henriksen of the ship-yard. Well, what good is that to Oliver?

Abel now rules the smithy, which his master, Carlsen, has finally made over to him at a reasonable rent, and he has acquired the curious steam hammer that runs on kerosene; it strikes rattling good blows and is just like having an apprentice about the place; Abel has work in plenty and earns good money. He is no skinflint wanting to keep each and every two-krone piece for himself. He earns the wherewithal for various items of furniture, for bedclothes, for a chest of drawers; he goes to Evensen the goldsmith and buys twelve grams of gold. He buys *what*? Gold. And Abel still manages to have a two-krone piece to spare for Dad's pocket.

You see, Oliver makes not a scrap of distinction between his children, and so when he is in need he goes, not to the absent Frank, but to Abel, whom he can find any morning at the smithy. And today more than a two-krone piece is at stake; as Oliver explains, Scheldrup Johnsen had sacked a cripple, his bread and butter are at stake, and what is he to do?

'Well,' says Abel, turning it over, 'the best remedy I can think of is for me to get married.'

What the devil! Dad frankly gasps on hearing this. 'What do you mean?' he asks.

'I've got everything ready and I'm not going to wait for her any longer,' Abel declares. 'I intend to have it settled.'

Oliver doesn't immediately grasp his son's idea, but he's an adaptable father; he at once forgets his own affairs and listens with concern to his son's. 'You'd be a mug to wait for her any longer!' he says.

'No, do you think so?'

'Don't I just! What is she and what are you? If you find a feather or a bit of down in the street – that's exactly what she is and nothing more.'

'Would you like to see the ring?' Abel asks. He produces it from a drawer in the bench by the window, and my, what a ring, thick and bright, heavy in the hand, gold. 'I've just finished it,' he says.

Oliver is speechless and incredulous, but poker-faced. Eventually he asks: 'What did old Evensen charge you for that ring?'

'Old Evensen? I made that ring myself!' Abel shows him the

mould he cast it in, shows him the filings he took from it, shows him the files with traces of gold on them. 'Here you can see the emery paper I polished it with; here are the different rags, coarse rags and fine rags; and I used chammy leather for the finish.'

It is true all right, every word of it; Oliver shakes his head and says: 'God bless my soul, Abel, it's just as if you can do anything that comes into your head!'

Abel is proud at being praised by Dad, but he lets slip the remark: 'Now it all depends on whether she'll have it.'

'Have it?' Oliver exclaims. 'If that person won't have it, you send her to me – just you do that. Not have a ring like this? Feel here, it's twice as heavy as the one I bought for your mother in foreign parts. You mustn't talk so blasphemously!'

Nothing more is said about Dad's bread and butter, but in spite of this his visit to the smithy has cheered the poor wretch up. Not that it takes much to do that; Abel's not losing heart in the face of imminent destitution is in itself a comfort and a support. Abel lose heart? Never.

Abel takes the handkerchief, a corner of which is projecting from Dad's breast pocket. Abel wants to borrow it for a moment, Abel has got something in his eye. And when Oliver gets his handkerchief back, yes, it feels heavier by a two-krone piece.

Thereupon he leaves, Oliver leaves. He is in a remarkable state of excitement; this visit to the smithy has done him good, he has money in his pocket again, tomorrow is Sunday, it's sure to be rowing weather – and as for the future, why, something will turn up! When he goes home to dinner, he takes some goodies for the children, and in the evening he rows out.

Night comes and he does not go home, the next day comes and he does not go home; no, he follows the usual pattern, lets the boat drift, fishes for food, goes ashore, cooks, eats, sleeps. It is incomparable, this wonderful idleness and sloth.

On the first morning sea and islands breathe the solitude of eternity; far away on the mainland stand a few meagre telegraph poles; from a parish outside the town he can just hear the church bell, disposing him to gentleness, disposing him to peace. The morning does not invite him to any kind of moral laxity, to oaths or blasphemies; no, no, all's right with the world, for example, and when he has eaten the remnants of last night's fish, he feels full and contented, and says: 'For what I have eaten may the Lord make me thankful!' Which is more than most people say each day.

Not every morning is alike; this one is Sunday, a morning of church bells and devotions, sigh after sigh is borne on the air; at his feet lies the sea, his homeland, his cradle, the breakers approach him, rising and falling, turning into foam and nothing on the beach. Good, all of it. Fancy, in the days of his youth he took a ticket in a raffle and won a tablecloth. And after that he rescued a full-rigged ship and brought her into harbour. Oliver Anderson did all these things.

He has slept again, it is good to eat and sleep. The sun is high in the heavens, it is so absolutely the day and the place for him, he will at least row in good earnest to the nesting cliff far out in the shipping lane. Today it shall be done, there is sure to be eiderdown on the little ledges up and down the cliff. 'Pray God,' Oliver sighs as he picks up the oars. His piety is perhaps a little calculated, as is the way with human piety; he is certainly not going to neglect his own interests. He knows that the coastal steamer has called at the town and gone again, so that he will meet no one; his voyage is a solitary one, without witnesses. Besides, what could witness do to him? Oliver is out on a fishing trip, that is Oliver's privilege.

Now as before, as nearly always these last twenty years, Oliver's life is partly within the law, partly on the borderline, occasionally a little outside.

Today he will not be stealing eiderdown with his usual style and proficiency; true, he cannot pass the precious commodity without taking it, but he snatches, he fills his bag with good and bad, clean and dirty. Something else happens that interests him more. Oliver's mind has never rejected adventure, and adventure has not yet rejected him. What is in store for him now?

The nests here are without birds, without eggs; the young are hatched out, conditions are perfect for Oliver. He examines the lowest nest, digs to the bottom, and finds paper in it – yes, paper, letters, what can this be? Mail, letters with stamps on them, how odd. He shoves the layer of down aside and gathers up the letters; they are registered mail, torn-up envelopes with blobs of sealing wax and the money extracted, registered letters which have never been opened. He reads some of the addresses and recognizes their owners, people in the town and the surrounding country. He is inspired to open a registered letter and comes upon banknotes; he opens others and comes upon banknotes ...

Adventure.

It takes Oliver all afternoon to make a proper job of the nesting cliff; he has grown avaricious, ransacking more and more of the nests within reach, from time to time finding what he is looking for and collecting it in heaps, getting richer and richer. He rows away from the nesting cliff in the twilight, bearing his booty, rows like a steamer, meets no one, no witnesses. He puts in again at the island which sheltered him last night.

From now until his dying day Oliver's heart will flutter at the memory of this experience. At first he guesses, mistakenly, that the letters came from a wreck. Then he remembers occasional newspaper items about faithless postmen emptying letters of their valuable contents and then throwing them into the sea. Ah, but Oliver's brain is practised in resolving equivocal matters; he soon sees how everything hangs together, that these are the remains of a certain theft of registered mail. Neither he nor anyone else is likely to have forgotten that great event, the postmaster's family has occasion to remember it, Oliver himself recalls a wad of notes from that epoch. But whoever the thief may have been – Adolf of the sea chest (he who called himself Xander), or the second mate (the postmaster's son), or whoever – what an ass he proves to have been, a bungler, a pitiful novice! Here he has had the chance of a lifetime and used it like a simpleton – stood on board in the dark, plundering only the fattest letters, and heaving the rest into the sea! He has treated the precious booty like a wastrel, treated it like a man to whom nothing is sacred. Oliver is filled with indignation at such behaviour. Whereas those dumb creatures, the eider ducks, show up as sensible and well-trained people, who take due care of a treasure. How wise of the eider ducks, to build their nests on a foundation of what they find, on a foundation of registered mail!

Oliver needs no food, no sleep, he just sits there till daybreak; then he carefully sorts his mail from the sea, a mail from heaven and from God, extracts the notes and sticks them in his inside pocket, collects the letters and burns them. Then he scatters the ashes and obliterates every trace. He himself may have been well served by his fishing trip, but certain other people may perhaps be content for the letters to have been burned.

Then he rows home, rows like a steamer. It is Monday morning, and Oliver, who is feeling limp after his excitement, says little to his family, though he is unusually mild and grateful for the food he is given; he has money in his pocket, of course, and can eke out his meal with sweetmeats. Next he goes to the warehouse.

More than once in the course of the day he slinks off behind sacks and barrels and counts his banknotes, smoothing them and winkling out the dog ears. One or two customers come in, greeting him with the sympathy due to a man who has been dismissed, feeling sorry for him. Oliver answers: 'Well, God will find a way for me.'

In his heart of hearts he expands. Here he is, back in his warehouse with money in his inside pocket, becoming more and more of a man; his clothes are completely threadbare, but his character improves, his nature becomes more firm, his carriage again grows more erect. No wonder, for Oliver is now on a peak, a summit, one visible only to himself; it turns into arrogance, he is downright cock of the walk. Not that he is tempted to go to the hotel and ape the rich Englishman by demanding horse and carriage for drives in the neighbourhood – nothing in excess. On his way home to dinner he is indeed seized by a whim of looking into a couple of shops and paying some old debts, but a glimmer of intelligence causes him to change his mind in time. For God's sake, his wealth is not *that* vast, it won't buy him an annuity, no indeed, but mercifully it is sufficient to give the poor wretch fresh heart, the courage to mutter, to stamp his crutch on the floor and say to himself: 'I refuse to be thrown out of the warehouse, I'll go to the consul!'

In the first place he bought and took home quantities of titbits, wow, previously unheard-of yummies in boxes and silver paper; from that hour preserved pears were no longer a fabrication and a fairy tale in the Oliver family. In this way he astonished people who had never knocked about all over the world, and Petra said mockingly that he must have found buried treasure on his last fishing trip. He was to work even greater wonders: less cautious than in this previous period of affluence, he bought a variety of clothing for the entire household and treated himself to a complete new outfit, not to mention a tie with silver tassels. Possibly it was meant for a girl, but evidently he couldn't imagine it around any neck but his own. Later in the day he went to Evensen the goldsmith, who also sold hymnbooks, spectacles, and musical instruments, and there he bought a gleaming brass horn, a clarinet, for the living-room wall. 'Let me see that you keep it bright,' he said to Petra.

The business of making a stupendous splash thus worked out of his system, there remained the consul. He boasted in advance of his intentions: he would go and see him, he had something to say to that man, that gentleman; he intended to make himself known, to tell him who he was ...

Meanwhile, he postponed the day and the hour; he appeared to be mulling something over and to be in two minds about it. Meanwhile, moreover, he received a letter from lawyer Fredriksen, Minister of State Fredriksen, who wrote to say that since he was now a Minister of State he wished to wind up all his affairs in his hometown. Therefore, Oliver must now either pay his overdue debt or leave the house he was living in.

Whereupon Oliver mulled things over no longer. He waited only till closing time; then he left the warehouse and went to see the doctor.

Yes, it may have been on shady business, but he went to see the doctor.

The doctor's surgery was as shabby and unscientific as ever: no dead man's skeleton, no microscope, only a half-finished portrait of the doctor himself hanging on the wall. Here of course he had sat, some years ago, to an apprentice painter, a wild young man who was going to paint a portrait of 'The Physician'; it had been a diversion in the doctor's impoverished life, nay more, it had affected him as an honour. But one day the painter had seen fit to interrupt the work in order to go to a neighbouring house and paint the Cross of the Dannebrog on a frock coat. This was more than the doctor could stand; it simply wouldn't do, thank you, one was not a fool, one was not just anybody. The doctor said: 'Take your picture and go!' 'Burn it!' countered the painter. 'Burn your own rubbish,' said the doctor, 'I'm not your charwoman.' Resenting this, no doubt, the apprentice painter then said: 'It isn't rubbish, it's a likeness; it's half-finished, it's a perfect portrait of you!' At first the picture had stood upside down in a corner, but the doctor's opinion of it seems gradually to have changed; he was not so abject but that he saw the sting in the painter's words; there might be something in them, a nucleus of truth. He belonged to a generation that was sceptical about everything except science, he subscribed to the legality of nature, even to the theory of the brown eyes; but his generation was innocent of cowardice, it could look life's emptiness and hopelessness in the face without a whimper. The doctor undoubtedly regarded himself as learned, a small-town superman, an accuser and castigator, but in his better moments he could also glimpse among his contemporaries greater figures than himself – an Englishman, a Frenchman, a German or two, a Dutchman; after all, the doctor was no fool, and for that matter he was quite capable of admitting that he was a little unfinished and hanging a half-finished portrait of himself on his wall. It was an action that approached true greatness.

What did Oliver want with him?

To be examined.

What did he want examined?

Hips and thereabouts. He wanted to have his injury examined and to get a certificate about it.

What for? No, the doctor wouldn't do it. Oliver could have chosen when the doctor chose; now it was just monkey business. Go back home!

Oliver was amazed. What was the meaning of this? How would the doctor manage without his hips? He explained that he and his family had been taken for the most God-almighty ride and could make good use of written evidence from the doctor.

No, go back home.

Oliver put his hand to his inside pocket and said he would pay for it; he became the open-handed sailor and said he would gladly give a hundred kroner for it.

'You have a hundred kroner?'

'That I have.'

But the doctor was actually blushing a little at his own question. What was he thinking of? Had he remembered a certain promise about a diamond ring for his wife, a youthful promise that was still unfulfilled? The slight blush settled delicately on his face and made it more attractive. Putting on his glasses, he asked: 'Didn't you catch a barrel of whale oil in your crotch and get ripped open?'

Oliver (in a bit of a spot over his old fib): 'It wasn't exactly a barrel of whale oil, but – no, it was a derrick that I fell astride and got smashed by. Afterwards I was operated on.'

'Take your clothes off!'

Oliver took his clothes off. The doctor felt him, squeezed him, and said: 'What is it you want me to tell you? That you're not a father? You know that for yourself!' And he could not resist a touch of greatness and infallibility: 'Not that it's ever been a secret to me, either.'

Oliver was canny enough to ask for it in writing.

What for? No, again the doctor wouldn't do it. 'How many children has your wife got?'

'We've got five children – she's got five.'

'My testimony would be too late now; the brown eyes have lost their fire in this town. Put your clothes on again!'

'It wasn't the brown eyes I wanted it for. I wouldn't dream of such a thing. No, we have two children with blue eyes.'

The doctor's ears pricked up, old small-town gossip that he was, but far be it from *him* to start asking questions; on the contrary, he said with apparent distaste: 'Please don't acquaint me with your family affairs!' Not that Oliver could have told him anything new; the doctor had doubtless heard a thing or two already and could afford to feign indifference now. He wrote out a statement and read it aloud; Oliver nodded his entire satisfaction and put his hand to his inside pocket.

The doctor stopped him. 'Surely you haven't the nerve to offer me payment for this piece of work?'

'Uh?' said Oliver, bewildered.

'No.'

So Oliver made tracks.

He made tracks for Scheldrup Johnsen and requested a few days off. 'Certainly!' said Scheldrup Johnsen, making it very plain how superfluous at all times was Oliver's presence at the warehouse. Oliver made tracks for home, where he notified his family that he intended to make a journey, and when his family clapped their hands in astonishment, he threw out his chest and let it be understood how exceedingly insignificant a journey was to a man accustomed to sailing all over the world. 'I'm just paying a flying visit to Christiania,' he said, 'to see a certain Minister of State,' he said. 'I'm sitting here with a paper in my pocket that I shall be showing him.' Oh, how obscurely Oliver talked, and how he boasted! He went to Abel and said: 'If there's anything you want from Christiania in the way of machines and so on, just say the word!' 'Well,' replied Abel, 'if you could buy me a steel rule. They don't have any here, and I'm completely stuck for one at the smithy.' 'You shall have your rule,' said Oliver with dignity. 'Of the best quality,' he added. 'I guess a father can do that much for you.'

So Oliver set out.

A few days later he returned in an excellent mood – yes, for he had got from his persecutor literally everything he wanted.

He had tried to see his son Frank; that went without saying; Oliver made no distinction between his children and tried to see Frank, too. But in vain. Frank was a teacher at a big school somewhere; anyway, he had finished at the university, they couldn't teach him anything more there. In the next place, however, Oliver was able to convey remembrances from Minister of State Fredriksen, a splendid fellow, talkative and kind as ever; and now he had written off the house. The family went wild with joy. Oliver (new boater at an angle): 'All it cost me was a few single words!' Family full of curiosity, full of questions. Oliver mute.

Once or twice before now Oliver had managed to pull the chestnuts out of the fire, by a technique all his own: a remarkably sly look which he directed slowly upward from the floor, accompanied by speech that was full of hidden menace. At such moments there was a depravity about him, a sick degradation, before which his adversary was bound to quail. No more on this than on previous occasions had he resorted to abuse of his creditor, or brought out a knife. What had he said? Trifles. In bed that night he gave way to his wife's ungovernable curiosity and retailed his interview with the Minister of State. What a couple, Oliver and his wife! Without constraint they bandied the subject about, and every so often Petra praised him for his apt answers and said: 'You've got what it takes all right!' And Oliver threw out his chest.

So what had he said? He had explained that he would find it quite in order if the Minister quietly let him off the debt, if the

Minister of his own accord presented him with the house, himself and Petra and the children—

'Children? They're grown up, surely?' said the Minister.

'Not all of them. Not the two with blue eyes. One of them is still quite small.'

'Really?'

Quite small. Almost nothing, for example. And the Minister had so much to think about now, what with the King and the government, the Minister ought to write off the house.

'Write it off? No.'

Oliver produced a doctor's certificate to the effect he was a disabled man. Well, the Minister read the document and handed it back and failed to see how it concerned him. 'No,' answered Oliver, 'because the Minister has so much to think about. That's why the Minister really oughtn't to think any more about the house in his hometown, but write it off for all time.'

'No, why should I?'

Oliver swivelled his eyes up at him from the floor and replied: 'Because otherwise the Minister will have something else to think about!'

Such had been their conversation.

Did Minister Fredriksen start at this point to wake up to the fact that his reputation was in danger? To be brief, he could hardly be involved in litigation over a house with a disabled man, a cripple – what would his old constituency say, what would his hometown say? So he wrote if off.

For a time Oliver rode on the crest of a wave, making no secret of the kick he got from his triumph. He still had money; he had spent a large proportion on his great journey, clothes for the family, the steel rule, the clarinet, goodies, one thing after another, but he still had money and his bearing was still erect. One thing hadn't changed, however: he remained under notice at the warehouse and due to leave any day. This was the calamity that would gradually finish him off and bow his neck.

So one day Oliver resolved on a brazenly dirty bit of business and went to the consul with his doctor's certificate. To the consul in person. The interview with Minister of State Fredriksen had gone so smoothly that Oliver couldn't resist attempting a repeat performance; mind you, nothing could have gone more deeply against the grain, but if there was no other way ...

Never before had he contemplated anything so base; he would gladly have spared Consul Johnsen's indiscretions, would have continued protecting those merry brown eyes from being dimmed. But what was he to do? In next to no time he would be out of work; surely the consul could acknowledge his involvement in the Oliver family's weal and woe to the extent of still having a warehouse job for the cripple. What could Oliver do in return? Everything. He could serve as the consul's apron, his devotion to his gallant chief was unaltered; he might relinquish his rights to him, be his watchdog, the guardian of his harem ...

He went to the consul.

And got nowhere. No, Consul and Double Consul Johnsen was not the same as of yesteryear; he was resting, he was superseded, his son now ruled the roost, the old tower had fallen. Even his outward appearance proclaimed that Consul Johnsen now counted for nothing; he was wan and grey, and his coat could have done with brushing. Anyone who knew no better might have thought that he alone had heeded the newspaper's call and got religion. Naturally he was still consul for two countries and wrote reports to his governments; he had the same potbelly as before – but what else? Nowadays it was all Scheldrup this and Scheldrup that, people passed the father on their way to the son without even stating their business. Why, lately the consul had once more heard people refer to him as Johnsen of the Wharf plain and simple. So much for people. What had happened to the crew of the *Fia*? they would ask. All right, the lads themselves had been gone for decades, but at least their families had until this day drawn some of their wages from the shipowner; now they were gone forever, sunk to the bottom of the sea, and, in the last resort, wasn't Johnsen of the Wharf to blame? At first the consul tried to give reasons, to explain his position, but after all, what was the use of struggling against such foolishness? They wouldn't even let him have his say; they answered back, they muttered. Gone were the days when to be master all one needed was a heavy gold chain on the waistcoat.

In Christiania luck had been on Oliver's side; here it deserted him. The consul listened, listened with an attentiveness that was almost pitiful to behold, looking more and more helpless; honestly, Oliver couldn't even bring himself to produce the doctor's certificate. 'You know,' said the consul, 'I've never treated you or your family badly, but now there's nothing I can do to help you, I no longer have a say in anything; let us hope for better days.'

Sad words, alas, for a faithful servant to hear!

Oliver's next proposed solution was to go to that scoundrel Scheldrup in person, and show him a genuine clenched fist. Would that help? Beyond question. One was not Oliver Andersen for nothing. But by now the blessed inside pocket was getting so thin, and by the same token his courage and willpower were so impoverished, that he let day after day go by without reaching a decision – until one evening Scheldup told him to hand over the warehouse key to Berntsen in the shop.

Oliver, therefore, was not to come back in the morning; he was finished.

It was no more than he had expected; nevertheless, it came upon him with paralysing suddenness. He hadn't even had the initiative to lay in a little cheap coffee and groats in good time, which meant that from now on his family would have to bite their fingers.

A month went by, an evil month; Oliver was peevish and *difficile*, not saying more than he could possibly help at home, and preferring to drift from street corner to street corner, since his clothes at least were presentable. There was no comfort in the bosom of his family, with the children increasingly pale, the clarinet hanging unpolished on the wall, and even Granny unable to refrain from sniffing and sighing, clean out of coffee as she was. Oliver cut her short: 'Right, in future you can get your coffee from the parish!' 'I'm so old now,' wailed Granny. 'Would to God I was in my grave!'

Then one morning the squeeze was a little bit tighter than ever, so that the family hadn't even a warm cup of something for breakfast. Petra came in from the pump, somewhat heartened perhaps from meeting the other women, whereas Oliver was silent, thinking no doubt that it was time Providence stepped in. Providence, however, seemed occupied exclusively by the lilies of the field and the hairs of the head which are *not* all numbered. Petra said, as if she had got the idea from some outside person: 'I'd like to know if I shouldn't go to that Scheldrup and talk to him.'

Oliver made no answer. His cheeks had shrunk; never before had he been so limp, his face so horribly lifeless; he no longer cared about anything. On coming in again at dinnertime he threw himself and his crutch into a chair and asked scornfully: 'Wasn't it you that was going to that fellow Scheldrup?'

Poor Petra was unprepared for this and could only answer: 'Ye-es?'

'But you never went?'

Recovering her composure, she began raising objections. Today? She couldn't very well go hotfoot; she needed to wash some clothes first, she was so untidy.

But next day, when she was nicely dressed and all set to go, Petra was once again a damned fine figure of a woman; Oliver might have noticed her mouth, how strongly it curved, up and down like a gallopade, Oliver might have kissed her – but Oliver was lifeless. So what did she get in return for being attractive?

Her visit to Scheldrup Johnsen was a washout, a visit to a stone, a block of wood; Scheldrup showed her the door, he had no use for Oliver, he couldn't afford to maintain him any longer – and that's all there was to it! Oh, Scheldrup had evidently not forgotten a certain resounding box on the ear that Petra had given him in his youth; now he was a fiancé and a small-minded fellow, quite unlike his father, who had often shown he could be openhanded.

So there was no option but for Oliver to work up enough fury in his soul to go in person and see Scheldrup – a momentous step which was to bring bitter tribulations on his own head. You see, he got nowhere by using his old technique of obscure threats accompanied by a sidelong glance up from the floor; Scheldrup was a modern, inflexible fellow with hardened feelings. Anyone who thought this gentleman was afraid of a scandal was making a mistake, unless indeed he stood to lose money by it. In this instance he could afford to feel safe, he had his Miss Olsen, come what may.

Oliver was bound to be worsted; he went about it the wrong way, he lost his composure, he screamed. Scheldrup gave him a sharp warning: 'Hush!' Oliver flung his precious doctor's certificate on the desk; Scheldrup Johnsen picked the document up and read it. Then he asked: 'What's the meaning of this?'

'I'm not a father,' said Oliver.

Scheldrup laughed and said: 'And what the devil's that got to do with me?'

This businessman had no conception of the unspeakable fate awaiting him, and perhaps no more than an inkling of the baseness and ignominy of the cripple's words, for he continued to snigger. Oliver subsided into his usual cowardice; he said everything he ought not to have said, mentioned his five children, started repeating himself, spoke of brown eyes, ah, lovely eyes, brown—

'Be off with you!' said Scheldrup.

'Brown eyes—'

'Yes, what about them?'

Oliver's bearing had slumped utterly, but this unfeeling folly provided fresh fuel for his impertinence. 'Easy now with that laughing! Who is it that has brown eyes in this town?'

'Me!' interrupted Scheldrup, laughing more than ever.

'No, not you, you know that perfectly well. What you have is neither here nor there. But what certain others have—'

'Now look here,' said Scheldrup, getting up, 'the doctor's wasting his time again; take his scrap of paper and go. I'm dead serious now.'

3 1

Within a matter of days it was all over town that Oliver was not merely minus a leg but was also a very special kind of disabled man, that he went around with a doctor's certificate to the effect that the children were not his. So what remained of him? The rumour reached Oliver's own ears via Mattis the carpenter.

This, too, this crowning ignominy! How had the closely kept secret been revealed? Can *any* secret be kept? Walls leak it out, the paving stones noise it abroad, every dumb object becomes vociferous, a young businessman may laugh and hurl it into the marketplace as a choice *plaisanterie*.

Mattis the carpenter at once laments that he has suspected an innocent man of Maren Salt's child, he is utterly sincere and gauche; anxious to atone for his injustice, he seeks Oliver out in the street and shakes him by the hand. The two men stand there, conducting their incredible interview; Oliver is completely at sea.

'The fact is, you see,' says Mattis, 'I wanted to shake hands with you. And you must excuse the way I've been.' He speaks with the utmost possible circumspection, taking it to such lengths that for a long time he is quite incomprehensible to the unsuspecting Oliver. Take a look at Mattis the carpenter as he stands there: an oddity, a splendid and ridiculous fellow, busily overlooking the fact that Oliver has wronged *him*, defrauded him of a pair of doors, cheated him of a gold ring, cheated him, you might say, of Petra herself; his only concern to excuse himself – he has had no peace since yesterday when he heard of Oliver's state—

'Of my state?'

'Yes, how disabled and operated on you are.'

Oliver stares at him. Eventually he says: 'What, you know about that?'

Why shouldn't Mattis know about it? It was the talk of the town, Maren Salt had brought it home from the pump yesterday, details and new accretions were continually spreading. Nor was it unduly tragic; it had its funny side too, its hilariously funny side. As for that Petra, creating her children unaided, it wasn't every woman who was capable of that, hee-hee!

Mattis doesn't exactly rub it in, but he expresses sympathy for the mutilated man and lets slip something about what a sad trick life has played on him. Or is the whole story a lie, perhaps?

Oliver stands there, head bowed, momentarily bewildered and uncertain whether to deny the facts of his case or admit them. He surrenders, abandons all bravado, and says: 'No, it's not exactly a lie.'

The carpenter brightens up perceptibly at this answer, as if some obstacle or other has suddenly been removed for his personal benefit. Is he at this moment thinking some strictly private thoughts? Then he says to Oliver: 'Well, well, poor fellow, what rotten luck you've had! But now let me tell you something: none of us knows what's going to happen to us, we're all in the hands of fate. The other day the youngster had got hold of the matches and was just setting fire to the shavings in the workshop. He might have burned himself to death!' Mattis chatters away, consoling

Oliver, calling him poor fellow, doing what he can. Oh, and to change the subject, he says he's about to start making a bed for young Abel. The lad came today and ordered it, wanted it finished in a couple of weeks.

'Really?' says Oliver; 'for young Abel?'

For young Abel. He is about to change his circumstances. It's quite extraordinary how fast young people grow up and become grown-up before your very eyes. What is one to say? But as if that isn't enough, those getting on in years are every bit as much in the hands of fate, says Mattis, chattering nonsense twenty to the dozen. And when Oliver doesn't answer, the carpenter says right out: 'I'm ashamed to confess it, but I too am about to change my circumstances.'

Oliver has the ability to forget his own affairs and listen to other people's. He asks in astonishment: 'You?'

'Yes, you may well ask!' nods the carpenter. 'But now it's a case of enough's enough. What was I to do, I'd like to know. That Maren won't give up the boy, and I, like a fool, have got rather used to him. I don't mean I've got *madly* used to him, but when a youngster sets fire to the chippings he'll burn to death, we all know that. And he's toddling around my ankles all the time, and on Sundays he takes my hand as if to say, Now it's time for us to go out. You never saw such a fellow. That's not to say I can't do without him, but that Maren doesn't want to get rid of him, either . . .'

Another long rigmarole, and then Oliver asks: 'So it's that Maren you're marrying?'

'What am I to do?' answers the carpenter. 'Yes, it's that Maren.'

But curiously enough, when Mattis the carpenter goes off, he doesn't seem unduly depressed over marrying Maren, he even seems in a hurry to get home. It may be that a burden has been lifted from him, a weight off his mind, God knows. Has it perhaps helped the carpenter over the worst to know that Oliver at least has had nothing to do with Maren and her boy? That whoever it may have been, it wasn't Oliver?

The cripple likewise is on his way home. There is no one, of course, who doesn't keep a wary eye on him, who doesn't hide from him, twisted as he is, so signally mauled, an abomination to his fellow creatures. Can he expect anyone to look at him willingly? His pendulous obesity is appalling, his whole being repulsive, the way he hops along the street insufferable. He is incomplete even as an animal, a quadruped, and he is not merely a cripple, he is a hollowed-out cripple, an empty husk. Once he was a human being.

Off he hobbles. Even Mattis the carpenter sheds a load as he leaves him.

As he passes the doctor's house he suspects him, perhaps, of having betrayed his secret and thinks of calling him to account. Oliver call anyone to account any more? Those days are gone. He sees the doctor at the surgery window and slinks off; perhaps it has dawned on him that he is on the wrong track.

He slinks off down the length of the street; the doctor stands at the window following him with his eyes. He is a spectacle, a problem, whom the doctor can argue about and assess in his own way. This devil on two sticks has been struck by something, a cyclone centre, a flash of lightning; he has become a wreck. At one time the town wits called him the jellyfish, a nickname coined, apparently, by his own skittish wife; the doctor considered it stupid. A jellyfish is not a wreck. A jellyfish is a kind of excrement, a vomit, it has no outline, no backbone; granted. But it's a colourful marvel of a vomit, a fabulous fried egg. What is Oliver? He hops about on land; he is a curiosity, a rebus. His deficiencies of limb are visible to all as he hobbles along, but he is not even physically present; only part of him is engaged in hobbling along. His other deficiencies the doctor's servant girl has now heard about at the pump. One day he came adrift from the common content of human life, summarily, by the cut of a knife; from that day forth he has stood outside humanity, he has lost his reality, become a pack of lies. Exaggeration? How so – is he not a wreck? Very well, examine him again, there is a rare perfection in his emptiness, a peculiar completeness; his misfortune has intensified it, has turned the former sailor into something nonexistent. He has been destroyed, and his destruction is a masterpiece, consciously created and prodigiously well performed.

Wait a bit. He is alive, and therefore not quite obliterated; he is a remnant with a sprawling wooden leg and crutch. One could compose a rune out of him, or a Hebrew character. Why has he been spared actual death? Ask human providence! What was the intention, was this man to be no more than an unsuccessful attempt, a rough sketch of annihilation? He is a remnant, this remnant has remnants, come and fetch them, he still has one leg, he can talk ...

Once he was a human being.

So much was left him that he always had the courage to grapple with life. Well done! He managed it most artfully; he lied to save his skin, simulated a man, wore long trousers. To cloak his case he dreamed up the yarn about the barrel of whale oil; he invested the case in a sublime dignity and called it fate. He had to rehabilitate himself, and this involved a fraud; in passing himself off as commensurate with other men, the poor wretch inevitably came to use his own yardstick and persuaded himself to believe in it. Maybe this gave him his own modest portion of happiness; at all events, he had no other. Artfulness from beginning to end, then? Artfulness from beginning to end. But not a bad bit of artistry.

Now everything had come to light, the work of art was unveiled, the artist revealed, the doctor's servant girl had heard the most unmentionable things at the pump, Petra had had babies through being visited by the moon, hee-hee. But Oliver himself was tops, he had stood in a warehouse in public view for twenty years and played the man. Treatment such as he had received would surely have driven anyone else into himself, into seeking solitude, seeking God. What else was chastisement for? But Oliver? No. He must be a hardened sinner. The doctor's wife brought the gossip from the pump, and the doctor said: 'It's a joke, the way people are unable to grasp his lack of resignation after becoming a wreck. Didn't he get snarled up with his God? Did it take a bit of an effort to come to terms with his adversary?'

So here stands the doctor, following the cripple with his eyes, chattering away to himself, still using the vocabulary of his brave young days, his philosophy of life unchanged. Oliver's fat and sterility made him an Oriental. But was he even that? He was a biological freak, an animal with wooden limbs. What good did it do him, anyway, rigging him out like that? It only gave him a swelled head. An invalid, certainly, but a veteran. He stood upright all the time, on his one leg, on his peg, he was nothing less than a stylite. Human providence, forsooth!

At this point Oliver disappears far up the street.

Oliver goes home. He notices nothing unusual about Petra, though of course she knows the whole story. Finding the atmosphere no different from any other day, he perks up again, realizes that he is hungry and in fine fettle, sees food on the table which may or may not be for him, and in any case, there is much to excuse him for throwing himself upon it. It is cold porridge. To forestall an outcry from Petra, he suddenly tells her that at long last Mattis is about to change his circumstances.

Petra is evidently wise to his stratagem and refuses at first to fall into line. 'Hullo,' she says, 'you're taking all the porridge. Well, I must say!'

Silence.

Still, Oliver's news is undeniably sensational, and Petra asks: 'Have you been talking with that fellow Mattis?'

'Yes.'

'Who's he going to marry?'

Oliver is silent for a reasonable length of time; then he answers, 'Who's he going to marry?' and is silent again.

'Oh well, it's nothing to do with me,' says Petra and returns to the porridge: now the dish is empty, and what will they do for supper?

Whereupon Oliver says: 'He's going to marry that Maren.'

It took Petra a little while to believe it, to grasp it; she was comically jealous of Maren, she excoriated Maren, spat upon Maren: a woman whose days were practically numbered. an old maid with a baby! But what a piece of luck for Oliver to come home with news like that! It distracted his wife's attention from everything else, and gave him a respite from his own troubles.

And this was not the only occasion: his respite lasted for days and weeks, during which he escaped being called to account. There must have been a Providence at work, a higher dispensation. Every time he grew nervous about his dishonour coming up for discussion, something or other occurred to help Oliver out of his dilemma. The first thing was that Abel got married. Nothing less: a great and solemn event that occupied the entire house of Oliver.

Abel got married at last.

He didn't get exactly the one he wanted, but a girl from outside the town, Louise, large and gentle, a farmer's daughter. She was his own age, they were a young couple, but they both had good arms and they were both broad-chested. Abel had not done so badly, that crazy, carefree fellow. He had talked about marriage all his life, but the day Dad told him he was out of work, he made up his mind to act. He startled his father for a moment, but this time he had beyond question hit on precisely the right idea.

The ring was not destined to adorn her for whom it had been made. No, Little Lydia refused to accept the ring when he brought it; she had already bought herself a ring with a red stone in it, and she had no intention of wearing a plain ring.

'What's wrong with it?' asked Abel. 'I made it myself, and I don't fancy there's much wrong with the soldering.'

Well, no, she thanked him, but she wouldn't accept it; people might easily think she was engaged. Besides, Little Lydia had no time to spare right now, she had to go to Police Constable Carlsen's again to practise the piano; she moved about the room with an air of haste. Then she stood at the mirror, putting on various bits of finery. The heels of her shoes were gloriously high – they might have been built by an architect.

Abel pleaded his suit as usual, his fear and bashfulness perhaps a little enhanced; naturally there was some nonsense mixed in with it, and he alternated between jest and earnest. What did she think, they were both old enough and Abel had a smithy, so now he would very much like to know.

Know what? She didn't understand him, not one word; Abel explained himself, and this time his delicacy took the form of not beating about the bush.

Little Lydia told him to stop, she had all she wanted and didn't intend to change her circumstances; she did sewing for the fashion department.

All right. But Abel wanted to get things settled there and then. He had a steam hammer, he had bought various things for the house, they could live at his home, in the old cottage; Mattis had made the bed—

This really seemed too much for Little Lydia, as if she were almost crippled by what she heard. She leaned forward and stared at him.

'Are you looking at me?' asked Abel.

'Yes. It beats me how you could think of such a thing! How you could imagine I'd say yes!'

They continued to discuss it, and she declared she could hardly help laughing at him. Things came to a head, and finally she gave him a very plain answer; indeed, she felt constrained to drop him a hint about the kind of father and mother he had.

Then, of course, there was nothing he could say; so he held his peace.

Not being a heartless girl, but a girl like any other, she began talking innocuously about other things: how her brother Edevart was on his way home, he had written from Boston. Abel answered politely and held his peace again. Well, she announced, she was ready now and must be off. Abel got up and made for the door; then, to show he was not completely crushed, he made one last attempt at a joke: 'Ah well, I can come back another day!'

He never came back.

He wandered away with heavy footsteps along the country road, hoping no doubt to walk off some of his sorrow and misery. He increased his pace, forcing himself to go faster and faster, as if he might find himself disinherited if he didn't hurry. Oh, and he must have been a little hurt, too, a little angry.

He stopped before a farm by the roadside. It was a farm that he remembered from his childhood: as a little squirrel he had once been here and begged in vain for a jacket that hung on a clothesline, had hinted at a little food and received none, had finally asked if he could buy a cup of coffee, and had been refused on the pretext that he was too small. Poor squirrel. But on that occasion he had vowed to come back to these disgraceful people when he was grown up. And now he came.

A girl was standing in the yard; he knew her by sight, had seen her in town from time to time and nodded to her, and she evidently knew him – she was just a little too preoccupied fiddling with the grindstone; also, she blushed. Louise, her name was. Needless to say, it was not entirely by accident that Abel stood before her now, few things happen entirely by accident; he stood there because he had been rejected elsewhere, he had come here in a spirit of defiance. And it may not have been entirely by accident either that young Louise came out at this moment. In any case, she cannot possibly have thought it necessary to examine the grindstone so meticulously. They struck up a conversation, and since Abel was again in no mood for beating about the bush, he managed to say quite a lot. She said little in reply; there was a pleasing hesitancy about her, and her mouth was a nest full of smiles. The first time they settled one thing and another, the second time more, and the third time everything. Abel was impatient to get the ring bestowed.

Now you might well think that Abel was saddled with a formidably large family – wife, parents, two sisters, and a grandmother – from the word go, and maybe they did feel the pinch during the first few weeks after the wedding; but Abel and the steam hammer worked like Trojans, besides which his father took to helping in the smithy. From the waist up he was as strong as a horse, and he had a special, machine-like aptitude for filing. It all went swimmingly. For good measure Bluebell now left home, which made one less mouth to feed. Behold little Bluebell going off with her Thumbtack to their own snug cottage on the heath, and leaving Abel, that oddity, crying in secret for a whole day. To comfort him, Dad said: 'Well, well, you've been good children to one another. And such children as you've all turned out!' 'She needn't have been in quite such a hurry,' retorted Abel.

It was not destined to stop at one sister; Abel had another, the Brunette, she of the family eyes and the oval face. Abel thought she could well have stayed put yet awhile, but this notion foundered on Edevart's coming home and taking her, Edevart the sailor; he had been away for many years, and now he came home, a hulking great adult, and took the Brunette. Incidentally, it was quite a little romance: for one thing, she was still so young, hardly any age, and for another, Edevart met with opposition both from his mother and from his sisters.

'So what?' he asked in extreme surprise. 'If she has a mother like that and no father at all, what's it got to do with me?' They explained in more detail, they made everything exceedingly plain for his benefit, but Edevart was a frisky young seadog and in love, and he didn't give a damn, he declared, about gossip or anything that he couldn't see with the naked eye. Finally, they told him that Little Lydia also had refused to enter that family by accepting Abel. 'So much the worse for her!' retorted Edevart.

No way round that one.

At the wedding, to be sure, both families were present, and Abel met Little Lydia again. They even had a brief chat together. She didn't ask him in so many words if he had forgotten her, but she seemed to be waiting for an explanation of why he hadn't come back again as promised. She spoke meekly and sadly, with an undercurrent of religion. Once she chanced to cough, whereupon she put her hand to her chest; he was to see that she was transformed, that she took life seriously and wept in the night and perhaps actually spat blood and so on. Naturally she was dressed up to the nines, for all her resignation and intermittently moist eyes; oh, she was too young to have renounced the world entirely, for she suddenly drew from her bosom some finery which had been dangling there and which Abel had taken to be lace and trimmings, but which proved to be a handkerchief, and with this she flicked some dust from the toes of her shoes. Oh, Little Lydia would pull through all right, and anyone who had smiled at her moist eyes might next moment have seen those same eyes go hard and dry; she knew how to look after herself.

Mr and Mrs Edevart left the town; indeed, they left the country and went to America. When Edevart saw how matters stood, with the home full of grown-up sisters who sat around sewing and being genteel, he cleared right out. For his sister's sake Abel had strongly discouraged the couple from taking this step, pointing out to her that they would never see each other again. It was all the same to him, he said, but it wasn't fair to the others! His ploy failed, their sister would go with her husband. 'You don't think of how shorthanded we shall be at home,' he said indignantly. Oh, Abel, the laughingstock of the entire household, of all the grown-up women who remained!

All these little marriages and everyday happenings meant nothing, of course, to the town and to other people, but they meant much to the Oliver family. For them they were momentous occurrences, and perhaps advantageous ones as well. Oliver, certainly, could not complain, he had escaped persecution of late, event had followed event in rapid succession without causing him any ill effects; on the contrary, he ate every day at Abel's capacious board and continued to receive from him frequent driblets of pocket money. What more could he ask for? No one looked askance at him, Petra held her tongue. Even if things were bad, he wasn't the one worst hit; he took fresh courage and his powers of resistance returned. When no less a person than the double consul himself was badly hit, he collapsed and threw up the sponge. An experienced postmaster received one night a thrust in his untested human thought and had been dumb and dim from that moment. Carlsen, the honest old blacksmith, could not endure wickedness, could not endure being suspected of a son who went around with Japanese pictures on his body; he became a child, twitched his lips, thanked God for good and evil, and waited for death. Oliver was made of sterner stuff, less delicate and sensitive, more carefree, in short, the right human clay; he could endure life. Who had taken a harder knock than he? But a tiny upward turn in his fortunes, a lucky theft, a successful swindle, restored him to contentment. Did he then bear the palm of victory? Oliver had knocked about the world; he had seen palms, they were not the sort of thing to go carrying around.

The days went by. Oliver enjoyed peace at home, the street urchins left off shouting insults, but old Olaus had a dig at him on every possible occasion. By now he might almost have been happy, but Olaus begrudged him this, and asked the cripple, for all the world to hear, about a certain doctor's certificate. Oliver went home and burned the certificate amid curses. He avoided his tormentor as much as possible, and next time he met him was lucky enough to have a packet of tobacco in his pocket to offer him. Their roles were completely reversed: Olaus was now top dog.

'I feel sorry for you,' said Olaus.

'How does that tobacco taste?' Oliver inquired. 'There's nothing wrong with it, is there?'

Olaus asked mercilessly: 'Are they all true, the things they're saying about you?'

After this Oliver might have feared that he had given away a packet of tobacco to no purpose, but he even hinted that it wouldn't be the last; he was now earning good money in Abel's smithy, and could help a good friend out with tobacco from time to time.

Fisherman Jørgen came up and heard the rest of Olaus's spiteful remarks; the appearance of this particular listener was a double mortification to Oliver, who in earlier years had done plenty of showing off to Jørgen, and was now connected to him by marriage. Did Olaus show one scrap of tact or delicacy in his impertinent questions? Of course not. His parting shot was to ask why Oliver bothered with clothes. Would it make any difference if he roamed the streets in the nude? With this Olaus sauntered off, impudent and cock of the walk.

Leaving Oliver in a rare old rage. Fisherman Jørgen said: 'That creature Olaus is not worth worrying about.' But it seemed he *was* worth worrying about; the cripple stood for a while glowering and working his jaws. 'I shan't forget him!' he said and nodded.

One got nowhere by standing around in amiable chitchat with that dotard Jørgen – all of a sudden Oliver limped away from him and into the main street. By a stroke of luck it was Saturday night and he was wearing his best clothes; he was not going to throw in the sponge. Stopping outside the shoemaker's window, he studied the ladies' boots, beckoned to the passers-by, and aired his views: just look at the length of these ladies' boots, how far up the leg they went. Oliver stood there smacking his lips over them and talking like a roué. Suddenly a boy hurled a damning nickname at Oliver, laughter followed, Oliver was struck dumb. 'Ay, boots and shoes will soon be too dear for ordinary folk,' said a voice behind him. It was fisherman Jørgen again. Oliver took fresh courage, he resumed his discourse on high boots, he smacked his lips anew; but, oh, it was only a feeble reflection of the way he had talked to Jørgen in earlier years – damned if he could understand it, he must have lost his fire. In desperation he sang out: 'Well, I'm off to the dance hall!'

He equipped himself thoroughly, buying scent and dousing himself with it till you could smell him for miles, buying goodies, buying shredded tallow, which he intended to spread on the dance floor. Hullo, he's bent on something, hell-bent on desperate deeds, heaven help us all, bent on love and bride snatching – out of the way there! God knows, perhaps faintheartedness has given him valour; his life is so pitiful as to be laughable, he is sweating and pale; he takes out of his pocket mirror, rubs his cheeks, dolls himself up a little. Then he opens the door and pounds his way in.

Every eye seems to turn in his direction. 'Oliver,' they say, 'Oliver, ha-ha!' He finds a bench and sits down. The dance goes on. 'Pull that crutch of yours in!' a young sailor lad warns him as he

waltzes past. 'What's he yelling for?' Oliver asks his neighbours. 'I
didn't go yelling in dance halls in my day.' After a while he gathers
some listeners. 'I guess you were a real wolf once upon a time,
Oliver?' they say. He wags his head and spins yarns about the Alca-
zar in Hamburg and the Greenhorn in New York, all the different
kinds of races and colours he's danced with and had for sweethearts, he's swung around Malays and Chinese, Indians and Negro
girls; an Indian girl was the prettiest he'd kissed in all his days . . .

Oliver is pale and sweating; it must tax such a lazy man to affect
so much excitement. They tell him – Well, well, but he mustn't
think about such things any more, and he replies – Why not? A
nature as fiery as his can't stop, will never stop; why, they can see
for themselves, he's going to dance halls now. 'Look here, lads, do
you want to try some extra-fine candy?'

He airs his views about the dancing, it's nothing to what it was
in his day, that fellow who yelled so loud has no idea how to waltz;
it's not the heels that do the dancing, it's the toes, and you should
hold up your lady so that she doesn't tire herself to death. This is
too pathetic for words. Oliver has half a mind to go out onto the
floor and show them how it should be done.

Laughter from the audience.

Oh yes, Oliver can do that, no problem. 'Look at that one's legs,
whew, smashing legs, for example. If I once got hold of them, you
know what would happen next, don't you? Tra-la-la, tra-la-la!
Look here, go and spread this tallow on the dance floor,' he says,
handing over his bag.

'Tallow?'

'Tallow. We always had some with us in case the floor was
heavy and slow.'

'Oh?' they say, and spread some of the tallow.

Well, now it goes as smoothly as you could wish, music and dancing melt together, the waltz is sustained by those legs, borne
around the floor by those pillars. It is remarkable how much the
tallow helps.

'You certainly know what's what, Oliver!' they say, bearing
with him as long as they can, because he's a cripple.

'They can't teach me anything,' he answers. And at this token
of appreciation he starts humming again and showing off and behaving as if he is prepared to wake the dead. 'Whoopee, what an

evening! Just look at that girl there, the one with the big bust; go and tell her I want a word with her.'

The girl comes, Oliver proffers his goodies, man-of-the-world to his fingertips, and says: 'Help yourself, young lady, a little refreshment!' The girl giggles, dips in the bag, and swings her hips as she retreats. Another comes, several more come; Oliver distributes his goodies and tells them, pale and dripping with sweat, how much he fancies them. 'You?' they exclaim, shrieking with laughter. Oh yes, he does, fancies them like mad. What does it matter if he's lame? He's none the worse for that. They should just have seen how a nurse in Italy trailed after him and wanted to marry him. He never had a moment's peace from kissing and cuddling.

The dancing starts again. Oliver looks exhausted, but he thunders out the beat with his foot, and in case that should fail to attract sufficient attention he goes one better and pounds it out also with his crutch. But now some of the lads start to resent his banging on the floor and taking up their partners' time with his saucy talk and his candy. He is warned to sit still and to stop making such a racket; waste of breath, he only becomes still more saucy. Honest to God, he's having a grand old time this evening, and there was a time when he was after the girls like a wolf – no, they needn't make a secret of it if anyone asks them, it's common knowledge. Help yourself, young lady, a little more refreshment—

Ouch – hullo, a couple's gone down. Shrieking and shouting. A second couple tumbles over the first. Pandemonium. What's this filthy muck they've slipped upon? Tallow. Where's it come from? The dancers make a beeline for Oliver, their clothes hideously daubed with tallow and dust; they swear in his face. The cripple retorts that in his day *he* used to dance on tallow; there's nothing they can teach him in that line, advancing, reversing, and so on. They demand payment for the damage he's done to their clothes; they call him idiot, swine, every name under the sun. At this, indeed, Oliver recovers some of his dignity and tells them who he is, Oliver Andersen – that he has managed Consul Johnsen's warehouse for more than half a lifetime, that they ought to be ashamed of themselves, behaving like this towards respectable folk—

'Get out!' they yell, and goodness, the names they call him as they figure out what kind of a remnant of a man he is, an empty sausage skin, an old wether. What's more, he's covered himself with scent, and there he sits, the rotten so-and-so, stinking like a polecat. Out!

Inevitably his adventure became the talk of the town, and the women at the pump were duly scandalized; it was beyond their comprehension that a poor old wreck like that shouldn't get religion and go to church – who else was church for? But curiously enough, once again Oliver escaped being called to account at home; it seemed that Petra had given him up completely. True, when he arrived home he filled the cottage with his abominable scent, and there's no denying that at first Petra staggered back a pace of two; but it never came to a fight. No, once again a higher dispensation had stepped in: news had come through that the philologist Frank, a son of the house, had received an interim appointment as headmaster of the local senior school.

And at that moment no one came and told Oliver that he was a childless man. Admittedly, his children were fabrication pure and simple on his part; still, he had them, throughout their childhood and adolescence he had meant something to them, they and he knew each other, they called him father among themselves and to other people, and now Frank was coming home to his native town in the grandeur of his learning. Oliver was filled with pride in his son. Petra and Granny, of course, would still have preferred to see him a parson, but there was nothing they could do about it. Oliver said with dignity: 'What a son!'

32

Flags are flying here and there about the town, at Grits-and-Groats Olsen's, at the double consul's, in fact at all the consuls' and at Henriksen of the Shipyard's. They are flying in honour of Scheldrup Johnsen and Miss Olsen, who have been in Christiania getting married and are expected home today as a married couple. The mail boat is already in sight when one more flag is hoisted, on Consul Heiberg's brig, which is lying at a corner of the quay, taking in whale oil.

The quay is already thronged with people, and more keep arriving. Of the consuls the only absentee is Davidsen, that wily small tradesman who always keeps out of the way of the big shots. The district magistrate and the doctor are also missing, but Frank, the young headmaster, has shown up. He has recently married Constance Henriksen of the shipyard, but his wife is not with him. Frank is not the least of those on the quay; philologically speaking, he reigns supreme over the entire town, the entire coastal town, a great man, learned to a fault in foreign grammars and languages as a school subject. He stands well to one side, near a mountain of whale-oil barrels waiting to be loaded onto the brig. He is wearing the new suit he was married in, and cannot therefore go too close to the barrels of whale oil; on the other hand, he needs their shelter on the windswept quay, being sensitive to drafts. His father stands at the other end of the quay and refrains from rubbing shoulders with his son. Oliver knows how to behave.

Oliver is again on the upgrade. He no longer holds an exalted position in a warehouse, but he spends whole days with Abel at the smithy; sometimes he files iron, and occasionally he rows out and fishes for whiting in the bay. 'My son the master blacksmith,' he says; 'my son the headmaster,' he says. He leans back on his sons and makes the most of their respectability.

He is comfortably off and he is contented; if fate will continue to leave him in peace, he will not complain. Needless to say, the street urchins refrain from shouting at the father of such a person as the headmaster, and needless to say, Oliver creates no more scandals at the dance hall. The only remaining source of anxiety is Olaus, and even he seems to have suspended hostilities. Yes indeed, the days go by, one after another. Oliver, likewise, is not the least of those on the quay; many are of smaller account. All these folks here, what are they? Nonentities, a class, banal small-town bigwigs in starched linen. Oliver is something special. Here, where everybody is much of a muchness, he is bound to be regarded as unique. A child of misfortune, if you like, chewed and spat out by life, left high and dry, but possessed of an undying instinct for survival. The local newspaper may reprint its programme once again and urge the advantages of taking a course in religiosity, it is happening elsewhere, folks need it, the times cry out for it; in short, it is necessary to begin at the end. Oliver no longer begins anything anywhere, beginning things is not his business, he stays where he is put, uncrushed by human thought, unconverted by the women at the pump. Naturally life, fate, and God are damned high-class questions and very necessary questions, but they will be solved by people who have learned to read and write; what use are they to Oliver? If a brain like his starts busying itself with the why and the wherefore, it will go into a tailspin, and then Oliver will be unable to continue with his work, to enjoy his food and candy, to be fit for what he is. Leave getting above oneself to others!

Yes, he's a contented man, it's written all over his face. He stands reasonably erect on his leg and his wooden leg, with the air of a man who now has powerful relatives behind him if he chooses to make use of them. And all of a sudden he is back in public esteem: he's the headmaster's father, the public reflects ...

And now the mail boat comes alongside. There by the rail stands the newly married couple, surrounded by their families; hats are raised ashore and abroad. Mademoiselle Fia has no qualms about making herself conspicuous by wearing red, purple; she has also started taking an interest in lapdogs, and now holds under her arm a shaggy little dirty-white fellow with hair over his eyes and a blue ribbon around his neck. She is as genteel as ever and speaks in a murmur, a lady and a countess without blemish; if she has a wish, it is to enjoy good health and a long life, to be granted many more years in which to practise her art and illustrate Indian fairy tales. Since she is innocuous and well-behaved, life will probably grant her this wish.

Her mother, Mrs Johnsen, has recovered her wits and is no longer weighed down by sorrows. Her face is no less yellow than before, but her hat is a large one again. Rumour has it that there was some hocus-pocus about the steamship *Fia* and the bankruptcy, that Mrs Johnsen imagined herself poor for three weeks and then found herself as rich as ever. She looms corpulently up alongside her daughter at the rail; it was she and her dowry who originally made a great man of C. A. Johnsen of the Wharf, she is genuinely worth a broad-brimmed hat, and even here she stands well clear of the Grits-and-Groats Olsens, as if to say: 'To be sure, we're related to them now, but we don't mix with them very much!' It was an outrageous trick that chance played when her husband went and lost his head and disposed of their country residence to that family. What do those people want with a country residence? Since buying it they have been there precisely once, and they didn't even drive there with horse and carriage; no, they went on foot, both Consul Olsen and his wife. Evidently the walk was quite enough for them, and now in Christiania they have made over the country residence to the newlyweds, it is their wedding present. What do these people want with a country residence if they can't use it?

But here comes Johnsen himself, the double consul, the only member of the party in a top hat. He carries a plaid on his arm and walks briskly; perhaps he has been delayed settling his bill, or he may have been having a bit of fun with the stewardess, damned if you can trust him. The double consul is a great man, director of a business with many branches. A fallen tower, he? A re-erected tower. He is again worth a million or some other round figure; in Christiania he wore the Cross of the Dannebrog on his chest. Might there actually be something in the talk of hocus-pocus over the *Fia* and the insurance, and if so, what does it consist of? Consul Johnsen has in any case lived to see better days again, he is no longer resting, he must have regained a bit more say in his own affairs and those of others. Once in a fit of soul-searching this man sought out the old postmaster, hoping to find peace; and once subsequently, when in a far worse scrape, he went up the back stairs to old Carlsen the blacksmith on the same quest, after which no one could call him a heedless man, he took his medicine; but it failed to help him. And as the days went by, well, he got out of his scrape and no longer needed help. What should he do with it? When he thought of the postmaster and his humble ways, he could afford to smile again. The postmaster searched and searched for peace; he had found a little star and walked by its light, it wasn't a strong light, it wasn't the sun and broad daylight, but it was enough to distinguish things by, very faintly. What frugality! For his part Consul Johnsen did no searching, it was far too much effort. He merely wished to inquire where peace was to be obtained on the market. Now he stands on deck, carefree and on top of the world again, looking as if he could survive three of four additional calamitous bankruptcies. A devil of a fellow, the double consul; he must have hit on some way of curbing that brash son of his and keeping him within bounds.

'We,' he says, apropos the business; 'my clerks,' he says. Moreover, there has been an abrupt change in people's behaviour towards him, they look up to him again instead of walking past him; at bottom it is emphatically not the son but the father whom people have liked and been fond of all their days. He has their own qualities, their own ordinariness, a good-natured creature without seriousness or constancy, but *primus inter pares,* a major town dignitary, chubby and rich, maybe he'll soon get another *Fia* ...

Consul Johnsen is also the only person to call a greeting to those on shore. He can do this, being the man he is. 'Can you see anyone to take our things?' he says to Scheldrup, and the next instant he has disappeared again. Perhaps he has left something in his cabin, or he wants to say a last farewell to someone. Damned if you can trust him.

Here at last comes Olaus, making his swashbuckling way along the quay. Has he overslept today, or has he been sitting playing cards up to the last moment? He takes the gangway and throws it aboard with a crash. The horse that is to drive the newlyweds out to their country residence shies, but Olaus takes no notice, and greets the sailor handling the hawser with a few forcible words: 'Hi, make fast the gangway instead of standing there like a boneless louse!'

Olaus has just been on a two-day binge and doesn't hesitate to make his presence felt. And an Olaus binge is a far cry from an ordinary Communion, with wine and in church; he drinks what he is capable of drinking. Now he turns up at the quay, oh boy, gloriously drunk and blissfully crazy, erect, smoking a short-stemmed pipe, hungry perhaps, but bullheaded and strong. His speech is loud and lumbering, his language coarse, his *r*'s numerous and guttural. What does he say? His words are intelligible enough, they stray neither to the left nor to the right. He pretends not to see Scheldrup Johnsen on board and speaks his mind about him. 'Oh, so you're driving that Scheldrup to the place in the country, are you?' he bawls to the coachman. 'A fine fellow! Ask him what happened about the insurance on the *Fia*. Haven't you heard? Scheldrup went and insured the boat himself, the crafty bastard, and pocketed the money.'

The entire quay hears this. It is no trifling matter, and perhaps no tall story either; at all events, Olaus is voicing a rumour that has grown more and more insistent. The tale about Scheldrup is by no means incredible, since in point of fact it is he who has managed the ship all along, a thing quite beyond his father's power. This being so, might not Scheldrup have paid an insurance premium? He was in a position to do so. By the same token, this would explain Scheldrup's coming home, taking his father's chair in the office, and writing out cheque after cheque in favour of the creditors. Finally, it would explain the father's getting his chair back when the affair came to light. Ah yes, this may have been the reason why Consul Johnsen suddenly got his second wind and became active again – he had curbed that modern son of his, he had recovered as much of the management as he wanted. Nothing spurs a man on like a success.

The newlyweds go ashore with their arms full of flowers, get into their carriage, and drive off bowing left and right, drive off to honeymoon and married life. Olaus quietens down somewhat. One by one the wedding party leave the ship. Olaus evidently starts finding this tedious; he leaves the gangway and makes off towards the forehatch in search of goods. Some crates are put ashore. Olaus is not struck for a few more ribald remarks; as usual there is no real malice in him, but he is swashbuckling and irresponsible, intent upon astonishing the bystanders with his outspokenness and making them laugh.

There in his corner stands Frank, the new headmaster, lean and liguistically learned. Olaus addresses him: 'Don't stand there dirtying those barrels of whale oil!' he bellows. A real witty dog this time – everyone sniggers. Oliver hears the shouted remark, so profoundly disrespectful towards his son, and limps a few hops nearer as if to intervene. He is wearing his foxy expression, and now he seems to entertain certain feelings for Olaus.

But Olaus, spurred on by success, continues: 'You're standing right in my lodgings, don't you know that? Yes, that corner's where that fellow Olaus and I bed down for the night under a tarpaulin. If you feel like coming down here tonight, I'll put you up, too!'

More disrespect.

Frank puts his hands behind his back to show his indifference and walks slowly away down the quay. He is not in the habit of answering except to exude learning, nor does he exude learning on a quay.

Olaus refuses to let him go; he laughs at his retreating back and says: 'Yes, don't I just think the world of you!' He catches sight of the father, of Oliver, hails him, tells him to look, there goes the son, Petra's and the moon's son. Oliver hears him and stands gazing at the ground. For Petra, however, Olaus has only appreciation and praise: he has known her since she was a little girl, pretty from the word go, he says, and far too good to come unstuck. But then she married Oliver, and that was on a par with becoming a widow for good and all. 'Bless you, Oliver, you're not a fit subject for anyone to soil their lips with. I feel sorry for a poor bastard like you; all you're capable of is sitting threading needles like a woman. Whereas Petra—'

At this point Olaus sees the doctor approaching along the quay and at once proceeds, drunk as he is, to drag the doctor into his farrago – he spares no one. Whereas Petra, she wasn't like the doctor's wife, who refused to have children; no, if she couldn't get them at home, she went into town and got them. That was how it should be, he couldn't care less what they said at the prayer meeting. Were they trying to make out that women shouldn't have children? To hell with that! Were they to do like the doctor's wife and weep and wail them away? Weep me here and weep me there, and drop her to the bottom of the sea, it was all she deserved! 'Isn't that right, Doctor?' he shouts insolently. 'Didn't you have to take a rag that time and mop her tears off the floor? Ah yes, now you turn away and don't want to hear any more. But I'll tell you one thing before you go – that the women who won't give their life and blood ought to go and bury themselves, they ought—'

'Take away the gangway!' orders the captain.

Olaus lifts the gangway unnecessarily high in the air, eases it down a little, and then lets it fall. The quay shakes. And the ship sails.

Ah, but today was the last time that Olaus would chatter away on the quay or demonstrate his strength; that same night he was silenced – Heiberg's barrels of whale oil came crashing down onto the tarpaulin he slept under and stove his chest in. This was a sad end for Olaus, though he could hardly have expected anything better. Much might be said to Olaus's detriment, but perhaps he too had been injured by his destiny, a horse destroyed while being broken in ...

As it happened, some of the brig's crew had heard the noise in the night, but then all was quiet and they went to sleep again. When day broke they found Olaus. He was somewhat flatter than usual, and there were traces of blood about the nose and mouth, but there were no gaping jaws; indeed, his teeth were clenched. In general he looked like a lazy man having a nap – dead as a door-nail of course, but with no sneer or ill will on his face; he seemed to be saying: 'Don't wake me until we're there!'

News of the accident spread rapidly through the town, reaching Oliver among others. Curiously enough, Oliver had been out for a turn in the night, and he too had heard in all innocence the noise made by the barrels of whale oil, but hadn't attached any significance to it. Oliver would never have wished such an end for a good pal, he said; a decent fellow through and through, he said. It was almost a pleasure to hear him speak so well of a poor wretch who couldn't even thread a needle, but doubtless it was Oliver's own choicely interesting experience of what an accident was that gave him his cue ...

So once again people were faced with questions about life, fate, and God, questions that some of them discussed in quite a talented way. There, once again you saw what a sagging tightrope life was, and we have to walk on it! Olaus was quiet now, but others continued to chatter. However, Olaus was much too in-significant a person for his death to cause any long-term searching of souls; people got tired of looking down the muzzle of a gun all the time, they started dancing again. Oh, that dancing lady, she continued to come to the town for the perpetuation of vanity and sin! It was as if she were driven by an inner call. There were times when things went badly for her, but she stuck them out – come what may, the show goes on! That time a little while back, when the *Fia* went down and the place became as quiet as the grave, she had lost all her pupils and had gone away looking distinctly ema-ciated; now she was back again, and in twice as much demand as before. Such is human nature, worldly and unchanged. Yes, and such is human nature that people dance just the same whether death has actually visited them in the night or has passed them by – for the time being.

There are impatient people who try to encroach on Providence and set up as reformers, planning a world very different from this, drawing up programmes, abolishing all wickedness. They do this not from arrogance, like cocks crowing against heaven; no, they pray, they flirt their way forward, they stand there turning over the music and whispering sentimentalities in her ear. But the music is played from no human score.

Who had more honestly deserved to be right in his programme than the old postmaster, and who had been more badly let down? Admittedly, a certain mail robbery had put it within his power to be an idiot for the rest of his life, but as an idiot he presumably had no idea of what a blessing this was. Or how was it – was he still contented, albeit on a new foundation? Were his perceptions and insights profounder, perhaps, than those of others? He seemed to dwell in another world, to be one with the wind and the stars, to be part of the universal flux that bore him along. Food? Yes, he even ate food – but how little he cared what it consisted of or whether he got it at all! A shadow, a spectre with clothes on, a deceased little person, of whom the most one could say was that he saw the light and blinked, he breathed in and out; when he caught a cold he sneezed. Anything more was beyond him. Was he then the unhappiest creature in the town? He never spoke about it; he had chattered himself out. Those who had seen him thought him calm and collected now; he looked sincere and natural, as if to say: I'm not sitting here like an idiot for nothing, I've got my reasons for it, I've come into my own.

And things take their course. Perhaps the postmaster was right in believing that life is governed by a great and just brain beyond the realm of existence. A number of people in the town actually started to incline to this belief. How else were they to explain the fact that when all was said and done things were looking up again? The shipyard, for example, had resumed operations. There were other glad tidings besides, but the reopening of the shipyard was nothing less than a godsend to the town. Kasper was back at work, all the workmen were receiving wages again. Henriksen himself had not exactly become a rich man at a stroke, but he had been given rich help; evidently Double Consul Johnsen was once more able to do good now that he sat in his own chair and had resumed command.

Time passes, then; everything passes; and many things even pass off well. What the supreme good is, we do not know. Going up and coming down are clearly parts of the whole to which everything belongs. A candle burns steadily in a candlestick. The door opens, the candle goes out. Whose fault is it? What fault?

'Let us be patient like the trees of the forest,' says Carlsen the blacksmith. He has his own way of looking at things; he is unintelligent and therefore has little to say, but he plugs away at being thankful to God for every day that passes. Of late he seems to have lost the grip even on his old craft and on everday matters. They are standing in the smithy discussing Olaus's death and many another topic, and Carlsen the blacksmith is telling about a time when he couldn't get coal. He ran out of coal and was unable to work for several days, he tells them; coal was not to be had in the town, no one had any coal. 'It wasn't many days before, thank God, some coal arrived, but it would certainly have taken much longer if I'd been the only one needing it.'

'Why should that be?' asks Oliver.

'Much longer,' the blacksmith quietly repeats. 'Because I hadn't deserved any better. It was on account of the others that I was helped.'

He stands there with his brand of wise understanding, gentle and humble, perhaps a little stupid, too, as so much wisdom is.

'And how's it going?' he asks Abel.

'It's going fine.'

'Is that apprentice of yours doing his job?' he asks humorously, pointing at the steam hammer. 'Well, God bless both you and the hammer!' says Carlsen the blacksmith. 'So everything's going fine,' he adds.

He starts peering under the bench by the window. Abel asks if he's looking for something and offers to help him. No, he's not looking for anything, it's nothing. Then he finds it – why, he must have seen it the whole time, but he pretends it's some trifle that he once threw away – it's a box containing various bags, little sacks.

'What's that?' asks Abel.

'What, that? It's just lying in the way.'

'Shall I burn it in the forge?'

His master ignores this and says: 'Just a few little bags, they each had their own, for things they'd carved. Yes, at one time they were very keen on carving, mostly just splinters of course, but some of the splinters were supposed to be boats, and some were axes, and some were people. After a bit we used to put them away; they were very particular about each having their own bag. Would you believe it, here they are still! I'll take them upstairs and throw them in the stove, of course—'

Abel offers to carry them for him, but Master takes the precious bags himself.

So Abel goes on working. A man comes, wanting iron rims on a new pair of cartwheels. A lighterman has broken his chain and needs to have it welded right away. Abel starts welding. To his father he says: 'When you have time, you might just polish those mountings a little.' Such is the tone, pleasant and conversational, now as before; no orders. And Dad isn't made to feel that he's just standing around; on the contrary, he's needed for this, he's needed for that. He answers: 'I'll find time for that!'

So Oliver files and polishes the mountings – the handles and corners for a chest. The chest is to go out into the country, where people still like to have solid blacksmith's work on their strongbox. And the day wears on at the smithy; it passes in work and talk between father and son. Earlier in the day Bluebell has looked in at the smithy on her way to the store, making three of them to do the talking. Since Bluebell is wearing a light-coloured dress, Abel gets up from the heap of coal to offer her his seat; afterwards he insists that she's got a smut on her forehead and puts a sooty finger right on the spot. So of course Dad has to produce his pocket mirror.

They enjoy their time together; no one gets in anyone else's way, and when Bluebell leaves, the others miss her.

In the evening Oliver means to go fishing; it is starting to drizzle, so the weather is right for it. Abel makes a deal with him in advance and pays for the fish. 'When you come ashore I want you to hang a nice string of fish on the municipal engineer's kitchen door. What do you want for it?'

'I don't want anything for it,' answers Dad.

'No, I suppose you'd rather knock at the engineer's door and make him pay through the nose,' Abel teases him. 'But I'm not having any of that. Here's two kroner, you're not getting any more!'

Oliver rows out. He is not gone for long; after a couple of hours the weather clears and he comes ashore. He threads the fish neatly on a line and hobbles off with it into the town. It may well be that Abel knows where he will go. He passes the municipal engineer's house and makes a beeline for the great colonnaded stone building. Blood is thicker than water; he goes to his son the headmaster and stops outside the kitchen door. Here he polishes his shoe with spittle; for a moment it looks incredibly bright and new, and his wooden leg needs no polishing. Then Oliver knocks at the door.

The maid is in the kitchen; the mistress comes in, Constance of the shipyard, big with child. Oliver possesses tact and manners; he has already removed his hat, and now he holds out the fish. The maid takes it. The mistress is not stuck-up, she thanks him personally for the gift; she knows her father-in-law, but she doesn't offer him a chair. 'Just think, if we'd had that fish in time for dinner!' she says for something to say. Oliver puts on a great air, just as if he himself belongs to the gentry, and replies – Yes, madam, in so far as it lies within his poor capacity he will come earlier next time. No, says the mistress, he is not to bring any more fish, she's not happy about it, lame as he is and all. Oliver pooh-poohs such talk, pooh-poohs it very discreetly of course, but at the same time he flails his arm as if to say he is only the tiniest bit lame and he will certainly come. 'But you heard me say I don't want it,' says the mistress. 'And I'm sure my husband wouldn't like it, either,' she adds. Oliver understands nothing and perseveres. Whereupon the mistress has no choice but to ask the maid some trivial question or other and, on getting the answer, to turn on her heel and go. For a time Oliver tries to exchange small talk with the maid; the mistress may have gone to fetch something for him, a bite of cake, a little souvenir; it would be mean to disappear while her back was turned. But even the maid is sparing of words. He recognizes her – the girl from the dance hall, the one with the big bust; he gave her candy that time. Naturally he makes no reference now to that lively evening; no, Oliver is a good boy in this house. He remarks that this is a fine kitchen, a delightful kitchen. 'Oh yes,' answers the maid. 'Is the headmaster at home?' he asks. Yes, he is. 'What's he doing? Reading, I expect?' The maid doesn't know and just goes on with her work. Oliver lingers for a bit; the mistress does not return. Finally he says good night and goes.

Nothing is the matter, nothing is wrong; Oliver feels only a touch of relief at being rid of his string of fish. He doesn't brood. If anyone were to come and offer him death, he would not accept it, by no manner of means; life is none too bad, in Oliver's opinion. It is not everyone who has it as good as he: a roof over his head, food and drink, a two-krone piece in his pocket, wife and children – and what children! He is made of the everlasting human clay.

There he goes, limping home. He is somewhat disabled, a trifle imperfect in himself; but what is perfection? The life of the town realizes its image in him: a crawling life, but none the less busy for that. It starts in the morning and continues till evening, when people bed down for the night. And some bed down under a tarpaulin.

Small things and great occur; a tooth falls from the mouth, a man out of the ranks, a sparrow to the ground.

Thomas Pynchon
The Crying of Lot 49 £1.50

The death of her ex-lover sets Oedipas Maas on a trail of delirious weirdness, through Dr Hilarius, Freudian shrink, Gengis Cohen, the eminent LA philatelist who likes his sex with the news on, not to mention Yoyodyne Inc, Randolph Driblette, and Messrs Wistfull, Kubitschek and McMingus, Attorneys ...

'The best American novel I have read since the war' FRANK KERMODE

'An exuberant, off-beat talent ... turbulent as storm-clouds' GUARDIAN

Emma Tennant
The Bad Sister £1.50

'Throwing together a radical feminist version of Charles Manson, late 60s craziness in communes in Notting Hill Gate and Scottish hills, the psychological repercussions of semi-acknowledged illegitimacy, the jaded and confused visions of the inveterate movie-goer and a bisexual assassin, Emma Tennant has created a novel of quite extraordinary power ...' TIME OUT

'... the black magic comes right off the page and bathes you in its menacing breath ...' GUARDIAN

Henry Green
Nothing, Doting and **Blindness** £2.95

The publication of *Loving, Living* and *Party Going* in one Picador volume in 1978 signalled the end of years of unaccountable neglect for this fine writer. Three further of his fine novels are published together.

Nothing – a brilliant comedy of manners about a well-to-do widower and his debutante daughter.

Doting – a satire on the perils of romantic involvement between youth and middle age.

Blindness – Green's first novel, telling of a clever artistic boy, blinded in a senseless accident, who turns to writing with powers heightened by his affliction.

'A rare, strange talent recovered for another generation of readers' GUARDIAN

edited by William McGuire and
abridged by Alan McGlashan
The Freud/Jung Letters £2.50

William McGuire's collection of *The Freud/Jung Letters* is highly regarded as a work of scholarship and is standard reading for any serious student of psychology.

Alan McGlashan's specially commissioned abridgement brings out the essence of this correspondence – a reflection of a relationship of crucial importance in the history of ideas in our century.

'The impression is of two immensely ambitious, self-willed, often inspired men, who had set themselves apart as innovators, roped together in a long climb into a new world' OBSERVER

Arthur Koestler
Janus: a Summing Up £2.25

'The human brain has developed a terrible psychological flaw, such that now it is working against the survival of the race. Something has *snapped* inside the brain. It is no longer necessarily a function which will lead to a better world, but something demonic, possessed' BOOKS AND BOOKMEN

'A summing up of a quarter of a century's study and speculations on the life sciences and their philosophical implications' GUARDIAN

'One of the major political *experiencers* and most widely informed spirits of the age turning to the crux of human survival on a ravaged planet' SUNDAY TIMES